Also by Dana Fuller Ross
in Large Print:

Arizona
California Glory
Expedition!
Hawaii Heritage
Illinois
Kentucky
Louisiana
Mississippi
Nevada
Outpost!
Sierra Triumph
Tennessee
Westward!
Utah

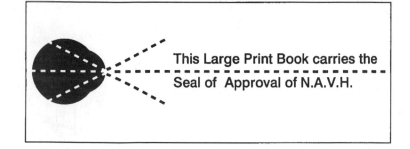

This Large Print Book carries the
Seal of Approval of N.A.V.H.

HONOR!

WAGONS WEST
THE EMPIRE TRILOGY

BOOK 1

HONOR!

DANA FULLER ROSS

Thorndike Press • Thorndike, Maine

Published in 2001 by arrangement with Book Creations, Inc.

Thorndike Press Large Print Western Series.

The tree indicium is a trademark of Thorndike Press.

The text of this Large Print edition is unabridged.
Other aspects of the book may vary from the original edition.

Set in 16 pt. Plantin by Christina S. Huff.

Printed in the United States on permanent paper.

Library of Congress Cataloging-in-Publication Data

Ross, Dana Fuller.
    Honor! / Dana Fuller Ross.
      p. cm. — (The Empire Trilogy ; bk. 1)
    ISBN 0-7862-3116-5 (lg. print : hc : alk. paper)
    1. Holt family (Fictitious characters) — Fiction.
    2. Washington (D.C.) — Fiction. 3. Conspiracies —
Fiction. 4. Large type books. I. Title.
PS3513.E8679 H67 2001
  813′.54—dc21
                                  00-053224

Author's Note

Honor!, the first book of WAGONS WEST: THE EMPIRE TRILOGY, immediately follows the events described in *Outpost!*, the third book in WAGONS WEST: THE FRONTIER TRILOGY. Thus, as both author and readers, we return to the early days of the Holt family as they, and the still-young nation known as the United States of America, face new dangers and challenges.

As always, my appreciation for the opportunity to continue the saga of the Holts goes to everyone at Bantam Books and Book Creations, Inc., especially George Engel, Elizabeth Tinsley, and Sally Smith, as well as good friends Greg Tobin, Pamela Lappies, and Paul Block, who assisted greatly in the development of the Holts' early history. Special thanks as well to L. J. Washburn, who provided an endless supply of ideas, advice, and encouragement during the writing of this novel.

This book is dedicated to you, the readers, who have waited patiently for the story of the Holts to continue. My thanks to all of you.

Dana Fuller Ross
Azle, Texas

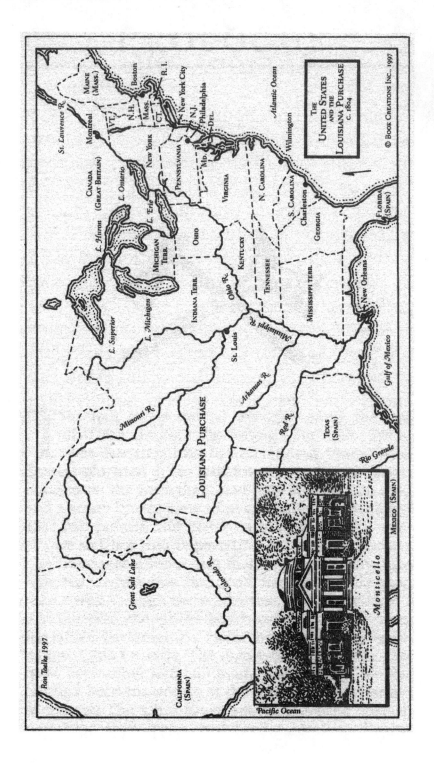

THE
UNITED STATES
AND THE
LOUISIANA PURCHASE
c. 1804

© BOOK CREATIONS INC. 1997

Ron Toelke 1997

St. Lawrence R.

MAINE
(MASS.)

Montreal

Boston

R.I.

New York City

N.H.

VT.

MASS.

CT.

N.J.

Philadelphia

DEL.

Atlantic Ocean

CANADA
(GREAT BRITAIN)

L. Ontario

New York

PENNSYLVANIA

MD.

Wilmington

L. Erie

VIRGINIA

N. CAROLINA

L. Huron

MICHIGAN
TERR.

OHIO

KENTUCKY

S. CAROLINA

Charleston

L. Superior

L. Michigan

INDIANA TERR.

Ohio R.

TENNESSEE

GEORGIA

MISSISSIPPI TERR.

FLORIDA
(SPAIN)

St. Louis

Mississippi R.

New Orleans

Arkansas R.

Gulf of Mexico

Missouri R.

LOUISIANA PURCHASE

Red R.

Great Salt Lake

Colorado R.

TEXAS
(SPAIN)

Rio Grande

Monticello

MEXICO (SPAIN)

CALIFORNIA
(SPAIN)

Pacific Ocean

HONOR!

An unforgettable, all–new epic adventure of hope, heroism, and heartbreak — with the men and women who blazed a path to the future across a land of infinite promise and peril. . . .

CLAY HOLT — Rugged, hot-tempered, wild as the land itself, the eldest Holt is the consummate man of the frontier, possessed of natural intelligence and a deadly skill with fist, knife, and gun. But drawn into the circles of Washington high society, he now faces an enemy more treacherous than any he has encountered before.

JEFF HOLT — As fierce in a fight as any man, he is more peacemaker than troublemaker. But now, in the service of President Jefferson, trouble has found him, and he won't back down. He must act quickly, boldly, and with absolute conviction . . . risking the ultimate sacrifice for brother and country.

MELISSA MERRIVALE HOLT — A stunning southern beauty who found happiness in the arms of her husband, Jeff Holt, she has matured into a savvy, successful businesswoman.

But when the family's North Carolina company faces sudden disaster, she is forced to make a terrible choice between love and honor.

SHINING MOON — Clay Holt's proud Sioux wife, she alone possessed the power and passion to tame his wild heart. Now, separated from her native land and from her husband, she must confront the terrible truth about the child she has taken in as her own.

PROUD WOLF — Shining Moon's younger brother, he is a man who has learned to fight by his wits. Earning an invitation to a prestigious New England academy, he is about to discover that his love for a white woman can lead others to savage hatred.

MATTHEW GARWOOD — Even though his father once started a bitter feud with the Holts, young Matthew has benefitted from Clay's generosity. But blood is thicker than gratitude, and as Matthew grows older, his hatred for the Holts begins to take deadly shape.

GIDEON MAXWELL — A man of charisma, charm, and utter ruthlessness, he is the puppeteer pulling the strings of power in Washington. Now he has an opportunity to expand his financial empire into the great western frontier . . . no matter how many laws are broken or how much blood is spilled.

DIANA MAXWELL — Gideon's breathtakingly beautiful daughter is the princess of Washington's high society . . . a woman offering the kind of temptations few men can resist. Alluring, calculating, and shameless, she's capable of leading an unsuspecting lover to betray his comrades . . . and destroy himself.

LIEUTENANT JOHN MARKHAM — A young, unseasoned army officer personally assigned by President Jefferson to assist the Holt brothers in their dangerous mission, he is captivated by the ravishing beauty of Diana Maxwell . . . an infatuation that could prove fatal.

Prologue

The four riders moved smoothly along the road that ran through the rolling Ohio hills. Spring was bursting into life all around them. Wildflowers bloomed in the meadows, tender green leaves budded on the trees that lined both sides of the road, and a warm breeze blew from the south. The winter of 1811 had passed, and better days lay ahead.

Or so Clay Holt believed.

There was a time — not that long ago, really, Clay reflected — when this fine road had been little more than a trail through the wilderness. He remembered it vividly, even though he had been only a child when his father, Bartholomew Holt, had brought the family here to Ohio to settle. The man who rode beside Clay now, his brother Jeff, had made that journey, too, but Jeff had been too young at the time to remember any of it now. The Ohio River valley had been sparsely populated then. There had been a small settlement, Marietta, and a few scattered farms and homesteads. That was all. Now Marietta was a good-sized town, and almost all the surrounding land was under cultivation. Forests had been cleared, and fields had taken their place.

That was progress, Clay thought. The wild things went away, and tamer, more civilized things appeared in their stead. For most folks, that was an improvement.

Not for everybody, though. No, sir, not for everybody.

"Can't get over how good it is to see you again, Clay," Jeff said. "Seems like it's been four or five years since we were together, not just two."

"It's been a busy two years," Clay said dryly. "Things have changed a lot for both of us."

Jeff laughed. "Reckon that's right. I never thought I'd see you out of buckskins again."

Clay grimaced slightly but made no reply. It was true that buckskins were not the most comfortable outfit in the world, but once a man got used to them, anything else just didn't seem quite right. At the moment Clay, a tall, broad-shouldered man of thirty with thick dark hair and a short beard, was wearing a homespun shirt of a butternut color, brown whipcord trousers, and high black boots. The garb was a concession to the fact that he was no longer in the Rocky Mountains, where he had spent most of the past three years working as a fur trapper. That was the life he loved, and only a desire to see his family again had brought him back to Ohio for this family reunion.

His brother Jeff was a couple of years younger and not as imposing physically, although his body was lean and powerful. Jeff was clean-shaven, with a shock of sandy blond hair under a broad-brimmed brown hat. His shirt, trousers, and boots were all store-bought; as a matter of fact, the entire outfit came from the mercantile emporium Jeff and his wife, Melissa, owned in Wilmington, North Carolina. Before he had gone back east and settled down, Jeff had never possessed much of anything store-bought. None of the Holts had, Clay mused. He hoped that civilized life had not softened his little brother.

But that was not really fair, Clay chided himself. Jeff had a right to live however he wanted to; he had gone through a great deal of hardship and tragedy in his life, and he had earned the right to some peace and happiness with his wife and son.

"Shouldn't that stagecoach be coming along pretty soon?" asked the third man. Cousin to Clay and Jeff, Ned Holt belonged to the Pittsburgh branch of the family. He was taller and brawnier than Clay and blonder than Jeff. For the past couple of years he had traveled extensively, first with Jeff, then as a sailor on ships owned by Lemuel March of Boston, another Holt relative. He had been eager to attend this family reunion and in particular to meet his famous cousin, the mountain man Clay Holt.

Beside Ned rode the fourth member of the party, a slight figure who looked almost like a child next to the three big men. India St. Clair had, in fact, passed as a child — and a boy at that — on more than one occasion. Today, however, her short dark hair was uncovered, and she was making no secret of the fact that she was a lovely young woman, despite the boots and riding trousers she wore. She and Ned were lovers and had been for some time, ever since she had met Jeff and Ned in New York while Jeff was searching for his missing wife. That quest had come to a successful conclusion, and Ned and India had found each other in the process. Now they sailed the sea-lanes together, although when they were at sea, India usually still disguised herself as a young man.

"I'm not sure when the coach was due," Jeff said in answer to Ned's question. "They don't keep to a tight schedule. But it was supposed to reach Marietta sometime today. I thought it would be a nice surprise for the children if we met it and rode on into town with them."

"I'll be awfully glad to see those youngsters again," Clay said with a grin.

Ned smiled. "You may not recognize them, Clay. They've been staying with my parents in Pittsburgh for quite a while now, and in the last letter I had from my mother, she said they were really growing. Edward's a young man now, and Susan's a regular lady, according to Ma. I reckon Jonathan's still something of a little tyke, though."

"It'll be good to see them again, no matter how much they've grown," Jeff said. He missed his little brothers and little sister. It had been far too long since all five of the children of Bartholomew and Norah Holt had been together.

If only their parents could have been here, too, the reunion would have been perfect. But Bartholomew and Norah had died several years earlier, victims of the senseless violence that sometimes plagued the frontier. After their deaths the family had scattered, and Clay's mouth tightened into a grim line as he thought about that. As the oldest child he should have done a better job of holding everything together, but circumstances were such that he could see no other way to proceed. He and Jeff had gone west to seek their fortunes as fur trappers, and the younger children had been sent east to live with their aunt and uncle, Ned's parents, in Pittsburgh.

And although they were coming back together now, it wouldn't last, Clay knew. When this visit was over, he would return to the Rockies with his wife, Shining Moon, and Matthew Garwood, the boy they had taken in to raise following the death of his mother. Jeff, Melissa, and their son, Michael, would go back to North Carolina, and Ned and India to Boston and the sea. Edward, Susan, and Jonathan would have to return to the home of Henry and Dorothy Holt in Pittsburgh. The Holt family's Ohio homestead would once again be left in the hands of Castor and Pollux Gilworth, the tenant farmers who maintained the house and land.

But for a while they would all be together, Clay reminded himself, and that ought to be a joyous occasion. For the sake of the others, he knew he would have to control his brooding and not surrender to the dark melancholy that sometimes gripped him.

India pointed into the distance. "I see some dust," she said. "Do you think that's the coach?"

Clay and Jeff reined their horses to a stop, and the other two followed suit. Clay studied the faint haze of dust rising into the air about a quarter of a mile in front of them. India had good eyes, he thought appreciatively. "That's probably the coach, all right," he said after a moment.

"Come on," Jeff said. "I want to see the expression on the children's faces when they realize we've come to meet them."

The four riders heeled their mounts into motion again, but they had gone only a short distance when Clay held up his hand and gestured for them to halt. "What's that?" he asked.

A distant popping sound came clearly to their ears through the warm air of the spring afternoon.

Clay and Jeff looked quickly at each other as they recognized the sound. "Gunshots!" Jeff exclaimed.

"I think you're right," Ned said excitedly. "Let's go!"

He smacked his boots against his horse's flanks and slapped the reins against its neck even as he called out the exhortation. The horse leaped forward into a gallop. India was right behind Ned, and there was nothing Clay and Jeff could do but follow. They exchanged another grim glance. They knew they might be riding into trouble, but that was nothing new.

Trouble seemed to follow the Holts. It always had.

The riders pounded over the road as it rose and fell on its course through the hills. They swept around a wide bend where the road avoided a particularly rugged upthrust of ground and found themselves galloping along a straightaway. A couple of hundred yards away, a stagecoach careened toward them, pulled by a team of four horses. The animals lunged forward under the whip of the driver, eyes wild, foam trailing from their mouths and flecking their sides.

The road was narrow enough that Clay, Jeff, Ned, and India could not see beyond the coach. But from the sound of the gunshots, which were much louder now, and the way the driver kept glancing frantically behind him, it was obvious what was happening. Highwaymen were trying to overtake the coach, no doubt intent on robbing the passengers.

The thieves were in for a surprise. That coach carried Holts, and there were more on the way.

Even here in the so-called civilized Ohio River valley, Clay was armed. A flintlock pistol was tucked behind the broad leather belt around his waist. It was primed and loaded, ready to cock and fire. He also had a pouch full of shot on his belt and a powder horn slung over his shoulder, but under the circumstances he doubted he would have a chance to reload the pistol. He had to make his first shot count. Jeff and Ned were likewise carrying pistols, but India was armed only with a slender dagger, deadly in close quarters but essentially useless in a fight like this.

Suddenly, as Clay raced to intercept the coach, he saw a dark head thrust out through one of the windows, followed by a young man's arms and shoulders. Clay could not see the youngster's face because it was turned toward the rear of the coach. The young man lifted the pistol in his hand and fired. Smoke and flame geysered from the barrel of the weapon.

A bouncing, careening stagecoach was not the best platform from which to aim a shot. Clay didn't expect the young man's attempt to hit anything. But it slowed down the pursuers momentarily, and that worked to the advantage of Clay and his companions.

"Jeff, stay with me!" he shouted over the thunder of galloping hooves and the loud creaking of the coach's madly spinning

19

wheels. "Ned and India, take the other side!"

Immediately, the others acted to follow Clay's orders. Jeff rode closely behind his brother, veering toward the left side of the road. Ned and India went the other way, toward the right, guiding their mounts to the very edge as the coach thundered down the middle of the road.

The coach's passage abruptly left the pursuing highwaymen facing four grim-faced avengers who had seemingly appeared from nowhere.

Galloping at top speed as they were, the two groups closed the gap between them almost immediately. Clay had just enough time to register the fact that there were six outlaws, all of them armed. The odds were in favor of the highwaymen, but the Holts had the element of surprise on their side.

Clay quickly hauled back on the reins, bringing his horse to a skidding stop. Smoothly he lifted his pistol and thumbed back the hammer. The flintlock roared in his hand. One of the robbers was driven backward by the heavy lead ball that slammed into his chest. He threw his hands up in the air and toppled from the back of his mount.

Alongside Clay, Jeff fired, too, and his

shot smashed the shoulder of another man. The outlaw managed to stay in the saddle, but just barely, and Clay knew he was out of the fight.

A few yards away, Ned's pistol blasted, but just as he pressed the trigger, the man he had drawn a bead on yanked his horse around in a tight, wheeling turn. Ned's ball tore through the throat of the animal, bringing a shrill, strangled scream of agony. The horse went down with a crash in the road, throwing its rider clear.

That was enough for the remaining highwaymen. Not realizing that Clay, Jeff, and Ned had already shot their volley, the thieves jerked their mounts around. "Let's get out of here!" one of them shouted. The man who had been unhorsed by Ned's shot scrambled awkwardly to his feet and then made a desperate leap toward one of his companions, who paused long enough to reach down, grasp his wrist, and haul him up behind the saddle. They raced for the trees at the edge of the road and darted among them, soon disappearing in the newly budded foliage.

Quickly Clay reached for his powder horn and shot pouch and began reloading the pistol, in case the robbers came back. From the rapidly diminishing sound of hoofbeats, however, he guessed they would not stop running anytime soon. He glanced around at his companions and asked, "Is anybody hurt?"

"They didn't even get a shot off," Jeff said. "I think we're all fine." Ned and India nodded in agreement.

Clay finished loading his pistol and then gestured at the body sprawled in the road. "Any point in looking at that one to see if any of us recognize him?"

"I don't see how we could," Ned said. "India and I have never been in these parts before, and you and Jeff have been away for a long time. Chances are he's just some wandering ne'er-do-well."

"Chances are," Clay agreed. He walked his horse toward the body anyway and swung down from the saddle when he reached it. He had never liked to leave things unfinished. Holding the pistol ready, in case the fallen highwayman was shamming, he hooked the toe of his boot under the man's shoulder and rolled him onto his back.

"Ned was right," Jeff said from horseback. "I've never seen that man before. He's certainly dead, though, no question about that."

Clay grunted. "No question." He tucked

his pistol behind his belt again and looked at the dead man.

The thief had been middle-aged, with a coarse, beard-stubbled face. There was nothing unusual or distinctive about him. His features bore the lines of a harsh existence, and in death he had a bitter, defeated look.

Could have been me, Clay thought. *If things had been a little different, that poor devil could have been me.*

But they had not been different. He had gone to the Rockies and met Shining Moon, finding a true home and the love of his life in the same place. There'd been a time when he had thought he had little to live for, but now he knew the truth.

The whole wide world was out there, and it was waiting for him.

But first . . .

"Let's make sure everyone's all right in that coach," Clay said as he reached for his horse's reins.

A few minutes later he and his companions trotted up to the stagecoach, which had come to a halt several hundred yards down the road. The driver, still looking shaken, had climbed down from the box and opened the door of the coach, and the passengers were climbing out. The dark-haired young man who had fired a shot at the high-waymen was already on the ground, and he turned toward the newcomers with a broad, excited smile on his face.

"Clay! Jeff!" he cried. "It really is you!"

Clay and Jeff stepped down from their horses and came toward the young man. "It's us, all right, Edward," Jeff said in greeting to his fifteen-year-old brother. He took Edward's hand, but instead of shaking it Jeff drew him into a back-thumping, brotherly hug.

Aunt Dorothy's letter to Ned had been accurate, Clay thought. Edward was a young man now, almost as tall as Jeff, and his chest and arms were filling out nicely. His dark hair was thick and wavy, and the first hints of a mustache darkened his upper lip.

The girl stepping down from the coach had the same sandy blond hair as Jeff. She let out a happy cry and flung herself toward Clay. He caught her and hugged her tightly, lifting her off the ground. "Clay?" she whispered.

"It's me, darlin'," he told his sister Susan. She was twelve years old now, and as Dorothy Holt had written, she was blossoming into a pretty young lady.

"I knew you were supposed to be here," Susan said as she hugged Clay's neck, "but it's been so long I couldn't bring myself to really believe I was going to see you again."

"Well, little sister, you can believe it," Clay told her. "I'm here, big as life —"

"And twice as ugly," Jeff finished for him. "Come here, Susan."

Reluctantly Clay let go of his sister and watched as she raced over to Jeff and embraced him. That left Jonathan, who, if Clay remembered correctly, was nine years old. As Clay turned toward the coach, a small, dark-haired blur shot out through the open door and attached itself to his leg, almost staggering him.

"Clay!" Jonathan whooped. "Clay!"

Reaching down, Clay grasped his youngest brother under the arms and lifted him into the air. Jonathan, too, had grown a lot in the time that Clay had been in the west. "Lordy, you're getting big," Clay said with a grin.

"Pass him over here," Jeff said, and Clay complied. Jonathan whooped again in delight as he was passed from one brother to the other.

Meanwhile, Edward and Susan were getting reacquainted with Ned, whom they had met in Pittsburgh while staying with his parents. Ned introduced the three younger Holts to India, who charmed them by saying,

"I've heard so much about you all, and I'm so glad to finally meet the rest of this remarkable family."

Three more people got off the coach as the Holts greeted each other exuberantly. They were strangers, and Clay paid little attention to them other than to note that they were a man, a woman who appeared to be his wife, and another man traveling alone.

"I thought we were all going to be robbed and killed," the woman said with some agitation. "Oh, dear, it was just horrible!"

Her husband put an arm around her. "We can't thank you gentlemen enough," he said to Clay and Jeff.

"Thought we were goners for sure," the driver added. "Those no-good scoundrels were layin' in wait for us back up the road a ways. Came out of the trees and started shootin' at us, yellin' for me to stop. But I just whipped up the team and drove right through 'em."

Clay was unsure whether he should congratulate the driver for his daring or be angry at him. Likely the highwaymen would have just robbed the passengers and ridden off without hurting anyone, and by fleeing, the driver had placed Edward, Susan, and Jonathan in greater danger.

On the other hand, there was always the

chance that the thieves had planned to murder their victims as well, and anyway, Clay didn't like the idea of giving in meekly. The driver had done the right thing, he decided, and the robbers who had been killed or wounded had gotten what they deserved.

Clay put a hand on Edward's shoulder. "I saw you take a shot at those men," he said. "You could have gotten your head blown off, sticking it out the window like that."

"Maybe," Edward agreed with a grin, "but what would *you* have done, Clay?"

After a second Clay had to return the grin. "I'd have taken a shot at them, too," he admitted. No Holt had ever greeted an attack passively. Likely no Holt ever would. "Get back on the coach, everyone," Clay continued. "We'll go on to Marietta and then out to the farm."

"That's right," Jeff added. "This family reunion has just begun."

Chapter One

Shining Moon sat in a rocking chair on the porch of the log house, moving gently back and forth. Of all the strange new things she had seen since journeying to Ohio with her husband, Clay Holt, this chair was perhaps her favorite discovery. She found the rhythm very soothing as she rocked and imagined that white women must find it quite helpful when calming cranky infants. There was nothing like it in the village of the Teton Sioux that was her home. She had never seen a rocking chair even in New Hope, the tiny settlement of white men near her Sioux village.

"You look very . . . content, Shining Moon," Melissa Holt commented from another rocking chair beside her. "Don't you miss your home, your own people?"

"Do you miss the land called North Carolina?" Shining Moon asked in return.

Melissa shrugged. "A little, I suppose," she admitted. "But any place is home as long as Jeff is there." She paused for a second, then went on, "I understand. You feel the same way about Clay."

Shining Moon nodded. She was wearing the homespun dress of a white woman that rustled and crinkled when she moved. It was not as comfortable as the soft, pliable doeskin garments and leggings of her people, but she was willing to wear it for the sake of Clay and his family. She did not want to stand out as different from the others or to frighten anyone who might think of her as a "savage."

Not that anyone would ever mistake Shining Moon for a white woman, not with her burnished copper skin, high cheekbones, dark doe eyes, and long, gleaming, raven's-wing hair.

Melissa Holt also had dark hair, but there the similarities between the two women ended — except for the fact that both of them were married to Holt men. Melissa's hair was dark brown, and she was several inches shorter than Shining Moon. Her skin was fair and lightly dusted with freckles. She was just as lovely as her Sioux sister-in-law, but in a different way.

Each was intimately acquainted with the wanderlust that sometimes gripped their men. Perhaps, Shining Moon reflected, she and Melissa Holt were more alike than either of them would have guessed.

She turned her gaze to the two boys

playing in front of the cabin. The women might have much in common, she mused, but the boys were as unlike as night and day and probably always would be. There was four years' difference in their ages, but that four years might as well have been twenty.

Michael Holt was fair, with a shock of blond hair so pale as to be almost white. Matthew Garwood's hair was so dark that, judged by that feature alone, might have easily been mistaken for Shining Moon's child. The boy was no relation to her, however. Matthew's mother was Josie Garwood, a young woman whose tragic life had led her from a farm near the Holt homestead in Ohio to a violent and unexpected death in the shadow of the Rockies. For a time Shining Moon had believed that Clay Holt was Matthew's father, but she knew better now. Both Matthew's parents were dead, and his only living relative was a crippled uncle, so Shining Moon and Clay had taken the boy to raise. That decision had been Shining Moon's. Clay had been reluctant, and given the bad blood between the Holts and the Garwoods, Shining Moon could not blame him for wanting as little to do with the boy as possible. But an innocent child, she had argued, should not be punished for the sins of his elders.

That had been her position early on, when she still thought of Matthew as innocent. Now, despite the warmth of the day, a chill shook her.

Still, despite what doubts she might harbor about Matthew, she thought it was safe to allow him to play with Michael while she and Melissa were only a few feet away, keeping an eye on them both. Michael had brought along a pair of carved wooden soldiers, his favorite toys, on the journey to Ohio. He and Matthew were marching them back and forth in the dirt to the beat of an imaginary drum. Matthew looked slightly bored; at seven years of age, he clearly considered himself too mature to be playing with a three-year-old.

As if she had read Shining Moon's thoughts, Melissa said, "I'm glad the boys get along so well."

Shining Moon nodded. "Yes. It is good for each of them to have a friend."

But they were not really friends, Shining Moon knew. She was relieved that Matthew was only bored and reluctant rather than dangerously resentful, as she had often seen him. It was foolish, she knew, but sometimes when his gaze grew dark, she thought he looked much older than his years, as if something ancient — and evil — dwelled inside him.

"Ho, there, lads!" The loud, hearty greeting penetrated Shining Moon's bleak reverie. One of the Gilworth brothers came around the corner of the cabin. She had not yet learned to distinguish between Castor and Pollux. Both brothers were massive and broad-shouldered, with thick, coarse black beards. They reminded her at times of the grizzly bears that roamed parts of her homeland.

"Castor!" Michael cried in reply. The boy had been able to tell the twins apart as soon as he had met them. Michael Holt was an unusually perceptive child, Shining Moon had discovered. He had eyes that saw clearly — with a few exceptions. He seemed to worship Matthew Garwood as much as he did Castor and Pollux Gilworth.

The little boy left the wooden soldiers where they lay and scrambled to his feet to run to Castor. The huge farmer scooped him up in one hamlike hand. "Pollux is getting ready to brand some of the calves," Castor said. "Do ye want to watch?"

"Oh, yes," Michael answered eagerly.

From the porch Melissa called, "You *brand* the cows, Mr. Gilworth? Why on earth do you do that?"

Castor lifted Michael to his shoulder and easily balanced the boy there. "The beeves run free, ma'am, and there's no way of knowing who they belong to unless we put the Holt brand on 'em."

"It seems rather cruel to me," Melissa said with a slight frown.

"Aye, I suppose it is," Castor agreed. "But it hurts them for only a short while, and what sort of caretakers would Pollux and I be if we allowed your husband's cattle to wander off with no way of identifying them?"

Melissa considered for a moment, then smiled. "I suppose you're right," she said. She thought of herself as a businesswoman, Shining Moon knew, so she could understand the necessity for such practices and accept them, unpleasant though they might be to her.

To Shining Moon, the whole discussion was pointless. How could one truly own anything? The earth and all that was above it, the sky and all that was below it — these things belonged ultimately to Wakan Tanka, the Creator, the Great Spirit who brought light and life to everything. But if these people of her husband's family wanted to pretend that they owned the land and the creatures who lived on it, then so be it. It was not her place to deny them their strange beliefs.

Castor Gilworth steadied Michael with one hand and reached out toward Matthew with the other. "Come along, lad," he said. "Don't ye want to watch the branding, too?"

Matthew looked down at the ground and shook his head. "No," he said shortly. "I'll stay here."

"You're sure?"

"I said so, didn't I?" Matthew snapped.

Shining Moon's lips tightened. She was about to scold Matthew but stopped herself. She had learned from experience that a strong reaction would only exacerbate his dark mood.

Castor shrugged, the movement of his shoulders rocking Michael a little and making the child cry out excitedly. Some children might be frightened on such an unsteady perch, but not Michael. Fearfulness was alien to his nature.

Castor and Michael went back around the cabin to the barn and the pens. Matthew stayed where he was, listlessly dragging the wooden soldiers back and forth in the dirt.

"I hope Jeff and Clay get back soon," Melissa said. "I'm ready to see the children again. Although I suppose they're not really children anymore. They must have grown so much since I saw them last. It's been years."

Shining Moon nodded. "Children grow quickly," she said.

Melissa took a deep breath. Quietly she said, "I've thought about asking Jeff if we can take them with us when we return to Wilmington instead of sending them back to his uncle and aunt in Pittsburgh. They really ought to be with their brother."

"Clay is their brother, too," Shining Moon said.

"Well, of course, but you wouldn't want to take them back to the . . . the wilderness —" Melissa stopped short and looked uncomfortable, glancing at Shining Moon as if she was worried that she might have offended her. "I mean, in North Carolina they could have a good education and all the other advantages of . . . of civilization."

"That is true," Shining Moon murmured. "The mountains and plains of my land are still wild and untamed, according to your ways. The children of my people live there and are happy, but the children of your people should be with their own kind."

"I've hurt your feelings —" Melissa began.

Shining Moon came to her feet. "No. Truly, you have not. You have spoken only the truth as you see it, and I cannot argue with you. Your world and mine will always be separate, Melissa." She smiled. "But that does not mean you and I cannot meet between those two worlds and be friends."

"I hope so," Melissa said. She reached up to grasp Shining Moon's hand and press it for a moment.

Shining Moon was still smiling, but inside, despite what she had told Melissa earlier, her heart was aching for her home.

John Steakley looked downright unhappy at the sight of him, Jeff Holt thought as he walked into the largest store in Marietta. And the man had good reason to feel that way, Jeff reflected, thinking back to the day several years earlier when he had come into Steakley's store seeking information about his wife, Melissa. Steakley had sent him on a wild-goose chase to New York. Not only that, but in his position as postmaster Steakley had also intercepted and destroyed numerous letters Melissa had sent to Jeff in care of the Marietta post office — all because Charles Merrivale, her father, had paid him to do so. All of this had come to light when Jeff and Melissa were finally reunited in North Carolina. Jeff would have been well within his rights to bring charges against Steakley. A hard fist to the jaw would have been equally justified, Jeff thought now.

Instead, he nodded curtly and said, "Afternoon, Mr. Steakley."

"Howdy, Jeff," the storekeeper replied, a false heartiness in his voice. "Good to see you again. I heard you were back. It's been a long time —"

"Yes, it has," Jeff interrupted.

"I got to tell you, Jeff," Steakley blurted, "I never meant any harm by what I did, and nobody was happier than me to hear that you and the Merrivale gal had finally gotten back together —"

Again, Jeff didn't let the man finish. "That's not why I'm here, Steakley," he said. "You own the only wagonyard in town. My brother and I want to rent a wagon."

"Sure thing. You can have the best one I got, no charge."

Jeff grunted as he took a small pouch from his belt and tossed it on the counter. "We'll pay," he said, his voice flat and expressionless, yet somehow menacing.

Steakley swallowed hard and nodded. "Whatever you want, Jeff. Yes, sir, whatever you want."

The only thing Jeff wanted at this moment was to get out of the store and head back to the Holt homestead. Clay, Ned, India, and the children were waiting outside for him. He concluded the deal with Steakley as quickly as possible, and the storekeeper hurried out the side door toward the barn where the wagon teams were stabled. "I'll have my hostler hitch you right up, Jeff," he called over his shoulder, his voice tinny with both false cheerfulness and utter fear.

Jeff strolled back out the front door of the store and rejoined Clay and the others. "We'll be ready to go in a few minutes," he told them.

Clay looked at him shrewdly. "Any trouble?"

"I didn't horsewhip Steakley, if that's what you mean," Jeff replied, summoning up a grin. "I reckon I might've felt like it, but I didn't do it."

"Fella likely doesn't know how lucky he is," Clay observed.

"Oh, he knows," Jeff said dryly. "He knows."

Several minutes later, the Holts were rolling westward out of Marietta toward the farm. Ned had tied his horse to the back of the wagon and climbed into the driver's seat. Edward sat beside him, while Susan and Jonathan rode in the back with all the bags. Clay, Jeff, and India rode horseback alongside the vehicle. The youngsters were still chattering excitedly, pointing out familiar landmarks in the beloved countryside where they had spent their earliest years.

Several times during the course of his married life, Jeff had come close to returning to the Ohio River valley with his wife and child, but something had always happened to prevent it. Now, with the business they had built up and the home they had established in Wilmington, it was unlikely they would ever come back to Ohio to stay. Jeff felt a slight sense of loss as he contemplated that possibility. This valley was home to him and always would be. But he was happy in North Carolina — happier than he had ever dreamed he could be, truth to tell. And Melissa and Michael were happy, too, which was even more important. He would not do anything to disrupt their lives.

But they could always come back for visits such as this one. Maybe someday, Jeff thought, he could even take them to see the mountains. Though he had never been drawn to the Rockies with the same compelling intensity that Clay was, he sometimes felt a pang of longing when he thought about the rugged, snowcapped peaks and the clean, crisp air of the high country.

It didn't take long to reach the Holt homestead, and the children grew even more excited as they approached the farm that had been their first home. The cabin was different now, of course; the log dwelling that

Bartholomew Holt had built when he first brought his family to the Ohio River valley was gone, destroyed in the same fire that had taken his life and that of his wife, Norah. The cabin in which the family was gathering now was the one Jeff, with the help of his father and brothers, had built for Melissa. Castor and Pollux Gilworth had added several rooms, sprucing it up until it was spacious enough to accommodate even as large a group as the Holts had become. Still, at the heart of the place was the original cabin in which Jeff and Melissa had begun their life as husband and wife, and every time he saw it, Jeff felt a pang of nostalgia.

That same feeling came over him now as the wagon rolled into sight of the cabin. Melissa was standing on the porch, her dark hair rippling in the spring breeze. She lifted a hand over her head and waved eagerly to the newcomers as she skipped down the steps. Jeff leaned forward in the saddle and returned the wave.

"Go ahead," Clay said from beside him in a mock growl. "Go say hello to your wife."

Jeff threw a grin at his brother and heeled the horse into a run. He swept up in front of the cabin and swung down from his saddle to gather Melissa in his arms.

Their kiss was warm and passionate. Jeff

never tired of the feel of his wife in his arms. They had been separated for a long time soon after their marriage, but he didn't think that was the reason. They were simply meant to be together, and each time they embraced it was like two halves of a whole coming back into one.

Melissa giggled as she pulled back a little. "If that's the way you greet me when we've only been apart for a little while, what will you do if you're ever gone for a long time again?"

"I won't be," Jeff told her. "You can count on that."

She smiled and chucked him on the chin, then leaned to the side so that she could look past him. "Oh, there are the children!" she exclaimed. "Edward looks so big. He's practically grown!"

"He'd be pleased to hear you say that. I reckon he feels the same way."

"And even Susan and Jonathan aren't little anymore." Melissa looked at Jeff again, her face suddenly solemn. "Time is passing, isn't it?"

He nodded, equally solemn, and said, "It's got a habit of doing that." He thought of his own son. "Where's Michael?"

"Out back with Castor and Pollux. I imagine he'll be here any minute, though, as

41

soon as he hears the others coming. He's anxious to meet his aunt and uncles."

True to Melissa's word, Michael came tearing around the corner of the cabin a moment later as the wagon rolled to a stop. Trailing him at a slower pace was Matthew. Then Castor and Pollux Gilworth lumbered around the corner, each lifting a hand in greeting.

Shining Moon came out to the porch from inside the cabin and smiled at Clay as he dismounted. He bounded up the steps and put an arm around her shoulders. Jeff thought his sister-in-law looked lovely in the dress Clay had bought for her, although he was not quite used to the sight of her in white woman's clothes. Ever since he and Clay had first met Shining Moon years earlier, she had always worn the beaded dresses of soft doeskin that the women of her tribe preferred.

The youngsters were piling out of the wagon. Melissa hugged each one in turn as Jeff stood back, a pleased grin on his face.

Meanwhile, Clay led Shining Moon down from the porch, his arm still around her shoulders. With his other hand he reached out toward Matthew, who stood nearby, eyes downcast, scuffing the dirt with the toe of one shoe. "Come on, Matthew," Clay said quietly but firmly.

The boy glanced up at him with a frown. Clay's expression was as stern as his voice. Matthew moved over beside Clay and Shining Moon but kept his hands jammed in his pockets.

After a moment Clay dropped his own hand. Small victories were better than none.

"You children remember Matthew Garwood, don't you?" Clay said.

Edward, Susan, and Jonathan exchanged glances. They remembered Matthew, all right, Jeff thought. They remembered all the Garwoods — and all the anguish they had brought the Holt family over the years. The Garwoods were gone now, though, except for Matthew and his uncle Aaron, who had become a staunch friend of Clay's and Jeff's in the Rockies. Jeff had assumed that all the old grudges had died along with Zach and Pete and Luther and Josie . . . but looking at Matthew now, he wasn't so sure.

Still, the Holts were going to make an effort at peace and reconciliation. Clay and Shining Moon had begun the process by taking Matthew in following the death of his mother. Edward continued now by stepping forward and holding out his hand to Matthew. "Howdy, Matthew," he said with a smile. "It's good to see you again."

Matthew stared at him for a second or

43

two, then smiled faintly and took Edward's hand. Jeff sensed that the adults were all heaving a mental sigh of relief. Susan stepped up and gave Matthew a brief hug, and then Jonathan pumped his hand and asked, "How are you, Matthew?"

"I'm all right, I reckon," Matthew said slowly. "How are you?"

"Mighty fine," Jonathan said. "Specially now that we're all back home."

Castor stepped up to the two boys and rested his big paws on their shoulders. "I reckon you figured out by looking at Pollux and me that we're pretty good cooks," he said. "I've got deep-dish apple pies in the Dutch oven. You boys want to help us polish 'em off?"

"Yes!" Jonathan said, and even Matthew nodded eagerly. Michael capered excitedly around the tree-trunk legs of Pollux Gilworth.

"That will be fine," Melissa said, "*after* we've all had our supper."

"Pie!" Michael said.

"After supper," Melissa repeated.

Pollux reached down and ruffled Michael's blond hair. "Come on, Whip," he said. "Let's go finish those chores in the barn whilst Castor rustles us up some vittles. Then we'll have that pie." He gestured toward Jonathan and Matthew. "You two come along, too."

Jonathan and Matthew followed Pollux and Michael around the corner of the cabin. Castor went inside, followed by Clay and Shining Moon, who were talking to Edward and Susan. The two older children were asking their Sioux sister-in-law about her life in the Rocky Mountains. They were clearly in awe of the beautiful, dark-haired woman their brother had brought back from the distant frontier.

Melissa looked at Jeff and raised one eyebrow. "Whip?"

Jeff shrugged. "Castor and Pollux have started calling Michael by that name. They saw me teaching him how to use a bullwhip the other day. He seems to like it."

"Jeff, he's too young to be doing such things. For goodness' sake, he'll put his eye out!"

Jeff laughed and slipped an arm around Melissa's waist, pulling her close to him. "I doubt that. The first thing I taught him was to be careful. Besides, once that child has his mind set on doing something, there's no talking him out of it."

Melissa sighed as she snuggled against her husband. "You're right. He's the most determined little boy."

"He gets that from his daddy."

"Oh? And what are you determined to do, Jefferson Holt?"

Jeff smiled, put his mouth next to Melissa's ear, and told her. She laughed, punched him lightly on the chest, then lifted her mouth to his for a brief kiss.

Then they went inside to join the rest of the Holts.

The reunion was going well, Clay reflected that evening. The meal Castor prepared, culminating in his delicious deep-dish apple pie, had been savored by everyone, and now they were all sitting around the big main room of the cabin, watching the fire crackling in the fireplace. The rocking chairs had been brought in from the porch, and Shining Moon was sitting in one of them, rocking happily back and forth. She had certainly taken to that chair, Clay thought as he watched her. All she needed to complete the picture was a baby cradled in her lap —

Clay's mouth tightened as he pushed that thought out of his head. The previous year, Shining Moon had lost the baby she was carrying, and Clay wondered if they would ever again have the chance to become parents. Shining Moon seemed healthy enough, and if it was the Lord's will, more children would come, he told himself. In the meantime, they had Matthew to raise . . .

"But I can't find them!"

Clay became aware of Michael's voice. The boy was talking to Melissa, and he sounded upset. He stood next to her chair, restlessly shifting from foot to foot.

"I'm sure they'll turn up," Clay heard Melissa say in a calm, soothing tone. "They have to be here somewhere."

"But they're *not!*" Michael insisted. "I've looked all over, and I can't find them."

Jeff strolled across the room to join his wife and child. "What's the matter?" he asked.

Melissa looked up at him distractedly. "Oh, Michael's just misplaced the toy soldiers he brought from home."

"Didn't mis . . . misplace them," Michael insisted. "I left them in front of the cabin when I went to watch Castor and Pollux branding the calves."

Melissa frowned. "I remember that," she said. She shot a glance at Shining Moon. "Matthew was playing with them."

Shining Moon stopped rocking and sat forward in the chair. "Matthew, do you know where Michael's toy soldiers are?"

Matthew was sitting cross-legged on the

floor not far from the fireplace, drawing figures on a slate with a piece of charcoal. He looked up and said sharply, "What?"

Clay walked over to stand beside him. "Have you seen Michael's toy soldiers?" he asked. "You were playing with them this afternoon." Clay didn't like what he saw in Matthew's eyes. The boy looked defensive.

Matthew shook his head. "I don't know what you're talking about. I haven't seen any stupid toy soldiers."

"They're not stupid!" Michael exclaimed. "And we were playing with them this afternoon!"

Matthew shrugged. "I haven't seen them since then. You must have done something with them."

"No," Michael insisted. "They were gone when I went back to get them. I thought you brought them into the cabin, Matthew."

"Well, I didn't."

Michael was unusually mature for his age and always had been, but he was still just a little boy. Tears welled up in his eyes as he said, "I can't find them. I *want* them!"

While Melissa tried to comfort her son, Clay hunkered on his heels next to Matthew so that he could look more directly into the boy's eyes. "If you know anything about this, you'd best tell the truth," he said heavily.

Without warning, Matthew slammed the slate down on the puncheon floor. "You won't believe me, no matter what I say! I'm just a Garwood, so that makes me a liar!" He leaped up and raced out the door before anyone could stop him.

Clay straightened, his face set in angry lines, and took a step toward the door himself when Castor Gilworth spoke up. "Ain't really none of my business, seeing as how I ain't family, but I'd let the boy go if I was you, Clay."

"Give him a chance to cool off a mite," Pollux added. "He'll be all right outside for a spell. Ain't no wild animals around that'd bother him, and all the Injuns in these parts are tame."

"Your friends are right, Clay," Shining Moon put in quietly. "Angry words will not help with that one."

Clay took a deep breath and glanced around the room. The mood of contentment that had prevailed only a few minutes earlier had vanished. Jeff and Melissa looked embarrassed, Michael was crying softly, and Edward, Susan, and Jonathan were staring at the floor, as if they wished they were somewhere else. After a moment, Clay nodded. "You're right," he said. "We'll let Matthew cool down. Maybe later we can get the truth out of him."

Jeff came over to his older brother and put a hand on his shoulder. "Maybe Matthew was telling the truth," he suggested.

"Maybe," Clay said, but he didn't believe that for a second.

"A couple of wooden soldiers aren't worth making a big fuss over," Jeff said quietly, so that Michael would not hear him. "Michael's got plenty more back in Wilmington. And they'll probably turn up later, anyway."

Clay nodded and said again, "Maybe."

No one was surprised a few minutes later when Melissa announced, "It's been a long day. I think we'll turn in. Come along, Michael." She took the boy's hand and led him into the room she and Jeff were using. Clay, Shining Moon, and Matthew were staying in the other bedroom. The younger Holts would sleep in the loft. Castor and Pollux had voluntarily moved to the barn for the time being.

The others followed Melissa's lead. Shining Moon came to Clay's side and took his hand. "Are you coming to bed, my husband?" she asked.

"In a little while," Clay replied. He took his pipe and his tobacco pouch from his pocket. "Think I'll smoke a little first."

Shining Moon nodded, sadness in her dark eyes. She missed her home, Clay thought, and she was as uneasy about Matthew as he was. Something ought to be done about that boy . . . but for the life of him, Clay did not know what it was. He had faced all sorts of trouble and danger in his hard life, but this business of being a parent was new territory for him.

Clay was alone in the room a few minutes later, packing his pipe, when Matthew slipped in the front door. Clay's back was turned, but he heard the door open and close and knew who was there. "Got anything to say for yourself?" he asked without turning around.

For a moment, there was silence. Then Matthew replied sullenly, "No."

"Go on to bed, then," Clay said. "We'll consider the matter closed."

"What about the brat's stupid toy soldiers?"

Clay's fingers tightened on his pipe, but he kept his temper in check. "If he doesn't find them, Michael will get over losing them."

"Well, I didn't do anything to them."

Clay wished he could believe that. He said wearily, "Just go on to bed, Matthew."

Clay heard soft footfalls as the boy padded across the room. The bedroom door opened and closed. Clay held his pipe in one hand and rubbed his bearded jaw with the other.

He could ride all night and fight all day, but trying to deal with the enigma that was Matthew Garwood left him mighty tired.

He squatted down beside the fireplace. The blaze had died down, leaving only embers and a few flickering flames. Clay reached out for a burning twig with which to light his pipe.

That was when he saw something among the ashes. Frowning, he carefully reached in and plucked out a charred piece of hardwood that had been carved into a recognizable shape. A few flecks of bright paint still clung to it.

It was a toy soldier's leg.

Chapter Two

Clay said nothing about the remains of the toy soldier he had found in the fireplace. He knew what must have happened: Matthew had brought the toys inside and concealed them among the kindling in the fireplace, knowing that a fire would be lit after the sun went down and that Michael's precious wooden soldiers would be consumed by the flames, leaving no evidence behind. The plan had almost worked, too.

But Clay knew the truth. What he didn't know was what he ought to do about it.

The only reason Matthew could have had for doing something so spiteful was a desire to hurt Michael. Matthew must have enjoyed watching Michael cry over his lost toys. Baffled by Matthew's apparent motive, Clay put what was left of the carved wooden figure in his war bag. He would figure out later what to do, he told himself.

But no answers came, and the problem haunted him over the next couple of days. There was no more trouble with Matthew; the boy seemed to be going out of his way to be cooperative, even friendly. But whenever Matthew's eyes met his, Clay could discern the old resentment, hidden now from everyone but him.

Clay knew that look. He had seen it often enough before in the eyes of Matthew's father — Josie's own brother, Zach Garwood.

Castor and Pollux Gilworth, proud of the improvements they had made on the farm, were pointing them out to Jeff and Clay.

"You boys have done a good job," Jeff told them, looking over the fields. "I doubt that Clay and I could have done any better."

"Probably not as well," Clay said. "I never was cut out to be a farmer."

"Our folks were some of the first settlers in this part of the country," Castor said. "They always had a good farm. Pa was a blacksmith, too, the best smith west of the Appalachians. Maybe you heard of him — Ulysses Gilworth?"

Clay and Jeff both shook their heads. "I'm afraid not," Jeff said. "But I'm sure he was as good as you say he was, Castor." He stood between the brothers and put his hands on their shoulders. "And you've done such a good job here that Clay and I have been talking about changing the arrangement we have with you."

"What?" Castor exclaimed. "You don't want us to take care of the place anymore?"

"I thought you were satisfied with what we've been doing," Pollux added.

Quickly Clay held up his hands. "That's not it at all. Jeff and I figured it's not fair to ask you to put so much into the place when you don't have any real stake in it. We want to give you part of the land, so it'll be your homestead, too."

Castor and Pollux looked at each other, smiles slowly spreading across their rugged, bearded faces. Then they turned to Clay and Jeff and shook their heads at the same time.

"Nope," Castor said. "That's a mighty generous offer, Clay —"

"But I reckon we got to turn it down," Pollux finished.

"Turn it down?" Jeff repeated, a puzzled frown on his face. "But why?"

"We want to be fair with you boys," Clay said.

Castor nodded. "We know that. And we appreciate it, too. But there's going to come a time when Pollux and me want to move on, and when that time comes, I reckon it'd be best if we weren't tied down."

"You see," Pollux said, "when some of your family decide they want to move back here to the farm permanent-like, Castor and me figure on heading farther west. There's a lot of country out there we've never seen."

"We've never been out of the Ohio River valley," Castor said.

"You want to be fur trappers?" Clay asked. That was about the only way to make a living west of the Mississippi.

Castor and Pollux both shook their heads again. "Nope," Castor said. "More folks are heading west all the time. Sooner or later, there's going to be farms and towns out there. We're going to help settle the place."

"That'll be the time to have a farm of our own," Pollux added. "Or a business of some kind. Maybe a freight line."

Jeff considered what the brothers were saying and nodded. "Well, you might have something there, boys," he agreed. "It'll be a long time before there's any real civilization beyond St. Louis, though."

"We've got time," Castor said confidently.

Pollux said, "So we thank you for your kind offer, but you see why we got to say no, thanks."

"If that's the way you want it," Clay said. "It may be a while before any of us comes back to take over the farm permanently, though." He knew *he* would not; it was fine to come back for a visit like this, but he would always return to the mountains. They were his true home now. He suspected that Jeff felt the same way about North Carolina. But it was always possible that Edward or Jonathan, or even Susan, when they got older, might want to reclaim the land their parents had settled.

"Like my brother said, we've got time," Pollux said. He pointed a blunt finger toward the cabin, several hundred yards away. "Somebody's coming."

Jeff shaded his eyes from the sun and squinted in that direction. "Sure is," he agreed. "Come on, let's go see who it is."

By the time they reached the cabin, the rider Pollux had spotted was sitting on the cabin porch, drinking from a dipperful of water that Susan had brought him. He looked up apprehensively as Clay and Jeff strode up to the porch.

"What are you doing here, Mr. Steakley?" Jeff asked. Clay could tell that his brother was trying his best to control his temper and remain polite. If Clay had been in Jeff's place — if Steakley had lied to him and helped keep him from his wife for several long months — Clay doubted he would make the effort. He gave Steakley a hard, unfriendly stare.

The storekeeper came hastily to his feet and handed the dipper back to Susan. "Th-

thank you, young lady," he stammered. He swallowed hard as he turned toward Jeff and Clay. He was wearing a coat instead of the usual apron he sported in the store, and a beaver hat was perched on his balding head. A leather pouch was slung on a strap over his shoulder. He opened the pouch flap, reached inside, and said, "I got something here for you, Clay."

That took Clay by surprise. "For me?" he said. "What in blazes could you have for me?"

"It's a letter, I think," Steakley said as he withdrew a folded paper from the pouch and held it out. "I pert' near forgot I even had it. It came a long time ago for you, last year sometime, I reckon. Seeing you folks in town the other day finally reminded me I had it, and then I had to look around for a while before I found where I had stuck it."

Clay hesitated, then stepped forward and took the letter from Steakley's hand.

"Nice to see you're taking your duties as postmaster a little more seriously these days," Jeff said dryly. "I seem to recall some letters written to me that never got where they were going."

Steakley sniffed and made an attempt to look haughty. "I did what I thought best," he said.

"You did what Charles Merrivale paid you to do."

Steakley sniffed again and looked down at the porch floor. There was no argument he could make to counter that charge. Everyone knew it was true.

Clay turned the folded paper over in his fingers. It was heavy, and on the back was a rough circle of wax into which a seal had been pressed. Something about the seal was familiar. Clay flipped the paper over again and examined the cramped handwriting. The letter was addressed to him in care of the postmaster of Marietta, Ohio; Marietta was spelled "Marryeta."

"Good Lord," Clay breathed, realizing why the seal was familiar and remembering where he had seen the tortured script and the misspelling before. "It's from Captain Lewis."

"Meriwether Lewis?" Jeff exclaimed in surprise. Steakley's eyes widened, too. Nearly everyone had heard of the famous journey of exploration led by Meriwether Lewis and William Clark over the Rockies to the Pacific in 1804. Clay Holt had accompanied them as a member of their Corps of Discovery. There were areas in the West that had been seen only by Clay and a handful of other white men.

"That's the captain's scribbling, all right," Clay said. He turned the letter over again, worked the wax seal loose with a fingernail, and unfolded the paper.

During the expedition, Captain Lewis had permitted Clay to read some of the entries in his journal, so Clay had some experience at deciphering the explorer's chicken scratchings. Still, it took him a couple of minutes to comprehend what Lewis had written. When he did, he looked up frowning and grim-faced.

"Wait a minute," Steakley said from the porch. "Didn't I hear that that Lewis fella is dead?"

"That's right," Clay said heavily. "Reckon you could say this is a letter from beyond the grave."

"Well, he wrote it while he was still alive," Jeff pointed out. "What does he want, Clay? Or what *did* he want?"

"Wants me to go to Washington City," Clay replied. "It says here that all the members of the Corps of Discovery received land grants as payment for their services during the expedition, in addition to their wages."

"Land grants?" Jeff repeated. "I don't recall your ever getting a land grant from the government."

Clay shook his head slowly. "Nope, I sure didn't. This is the first I've heard of it. But according to the captain, I was supposed to receive one just like the other men. My name was on the list that he turned in to the government when we got back. All he can figure is that somewhere along the way I accidentally got left out." He looked sharply at the storekeeper. "You say this letter came for me last year?"

Steakley's Adam's apple bobbed nervously in his throat. "That's right. Don't remember exactly when. Sorry, Clay."

"Captain Lewis died year before last in Tennessee, while he was making a trip up to Washington City," Clay mused. "Folks say he shot himself because he got into some sort of trouble. I don't know about that, but I reckon writing this letter must've been one of the last things he did before he died. Says all I have to do is go to Washington and claim what I've got coming to me."

"Are you going to?" Jeff asked. "Go to Washington City, I mean?"

Clay looked at his brother and answered honestly, "I don't know." This news was a bolt out of the blue. He had never given much thought to owning land other than the farm his parents had built. He had been content to live his life in the mountains and the prairies, which, according to the beliefs of his wife's people, truly belonged only to the Great Spirit.

"Seems to me you ought to," Jeff said. "If you've got something coming to you, you ought to claim it. Of course, it's none of my business . . ."

Distractedly, Clay shook his head. "No, that's all right. You're my brother, and you have a right to say whatever you want. But all I know right now is that I have to talk this over with Shining Moon."

"Good," Jeff said. "I reckon that'd be for the best."

It would almost have been better, Clay suddenly thought, if Steakley had never remembered having this letter. Then he would not be faced with such a difficult decision. Things were generally a whole lot simpler when they didn't change.

Unfortunately, life rarely worked out that way.

Shining Moon was in the cabin explaining to her sister-in-law how to make pemmican. Melissa's nose wrinkled in distaste as Shining Moon described the mixture of jerked meat, buffalo fat, and chokecherries. Melissa would probably never learn to appreciate how tasty and nourishing this staple of her people's diet could be, Shining Moon thought. But then, she allowed, so many ways of the whites would forever remain a mystery to her.

Clay came into the room, carrying a piece of paper in his hand, and as always, Shining Moon's heart gave a little leap at the sight of her husband. The feeling was fleeting, however, because she could tell by his expression that something was bothering him.

She stood up to greet him and put a hand on his arm. "What is it?" she asked.

Jeff came into the room behind Clay and went to Melissa's side, resting his hand on her shoulder as she sat in the rocking chair. Quietly she said, "I saw Mr. Steakley outside a few minutes ago. What's going on, Jeff? Is there trouble in town?"

"Clay got some news," Jeff replied cryptically. "Reckon I'd better let him tell it." He looked at his brother. "Melissa and I can give you some privacy if you want it, Clay."

"No, that's all right," Clay said. "Secrets usually get folks into more trouble. I'd just as soon not keep any from my family."

Shining Moon looked into his eyes. "Tell me, Clay Holt," she said.

Clay lifted the paper he held in his hand and said, "I've got a letter here from Meriwether Lewis, one of the captains from that expedition I went on back in '04. He says the government was supposed to give me a land grant in return for my services, but somehow a mistake was made and I never got my land. Seems they've found the mistake now — or they did a couple of years ago, when Captain Lewis wrote the letter — and I can claim the land by going to Washington City."

"Clay, that's wonderful!" Melissa exclaimed. "I've always thought you explorers more than deserved any compensation you received."

Shining Moon looked at the letter in Clay's hand. She understood the words he had spoken but was struggling to grasp the concept behind them. "The government will give you land?" she asked.

"That's right," Clay said. "Leastways, according to Captain Lewis it will."

"Where is this land?"

Clay shrugged. "I don't rightly know. The captain's letter doesn't say, and since this is the first I've heard about the land grants, I just don't know."

"They would pay you . . . with something that is not theirs to give?"

"Well . . . the government figures it *is* their land to give, since we bought it from that Frenchman Napoleon."

"We bought it?" Shining Moon said.

"The United States government did."

Clay sighed, and Shining Moon felt a flash of anger. He was growing frustrated with her because she could not understand the ways of his people. Could he not see how foolish it was to speak of owning land, especially when it was owned by "the government," which to Shining Moon was something imaginary, made up by the white men to keep themselves from killing each other. Clay had told her in the past that it was like the council of elders that ruled her band of the People, but Shining Moon could not imagine the white leaders in this place called Washington City smoking the pipe of wisdom, blowing smoke to the four winds, and being guided by the honored spirits.

Shining Moon pushed aside her momentary irritation and concentrated on the matter at hand. "You will leave here and go to Washington City?" she asked Clay.

"I don't know yet," Clay said. Shining Moon could see how troubled he was by the decision facing him.

"It's none of my business —" Jeff began.

"You're my brother," Clay said. "As much as we've been through together, there's nothing you can't say to me, Jeff."

"All right. I was just going to say that it looks to me like you don't really have a choice, Clay. You've got to find out what your rights are. The government might let you claim the land anywhere you want. You could own your own private chunk of the Rockies."

Clay looked doubtful. "I don't know. Wouldn't seem right somehow, owning part of the Shining Mountains like that."

"What about New Hope?" Jeff asked. "From what you've told me, it's turned into a right busy little settlement."

"You want me to claim New Hope and throw people out of their homes?" Clay exclaimed. "Blast it, Jeff —"

"Hold on, hold on." Jeff raised both hands to forestall Clay's protest. "That's not what I meant at all, and if you'd just stop and think for a minute, you'd know I would never suggest anything like that."

"Well . . . I reckon not," Clay said sheepishly.

"What I meant was, you could claim land near New Hope, so that as the settlement grows, you'd have some say over *how* it grows."

"Sounds like you want me to start acting like a businessman or something," Clay muttered.

"It wouldn't hurt you to start thinking about the future," Jeff said.

Clay grunted. "You've changed a mite, little brother, that's all I've got to say." He turned back to Shining Moon. "What about you? What do you think I should do?"

"I do not know," she said truthfully, hoping she was not letting him down. "How long would you be gone?"

"I'm not sure." Clay shrugged. "A couple of weeks, maybe?"

"More like three or four, to get from here to Washington and back," Jeff put in.

"That's a long time." Clay looked down at the letter in his hand. "But Captain Lewis wanted me to go . . ."

"You should go," Shining Moon said abruptly. She could tell that, deep down, Clay was anxious to travel to Washington and clear this matter up. If that was what he wanted, then she wanted it, too.

He looked up at her in surprise. "What about you and the boy?"

"We will remain here until you return for us," Shining Moon declared.

"You could come with me," Clay suggested.

She shook her head. "No. You will travel more quickly without us, and the sooner you return, the sooner we will go back to the mountains." Shining Moon would not have admitted it, even to Clay, but the thought of traveling farther east, to one of the largest cities of the white men, terrified her. She had known many good white men — Clay, of course, and Jeff, and Father Thomas, the priest in New Hope — but she had also suffered greatly at the hands of whites. This farm in the Ohio River valley was as close as she ever wanted to get to their civilization.

Clay put his hands on her shoulders. "Are you sure about this?" he asked solemnly.

"I am certain," she told him.

"I could come with you, Clay," Jeff mused. "I've never seen Washington City."

"Just a moment," Melissa said. "I thought you said we wouldn't be separated again."

Jeff turned to her and said earnestly, "It wouldn't be for long, Melissa. You and Michael can go on back to North Carolina, and I'll join you there after Clay finishes his business in Washington. That won't take nearly as long as coming back here to get the two of you and then going home."

Clay gave a short bark of laughter. "Sounds to me like the only reason you want me to go to Washington is so you can invite yourself along for the trip."

Jeff grinned. "You're not the only one in the family with the itch to see the world, Clay." He looked at his wife again. "Well, Melissa, what do you think?"

She looked sternly at him for a moment, then sighed and smiled indulgently. "I could never deny you something you want so badly, Jeff. If Shining Moon can give her blessing for this trip, then I suppose I can, too."

Jeff bent down and gave her a quick kiss. "Thanks, darling. I'll get back to Wilmington as quickly as I can."

"Michael and I will be there waiting for you," Melissa promised.

Clay looked at Shining Moon again, and she smiled bravely at him.

"You and Matthew will be all right with Castor and Pollux until I get back," he said.

She nodded. "I know."

"We'll be back in the mountains before all the spring pelts are gone."

Shining Moon knew he meant his promise, but somehow she doubted that he would be able to keep it. Something inside her wanted to beg him not to go, to plead with him to forget about this unexpected grant of land and return with her to the prairies and mountains that were their true home.

But she would not do that. He would do what he must, and so would she.

"What about the children?" Clay asked as he turned to Jeff.

"Melissa and I were giving some thought to taking them to Wilmington with us," Jeff said, "but I suppose under the circumstances it'd be better if they went back to

Uncle Henry and Aunt Dorothy's home in Pittsburgh for the time being. They can join us later, once I'm back in Wilmington."

"Have you asked Edward about that? He's liable to think he's a grown man now and ought to have some say in where he lives."

Jeff nodded. "You're right. I'll talk to him. I still think it's best that all three of them head back to Pittsburgh, though."

"I reckon you're right," Clay agreed.

Melissa sighed. "I suppose this means our family reunion is over."

Clay and Jeff both looked at her, and Shining Moon noted that they at least had the good grace to seem a little embarrassed. They were excited at the prospect of a new adventure — although from everything Shining Moon had heard, a trip from Ohio to Washington ought to be peaceful enough — but they knew their decision affected others besides themselves.

"You're right," Jeff said. "The reunion is over. But it was a good time for all of us, wasn't it?"

Shining Moon wished she could agree, but instead she found herself thinking of the homeland she missed so badly. And she was thinking of Matthew, too.

Clay was going to leave her here with Matthew. She would be responsible for him now. That was fitting, she told herself, since it had been her idea to take him in following the death of his mother.

But she thought of the dark menace she sometimes saw in his eyes, and she had to repress a shudder. She hoped Clay would hurry back and take her home. She hoped that with every fiber of her being.

Chapter Three

"This visit wasn't nearly long enough," Susan said, a catch in her voice. She threw her arms around Clay's neck and hugged him tightly.

"I know, honey." He patted his sister awkwardly on the back. "We'll all be together again, and it won't be as long between visits next time."

"Promise?" Susan asked.

"I promise." Clay had never been comfortable making pledges like this. He had seen enough of life to know how uncertain it was, and he knew that often a promise, no matter how sincere, didn't mean a blasted thing in the face of harsh reality. But for now it was something he was willing to say to make his sister feel better, whether or not anything ever came of it.

Susan sniffled a little as she left Clay's arms and stepped over to hug Jeff. Jonathan came up to Clay and stuck his hand out, and Clay could tell that his youngest brother was trying to handle this farewell like a man. But Jonathan wasn't a man; he was nine years old, and tears that he could not hold back shone in his eyes.

"So long, Clay," Jonathan said. "You'll have to come to Pittsburgh sometime and see us."

"Or Wilmington," Melissa put in. "You'll be living there with us soon enough, Jonathan."

"That's right," the boy said, smiling. He and Susan had been thrilled to hear that Jeff and Melissa wanted to take them to North Carolina to live. They adored Uncle Henry and Aunt Dorothy, but living with Jeff's family would feel more like old times.

Solemnly, Clay shook Jonathan's hand. "I'm counting on you to look after things," he said.

Jonathan nodded, equally solemn. "I won't let you down, Clay."

The family was gathered in Marietta to say farewell to its younger members. The stagecoach that had brought them to Ohio would soon be rolling out, eastbound now after traveling on to Cincinnati and turning around there. It would follow the post road back along the Ohio River to Pennsylvania, carrying Edward, Susan, and Jonathan among its passengers.

Although Susan and Jonathan were sorry to see the family visit come to an end, Clay knew they did not mind being sent back to

Pittsburgh. But Edward was a different story. He stood off to one side of the porch in front of Steakley's store. He had not welcomed the news that Clay and Jeff were traveling to Washington. Or rather, Clay thought, he had not welcomed their decision to go without him.

As soon as Clay had told the younger members of the family about the trip, Edward had insisted on accompanying them. "I'm old enough now to go with you," he said. "I can ride and shoot just fine."

"We're going to Washington, not the frontier," Jeff had told him with a grin. "I don't think there'll be much need for shooting."

"You know what I mean," Edward had said. "I won't hold you back, I swear I won't."

As far as Clay was concerned, speed was of the essence. That was the reason he and Jeff would be journeying overland, on horseback. They could have ridden the same coach that would carry the children back to Pittsburgh; from there the route went on to Philadelphia and New York. Or they could have taken a keelboat back up the Ohio to Pittsburgh and then traveled overland. But they would make the best time, Clay had decided, by riding their horses all the way. They would take a couple of spare mounts, and by switching back and forth to keep the animals fresh, they would cover the miles in a hurry.

And that was important, because Clay wanted nothing more than to get this business of the land grant cleared up quickly so that he could return to Marietta and then begin the long journey back to the mountains with Shining Moon and Matthew.

Clay strode over to Edward now and extended his hand. "You're the one I'll really be counting on," he said in a low voice so that Jonathan wouldn't hear. "You take care of your brother and sister, hear?"

Grudgingly, Edward took Clay's hand. "I still say they'd be just fine going back to Pittsburgh by themselves. That was no reason to tell me I couldn't come to Washington with you and Jeff."

"Maybe next time."

"How do you know there'll *be* a next time?" Edward challenged.

"There will be," Clay said.

"I'm not Susan or Jonathan," Edward shot back. "I know that promises don't really mean very much. You know it, too."

Clay stiffened. Was his outlook on life really that bleak? True, he had seen more than his share of trouble and tragedy, but he had experienced joy and hope, too. A fellow couldn't give up just because things didn't work out all the time.

"We'll see the elephant together, don't you worry about that," he said as he shook Edward's hand. "Your time's coming."

Edward didn't look convinced, but he tempered his resentment enough to throw an arm around Clay's shoulders and slap him on the back. Clay returned the gesture.

When he turned away from Edward toward the street, he saw Matthew standing there by himself, head down, scuffing the toe of his shoe in the dust. That was a typical pose for the boy. He never joined in when he could stand apart. Shining Moon stood at the edge of the porch, watching him. Clay saw the worry on his wife's face. She was probably wishing she had never suggested that she and Clay raise Matthew after Josie's death. Clay himself had wished many times that he had not agreed. But it was too late now; Matthew was their responsibility.

Only now he was about to leave, and Shining Moon would have to take care of Matthew by herself for a while.

At least Castor and Pollux would be around to give her some help, Clay told himself. With those two on hand, he doubted that Matthew could get into too much trouble. He would never have decided to go to Washington otherwise.

Jeff shook hands with Edward and Jonathan, and Melissa hugged both boys. Michael imitated his father and stuck out his hand, shaking solemnly with his uncles. Ned and India said their farewells, too, as the driver of the stagecoach emerged from Steakley's and looked around at the large gathering of Holts.

"Ready to roll, folks," he said. "Them that's going better get on board."

The children's bags had already been loaded into the boot at the back of the coach. Ned opened the door of the passenger compartment and held it as Edward, Susan, and Jonathan climbed aboard. Clay moved beside Shining Moon and put an arm around her shoulders. Jeff did the same with Melissa and then dropped his free hand on Michael's shoulder as the boy leaned against his leg. Clay noticed and wondered what it would feel like to be that close to Matthew. He would probably never know, he thought. Matthew had never softened toward any of the Holts; always withdrawn and suspicious, he shunned all attempts at affection and warmth. Clay squeezed his wife's shoulder as he thought again of leaving Matthew in her care.

His sober reflections were cut short by the

children's shouted good-byes. The coach was rolling down the road, the three younger Holts waving madly out the windows. Clay and Shining Moon waved back. Before the day was through, Clay and Jeff would be on their way as well, and within a couple of days Melissa and Michael, along with Ned and India, would follow suit. The time of coming together was over.

The Holts were on the move again.

The young man prowled stealthily along the ridge, just below the crest. From time to time he raised his head to peer over the top into the shallow valley on the other side. The buffalo were still there, grazing peacefully on the lush grasses. The young man smiled and tightened his grip on the bow in his hand.

His name was Proud Wolf, and he was a Teton Sioux. He had seen twenty summers and was a man full-grown, although he was neither tall nor brawny. What he might lack in size, however, he made up for in speed, cunning, and intelligence. Had he not penetrated into the far reaches of the Blackfoot stronghold, in the land the white men called Canada, to help Clay Holt ruin the murderous plans of the evil one known as McKendrick? Clay was the husband of

Shining Moon, Proud Wolf's sister, and even more importantly, he was Proud Wolf's friend.

Wearing only buckskin leggings, a loincloth, a quiver of arrows, and a necklace made of elk teeth, Proud Wolf stalked the buffalo alone. He spent much of his time these days in solitude. Clay and Shining Moon had returned to Clay's homeland in the east, in the land the whites called Ohio, and although Shining Moon had asked Proud Wolf to go with them, he had declined the offer. True, he was curious about white men and their ways, but something bound him to these prairies and the mountains that loomed over them.

He was waiting for Raven Arrow to return to him.

Raven Arrow — the warrior maiden who had been known as Butterfly when she first began her pursuit of Proud Wolf — had given her life to save her companions during their journey of vengeance to Canada. Since then, Proud Wolf had been haunted by visions of a pale, ghostly mountain lion — a spirit cat. He sensed that the cat was not the spirit of Raven Arrow herself, but he had decided that the visions came to prepare him for the return of Raven Arrow. Somehow she was going to come back to him.

And until that day he would hunt alone, returning only occasionally to the village of his father, Bear Tooth, near the white settlement known as New Hope. He had friends in both the Sioux village and New Hope, among them Aaron Garwood and the priest, Father Thomas, but none of them could help him grasp the true significance of the visions. He had not sought them; he had not asked the spirit cat to come. But since it had, he would discern its message himself, seeking aid from no one.

His solitary days were not without their pleasures. He enjoyed the hunt, and now, as he silently slid an arrow from the quiver and nocked it on his bowstring, he felt the familiar drumming of anticipation within his breast. He had drawn within bowshot of the small herd of buffalo. The wind was right, and the buffalo were stupid. Proud Wolf knew that he could fell several of them with his arrows before they realized what was happening. There was a Sioux hunting party nearby; he had seen their sign that morning. He would find them and bring them to the buffalo he killed, so that they could return to their village with plenty of hides and meat. He would help his people, even though for the time being he chose not to dwell among them.

With his muscles tensed and the bow-string drawn back halfway, he was ready to step over the ridge and let fly with his first arrow. Then he heard a noise in the distance.

Gunshots.

Proud Wolf stiffened. He had seen no sign of white men in the area in recent days. Other than the settlers at New Hope, the only whites he knew of were the fur trappers who traveled up and down the mountain streams, setting their traplines. Few of them ventured out here on the prairie, since the beaver were much more numerous in the mountains. But the dull, heavy roar of charges of black powder exploding could only mean white men. Few Indians in the area carried guns.

Uncertain whether or not to investigate, Proud Wolf hesitated just below the crest of the ridge. Suddenly, the sound of racing hooves came to his ears from the far side of the rise, and he knew the buffalo were on the move. The shots would not have frightened them; Proud Wolf had seen white hunters stand and shoot down a dozen or more of the shaggy beasts before their puny brains comprehended the connection between the loud noises and the deaths of their fellows. But something had spooked them, and as he turned back toward the ridge, Proud Wolf saw what it was.

A huge mountain lion crouched there, its tail lashing back and forth. The cat was as white as the snow that capped the distant mountains. As Proud Wolf's eyes widened in shock, it let out a loud, growling cry.

The spirit cat! It had returned, but this time, instead of the spectral shape that had haunted Proud Wolf's visions for many moons, it had taken physical form. It was real, and its cry — and scent — were enough to send the buffalo stampeding away. Proud Wolf cried out in frustration and fear. The cat swung its massive head toward him.

Pale eyes met his.

Suddenly Proud Wolf understood. The spirit cat had stampeded the herd for a reason. There was something else he was meant to do, something more important than hunting the buffalo.

And it was connected with the gunshots he had heard.

His pulse hammering madly in his head, Proud Wolf turned and began to run. His every instinct cried out a warning that he should not turn his back on the beast, but he knew somehow that he had nothing to fear. It was not going to attack him.

Go. Go, a voice said in his head. *Follow this*

*trail where it may lead you. The mountains —
and she who waits for you — will be here when
you return.*

With both command and reassurance
echoing in his mind, Proud Wolf raced
across the prairie, toward the sounds of
battle.

I hope I'm not making a mistake, Jeff Holt
said to himself as he slung his saddlebags
across the back of the horse he had selected
for the first leg of the journey. It was a good-
sized bay mare with a white blaze on its face.
Clay was nearby, saddling a rangy, jugheaded dun gelding with a dark stripe down
the center of its back.

After long months of forced separation
from Melissa, months during which he
couldn't be sure he would ever find her, Jeff
had sworn he would never again be apart
from his family. Only the direst circumstances had forced him to break that vow in
the past.

But now he was *choosing* to leave his wife
and son, if only for a while, and that was an
important distinction. He felt as if he was
letting Melissa and Michael down, and he
was starting to wonder if he ought to tell
Clay that he had changed his mind.

"I left my powder horns inside," Clay

said. "Reckon I'd better go get them." As he strode toward the cabin, he passed Melissa, who was walking out to Jeff.

Jeff snugged his saddlebags in place and turned to look at his wife. Melissa was smiling, although he could see a tinge of regret in her eyes.

As if she had heard the thoughts going through his head a few moments earlier, she laid a soft hand on his arm and said quietly, "This is a good thing you're doing, Jeff."

"What, abandoning you and Michael?" The question came out more harshly than he had intended, but he was feeling guilty and more than a little peeved at himself.

"You're not abandoning anyone," Melissa said firmly. "Ned and India have decided to come back to Wilmington with us and catch a ship to Boston from there, so Michael and I won't be traveling alone."

Jeff felt a surge of relief. "Well, that's good to know. You'll be safe enough with those two around. I reckon they can handle just about anything I could. Ned's a good man in a fight, and India's smart as they come."

Melissa's fingers tightened on his arm. "I'll miss you, of course. I'll miss you terribly, and so will Michael. But it's only for a few weeks, and it's for a good cause."

"Indulging my need to roam the world,

you mean?" Jeff asked with a smile.

"Helping your brother is what I mean." Melissa cast a glance over her shoulder toward the cabin, then looked at Jeff again. "Out there on the frontier there's no one I'd trust more with my life than Clay Holt. But Washington isn't the frontier, Jeff. Clay's going to be lost when he gets there, and you know it. He'll need your help getting everything straightened out with this land grant."

Jeff frowned. Melissa might have a point. Clay could track almost anything over any kind of terrain, and there was no one more skilled when it came to riding and shooting — or fighting. But he had no experience at all in dealing with politicians and government officials. Neither did Jeff, of course, but he had been in business and had learned something of the art of talking to people and getting what he wanted from them. Clay was sometimes too blunt for his own good.

"I reckon that must've been in the back of my mind when I invited myself to go along with him," Jeff admitted, "but you've got to know the truth, Melissa. I've never been to Washington before, and I wanted to go."

She tipped her head back and laughed softly. "Do you think I don't know that? But it doesn't really matter why you spoke up, Jeff. What's important is that Clay needs you, and you can't let him down. I wouldn't want you to."

Jeff put his hands on her shoulders and shook his head in wonder. "You're a mighty special woman, Melissa Holt," he said fervently. "And I'm mighty glad I married you."

"Then you'll hurry home once you and Clay are finished in Washington."

"You can count on that," Jeff said, and his mouth came down on hers to seal the promise.

After a long, heated moment, Melissa put her hands on his chest and moved back a little, breaking the kiss. "You're shameless, Jeff!" she exclaimed breathlessly. "We're right out here in plain sight."

"Yep, and in broad daylight, too," he agreed with a grin.

At the sound of voices Melissa pulled away some more, a blush spreading prettily over her face. Jeff slipped his left arm around her shoulders and waited as Clay, Shining Moon, Michael, Ned, and India came out of the cabin.

As Ned came up to them, Jeff extended his right hand. "Melissa tells me that you and India are making the trip back to Wilmington, too. I'm obliged, Ned."

"No need to thank me," Ned said, grinning as he shook Jeff's hand. "It was India's idea. To tell you the truth, I think she and Melissa are hatching some sort of scheme between them. They're plotting against us, Jeff."

"And you're a madman," India said dryly in her crisp English accent. "What sort of plot could a couple of helpless women such as ourselves come up with?"

"Helpless?" Ned repeated. "You're about as helpless as a grizzly bear!"

India looked as if she didn't know whether to punch him in the face or kiss him. She settled for sighing and rolling her eyes.

Jeff lifted Michael in his arms. "You're going to be a good lad while I'm gone, aren't you?"

"Yes, sir," Michael said solemnly.

"You'll take care of your mother and do everything she tells you?"

Michael nodded.

"And you won't go exploring where you're not supposed to and get into trouble?"

Michael stuck a finger in his mouth and didn't say anything. Obviously that was a more difficult promise for him to make. The adults laughed, knowing Michael's restless nature and his penchant for getting into places that were forbidden to him.

"Don't worry, Jeff," Melissa said. "I'll

keep a close eye on him."

"Better make it two eyes," Jeff said. "He's tricky."

"Am not!" Michael protested. "Just like to look at things."

"All right." Jeff hugged his son tightly, then turned and handed him to Melissa. A few feet away, Shining Moon was in Clay's arms. Jeff could not see her face, but he could see Clay's, and he knew this parting was hard on him. Right about now Clay had to be wishing he had said to hell with that government land grant.

But Clay wasn't the sort to back out of something once he had committed himself to it. He kissed Shining Moon and then stepped over to the dun, taking its reins in his hand. "We'd better be riding," he said gruffly to Jeff and swung up into the saddle.

Jeff gave Melissa one last hug after she set Michael on the ground. He put his hand under her chin, cupping it momentarily as he looked deeply into her eyes. Then he turned and mounted up as well.

Ned handed the reins of the spare horses to Jeff and Clay, then stepped back and put his arm around India's slender waist. Melissa stood with Michael, his hand clutched in hers. Shining Moon stood straight and alone, her dark-eyed gaze fastened on Clay.

Clay lifted a hand in farewell as he wheeled his horse around and kneed it into motion.

Jeff smiled and waved before he turned his horse and fell in alongside his brother. Both men heeled their mounts into a trot that carried them along the road leading to Marietta. They had gone about fifty yards when a shout of "Good-bye!" in a child's voice made Jeff pause and look back over his shoulder. He saw Michael waving frantically at him, and he returned the wave with a bittersweet smile.

"Hard as hell, ain't it?" Clay asked from beside him. Jeff noticed that Clay had not turned around. Maybe he didn't trust himself to.

"It's hard, but we're doing the right thing, Clay," Jeff said as he forced himself to face the road again. "It would always eat at you if you just ignored Captain Lewis's letter."

"The captain's dead," Clay said flatly. "It won't make a bit of difference to him whether I go to Washington or not."

"Yes, but he wanted you to have that land grant. You were supposed to have it, and I reckon Captain Lewis felt it was unfinished business for him, too, as long as you hadn't claimed it."

"You mean I'm doing this so the captain can rest easy."

"I guess you could say that," Jeff agreed. "Besides, you don't know how things will work out. The whole business could turn out to be more important for you than you think. And for other folks, too."

"Or it could be more trouble than it's worth."

"Well . . . that's true of just about anything, isn't it?"

Clay didn't answer for a moment. Then, with a faint smile, he said, "I reckon."

Neither of them looked back again as they rode on.

Chapter Four

The gunfire had become more sporadic as Proud Wolf ran easily over the rolling hills. If the shooting stopped altogether, that would be a bad sign. It would mean that the white men had been overwhelmed by whatever enemy had attacked them.

Of course, Proud Wolf reminded himself, it was always possible that what he was hearing was a hunting party. White men could be shooting buffalo, which they sometimes did for the sport of it — though what sport there was in slaughtering such dumb animals, Proud Wolf had never understood.

But he had heard no sounds of a stampede, nor seen any haze of dust in the air, and any herd of buffalo would have begun running by now, after this much shooting. Besides — if such a thing were possible — the gunshots had sounded to him somehow *desperate.*

As if men were fighting for their lives.

He was close now, but the firing had dwindled away to an occasional blast. Proud Wolf raced up another rise, then dropped to his hands and knees before he reached the top of it. Carefully, he peered over.

A small stream bordered by stunted trees trickled through the valley on the other side. A wagon was parked beside the stream, about an arrow's flight from where Proud Wolf crouched and watched. A team of mules and several horses were milling around nervously in a makeshift pen that had been created by stretching ropes between some trees on the creek bank.

To Proud Wolf's left, a dry coulee ran down the slope to join with the bed of the stream. Proud Wolf spotted the eagle feathers adorning the hair of several Indians who were using the coulee for cover and firing arrows toward the wagon. At first glance he could not identify which band they came from, or which tribe.

There appeared to be two, perhaps three white men lying under the wagon, returning fire with flintlock rifles. Sprawled facedown on the ground nearby was another white man, this one with a pair of arrows embedded in his back. Proud Wolf could tell at a glance that he was probably dead.

This fight had nothing to do with him, Proud Wolf told himself. He had no way of knowing who had started it or who was in the right. Despite his friendship with Clay and Jeff Holt and Aaron Garwood, he had no natural sympathy for white men. He knew from experience that any trouble between his people and the whites was usually provoked by the latter.

And yet, from the way things looked, it appeared that the Indians had ambushed the white travelers' camp. That struck Proud Wolf as a cowardly way to attack an enemy, and he refused to believe that any of his fellow Sioux were capable of such baseness. Indeed, as he watched, the warriors in the coulee grew brave enough to venture out of its shelter and dash toward the wagon, and he recognized them as Crow. Most of the Crow hunting grounds were north and west of this area; these three were likely a raiding party, out for the blood of any unlucky souls who happened to cross their path.

No more shots were fired from under the wagon. Either the white men had run out of powder or shot or they could no longer fight back.

Barely thinking about what he was doing, Proud Wolf came up out of his crouch, smoothly lifting his bow and letting fly with an arrow. It raced straight and true and thudded into the side of one of the attacking Crow warriors. With a grunt of pain that Proud Wolf could hear even at this distance, the Crow staggered and fell. Proud Wolf let out a war cry. Already he had another arrow nocked and ready to fire as the other two warriors spun toward him.

Another shot came from under the wagon, and one of the Crow was driven sideways by the rifle ball that slammed into him. The remaining warrior frantically looked back and forth between Proud Wolf and the wagon, uncertain where the greater danger lay. Apparently reasoning that whoever had fired the shot would need time to reload, the Crow concentrated on Proud Wolf and released an arrow at the same moment the young Sioux did.

The arrows flew past each other in midair. Proud Wolf flung himself to the side, and the Crow's shaft whipped harmlessly past. As he scrambled to his feet, he saw to his disgust that his arrow had missed, too. The warrior was already up and racing toward the wagon. He had dropped his bow and jerked a tomahawk from a thong slung from his waist.

One of the white men scrambled from under the wagon and ran desperately along the creek bank. That was either a foolish or a brave thing to do: foolish if he thought it would save his life, brave if he was trying to lead the Crow away from whoever was left under the wagon.

Proud Wolf dropped his own bow and sprinted down the hill as the Crow narrowed the distance between himself and the fleeing white man. Under the circumstances a bowshot was too risky; the arrow might miss the Crow and hit the white man instead. But the Crow was considerably larger than Proud Wolf, and hand-to-hand combat carried its own peril.

He had come too far to turn away now, Proud Wolf told himself. As Clay and Jeff would say, he had taken cards in this hand, and now he would have to play it out.

The Crow caught up with his quarry and lunged forward, reaching out to grab his shoulder and jerk him around. The tomahawk went up, poised to strike. In another second it would swoop down and shatter the skull of the white man. Proud Wolf caught a glimpse of the man's face. He was middle-aged; the stiff bristles of white hair reminded Proud Wolf of a porcupine's quills.

Then there was no time to see anything else, because Proud Wolf threw himself in the air and crashed into the broad back of the Crow.

The raider staggered, and the two men tumbled to the ground. Proud Wolf rolled quickly to one side and pulled his own tomahawk from his belt as he came up on his knees. A few yards away the Crow, momentarily stunned by the impact of Proud Wolf's leap, grabbed the tomahawk he had dropped and lurched to his feet with a snarl. The white man who had been his quarry only moments earlier was forgotten now. The Crow was focused intently on Proud Wolf.

As Proud Wolf came to his feet and the Crow warrior launched himself at him, the white man picked up a broken branch from the creek bank and smashed it into the back of the Crow's head.

Proud Wolf yipped in surprise and pleasure. The blow sent the Crow stumbling toward him, dazed, his tomahawk dipping heavily toward the ground. Proud Wolf stepped forward and slashed his own weapon across the Crow's face.

The Crow must have seen the blow coming, even in his stunned condition, because he jerked his head back in time to avoid a crushing blow to the skull. The heavy stone head of the tomahawk pulped the Crow's nose, however, and blood streamed down over his mouth and chin. Howling in pain and rage, the Crow barreled into Proud Wolf, knocking him backward. Proud Wolf went down.

Knowing that if he wound up trapped

under the Crow's weight he would never survive the fight, Proud Wolf jerked his legs up and managed to shove his moccasin-shod feet into the Crow's belly as the warrior lunged at him. With a grunt, Proud Wolf threw the man to the side. Continuing the same motion, he rolled over and looked around desperately as he realized that he had dropped his tomahawk. The Crow had landed heavily on the ground nearby, but he was already recovering and gathering himself to attack anew.

Proud Wolf had lost track of the white man, but a shout of "Here it is!" made him jerk his head around. The white man had picked up Proud Wolf's tomahawk and was running toward him with it, holding the weapon out in front of him. Suddenly, the white man tripped and sprawled in the dirt, the tomahawk flying out of his hand and spinning away toward the creek.

The Crow shouted in triumph. He drew back his own tomahawk and brought it forward in a savage blow aimed at Proud Wolf's head. Proud Wolf twisted lithely and ducked, lowering his shoulders and lunging closer to the Crow so that the tomahawk went over his head and struck a glancing blow on his back instead. He slipped his knife from the sheath on his hip and drove it upward into the Crow's belly, ripping the blade from side to side.

The Crow gasped, then sagged against Proud Wolf. He pulled the tomahawk back in an attempt to wield one last blow before he died, but Proud Wolf put a hand against his sweat-slicked chest and shoved hard, jerked his knife free, and whipped it across the man's throat. Blood fountained over Proud Wolf's hand. The tomahawk slipped from the Crow's suddenly nerveless fingers and thudded to the ground.

Proud Wolf darted back a couple of steps as the Crow collapsed. The man went to his knees, air rasping through the hideous wound Proud Wolf had opened in his throat. Then he pitched forward on his face. The death rattle came from him, and his muscles spasmed several times before he lay still.

Chest heaving, Proud Wolf drew several deep, ragged breaths, then bent over and wiped the blood from his knife and his hand on the grass at his feet. He sheathed the knife and looked around. The white man had gotten to his feet and was now staring openmouthed at him. After a moment the man's jaw snapped shut, and he swallowed hard. Then he said, "Do you speak English? You're not going to kill me now, are you?"

"I speak your tongue. I saved you from

this . . . dog of a Crow," Proud Wolf replied, still breathing hard. "I would not have done this . . . had I wished you any harm."

The white man closed his eyes and heaved a huge sigh. "Thank the Lord," he said. Then he opened his eyes, looked at Proud Wolf, and went on hurriedly, "And thank you, too, young man. You saved my life. And that of my friend Nicholas." He glanced nervously at the bodies of the other two Crow and added, "Shouldn't we make certain that those other savages are indeed dead?"

"If they are not, they soon will be," Proud Wolf said. Trying to conceal how shaky he still was, he strode over to the fallen warriors and examined them briefly. As he had guessed, both of them were dead. He told the white man, "They will trouble us no more."

"But if they had been alive?"

"I would have cut their throats," Proud Wolf said matter-of-factly.

The white man paled. "Oh, my," he muttered. "Well . . . I knew this land was a wilderness when I came out here. I suppose such practices are only to be expected."

The way the man talked reminded Proud Wolf of someone, but for the moment he could not think who. Certainly not Clay or Jeff Holt. Father Thomas, perhaps. The priest was an educated man, and this stranger sounded as if he, too, had had much schooling.

Pulling a handkerchief from his pocket, the white man mopped his face with it, then said, "I have to see if Nicholas is all right. He was wounded, I'm afraid."

Proud Wolf picked up his tomahawk and tucked it away, then followed the white-haired one back to the wagon. The man knelt and crawled under the vehicle, saying to his companion, "Nicholas, how badly are you wounded?"

"Reckon I'll . . . live, Professor," Proud Wolf heard the man reply. The man called Nicholas had the broken shaft of an arrow buried in his left shoulder. It would have to be pushed through his body before it was removed, Proud Wolf knew. If the arrow was pulled straight out, the barbs on the head would rip out huge chunks of flesh and leave a much more severe wound.

Nicholas probably knew that, too. He wore buckskins and had the grizzled, bearded look of a frontiersman. Proud Wolf suspected that he and the dead man, who was also wearing buckskins, had been hired as guides and for protection by the white-haired man.

Professor. That was what Nicholas had called the white-haired man. Proud Wolf realized suddenly whom the man's speech reminded him of.

This stranger's words and way of speaking were much like those of Professor Donald Franklin, the leader of an ill-fated scientific expedition in which Proud Wolf, Clay Holt, and Shining Moon had served for a time as guides. Two years had passed since the three of them had encountered the group of white travelers, but Proud Wolf would never forget Professor Franklin.

Professor Franklin, who was now buried far to the north and west.

Proud Wolf shook his head as he pushed aside the memories of that evil time.

"Let me help you out, and we'll get that wound patched up," this professor was saying as he extended a hand to Nicholas. "Then we'll have to bury poor Tom."

Nicholas slowly crawled out into the open. "He never knew what hit him," he grunted. "Got that to say for it, anyway." He glanced at Proud Wolf. "Who's this, and where'd he come from? Last I knew 'fore I passed out, those bucks were fixing to charge us."

"That they did," the professor said as he propped Nicholas in a sitting position against one of the wagon wheels. "Then our young friend here came out of nowhere and saved our lives. I used your rifle to down one of the

Indians, but this young man killed the other two."

"You shot one o' them bucks?" Nicholas sounded incredulous. "Thought you said you'd never shot a gun before in your life, Professor. That's why I had you loading for me."

"Beginner's luck, I suppose," the professor said with a weary smile. He reached out toward the arrow in Nicholas's shoulder but hesitated before he touched it. "I . . . I'm not sure what I should —"

"Push it on through," Proud Wolf and Nicholas both said at the same time.

They looked at each other, and Nicholas's bearded face contorted in a mixture of grimace and grin. "Teton Sioux, aren't you?" he asked.

"They are my people," Proud Wolf said.

"Thought so. You know Bear Tooth, the old chief? Has a village near a settlement called New Hope?"

"That's where we're going," the professor put in.

"I know New Hope," Proud Wolf said dryly. But he was surprised that these white men did.

"What luck!" the professor exclaimed. "Perhaps you can take us there."

Proud Wolf hunkered on his heels in front

of Nicholas and moved the professor aside. "Let me do this," he said as he reached out to grasp the broken arrow shaft.

Nicholas chuckled. "Not even going to . . . give me some whiskey first for the pain?"

Without hesitation, Proud Wolf pushed the arrow through the white man's shoulder. It emerged from Nicholas's back with a ripping sound, but that was from the buckskin shirt being torn, Proud Wolf knew. Nicholas let out a low cry between gritted teeth and sagged forward. Proud Wolf reached around him, caught hold of the arrowhead, and pulled the shaft free.

"Now the whiskey," Proud Wolf said.

"C-clean it out . . . good," Nicholas said huskily. "I ain't of a mind to . . . let it fester."

Proud Wolf glanced at the professor, who had turned ashen again. "If there is whiskey in the wagon, bring it."

"Yes. Yes, there is." The professor blinked a couple of times. "Strictly for medicinal purposes, of course. But if this doesn't fit the bill, I don't know what would."

A short time later, Proud Wolf finished bandaging the wounds in the front and back of Nicholas's shoulder. He would have liked to pack some healing herbs in the wounds, but the white man's whiskey would have to do for the time being. He had poured it liberally over the jagged holes in the flesh, then given the bottle to Nicholas. The frontiersman had quickly drained half of what was left.

Traveling in the wagon, they could reach New Hope in a day and a half, Proud Wolf estimated. If Nicholas lived that long — and Proud Wolf was fairly confident that he would — then Father Thomas could care for him and nurse him back to health.

In the meantime, Proud Wolf had postponed satisfying his curiosity long enough. There was still a dead man to bury, but that could wait a bit longer. He turned to the professor and said, "Who are you? Why have you come to this land? What is it you seek in New Hope?"

"We're looking for someone," the professor said. "Or actually, I should say that *I'm* looking for someone. My name is Abner Hilliard, Professor Abner Hilliard. I'm an instructor of natural science at Harvard University and fellow of the American Philosophical Society. Although you wouldn't know anything about that." He nodded toward Nicholas, who was taking another long drink from the bottle of whiskey. "I hired Nicholas and Tom in St. Louis to bring me out here, since they've trapped in this region and know it quite well. We had made it this far without any trouble, but I suppose our luck simply couldn't hold."

"Whom do you seek in the village of New Hope?" Getting solid answers out of this man was not easy, Proud Wolf thought. He had an abundance of words, but they poured out of him at such a rate as to be almost worthless.

"Well, I don't know if we'll find him in New Hope or in the village of Bear Tooth, the Sioux chief. The lad I'm looking for is Bear Tooth's son."

Proud Wolf's eyes widened in shock.

"His name is Proud Wolf," the professor went on, "and I've come out here to make him what I hope is a most interesting offer."

Chapter Five

Before the day was over, Clay and Jeff passed the stagecoach carrying their younger brothers and sister back to Pittsburgh, eliciting shouts of greeting from the three youngsters. They grinned and returned the waves as they rode by, but not without regretting that once more their family had to go off in so many different directions. Clay hoped that this time they would see each other again before too long.

From Wheeling they took a trail that led directly east to Pittsburgh rather than the main road that followed the northward curve of the Ohio River. By Jeff's estimate, that shortcut took at least a day off their journey.

Jeff had been to Pittsburgh before, had in fact even stayed for a time in New York, so for him the sight of a large city was not as awe-inspiring as it was for Clay. As they paused on a rise overlooking the great triangular point of land where the Allegheny and Monongahela Rivers came together to form the mighty Ohio, Clay gaped as he took in the maze of streets, the row upon row of substantial-looking buildings, and the bustle of humans, horses, wagons, and carriages. The banks of the Monongahela, which flowed on the south side of the city, were crowded with wharves, warehouses, and shipyards. Even from a distance, the brothers could hear the hum of activity.

"Lord," Clay said a hushed voice. "I never saw so many buildings, or so many people."

"Pittsburgh is a good-sized city," Jeff agreed.

"I hope never to see a bigger one!" Clay said fervently. "How does a fella keep from getting lost down there in that mess?"

"There are signs. You could manage easier than you think."

Clay reined the dun toward a path that skirted the city to the south, across the river from the warren of buildings. "I won't have to," he said over his shoulder, "because I'm not going down there. Washington's southeast of here, right?"

Jeff heeled his horse into a fast walk so that he could ride alongside his brother. "That's right. There's a good road leading down that way. But you mean to tell me that you're not going in to Pittsburgh to say hello to Uncle Henry and Aunt Dorothy?"

Clay shook his head ruefully. "I feel a mite bad about that, but I promised Shining Moon

I'd get to Washington and back as fast as I can. That doesn't leave any time for visiting."

Jeff shrugged. "Suit yourself. I'm just along for the ride, so I'll do whatever you say."

"Sorry, but I'm moving on."

"That's fine with me."

Clay did feel guilty about not calling on his aunt and uncle, especially since Henry and Dorothy had been kind enough to take the children in four and a half years earlier when Clay and Jeff had first headed west. Perhaps, he mused, if he was able to settle the business of the land grant quickly enough in Washington, there would be time for a visit on the trip back to Marietta.

As Jeff had said, there was an excellent road leading southeast through the Allegheny Mountains from Pittsburgh. The terrain was rugged, but the road followed the natural passes between the mountains.

"This used to be called Braddock's Road," Jeff commented to Clay a couple of days later, as they rode along the winding route. "That English general Braddock laid it out with some help from George Washington, back when they were fighting the French and the Indians out on the frontier."

Clay nodded. "I remember Pa spinning

yarns about those days, about how he went on some surveying trips with Washington and fought with him during a couple of wars."

"Those were mighty exciting times, I reckon," Jeff said wistfully. "The country's settled down a lot since then."

Clay gestured toward the fine road on which they were traveling. "It sure has. Folks are settling all over what they used to call the Old Northwest."

"There'll come a time when there're cities all the way from the Atlantic to the Pacific," Jeff prophesied.

Clay grunted and shook his head. "I'd just as soon not live to see that," he declared.

After they had put the Alleghenies behind them, they soon reached the Potomac River. "From the maps I've seen," Jeff said, "this road follows the river all the way to Washington. We ought to be there in another three or four days, if we keep pushing the horses the way we have."

"Can't be soon enough to suit me," Clay said. "We've been away from Marietta a little over a week. At this rate we'll be gone almost a month."

Jeff thumbed back his hat. "Well, it can't be helped, not if you want to claim that land grant."

"Sometimes I'm not sure this was a good idea in the first place," Clay said gloomily. He sighed. "But we've come this far, so I reckon it's too late to turn back now."

"It'll all work out," Jeff assured him. "You'll see."

Clay wanted to believe that his brother was right. But he couldn't help wondering how things were going back in Marietta, and how Shining Moon was coping with the task of keeping up with Matthew Garwood . . .

"Matthew! Matthew!"

Shining Moon sighed in exasperation as she stood in the open double doors of the barn. She had been calling the boy for several minutes. She had seen him around the barn earlier in the afternoon, but now there was no sign of him.

One of the Gilworth brothers was forking hay into a stall. He paused and leaned on his pitchfork, sleeving sweat from his forehead. "Why're ye looking for the boy, ma'am?" he asked.

"I want him to bring some eggs from the chicken house," Shining Moon replied, "but now he has vanished."

The bearded man nodded solemnly. "Aye, if there's work to be done, that lad's going to be hard to find. Now, if 'twas young Whip you were talking about . . ."

Shining Moon did not need to be told how helpful Michael Holt was. Jeff's son was always anxious to please. A bit more sharply than she intended, she said, "If you see Matthew, please send him to the house."

"Aye. I'll do that, ma'am."

With a rustle of skirts and petticoats, Shining Moon turned and walked back to the cabin. Several days had passed since Clay and Jeff had left for Washington, and Melissa, Michael, Ned, and India had departed for North Carolina the day after that. Since then, Shining Moon had tried to keep busy around the Holt farm, hoping her chores and projects would blunt her boredom and her homesickness. So far, the effort had been only partially successful. Castor and Pollux were so conscientious about their jobs that there was little left that needed doing around the place. The house was in good repair, better than might have been expected given the fact that two men had lived there alone for several years. And because Shining Moon knew almost nothing of the practice of farming — her people were hunters and always had been — she could not presume to offer the Gilworths advice on matters relating to crops or animal husbandry. She had experimented with cooking on the cast-iron woodburning stove, but other than that she had largely been at loose ends.

What would the Gilworths think of her, she suddenly wondered, if she took off these white women's clothes and donned her buckskins once more? She could go into the woods, cut a limb from a tree, and fashion a bow. She had never been a warrior like the young woman called Raven Arrow, but she could certainly handle making a bow without too much trouble. Once she had strung it, she could carve arrows and venture into the forest to hunt.

And what would she hunt? At what sort of target would she fire those arrows? Some farmer's milk cow? A huge, plodding dray horse? Shining Moon shook her head. The whole idea was ridiculous. No, she told herself sternly, she would simply have to conduct herself as a white woman would, no matter how strange and uncomfortable that felt, until Clay returned from Washington and took her back to her home.

The soft thud of hoofbeats and the creaking of wagon wheels caught her attention before she reached the cabin. She turned, curious about who could be paying a visit to the farm, and saw a small wagon — a two-wheeled cart, actually — approaching from the east. A tiny figure was perched on the front of the cart, handling the reins of the mule that was pulling it. At first glance Shining Moon took the driver to be a child, but as the cart came closer, she saw the wrinkled face of an elderly woman peering out at her from under a dark blue bonnet. Shining Moon stood where she was as the old woman drove the cart up to the cabin.

"Whoa there, ya dadblasted, jugheaded, sorry excuse for a beast o' burden!" the old woman bawled to the mule as she hauled back on the reins and brought the cart to a stop. With a spryness that belied her years, she scrambled down from her perch and turned toward Shining Moon with a hearty greeting. "Howdy, Injun!"

Shining Moon gasped. She was not accustomed to being addressed in such a manner, though she knew the word was one the whites commonly used for her people. Drawing herself to her full height, she nodded and said, "Good morning."

The old woman's right cheek was bulging oddly. As Shining Moon watched in fascination, the lump shifted to the other cheek, and then the woman leaned to the side and let loose with a brown stream of chewing tobacco. She grinned. "You'd be Shinin' Moon Holt, I reckon," she said.

"I am called Shining Moon."

The old woman extended a gnarled, callused hand. "Cassandra Doolittle. Folks call me Cassie."

"I am pleased to meet you," Shining Moon said as she shook hands. She was puzzled. Why was this old woman here?

To ask such a question would be impolite, however, so Shining Moon simply stood there and waited. It didn't take long for Cassie to get to the point of her visit. She turned to the cart and reached in the back. "Heard you were stayin' here whilst yer man was gone, so I come over to pay you a neighborly visit. I brung you some sweet taters." She took a burlap bag out of the cart and handed it to Shining Moon, swinging it around as if it weighed nothing. Shining Moon took it and quickly tightened her grip when she realized how heavy the bag actually was. Cassie continued, "Invite me in for a dram, and maybe I'll tell you how to make the best sweet tater pie you ever et, Injun."

"My name is Shining Moon," she said again, a bit more curtly this time.

"Yep, I know. Didn't mean no offense. When me an' my man Horace come out here with ol' Colonel Putnam back in '88, none of us knew for sure whether or not the redskins hereabouts was hostile. Turns out most of 'em wasn't, but they was all just Injuns to me then, and sometimes I slip back into my old ways. Don't mean nothin' by it, but I'll try to remember. Now, about that dram . . ."

Shining Moon shook her head. "We have no whiskey here."

Cassie licked her lips and looked sorry to hear that. "Well, I reckon a cup o' cider'll do, in a pinch. You *do* have cider, don't you?"

Shining Moon nodded. "There is a jug in the cellar. I will bring it."

"Is one o' them worthless Gilworth boys around? My mule needs tendin' to." Cassie raised her voice into an ear-jarring screech. "Castor! Pollux! One o' you scrawny sons get out here and see to this mule o' mine!"

The Gilworth brother to whom Shining Moon had spoken a few minutes earlier came hurrying out of the barn. "Miz Doolittle!" he said. "I, uh, thought I heard you a few minutes ago —"

"Then why was you lollygaggin' in the barn instead o' comin' out here to help a pore ol' woman? Get this mule some water and grain, boy!"

"Yes'm." The massive, bearded farmer scurried about, following the orders of an old woman little more than a quarter his size.

Smiling to herself, Shining Moon took

the bag of sweet potatoes down into the cellar and returned with a jug of cider. Cassie followed her into the cabin, boldly looking around, seeming to take everything in with voracious interest. The two women sat at the table in the main room.

Cassie smacked her lips over the cider. "Could be better, but 'tain't bad. Tell me, gal, what tribe're you from?"

"I am of the Teton Sioux. I am the daughter of Bear Tooth, the chief of my band."

"Well, what in blazes are you doin' back here in Ohio, 'stead of out yonder in the wilderness?"

"I go where my husband goes," Shining Moon said simply.

"But Clay ain't here."

"He is away for a time . . . on business." Shining Moon wasn't sure where she found those words, but they seemed to fit.

Cassie nodded. "Ain't that jus' like a man? Drag a pore woman halfway across the country an' then up and leave her whilst he goes gallivantin' off somewheres else."

"Clay Holt will return soon," Shining Moon said, hoping that was true.

"Well, until he does, if'n you need anything, you come see ol' Cassie. Those no-account Gilworth boys know where my farm is. You make one of 'em bring you over there anytime you want to see me."

Shining Moon felt obliged to rise to the defense of the two tenant farmers. "The Gilworth brothers seem to be very hard-working."

"Oh, they're all right, I reckon." Cassie gave a shrill cackle of laughter. "I jus' like to hooraw 'em a mite. They're so big ever'body else 'round here walks mighty soft around 'em. But I don't, no, ma'am! Cassie Doolittle don't walk soft for nobody!"

Shining Moon could easily believe that. "Do you and your husband have a farm near here?" she asked.

"Oh, Horace is dead. Has been for nigh on twenty years. He was choppin' wood one day a couple o' years after we came here, when he missed and practically lopped his whole damn foot off. Horace was a good man, Lord rest his soul, but he never was much of a hand with an ax. Bled to death on the way back to our cabin. I heard him yellin' his fool head off an' got to him just in time to hold him for a minute 'fore he passed on."

"I am sorry."

Cassie shook her head impatiently. " 'Twas a long time ago, gal. I do sometimes miss him, I reckon. He couldn't chop wood, like I said, and when you come right down to it, he weren't worth a damn as a farmer.

But he could sure keep a gal warm on a cold winter night." She cackled again. "Heated me up real good, sometimes two or three times 'twixt dusk and dawn!"

Shining Moon felt a flush creeping over her face. She was not accustomed to such candid talk about what went on between a husband and wife in the privacy of their blankets. *Especially* not from someone like this old woman.

"Got any young uns?" Cassie asked, changing the subject.

Shining Moon shook her head. "Not of my own, but there is a boy we care for."

Cassie's eyes narrowed. "Yep, I heard about that. Took in the little Garwood boy, didn't you? Josie's bastard?"

"His name is Matthew," Shining Moon said sharply.

"I remember him. There were stories about his ma and Clay Holt —"

"Clay is not Matthew's father!" Shining Moon was surprised by her own vehemence. But she remembered how much trouble that old lie had engendered between her and Clay, and she did not want anyone else believing it.

"Oh, hell, I know that," Cassie snorted. " 'Twas Josie's own brother Zach got her with child. Some o' the folks 'round here figured that out after a while, but they didn't want to admit it, even to theirselves. Folks don't like to think the worst of people, even when it's scum like the Garwoods they're talkin' about."

Shining Moon took a deep breath and brought her anger under control. "We are trying to raise Matthew as best we can. It is the Christian thing to do."

"Yep, I reckon." Cassie gave her a solemn look. "But you be mighty careful, gal. Blood runs true. You mind ol' Cassie. Blood runs true."

Shining Moon shivered a little. She feared that the old woman was right — at least where Matthew Garwood was concerned.

The young man limped heavily across the clearing, supporting himself with a crude wooden crutch tucked under his right armpit. His right leg was gone, amputated just above the knee. His left arm was thinner and obviously weaker than the right one. Despite those handicaps, his skin was tanned and healthy, his eyes were lively and bright with intelligence, and a wide grin lit up his face. He stopped in front of a large building constructed of roughly planed wooden planks and balanced himself easily as he lifted his crutch to rap on the door.

119

After a moment it was opened by a tall, broad-shouldered man with a thatch of rumpled red hair. He wore a sober black suit with a white clerical collar. He smiled when he saw his visitor. "Good morning, Aaron. What brings you here?"

"Oh, I was feeling good this morning, Father, so I thought I'd see if you needed a hand around the church," Aaron Garwood said. "You told me some exercise would be good for me."

"Indeed it would," Father Thomas Brennan agreed, "but you have to be careful not to exert yourself too much. You've made a remarkable recovery so far from your injuries, Aaron. You don't want to do anything to jeopardize it."

When Clay Holt and Proud Wolf had first brought Aaron to him, Father Thomas had not expected the young man to live. Aaron's right leg had been crushed in an avalanche, and the wounds he had suffered had become infected. It had taken all the medical training Father Thomas had received before entering the priesthood to save Aaron's life. He'd had no choice but to amputate the leg, a risky procedure under the best of circumstances but even more dangerous in the wilderness.

But Aaron had come through the surgery

well, and physically, at least, he had progressed to the point where Father Thomas expected him to live out a normal life span, barring further injuries. Mentally and emotionally, however, it had been a different story. Already handicapped by a weak left arm that had not healed properly from a bad break several years earlier, Aaron had looked at the empty space where his right leg had been and decided that life was no longer worth living.

For months, even as Aaron's body was healing and growing stronger by the day, Father Thomas had waged a war for the young man's soul, fighting the ever-increasing despair that threatened to drag Aaron down into a dark hell from which he might never return.

Today it seemed that somehow Aaron had thrown off the shackles of gloom and bitterness, and Father Thomas couldn't afford to waste this opportunity. He stepped back from the doorway and said, "Come in, come in. I'll be glad for the company and pleased to have you give me a hand. I'm working on my sermon for this Sunday."

Aaron hesitated, his smile suddenly replaced by a frown. "Oh, now, Father, I won't be much good for something like that. I was never much of a hand with words, especially preachifying. That's *your* department."

"Yes, but you can listen to what I have so far and give me your opinion, can't you?"

"Well . . . I reckon." Aaron shrugged awkwardly. "If you're sure you want me to."

"Of course I do. Come in," the priest repeated.

Aaron followed him into the sanctuary. The church sat somewhat apart from the rest of the settlement of New Hope, which consisted of a trading post and a dozen or so log cabins on the bank of one of the creeks that ran through this broad mountain valley. The valley was a gorgeous spot, ringed by mountains; the tallest, most majestic snow-capped peaks rose to the west. A cold, fast-moving river flowed parallel to that range, and the valley was well watered by numerous smaller streams that flowed into the river. The lower slopes of the mountains were covered with dense groves of pine and aspen, and at this time of year the meadows were carpeted with brilliant wildflowers. The air was so clear that an eagle wheeling through the sky a mile away was clearly visible. Father Thomas was convinced that there was no more beautiful place on the face of the earth, and he almost hated to close the door and shut out the view.

At the moment, though, it was more important that he take advantage of Aaron's good mood and perhaps find out what had lifted the young man's spirits. He led the way to his small quarters at the rear of the church. Several sheets of paper were spread out on the small writing desk, as well as a quill pen in its holder and a small bottle of ink Father Thomas had purchased at Malachi Fisher's trading post with beaver pelts brought to him by grateful parishioners.

"Have a seat," Father Thomas told Aaron, casually waving a hand at one of the two rough-hewn chairs with seats of woven rope. The priest sat in the other one, smiled at Aaron, and said bluntly, "Tell me what's got you so cheerful this morning."

"Grass Song gave this to me," Aaron said. He reached inside his homespun shirt and brought out a circle of rawhide, several inches in diameter, which had been stretched over a wooden frame. It was decorated with intricate, colorful beadwork and attached to a rawhide thong by which it hung around Aaron's neck.

"That's beautiful," Father Thomas murmured as he leaned forward in his chair to study the ornament.

"She says it's a spirit shield, only instead of protecting my body from the arrows and lances of my enemies like the shields of the warriors do, it protects my heart from unhappiness." Aaron grinned again. "So you see, Father, I *have* to be cheerful. I have no choice in the matter."

"Because of this . . . spirit shield?"

"And because of Grass Song," Aaron said.

Father Thomas nodded slowly. He understood now. He had seen the maiden known as Grass Song in the village of Bear Tooth. She was a lovely young woman, seventeen summers old, always friendly and smiling. Father Thomas hoped Aaron wasn't mistaking her naturally pleasant nature for something more serious.

Still, perhaps the gift of the spirit shield did mean something. Father Thomas hoped Aaron was right, for clearly Grass Song had lifted his spirits considerably.

"Of course," Aaron went on, "I don't know what Grass Song would want with somebody like me." A hint of the old bitterness crept into his voice. "After all, I'm just a cripple."

"Nonsense," Father Thomas said sharply. "You're an intelligent young man with a good heart. I would think that any young woman would be happy to have you as a friend."

"But nothing more than a friend."

Father Thomas frowned. "This is not an area in which I have a great deal of, ah, expertise, Aaron . . ."

"Just as I told you I don't know anything about preaching. But I know this, Father." Aaron sighed. "Out here on the frontier, I'm not much use to anybody the way I am now. When Clay comes back, he's not going to want to take me hunting and trapping with him. I could never keep up on this crutch." He had placed the crutch on the floor next to his chair, and now he nudged it with his foot. "That's why I'm going to get rid of it."

"Get rid of it?" the priest repeated. "But how —"

"How will I get around? I've been doing some thinking on that. If I had a pegleg, I think I could get around a little better. I'm thinking about carving one and giving it a try."

"Oh," Father Thomas said, cocking his head. "I see."

"That way I could at least do a little hunting and fishing, maybe run some traplines." Aaron looked down at the floor. "And provide for a family."

Father Thomas considered. He wanted to tell Aaron not to get too far ahead of himself, not to count on things that might not be possible. But he was so glad to see Aaron showing some initiative again that he didn't want to say anything that might dampen the young man's enthusiasm. Even if Grass Song was *not* seeing Aaron as a potential mate, no doubt someday some other young woman would. Their chances for happiness would be greatly enhanced if Aaron had learned how to cope with his disabilities.

"Well, I think that's an excellent idea, Aaron," Father Thomas said. "There's no reason in the world I can see why you shouldn't give it a try. If there's anything I can do to help, just let me know."

Aaron smiled sheepishly. "It's a help just knowing you don't think I'm a damn — I mean, a darn fool for wanting to try."

"The Lord helps those who help themselves," Father Thomas said assuringly.

"That's what I've heard." Aaron gave a decisive nod. "I reckon on finding out for myself."

Chapter Six

Clay Holt looked at the teeming hordes and experienced a sensation he seldom felt, even in the most desperate situations.

He was afraid.

"There's just too damn many *people!*" he hissed to his brother as they rode along Pennsylvania Avenue in Washington City. The nation's capital had been moved here from Philadelphia in 1800, and the city had grown steadily in size and population since then.

The road Clay and Jeff had followed from Pittsburgh had turned into the broad, tree-lined city street of hard-packed dirt on which they now rode. They had already passed an impressive Georgian mansion built in the Palladian style at the west end of the avenue, and Jeff had pointed it out. "I reckon that's the president's house. You want to go say howdy to President Madison?"

Clay had snorted. "I imagine the president's got more important things to do than pass the time of day with a couple of dusty frontiersmen like us. At least I hope so."

A little farther down the street, Jeff gestured toward a massive stone building on a small rise at the far end of the avenue. The structure was dominated by a large dome in the center, which was flanked by two smaller domes. "That'd be the Capitol Building," Jeff said.

"Where do you think I should go to find out about that land grant?" Clay asked, casting wary glances at the crowds of pedestrians on the plank sidewalks and the buggies and carriages that crowded the street.

"I don't know for certain, but I'll wager we can find out. I suppose the first thing we need to do is find an inn. Then we can see about locating the right government office. If we can't find anybody who knows, we *will* go ask the president."

Clay shook his head. The idea of brazenly going up to the leader of the whole blasted country and asking him for directions made him nervous, but it was just the sort of thing Jeff would do.

Clay angled his horse toward the side of the street. As he approached the sidewalk, he lifted a hand and called to a man passing by, "Pardon me, mister, but could I ask you a question?"

The man, well fed and well dressed, cast a skeptical eye at Clay. He raised one eyebrow as he took in Clay's homespun shirt, old-fashioned tricorn hat, powder horns, and the long-barreled flintlock rifle resting across the saddle. "And who are you supposed to be, my good man?" he asked. "Daniel Boone?"

"I've heard of the fella, but I'm not him," Clay said. "My name's Clay Holt. My brother and I are looking for a place we can get a room."

"Well, the Stafford House is one of the finest hotels in the city," the man replied, looking them up and down, "but I doubt that such, ah, gentlemen as yourselves would be comfortable there."

Jeff had ridden up beside Clay, and he bristled at the man's condescending tone. "What do you mean by that, mister?" he demanded.

Clay gave Jeff a warning look. That was a change, he thought wryly; usually it was Jeff reining *him* in. But right now he just wanted to find a place to stay so that he could get off this crowded street for a while.

"What about a good inn?" he asked.

"Try the Copper Gable tavern on Eighth Street," the man suggested. "The proprietor rents out rooms upstairs." A leer spread across his face. "And the serving girls are more than accommodating about accompanying a fellow upstairs if he has a few coins in his pockets."

129

One of the pedestrians passing by on the sidewalk nodded pleasantly to the man and said, "Good afternoon, Senator."

The man returned the passerby's nod, cleared his throat, and said solemnly to Clay and Jeff, "Don't misunderstand. I've only heard *stories* about the Copper Gable."

"Sure," Clay said dryly as he reined the dun away from the sidewalk. "Much obliged, Senator."

As they rode away, Jeff jerked a thumb over his shoulder. "That was a politician."

"Yep," Clay nodded. "Sure was."

They hadn't asked for directions to the Copper Gable, but it wasn't difficult to find. Another man pointed it out to them on Eighth Street a couple of blocks north of Pennsylvania Avenue. Clay and Jeff reined up in front of the building and swung down from their saddles, stretching muscles weary from long hours on horseback.

The Copper Gable was a square, sturdy-looking, two-story stone building. There was one gable in the center of the dark green roof, and the sides were covered in a material that did indeed appear to be copper, although Clay wondered if it was merely painted that color. There was no sidewalk here. The door of the tavern opened directly onto the street.

To one side of the door stood a hitching rail. Clay and Jeff tied the four horses to it and went inside, carrying their rifles and war bags.

Despite the brightness of the day, shutters on the windows kept out the light inside the inn. The big main room was dimly lit by candles placed on wagon wheels suspended from the beamed ceiling. Tables made from barrels and slabs of wood were scattered haphazardly around the room, and booths of dark hardwood lined the walls. On one side of the room was a large fireplace with a massive stone mantel. The bar was opposite the fireplace. A staircase against the back wall led up to the second floor. The sounds of talk and laughter and the bluish-gray haze of pipe smoke filled the air.

Clay and Jeff looked at each other and grinned. The Copper Gable reminded them of taverns they had visited in Ohio and St. Louis. There was nothing fancy about the place. Both men sensed that they would be comfortable here.

They headed for the bar, where a ruddy-faced bartender with curly, graying red hair was holding court as he filled buckets of beer from a cask. He was saying, "So then I says to him —" but stopped short when Clay and Jeff stepped up to the bar. With a pleasant nod he said, "Howdy, gents. What can I do for you?"

Jeff said, "Someone told us that you rent rooms here."

"Aye, that I do."

"My brother and I need a place to stay while we're in Washington."

The bartender studied the Holt brothers for a moment, his dark eyes cautious. "I'd have to see the color of your money," he finally said.

"Fair enough." Jeff brought a coin from his pocket and flipped it onto the bar. The bartender scooped up the coin, studied it for a second, then broke into a broad smile.

"Welcome to the Copper Gable, gents," he said. "I'm Harry Ledbetter, the owner and proprietor. Just go to the top of the stairs, turn left, and take your pick of the rooms. They're all vacant on that side of the building."

"Much obliged," Clay said. Though the tavern was full of people, this crowd didn't have the same effect on him that the one in the street had. He was starting to feel better about this visit to Washington.

"Before you go, what say I stand you both to a mug of beer?" Harry Ledbetter suggested.

"You'd better say yes," one of the men at

the bar said with a laugh. "Ol' Harry ain't known for his generosity, so you'd be wise to take advantage of it."

"That's a scurrilous lie," the tavern keeper said with a good-natured scowl. "Ask anybody in Washington. They'll tell you Harry Ledbetter ain't got a stingy bone in his body. I'm the most generous soul you'll find in the whole city."

Clay couldn't have judged one way or the other, but he knew that a beer would go a long way toward cutting the dust of travel from his throat. He nodded and said, "That'd be fine, Mr. Ledbetter. Again, we're much obliged." He added as Ledbetter drew the beers, "By the way, my name's Clay Holt, and this is my brother Jeff."

"Pleased to meet you, Mr. Holt," Ledbetter said as he slid the mugs across the bar to Clay and Jeff. "What brings you to Washington?"

Clay and Jeff glanced at each other. Tavern keepers usually knew as much as or more than anyone else about what went on in a city. Maybe Ledbetter could help them, Clay thought. He said, "We're here to do some business with the government. Do you happen to know where we'd need to go to talk to somebody about a land grant?"

Ledbetter's bushy eyebrows rose. "A land

grant, is it? You fellas have some government land coming to you?"

"My brother here does," Jeff said. "He was with the Corps of Discovery."

The men standing around the bar turned to them with great interest. "The Corps of Discovery," one of them repeated. "You mean you went to the Pacific with Lewis and Clark?"

Clay nodded. "That's right."

"You're lucky you got back alive," another man said. "I've heard that there's nothing out there beyond the Mississippi but wasteland and savage redskins."

"You couldn't pay me enough to go out there," a third man put in. "If you ask me, Jefferson was a damned fool for buying all that worthless land from the French in the first place. And then Bonaparte turned around and used the money he got from us to go to war against the rest of Europe." The man shook his head. "A big mistake, that's what it was."

Clay's jaw tightened, but he didn't say anything. He refused to get into an argument over the merits of the Louisiana Purchase. He was glad that the plains and the mountains were now part of the United States. Some of these people back east might think of the west as a wasteland, but

Clay knew better. As far as he was concerned, it was about as close to Paradise as anybody was likely to find on Earth.

"I suppose you'd need to talk to the clerk in the Government Land Office," Ledbetter said. "If they don't handle land grants, someone there ought to be able to tell you who does. Just go back up to Pennsylvania Avenue and turn toward the Capitol. The Land Office building will be on the right, a couple of blocks up just before you get to Fifth Street."

"Thanks," Clay said. He drained the rest of the beer in his mug, then continued, "We'll put our gear away, then see what we can find out."

He and Jeff placed their empty mugs on the bar, then turned toward the staircase. Before they could reach it, one of the serving girls who had been moving around the room sidled up to them. Her blond hair was piled high on her head in a mass of ringlets, and the white swells of her large breasts were visible in the low, square-cut neckline of her cotton dress. "You boys going upstairs?" she asked. "Need any help finding your room?"

"I reckon we can manage, but we're obliged anyway," Clay said.

"Both of us are married," Jeff added.

The serving girl laughed. "That never stopped anybody before, now, did it?"

"There's a first time for everything, I reckon," Clay told her.

She let her gaze play brazenly over their tall, broad-shouldered forms and sighed in what seemed to be genuine regret. Then she moved on to find a more willing customer for what she was selling. Clay and Jeff couldn't help but watch her go, and then they exchanged glances. The young woman was undeniably attractive. The big city, Clay thought, held all sorts of unexpected temptations.

All the more reason to get this over with and get back home as soon as possible, he told himself.

After leaving their rifles and bags in one of the rooms upstairs at the Copper Gable, Clay and Jeff walked up Pennsylvania Avenue to the Land Office. They still had to make arrangements for stabling their horses, but Clay had decided that could wait for a little while. He was anxious to find out what was going to be involved in claiming the land grant.

The Government Land Office was in a nondescript building that sat in the looming shadow of the Capitol. Behind a counter inside, they found a man with iron-gray hair and flaring, bushy side-whiskers seated on a stool and entering notations in a large black book spread open before him. He didn't look up when Clay and Jeff came into the office; in fact, he gave no sign that he was even aware of their presence until Clay cleared his throat. Then, still without glancing up, he asked, "What may I do for you?"

"Are you the clerk of the Government Land Office?" Clay asked.

"That's right."

"I'm here about some land that's coming to me. My name's Clay Holt."

The man finally looked up. "Is that name supposed to mean something to me?"

"No reason for it to, I reckon. But I've got a land grant coming to me because I went with Captain Meriwether Lewis and Captain William Clark on their expedition to the Pacific Ocean."

The clerk's eyebrows drew together in a frown. "That's impossible. All those land grants were handled years ago."

"I know. My name accidentally got left off the list of members of the Corps of Discovery."

"I see." The clerk's eyes narrowed in suspicion, and he went on harshly, "So I'm supposed to believe that you went with Lewis and Clark, and in return I'll just hand over a chunk of government land to you."

Clay felt a surge of anger. It was clear the man *didn't* believe him. "I'm not in the habit of lying, mister," he said tautly. "I got a letter from Captain Lewis telling me to come here to Washington to straighten everything out."

The clerk snorted in disbelief and looked down again at the book in front of him. "That's ridiculous. Meriwether Lewis is dead. He blew his brains out year before last."

Clay felt his right hand clench into a fist and his arm come up. He intended to slam that fist down on the counter to show that he meant business. But before he could, Jeff lightly grasped his wrist and stopped him.

"My brother has proof of what he's saying," Jeff said. "He brought the letter from Captain Lewis with him."

Obviously irritated, the clerk put his pen down. "Is that so? How am I supposed to know this letter is genuine? Anyone could forge a letter like that."

"It's no forgery," Jeff said. "Why don't you just take a look at it?"

With a frustrated sigh, the clerk nodded. "All right. Let's see this so-called letter."

Clay reached into his shirt and pulled out

the Sioux medicine bag he wore on a thong around his neck. Shining Moon had given him the small pouch. He opened it and took out the letter, unfolded it, and smoothed it on the counter. The clerk took a pair of spectacles from his coat pocket, perched them on the bridge of his nose, and leaned forward to study the document.

"Whoever wrote this can't spell worth a damn," he said after a moment.

"Captain Lewis never was much on spelling," Clay said.

"You believe this is the real thing, don't you?"

"I know it is. I read enough of the captain's journal entries to recognize his handwriting. He sent it to the settlement in Ohio where my family lives, and I didn't get it for over a year because I was away from home."

"Well, this is certainly interesting," the clerk mused. "I don't know whether to believe it or not." He picked up the letter. "I'm going to have to keep this and look into the matter, so that I can determine if your claim is genuine."

"The letter's real, and so's my claim," Clay insisted.

"We'll see," the clerk said, still sounding dubious.

Clay had kept a tight rein on his temper all

during the conversation, but the clerk's arrogance was intolerable. He said hotly, "I don't like being called a liar —"

Again Jeff interceded, grasping Clay's arm and smoothly moving between him and the Land Office clerk. "My brother's telling the truth," he said. "You look into it all you want. You'll find out that he's right."

The clerk sniffed. "Come back tomorrow. I'll see what I can find out by then."

Clay began to protest, but Jeff said quickly, "All right. We'll be back in the morning." He steered Clay to the door and out onto the street.

"Damn it!" Clay exploded when they were outside. "I don't trust that fella. How do we know he won't burn the captain's letter or do something else with it?"

"He's not going to do that, not until he finds out whether or not the letter's genuine. If it is —"

"If?" Clay said sharply.

"You and I know it is, but that clerk doesn't. He's not going to risk his job by destroying the letter until he knows one way or the other. If he got rid of it and denied your claim, and it turned out later he was wrong, he'd be in trouble."

"Maybe," Clay grumbled.

"And since we know the letter *is* genuine,

all we have to do is give him a little time to find out the same thing. Chances are, when we come back tomorrow morning, he'll treat us a mite different."

"He'd damn well better," Clay muttered. "Otherwise he and I are both liable to be sorry . . . but he'll be sorrier."

Jeff's prediction proved to be ill-founded. The clerk was no more helpful the next morning. He informed them coldly that he was still looking into the matter and asked them to return later. For a moment Jeff was afraid he would have to pull Clay bodily out of the office to keep him from vaulting over the counter and strangling the man. But eventually Clay came along peacefully, though he was red-faced with anger.

This was why he had come along, Jeff told himself wryly. Melissa had been right: Clay needed his help getting through the maze of bureaucracy that seemed to be devoted to keeping him from his goal.

The delay chafed at Clay, and every day that went by only confirmed his conviction that it had been a mistake to come to Washington in the first place. No grant of land could be worth such a long separation from Shining Moon and his home.

But on the fourth day the clerk greeted

them with a smile — albeit a grudging one, Jeff thought — and said, "Well, everything appears to be in order, Mr. Holt. You are indeed entitled to a land grant of two thousand acres."

Clay looked at his brother and sighed in relief. "Where?" he asked the clerk.

From under the counter the clerk hauled a huge book of maps. "Anywhere you choose within the boundaries of the Louisiana Purchase that hasn't been previously claimed. You understand, the government surveys of the area are still woefully incomplete, but perhaps you can find an area to your liking on one of these maps."

"I know where I want it," Clay said without hesitation. He paged through the book of maps and after a moment stabbed at one of them with his finger. "Right there." It was the area north of New Hope, along the river where Bear Tooth's people had their village. As long as that land belonged to him, at least in the eyes of the white man's government, no one could come along and take it away from the Sioux.

The clerk frowned. "Are you familiar with this land?" he asked. "This is one of the areas where the survey is incomplete —"

"I'll give you all the information you need, including all the landmarks," Clay told him. "That ought to be enough."

"Very well." The clerk drew a deed book in front of him and picked up his pen. "We might as well get started."

By the end of the afternoon, Clay and Jeff had taken the land office clerk almost step by step over the territory Clay was claiming. The man had made copious notes and had also drawn several maps. When he was finished, he said, "All this information will have to be entered in our records, and then the formal land grant itself will be drawn up."

"When can I have it?" Clay asked.

"Everything should be ready by . . . let's see . . . the day after tomorrow."

Clay suppressed a groan. Another delay. But there was nothing he could do about it, so he simply said, "We'll be here to pick it up."

"Very good." The clerk hesitated, then held out his hand. "I'm sorry I doubted you at first, Mr. Holt. I understand now that you're something of a famous man. You've explored a great deal of the West, I'm told."

Clay shook the man's hand. "I've seen my share of country," he allowed. "And I'm anxious to see it again."

"I'm sure you are," the clerk said with a smile. "Well, be here the day after tomorrow, and everything should be ready for you."

With a nod, Clay left the office. Jeff walked alongside him as they turned down Pennsylvania Avenue toward the side street where the Copper Gable was located. Dusk was settling over Washington, and lights were beginning to appear in windows as lamps and candles were lit for the evening. The air was warm and muggy.

"You see, everything's going to work out all right," Jeff commented, "and we didn't even have to bribe that clerk."

"I wasn't going to pay the fellow off for doing his job," Clay said disgustedly.

Jeff smiled. Clay knew the frontier like the back of his hand, but he didn't completely understand how things were done among more gentrified folk.

"You did the right thing, picking that land near New Hope," Jeff went on. "It's liable to be worth a lot of money someday."

"All I care about is that Bear Tooth and his band will always be able to live there."

Jeff put a hand on his brother's shoulder, feeling a little ashamed. He should have known that Clay wouldn't be concerned with potential profits from the land grant. *Maybe I've been in business too long*, Jeff told himself. "That's right," he said to Clay.

They turned onto the side street. As they

headed for the tavern, they passed the mouth of an alley that was cloaked in shadows. Suddenly, from the depths of the alleyway, they heard a woman cry out in pain. An instant later she called desperately, "Help me! Oh, God, somebody help me!"

Clay stiffened and lunged into the alley before Jeff had a chance to move. City living had dulled his instincts so that he was slower to react than his brother. But he was right behind as Clay plunged toward the sounds of a struggle.

Other instincts, instincts Clay did not possess since he had never lived in a city, abruptly shrilled a warning in Jeff's head. This could be some sort of trap —

That was the thought going through his mind when something slammed into the back of his skull and sent him tumbling forward into the darkness of the alley.

Chapter Seven

Professor Abner Hilliard was at the reins of the wagon moving through the wilderness. Nick Palmer was in no shape to handle the job with his wounded shoulder. Proud Wolf and the professor had buried Tom Fairley, the guide who had been killed by the renegade Crow warriors. Then they had helped Nick into the back of the wagon, propping him up against the professor's trunk. The bouncing, jolting ride was doubtless uncomfortable for him, but he was enduring the pain without complaint, his stoicism bolstered by the bottle of whiskey cradled in his lap. He took a healthy nip from it every now and then.

Hilliard had asked Proud Wolf to ride beside him on the wagon seat. Proud Wolf had hesitated before accepting. He would have had no trouble keeping up with the wagon on foot, and he was not accustomed to riding on a white man's conveyance. But he wanted to hear more about this proposition the professor had for him.

"Simply put, I want you to come back east

with me and attend school there," Hilliard said as he guided the mules. "Your tuition and all your living expenses would be paid for by a scholarship from the American Philosophical Society."

"The society to which Professor Franklin belonged," Proud Wolf said.

"Exactly. Donald was a valued member, very well liked and respected, and everyone in the society was terribly saddened to hear of his tragic passing."

"It was an honorable death," Proud Wolf said. "He died so that his daughter and others might live."

Hilliard nodded. "Yes, I understand that. But it was still a great loss to the academic world . . . and to those of us who were his friends." The professor cleared his throat. "All of Donald's journals were brought back to St. Louis with his daughter Lucy by your friend Clay Holt. Lucy is doing as well as can be expected, by the way. I'm not sure she will ever completely recover from the ordeal she experienced, but I'm told she's making progress. At any rate, Professor Franklin's journals eventually found their way back to his colleagues at Harvard, myself among them, and we were able to devote a great deal of study to his observations."

This white man was very fond of the

sound of his own voice, Proud Wolf thought. But he kept silent and allowed Hilliard to continue.

"What was most intriguing were his comments about you, Proud Wolf. He was quite impressed with your native intelligence. It was Donald's theory, you see, that a person's natural abilities are independent of his or her surroundings, but that the development of those abilities is determined by the opportunities to which they are applied. In other words —"

"An apparently mindless savage such as myself might actually be as intelligent as, say, a college professor?"

Hilliard looked sharply at Proud Wolf, his expression a mixture of surprise, pique, and amusement. "Donald's notes mentioned that you were exceptionally well-spoken," he said after a moment. "He didn't say anything about how blunt you can be." He grunted and shook his head. "But you're right, you know. That is exactly what Donald believed. I do, too. That's why I want to prove it by taking you back east and giving you an education at one of the finest academies in the country."

"You would turn me into a white man," Proud Wolf suggested.

The professor shook his head emphatically.

"Absolutely not. Education has nothing to do with the color of one's skin. You will always be a Teton Sioux, no matter how much you know or how you dress and act or where you live."

Proud Wolf was not certain he agreed, but he let it pass for the moment. He waved a hand at the landscape around them and said, "Some people would believe that living here is an education in itself."

"And they would be correct. The skills you need to survive here are for the most part entirely different from those required by a civilized life. And yet, white men can learn the skills of your people and thrive in these surroundings. Clay Holt is proof of that. So are John Colter and all the other so-called mountain men. The reverse should be true as well. An intelligent young man from these surroundings — a young man such as yourself, Proud Wolf — should be able to learn everything that is necessary to thrive in Cambridge, Massachusetts. And of course, after you've finished your schooling, you could always come back here to live, if that was your wish."

Proud Wolf had his doubts about some of the things Hilliard was saying, but he had to admit that the professor made a good argument. And he wanted to believe that he could indeed survive in the East. Hilliard had said that he hoped Proud Wolf would find his proposition interesting. Proud Wolf was intrigued, yes — but he was not quite ready to accept the offer.

"We will speak of this again when we reach the village of Bear Tooth," he told Hilliard. "Until then, I will think on all that you have said."

"That's fair enough," the professor said.

Behind them in the wagon, as it lumbered on toward the mountains, Nick Palmer began to sing in a drunken voice.

Jeff never lost consciousness completely, even though the vicious blow to the back of his head had sent him sprawling forward to the ground. He caught himself, feeling a stone painfully scrape the palm of his left hand. He heard fists thudding against flesh, and somebody hissed harshly, "Stove their heads in, damn it, then grab their purses!"

Sensing more than hearing another blow coming toward him, Jeff threw himself to the side and rolled quickly until he came up against the wall of a building. He pushed himself to his feet and blinked rapidly, trying to clear his vision, which had blurred when he was struck from behind. Just in time, he focused on a dark shape whipping through the air toward him and ducked so that the club slammed into the wall just above his head. The man who had swung the club was close enough that Jeff could reach out and smash a fist into his midsection.

The man grunted and doubled over. Jeff grabbed his coat and slung him to the side, sending him stumbling away into the darkness, out of control. A second later he heard a muted crash as the man fell over something, probably a barrel or a crate. Figuring that his opponent would be out of the fight for at least a few moments, Jeff looked around for Clay.

The sounds of a struggle were enough to guide him. Clay was on the other side of the alley, trading blows with at least two men. Jeff could barely make them out in the dim light that seeped in from the street. He started toward Clay, intending to help him fight off his assailants, but before he had taken two steps, a patter of footsteps came from behind him and something suddenly landed on his back.

"I've got this one," a woman's voice cried, practically in Jeff's ear. "One of you louts give me a hand!" Her arms went around Jeff's neck and began to choke him with surprising strength.

He tore at the woman's arms, straining

until he managed to draw a small breath between clenched teeth. One of her arms came loose from his neck, but the woman instantly shifted her attack to his face. Fingernails like the talons of an eagle clawed at his cheeks and gouged at his eyes, and he had to twist his head to avoid them.

Jeff had faced enough dangers in his life for any two normal men, but he had never been in a situation quite like this. The woman, no doubt the one whose false cries for help had lured Clay and Jeff into this alley, was doing her best to blind and disable him. He had to strike back, yet for some reason he hesitated.

But as the fingernails raked his nose and cheek, Jeff decided that a dark alley in the middle of a city was no place for chivalry. Knowing there was a wall somewhere close behind him, he set his feet and then threw himself backward. The woman gasped in surprise, then in pain, when he slammed into the brick wall. Her grip loosened, and as he stumbled forward again, she slid off his back.

Jeff had rid himself of the woman just in time to deal with the renewed attack of the man he had punched in the belly a few moments earlier. The man came lunging back, once again swinging a club. Jeff threw up his left arm to block the blow, taking it on his forearm instead of his head. Pain shot up to his shoulder from the impact, and his left hand went numb.

His right hand was still functioning, however, and with it he threw a roundhouse punch that caught his opponent on the jaw. The man went down again, and this time the limp, heavy way he fell told Jeff he wouldn't be getting up for a while.

In the meantime, Clay had his hands full with the two men who had jumped him. He had managed to fend them off for a while, trading punches with first one and then the other, but when both men pressed their attack at once, Clay was forced back against the far wall of the alley.

There was one way to even the odds, Clay thought. He brushed aside his coat and closed his fingers around the wooden grips of the long, heavy-bladed hunting knife sheathed on his right hip. He slid the weapon from its sheath and lashed out with it in one continuous motion. The blade met a momentary obstruction and then ripped through it, powered by the muscles of Clay's arm and shoulder. He heard a man scream.

Clay slashed toward the other direction, forcing the second man to leap back frantically to avoid the blade. While the man was off balance, Clay hooked the toe of his boot behind his opponent's leg and yanked. The man went over backward with a startled cry. His head hit the wall of the building with an ugly thud, and he landed in a nerveless heap.

The fellow Clay had wounded with the knife was stumbling around moaning, "He cut my arm off! He cut my arm off!" Clay doubted that; he hadn't felt the knife grate on bone when he ripped through whatever he had hit. He allowed that there was probably a fairly serious cut on the man's arm and that he might bleed to death without a doctor's attention.

But Clay was not about to waste his sympathy on a common thief. He stepped closer to the wounded man and kicked him in the groin. The man screamed again and fell over, clutching at himself. "Reckon that'll take your mind off your arm," Clay grated.

A rustle of skirts sounded close by, and he lunged out with his free hand. His fingers closed around what he realized immediately was someone's arm. A woman cried out, but Clay spun her around, shoved her roughly against the wall, and pinned her there, his left forearm across her throat. He brought the knife up with his right hand.

"Wait, Clay!" Jeff said urgently. "Don't kill her!"

"F-for God's sake, m-mister," the woman

rasped. "Listen to your brother!"

Clay leaned closer and growled, "How'd you know he's my brother?"

"I . . . I . . ."

The woman didn't need to answer. Clay's eyes had adjusted to the darkness, and he could make out her features in the shadows. "You're the serving girl from the Copper Gable," he said. "The one who wanted to go upstairs with us the day we got here."

"It's her, all right," Jeff agreed as he, too, moved closer. "I think I heard Ledbetter call her Rachel."

"Is that your name?" Clay demanded, tightening the pressure on her throat for a second, then releasing it. "Are you called Rachel?"

"Aye! That . . . that's my name." She was breathing raggedly, fighting for every bit of air that Clay allowed her.

"Well, Rachel, why did you and your friends try to murder us? Are you simple thieves?"

"That's right, sir! Aye, we wanted naught but your purses. We'd not have truly harmed you —"

"That's a lie," Clay snapped. "You tried to brain both of us." He glanced over his shoulder at Jeff. "Are those bastards still unconscious?"

"They're no threat right now," Jeff reported after checking the recumbent forms of the three thieves. "They'll probably start coming around in a few minutes."

Clay turned his attention back to Rachel. "You're a pretty one. I'll wager it hurt your feelings when Jeff and I didn't take you up on your offer. You decided right then that you'd get even with us, didn't you?"

Even with the blade of his knife only inches from her face, the woman managed to summon up a trace of defiance as she said, "What if I did?"

"I could carve that pretty face of yours so that *no* man would want you. Ever." Clay's voice was low and menacing.

"You . . . you wouldn't do that to me," Rachel said, but she didn't sound convinced.

Clay's jaw was tightly clenched, and a muscle jumped in his cheek as a long moment passed in silence. Then he sighed and said, "You're right. I won't . . . this time. But if you try anything like this again, I might do worse."

He stepped back, removing his arm from her throat and lowering the knife. Rachel sagged forward, breathing heavily and bringing her hands to her face.

Clay swept the point of the knife around to indicate the three men who were still sprawled, semiconscious, on the alley floor. "When these skunks wake up," he said, "you'd better convince them to find some other line of work besides robbing innocent folks. I may be around Washington for a while, and if I hear of any more robberies in this neighborhood, I'll find all four of you and settle things once and for all. Do you understand?"

"I . . . understand," Rachel said. Her voice was still hoarse.

"Good. See that you remember." Clay pulled his coat back and slid the knife into its sheath. "You're all lucky we weren't carrying our pistols tonight. Thought we wouldn't need them, since we're in the middle of a *civilized* city," he said scornfully. "We won't make that mistake again, will we, Jeff?"

"Not likely," Jeff said.

Clay inclined his head, Jeff nodded, and together they backed out of the alley, leaving Rachel and the three men where they were. When they reached Pennsylvania Avenue, Clay asked, "Is there a constable in this town, or any other law?"

"I'm sure there is, but what good would it do to summon him now? Everything is over." Jeff shook his head in relief. "I'm just glad there wasn't more bloodshed. For a moment there I thought you really intended to cut that young woman's throat."

Clay grunted. "Maybe I did."

"I don't think so. You were just trying to scare her, put the fear of God — and Clay Holt — in her."

"It doesn't matter," Clay grumbled. "She'll still come to a bad end, and those three with her. It's only a matter of time."

"You're probably right. Still, I don't think they'll bother us again while we're here."

"Jeff, as soon as I have that land grant in my hand, I'm leaving Washington." Clay rolled his shoulders wearily. "It's time I got home."

The evening crowd was beginning to gather in the Copper Gable when Clay and Jeff strode in a few minutes later. They were crossing the room toward the staircase when they heard their names being called. When they turned toward the bar, they saw Harry Ledbetter beckoning them.

"What's this about, do you reckon?" Clay asked from the corner of his mouth.

Jeff shook his head and said, "Only one way to find out." Together they made their way across the room. It wasn't difficult getting through the crowd. People tended to move out of the Holts' way.

"I'm glad I saw you lads come in," Ledbetter said as they walked up to the bar. "Can I get you a drink?"

"Is that all you wanted?" Clay asked in disgust. "To sell a bucket of beer?" He started to turn away.

Ledbetter leaned forward quickly and put a hand on Clay's arm. "No!" he exclaimed. "That's not it at all."

Clay looked down pointedly at Ledbetter's fingers, and the tavern keeper let go.

"Begging yer pardon, Mr. Holt," Ledbetter went on hurriedly. "I really do need to speak to you and your brother. I guess my old bartender's instincts just got the better of me for a second."

"What is it you want?" Jeff asked.

"A fellow came in earlier today, while you were gone to the Land Office." Ledbetter bent over and reached under the bar. "He left this for you." With a flourish he held out a folded piece of paper toward Clay.

Clay's eyes narrowed. In the smoky light of the tavern he saw his name written on the paper in a bold, forthright hand. He didn't recognize the writing.

This trip to Washington had begun because of a letter for him, Clay thought. What might *this* message represent?

As Jeff had said, there was only one way to

find out. He took the paper from Ledbetter and turned it over. It was fastened shut with plain red wax. There was no seal.

Whatever the letter contained, Clay wasn't going to stand here in the middle of a crowded tavern and read it. He gave Ledbetter a curt nod and said, "Thanks," then turned toward the stairs again.

"Aren't you going to see what it says?" Ledbetter asked, clearly disappointed that his curiosity was going to go unsatisfied. "The gent who brought it had the look of an important man about him."

"What did he look like?" Jeff asked. He brought out a coin and slid it onto the bar, where Ledbetter promptly made it disappear with all the speed and dexterity of a sleight-of-hand artist.

"He was a tall man with a very thin face," Ledbetter said. "Very well dressed, and when he was going out, I caught a glimpse of a fancy carriage parked outside. The fellow had the look of real money about him."

Clay and Jeff glanced at each other, and Jeff shrugged. He didn't recognize the description, and neither did Clay.

"Thanks," Clay said again. He turned and strode back across the room to the staircase, Jeff right behind him.

Once they were back in their room, with

the door shut firmly behind them, Jeff tossed his hat onto the bed and said, "I wonder what this is about."

Clay looked at the folded paper rather nervously. "I don't know," he said, "but I'll wager nothing good will come of it."

"You can be the gloomiest fellow sometimes." Jeff gestured toward the paper. "Go ahead and open it."

Clay broke the red wax and unfolded the paper. The message was addressed to him and was written in the same bold hand that had inscribed his name on the outside. His eyes scanned the words, and although their meaning was quite clear, for a moment his brain refused to comprehend them. He frowned darkly.

"Well?" Jeff demanded. "What is it?"

"It's an invitation," Clay replied as he looked up, still frowning. "We're going to see the president."

Chapter Eight

The nicest thing about traveling, Melissa Holt thought as she looked around the bedroom she shared with Jeff in the large house in Wilmington, was coming home again. She was relieved and happy to be back in North Carolina.

"It's so good to have you home, dear," her mother Hermione said, echoing Melissa's thoughts. "I missed you and little Michael so much."

"Whip," Melissa said with a smile.

"What, dear?" Hermione cocked her head, looking confused. She was still attractive in middle age, Melissa thought, her red hair only lightly touched with gray.

"Michael has decided he wants to be called Whip. That's what Castor and Pollux Gilworth called him, because they saw Jeff trying to teach him how to use a whip."

"Well, that's hardly an appropriate name for a little boy, I should think," Hermione said. She put a hand to her throat. "It sounds more like something you would call a . . . a ruffian."

"Yes, but he likes it, so don't be surprised if he asks you to call him by that name. I'm trying to discourage it, though, Mother, so we'll continue to call him Michael."

"I couldn't agree more," Hermione said crisply. "A child shouldn't be using a whip, anyway. He'll put his eye out!"

Melissa suppressed a smile. "He's surprisingly good with it. But I agree with you, Mother, he's too young for it now. Perhaps when he's older . . ."

"Well, we'll see. Now, as soon as you've unpacked, you must come downstairs and tell me all about your trip." Hermione put her arms around Melissa and hugged her. "I know I said it before, but it's just so good to have you home."

Her mother left, and Melissa got busy with the business of unpacking her bags. As she did so, she wondered where Jeff was now and what he was doing. That thought had come to her often during the journey from Ohio to North Carolina, which had taken almost a week in a stagecoach. Melissa, Michael, Ned, and India had traveled from Marietta southeastward through Kentucky, following the old Wilderness Road laid out by Daniel Boone, through the Cumberland Gap into Virginia, and then on to North Carolina. Ned and India had ridden horseback most of the way, only occasionally tying their mounts on behind the coach and riding inside with the others. The country-side had been beautiful, with mountains the deep green of the forests that covered them and broad grassy valleys where mist floated in the early mornings. Melissa had enjoyed the trip, even though she missed Jeff. But the journey had been tiring, too, and she looked forward to a good night's sleep in her own bed.

She was also anxious to visit the store and check on how the family business had fared in their absence. It was now known as the Holt-Merrivale Trading Company and included both the emporium in Wilmington and a busy freight line that extended west to the settlements in Tennessee and Kentucky. Jeff had pioneered that end of the business, back when Melissa's father was still alive and running the store in Wilmington. Now she and Jeff were in charge of the entire operation, with Hermione serving as a silent partner.

The bedroom door opened, and Michael hurried inside. "Mama!" he cried with his usual exuberance. "When can we go to the store?"

Melissa smiled. The emporium was one of Michael's favorite places, with its cavernous ceiling, its maze of aisles, and its shelves stocked with every conceivable sort of merchandise. "It's rather late in the day," she told him. "I thought we'd wait until tomorrow to go."

"I want to go today!" Michael said. "I promised Ned I'd show him all my favorite things."

"Ned has been to the store before," Melissa pointed out.

"But I want to show him!"

Melissa started to shake her head, then sighed and decided that it wouldn't hurt to make a short visit. Besides, it might be best to drop in unannounced and perhaps get a more accurate sense of how business had been. By tomorrow morning, word that she was back in Wilmington might have spread.

"All right," she told Michael. "We'll go to the store. Ned can drive the carriage."

Michael let out a whoop of excitement and ran out of the room, obviously intending to find Ned and tell him the good news.

The rest of the unpacking could wait until later, Melissa told herself. She had always found it difficult to deny her young son anything he wanted.

"I would have thought the place would be busier, even this late in the day," Melissa said, frowning in concern as Ned brought the carriage to a stop in front of the Holt-Merrivale Emporium. Usually there were several wagons backed up to the high porch in front of the store, ready for loading with the supplies their owners were purchasing.

Today, however, Melissa's carriage was the only vehicle stopped at the emporium. India St. Clair, who was riding in the seat across from Melissa and Michael, leaned forward to look out the window of the carriage. "Perhaps it's just a slow day," she suggested.

"Perhaps," Melissa said, but she was still disturbed by the air of emptiness about the store.

Not that the place had been cleaned out by thieves or anything like that, she saw a few moments later as she entered the building with the others. The shelves were well stocked — a bit *too* well stocked, she thought. Running out of a few items now and then meant that the merchandise was selling at a healthy pace.

What was missing in the emporium was customers.

As Melissa looked around, she saw two women standing at the long counter in the rear of the store. They appeared to be the only customers at the moment, and they were outnumbered by the three clerks behind the counter. One of the men spotted Melissa and stared at her with wide eyes for a second before he recovered his composure and hurried out from behind the counter. He came quickly down the long center aisle, nervously rubbing his hands together. "Mrs. Holt!" he greeted her. "We didn't know you were back."

That was obvious, Melissa thought, then told herself that she was being uncharitable. Her employees were not to blame for the lack of customers. They couldn't very well go out, drag people in off the street, and force them to buy something, now could they?

"Hello, Mr. Hayward," she said to the man, who was her chief clerk. "I just returned to Wilmington this afternoon."

"And where is Mr. Holt?"

"He's not here at the moment." Melissa gestured toward Ned and India. "You remember my husband's cousin Ned and Miss St. Clair."

"Of course," Hayward said. He nodded politely to the couple, then reached out and ruffled Michael's hair. The boy squirmed away from his touch. "And this little lad, of course."

Michael took hold of Ned's hand, then grabbed one of India's as well. "Come on," he said, tugging the two adults along with him. "I want to show you things."

Ned and India went along tolerantly, and Melissa watched them go with a smile. As she turned back to Hayward, the smile vanished. "What's wrong here, Mr. Hayward?" she asked. "The store is nearly empty. Where are all the customers? Is something going on in town that I'm not aware of?"

The clerk sighed. "I'm sorry to have to tell you this, Mrs. Holt, mighty sorry, but this isn't too unusual these days. Our sales have been dropping steadily."

Hayward was something of a toady, and Melissa was not very fond of him, but he was competent, reliable, and, as far as she could tell, unwaveringly honest. She knew he was telling her the truth.

"Why?" Melissa asked sharply. "Why are sales dropping?"

"It's that son of a —" Hayward caught himself before he uttered the epithet, then went on, "It's Jeremiah Corbett, ma'am. Since you've been gone, he's dropped his prices so drastically that we can't compete with him."

Melissa frowned in surprise. She knew of Jeremiah Corbett. The man owned a general mercantile store in Wilmington, a direct competitor of the Holt-Merrivale Emporium. But Corbett's store was smaller and not as well stocked, so Melissa had never considered him a serious threat. Besides,

Wilmington was growing, and there was more than enough business for both of them, she believed. She had seen no reason to engage in cutthroat tactics against the other merchant, and neither had Jeff.

"Corbett's prices are so low that if we match them, we'll be losing money on almost everything we sell," Hayward went on.

"How is it possible for Mr. Corbett to keep his prices so low?" Melissa asked. "We've always priced our goods so that we'll make a reasonable profit, no more."

Hayward shook his head. "I don't know, ma'am . . . unless it's that new shipping line."

"New shipping line?"

"The Rattigan line. It's owned by an Englishman. His ships have recently started sailing in and out of the port here, and it's rumored he's in partnership with Corbett. Rattigan ships are said to be supplying the goods that Corbett sells."

Melissa nodded in understanding. Holt-Merrivale had a similar arrangement with Lemuel Marsh, whose wife Irene was cousin to Bartholomew Holt, Melissa's late father-in-law. Marsh ships plied the coastal waters from New England to Florida, and by working in concert with the shipping line, Melissa and Jeff had been able to hold their prices down in the store.

But apparently not enough, if Jeremiah Corbett was undercutting them and luring away their customers. Clearly a great deal had happened in the weeks since she and Jeff had left for Ohio.

"I'll have to look into this," she said. "Perhaps there is some way we can compete with Mr. Corbett."

"Not if we can't get the goods to sell," Hayward said gloomily.

Melissa raised her eyebrows. "What do you mean by *that?*"

The chief clerk looked uncomfortable, as if he wished he hadn't said anything. "Two shipments of merchandise bound for the store here had, ah, accidents."

Melissa tensed, not liking the sound of this at all. "What sort of accidents?" she asked tautly.

"A ship went down at sea, and the cargo was lost."

"A Marsh ship?"

Hayward nodded. "It's assumed that it sank during a squall we had a couple of weeks ago."

"That's not known for certain?"

"No wreckage was ever found. But the ship disappeared, so what else could have happened?"

Pirates. Melissa thought the word but didn't say it. Another ship could have waylaid the

Marsh vessel, looted its cargo, and then either sunk it or burned it. That seemed at least as likely an explanation for the ship's disappearance as going under during a storm.

"What about the other shipment?"

"Those goods arrived in Wilmington safely," Hayward said, "but they were never delivered here to the store. They were unloaded into a warehouse and were to be carted over here the next day." He swallowed. "The warehouse burned that night, burned to the ground along with everything in it."

"Was the fire an accident?"

"Who can say?" Hayward shrugged miserably.

He was afraid to come right out and admit what they were both thinking, Melissa knew. The warehouse fire could be attributed to simple fate, just as the disappearance of the Marsh ship could be attributed to the forces of nature. But Melissa had a feeling that neither fate nor nature was to blame in either case.

The hand of man was behind these troubles. Or rather, the hand of *one* man.

And more than likely his name was Jeremiah Corbett.

Cassie Doolittle had become a regular visitor at the Holt farm, for which Shining Moon was grateful. She had grown quite fond of the old woman, despite her colorful, sometimes coarse speech. Shining Moon had even learned not to mind so much when Cassie occasionally slipped and called her "Injun." The old woman's visits were a welcome distraction from Shining Moon's continued uneasiness about Matthew Garwood.

Matthew was more sullen than ever. He seldom said more than a dozen words to Shining Moon during the course of a day, and he disappeared into the woods for long stretches of time. Twice, Shining Moon had grown so concerned about his absence that she had asked the Gilworth brothers to help her look for the boy. Both times they had finally found him deep in the forest, sitting beneath a tree. He only glared at them and steadfastly refused to explain what he was doing. Shining Moon suspected that he could not abide being around her.

It would be simpler, she found herself thinking one day, if Matthew just ran away and never came back. She was appalled at herself for allowing such a thought to enter her head, but there was no denying the truth of it. They might all be better off if Matthew were gone.

But that would mean giving up, and she

was much too proud to do that. She would get through to Matthew somehow, she decided. She would make him understand that he was loved and cared for, that he no longer had to hate the Holts simply because they were Holts. He was one of them now, in every way that counted . . . except blood.

Today, when she heard the creaking of Cassie's cart through the open window of the cabin, Shining Moon broke into a smile and put aside the clothing she was mending. She stood up, went to the door, and swung it open in time to see the old woman nimbly climbing down from the cart.

"Hidy," Cassie called to her. "How are you today, Shinin' Moon?"

"I am well," Shining Moon answered as she stepped out to the porch. "Come inside. I will fetch the cider."

"No need for that." Cassie reached into the cart and brought out a clay jug with a carved wooden stopper. "I brung somethin' for us to drink."

Without hesitation Shining Moon shook her head. "I cannot. I will not drink whiskey. I have seen too many times what it does to my people."

"Well, then, I'll drink some of it, and you can give what's left to the Gilworths." Cassie shook the jug back and forth. Shining Moon could hear the liquid sloshing inside. " 'Tain't full. A sip or two o' corn squeezin's won't hurt big fellas like them two."

Shining Moon knew that Castor and Pollux kept a jug of their own in the barn. Clay seemed to think it did no harm. "I am sure they will thank you for your generosity," she told Cassie.

"Brung you a peach pie, too." Cassie took a cloth-covered plate from the cart. "Best you ever et."

"I am sure it is." Shining Moon had heard Castor and Pollux praising Cassie's cooking skills.

Cassie looked around suspiciously and asked, "Where's that boy?"

"Do you mean Matthew? Castor and Pollux have taken him to the fields to help them plow. I thought it would be a good idea if he did some work."

Cassie grunted. "Might help straighten him up, all right. I'll come in and visit a while, then. Didn't want to intrude if the boy was here. I got the feelin' he don't like me."

Unfortunately, Shining Moon had the same feeling. Of course, she could have told Cassie that it wasn't her fault, that Matthew did not like *anyone*. But it was true that Matthew seemed particularly antagonistic toward Cassie. More than once, after Cassie had come for a visit, Matthew had called her an old witch — and worse.

"Please come in," Shining Moon said. "We will talk."

Cassie handed her the pie and carried the jug herself. She followed Shining Moon into the cabin, and soon they were seated at the table. Shining Moon brought cups of coffee from the stove to have with their pie. Cassie pulled the cork from the jug with her teeth and poured a healthy dollop of whiskey into the coffee.

The time passed pleasantly for Shining Moon. Cassie reminded her of some of the old women of her tribe, who could tell story after story about the Sioux people — where they had come from, their battles, their heroes and great chiefs. Cassie, who had been one of the first white settlers of the Ohio River valley, had many tales of those early years. Some of the stories were exciting, others were humorous, and others were quite ribald. Shining Moon had grown accustomed to Cassie's bluntness, but she still found her face warming as she giggled at the old woman's lewd stories.

The pie was as good as Cassie had claimed. Shining Moon ate two pieces while Cassie looked on, beaming with pride. "I will save the rest for Matthew and Castor and Pollux," Shining Moon said.

"If'n you want any more for yourself, you'd best hide it," Cassie advised. "Once them Gilworth boys get a whiff o' that pie, there won't be none left."

A few minutes later, Shining Moon heard voices outside and knew that the brothers had returned from the fields. Matthew would be with them. Cassie realized that, too, so she stood up and said, "I'll be goin' now."

"You do not have to leave," Shining Moon told her.

"Reckon it'd be better if I did. Weren't never any love lost 'twixt the Garwoods and the Doolittles. We didn't do any feudin' with 'em, like the Holts did, but there was enough bad blood so's I don't want to be around that boy."

Shining Moon felt a pang of regret, then a sudden surge of resentment. It was not fair that Matthew's mere presence was enough to cause the only friend she had made here to depart so abruptly. Of course, she told herself, it was not fair either to blame Matthew for who his parents were. If anyone was at fault here, it was Cassie for being so intolerant. The boy was, after all, an innocent child.

Still, Shining Moon could not bring herself to be angry at Cassie. The old woman had brightened her days considerably and helped the time pass while Clay was gone.

"Very well," she said to Cassie. "But please come back soon."

"I'll do that." Cassie pushed the stopper back in the jug and slid it across the table to Shining Moon. "Don't forget to give that to Castor and Pollux."

Shining Moon nodded. "I thank you on their behalf."

The voices were coming from the rear of the cabin now, in the direction of the barn. The Gilworths were probably stabling the mule they had taken out to the field. Cassie hurried out before they could finish that chore and come inside with Matthew. She climbed up onto the seat of her cart after untying the mule, and within moments the vehicle was rolling away, bouncing on the rough spots in the road. Shining Moon stood in the doorway and watched her go.

Matthew appeared at the corner of the cabin. He glanced at the departing cart and sneered, "That old woman was here again."

"Mrs. Doolittle is my friend," Shining Moon said. "I like it when she visits us."

"Well, I don't. She's old and ugly, and I don't like her."

"She has never done any harm to you or your family," Shining Moon said patiently.

"*Which* family?" Matthew shot back. "I bet she's just like everybody else around here. I bet she told bad stories about my ma."

"You do not know that," Shining Moon said, "and even if it is true, it was long ago."

"Not that long. I ain't forgot."

"Perhaps you should. It is not good to hold bad thoughts inside you."

Matthew pushed past her and went into the cabin. Shining Moon let him go. He already resented being forced to work in the fields with Castor and Pollux and would be sullen for the rest of the day. She would only make matters worse, she knew, if she tried to reason with him.

Shining Moon went down the steps and toward the barn behind the cabin. One of the Gilworth brothers emerged, greeting her with a polite nod. "Howdy, ma'am," he said. "Castor'll be along in a little while. He stayed behind to burn a big ol' stump we uprooted this afternoon."

So this was Pollux. Shining Moon glanced over her shoulder toward the cabin. "Matthew did not seem to have enjoyed working with you this afternoon," she commented.

"That little fella don't enjoy much of anything."

178

"I know. I do not mean to say that you and your brother did anything wrong, Mr. Gilworth. I was hoping that some work might be good for Matthew. The young boys of my people are often given such tasks, so that they will know how to act as men."

"Yes, ma'am, and it's a good idea," Pollux agreed. "But Matthew didn't really do much work. He ran off into the woods again, and me'n Castor had to go after him."

Shining Moon made a soft sound of dismay. "He hid again?"

Pollux turned his eyes toward the ground and shifted uncomfortably. After a moment he said, "I reckon it's worse than that this time."

More bad news concerning Matthew. Shining Moon did not know how much more she could take. But it would do no good to ignore whatever had happened in the woods this afternoon, so she said, "Tell me."

"It took a while for Castor an' me to find him," Pollux said, "and we might not have even then if we hadn't heard some . . . well, noises."

"What sort of noises?" Shining Moon asked.

"Animal noises. Howling and crying. Like the critter making 'em was in pain. A lot of pain."

Shining Moon felt a chill creep up her backbone. "Matthew was in pain?"

Pollux took a deep breath and lifted his gaze to hers. "No, ma'am. He'd caught himself a raccoon somehow. A little one, not much more'n a baby. And then he . . . took his knife to it."

"He . . . killed this raccoon?"

"No, ma'am. That wouldn't have been so bad. I've killed and skinned many a 'coon." Pollux shook his head solemnly. "The critter was still alive when we found Matthew with it, even though we'd been hearing it scream for a good ten minutes. Castor grabbed it away from him and stomped its head, to put it out of its misery. Matthew just stood there with that knife in his hand, blood dripping off the blade, and looked like he wanted to come after *us* next and skin us alive, like he was doing to that 'coon. I'm sorry to have to tell you this, ma'am, but we figgered you ought to know about what the boy was doing."

The icy feeling along Shining Moon's spine had spread to her entire body. Numbly she wondered if Matthew had tortured animals on those other occasions when he had disappeared into the woods.

Unbidden memories flashed into her mind, triggered by the thought of blood on the blade of a knife. She had seen such torture before, but inflicted on humans. She had suffered some herself when she had been tormented and violated by her Blackfoot captors. Most of the time she managed to keep those bitter images at bay, but now she had to turn away from Pollux Gilworth so that he would not see how agitated she was.

"I'm mighty sorry, ma'am," Pollux said again. "If there's anything I can do —"

Shining Moon shook her head. "There is nothing."

"Castor and me didn't say much to the boy, even though we were pretty mad at what we saw. Didn't figure it was our place to talk to him. But if you want us to . . ."

"No," Shining Moon said firmly. "I will speak to him."

Anger welled up inside her as she walked into the cabin. She found Matthew in the kitchen, about to cut himself a piece of the pie Cassie had brought. He looked up in surprise as Shining Moon reached out and took the knife away from him.

"Pollux told me that you would not work," she said. "He told me, too, how they found you in the woods."

"They're lying —" Matthew began.

"No. I know they speak the truth." Shining

Moon slammed the knife down on the table, making Matthew jump. "From now on, you will do as you are told, and you will not harm any creature. Do you understand?"

"You can't make me —"

Again she did not allow him to finish. "Yes, I can. The children of my people obey their parents, and *you* will obey *me*."

He looked so shocked by her vehemence that for an instant she was tempted to reach out and touch his face, just so he would know she did not hate him. But she suppressed that impulse. It would not hurt for Matthew to be a little afraid of her.

"Now, go and gather the eggs from the chicken house," she told him. "That will be your chore every day from now on."

She thought for a moment he was going to argue with her, but then he ducked his head and said quietly, "Yes, ma'am." He went out to perform the task she had given him.

Shining Moon took a deep breath. That confrontation had been surprisingly difficult, but she felt better now that she had done something to try to take Matthew in hand.

Perhaps things would be different from now on.

Chapter Nine

"The president?" Jeff repeated. "We're going to see President Madison?"

Clay shook his head and extended the note toward his brother. "Thomas Jefferson," he said. "He wants us to come see him at his place in the country."

Jeff took the note and studied it. It was indeed an invitation from the former president, Thomas Jefferson, requesting that both Holt brothers pay a visit to Monticello, which Jeff figured was the plantation where the president lived now that he had retired from public life.

"I was named after the president," Jeff said as he looked up at Clay, a touch of awe in his voice.

"I know."

"I surely never expected to meet him. Are we going?"

Clay shrugged. "What choice do we have? When someone like Thomas Jefferson invites you to his house, you don't turn him down."

"No, I reckon not." Jeff looked at the letter again. "I'm just surprised that he would want to see us. What do you think he wants?"

"Only one way to find out." Clay sighed. "I hope this doesn't slow us down too much. I planned on being ready to ride as soon as we'd picked up those land grant papers."

Neither of the Holt brothers slept particularly well that night. The attack in the alley had unsettled them to begin with, and the unexpected, mysterious invitation from one of the country's most prominent public figures only added to their restlessness. Both men tossed and turned until long after midnight and were hollow-eyed when they arose the next morning and went downstairs in search of breakfast and hot coffee.

Harry Ledbetter was behind the bar, looking equally tired and bleary-eyed. He gave the brothers a sullen nod and commented, "You fellas are up mighty early."

"We have some more business to attend to," Clay said. "Do you know how to get to a place called Monticello?"

Ledbetter's eyes widened, and he was suddenly more alert. "Monticello?" he said. "You mean President Jefferson's estate?"

"That's right," Jeff said. "You've heard of it?"

Ledbetter snorted. "Who hasn't heard of Monticello? Jefferson's built himself a bloody great mansion out there. It's more like a palace than a house — or so I've heard. I've never been there, of course. The likes o' me don't get invited to see a president." He eyed the Holts with suspicion. "Is that where you're going? That fella who brought the note for you yesterday — did Jefferson send him?"

Clay ignored Ledbetter's question. "Just tell us how to get there," he said.

"Fine," the innkeeper snapped. "I was just curious. I don't see what a man like Thomas Jefferson would want with a couple of backwoodsmen like you boys. No offense, of course," he added grudgingly.

"So how do we find the place?" Clay asked, trying not to give in to his impatience.

In a few quick sentences, Ledbetter gave them directions. Monticello was in Albemarle County, near the town of Charlottesville, he told them. "Head southwest and keep the Blue Ridge Mountains on your right. If you do that, you'll get there. It's nigh onto a hundred miles, though, so it'll take you a few days."

"A few days?" Clay suppressed a groan. He had thought that he and Jeff were on the verge of leaving Washington and heading back to Ohio, and now here they were, faced with a delay of another week or so. The only alternative was to refuse Thomas Jefferson's invitation. At this moment Clay was tempted to do exactly that.

He glanced at Jeff, who seemed to know what he was thinking. Without being asked, Jeff said, "It's your decision, Clay. I'll do whatever you want."

"I reckon we're going to see the president," Clay said glumly. "I just hope he's got a good reason for wanting to see us."

They left Washington less than an hour later, crossing the Potomac on a ferry with their saddle horses and pack animals, then rode southwestward on a broad, hard-packed turnpike. The pleasant weather enabled them to make good time, but not good enough to suit Clay. He thought often about the land grant documents waiting for him in Washington City. If not for the message from Thomas Jefferson, he would be on his way back to Shining Moon by now.

Switching horses frequently allowed them to travel at a rapid pace, and the miles of Virginia countryside fell steadily behind them. As Harry Ledbetter had instructed them, they kept the mountains of the Blue Ridge to their right. The dark blue peaks rose steeply in the distance, the rounded tops sometimes visible and sometimes cloaked in clouds of mist. The terrain through which Clay and

Jeff rode was mostly flat, with a few gentle hills here and there. It was cut by numerous streams that Clay would have called creeks but which the locals referred to as runs. Some were crossed by covered bridges, while others had to be forded at low-water crossings. Many of the fields they passed were cultivated, but some of the land was still wild, covered with virgin forests and choking underbrush. Now that they were away from the city, Clay should have felt more at ease, but his spirits were still dampened by the great distance between himself and his wife.

On the third day of the journey, Clay and Jeff were riding along a broad valley between the Blue Ridge and a range of smaller mountains to their left. Late in the afternoon they reached Charlottesville, a picturesque town nestled among thickly wooded hills. They secured a room in a tavern that faced the town square, and the thick-set, middle-aged woman behind the bar gave them directions to Monticello.

"Just take the south road out of town, and ye cannot miss it. 'Tis on a hilltop. Ye can see it for miles around." She looked at Clay and Jeff with narrowed eyes. They were covered with the dust of their journey, and Jeff had not shaved since leaving Washington. "Pardon me for asking, but what're a pair of lads such as yourselves doing visiting Mr. Jefferson? Most of his callers are government fellas or important folk from other countries."

"He asked us to come see him," Clay replied honestly. "We don't know any more than that."

"Well, I reckon you'll enjoy your visit. You ain't never seen a place like Monticello before, I'll wager that! It's taken him near thirty years to get the place put together the way he wants it."

"That's what we've been told," Jeff said. He was looking forward to this visit with the former president, even if Clay wasn't. And from here he would go on home to North Carolina, they had decided, rather than accompany Clay all the way back to Washington. Jeff felt badly that he would be reunited with his family long before Clay could return to Shining Moon, but it seemed the most sensible way to do it.

Since it was late in the day, they decided to wait until the next morning before paying their visit to Thomas Jefferson. Once again, Clay was restless as he tried to sleep. The prospect of meeting such a famous person as Jefferson did not bother him; he had always taken folks as they were and never worried about such things as power and influence. Meriwether Lewis and William Clark had achieved wide renown by the time they returned from their expedition, but to Clay they had simply been Captain Lewis and Captain Clark.

What did worry Clay was the question of *why* Jefferson had summoned him and Jeff. Clay knew it was not simply because the former president wanted to meet them. A man like Thomas Jefferson had no reason to have ever heard of the Holt brothers. No, something was afoot, and Clay's every instinct told him that trouble of some kind lay ahead.

After washing up and putting on clean clothes the next morning, they set off for Monticello. It did not take them long to reach the estate, and as the woman at the tavern had told them, they could see it for quite some time before they arrived. The road wound through a forested area that seemed to be alive with small animals, and through the trees Clay and Jeff caught glimpses of an imposing brick structure on top of a hill in the distance. They were already on Jefferson's property, Clay figured, and his guess was confirmed when the road passed through an orchard of peach, apple, and cherry trees. Several men working in the orchard nodded in answer to Clay's question.

"Mr. Jefferson had these trees planted, all right," one of them said. "I never saw such a fella for growing things."

"Is that his house up on the hill?" Clay asked, pointing through a gap in the fruit trees.

"That's right."

With a nod of thanks, Clay and Jeff rode on, passing a large pond a few minutes later. The road cut through another band of trees, and a sudden crashing in the undergrowth made both men draw rein.

"Look there," Jeff said excitedly, pointing into the trees. "Isn't that an elk?"

Clay grinned in recognition. "Sure is," he said as he watched the massive creature with its graceful sweep of antlers bound away through the woods.

A little farther along the road they spotted a buffalo grazing peacefully in a meadow. For a moment they stared at the shaggy beast in amazement, remembering the vast herds they had seen on the western plains. This solitary animal looked out of place in the Virginia countryside, but it seemed content enough as it cropped on the lush grass.

The road sloped upward toward the top of the hill on which Jefferson's mansion sat. Clay could see the redbrick building clearly now. A large dome dominated the center of it, built over what was probably an entrance hall. The wings of the house ran to the right and left of the dome, which shone white in the sun. A porch had been built in the front of the house, and graceful white columns supported a balcony that extended over it. With the exception of the porch, the house was surrounded by trees and shrubbery. A path paved with fine gravel curved through immaculately kept grounds toward the porch. It was an impressive estate, right enough, Clay mused, a fitting residence for a man who was not only a former president but also one of the most famous living Americans.

Someone had apparently seen Clay and Jeff coming, because as they drew rein in front of the porch, the door opened and an elderly servant in fine livery stepped out. The black man's white hair was cropped close to his head, and his face was seamed and leathery. He gave Clay and Jeff a half-bow as they dismounted, then asked in a deep, rich voice, "Would you be the Holt brothers, suhs?"

"That's right," Clay said. "I'm Clay Holt, and this is my brother Jeff."

"We're here to see President Jefferson, at his invitation," Jeff added.

The servant nodded. "You-all are expected. Come in, please." He stepped aside and ushered them into the house.

Clay expected that the servant would show them to a parlor or some other room where they would wait for the president. To his surprise, as soon as he and Jeff stepped into the high-ceilinged entrance hall directly beneath the mansion's prominent dome, a tall, broad-shouldered man strode toward them, hand extended. Though he had to be close to seventy years of age, he stood straight and moved with the grace of a younger man. His hair, which fell almost to his shoulders, was still thick, and its original red color was just visible through the gray. The man's handsome features were tanned and weathered by sun and wind.

"Clay Holt," Thomas Jefferson said as he took Clay's hand. "I'm very pleased to meet you." He turned toward Jeff. "And you're the young man who was named after me."

"Yes, sir," Jeff said, trying not to stare as he shook Jefferson's hand. "How did you know that?"

"I make it a habit to learn as much as I can about the people who visit me, and as you might well imagine, I still have access to a considerable amount of information, even though I'm simply a retired country squire now."

Clay knew better than that. Thomas Jefferson would never be a simple anything; too much intelligence and vitality shone in his eyes.

"Let me show you around," Jefferson went on. "I'm rather proud of this house, and I like for all my visitors to see it."

Clay would rather have proceeded to whatever matter had prompted Jefferson to invite them to Monticello, but one didn't rush a president. He fell in with his brother as they followed Jefferson across the entrance hall.

"Take a look up there," Jefferson said, turning and raising a hand to indicate the wall above the entrance. The door was flanked by two large windows, and attached to the wall above them were two sets of moose antlers. "Those antlers were presented to me by Captain Lewis and Captain Clark after their return from the Pacific. I daresay you were with them when the trophies were taken, Clay. You don't mind if I call you Clay, do you?"

"No, sir," Clay replied as he looked up at the antlers. He didn't recall the particular animals they had come from, nor did he have any idea when Captain Lewis and Captain Clark had taken them. Truth to tell, Lewis and Clark had packed up so many crates of specimens to be brought back to civilization that Clay and the other men in the party had soon stopped paying much attention to that aspect of the journey. Jefferson was looking at him expectantly, though, so he had to say something. "We made many a meal on moose steaks."

Jefferson sighed. "A part of me wishes I could have gone with you. I would have dearly enjoyed seeing all that pristine wilderness. But I had duties of state to attend to, of course, and I *was* a little old to go traipsing off across the continent, I suppose."

"It would have been an honor to have you with us, Mr. President."

"I'm not the president any longer," Jefferson said with a smile. "Call me Tom."

Clay was sure he could never bring himself to call the former president by that name. He nodded noncommittally and said nothing. He glanced at Jeff, who still seemed overwhelmed by their surroundings and Jefferson's presence.

"Now, that clock up there, that's my own design," Jefferson went on, pointing to a large clock that hung over the door. "Those counterweights are actually cannonballs, and they show not only the hour but also the day of the week. I suppose it would be a bit large and cumbersome for most houses, but it seems to fit nicely here."

It certainly did, Clay thought. Like the rest of Monticello — including its designer and occupant — the clock was larger than life.

"Come into the parlor," Jefferson continued, leading them toward an arched doorway. "I suppose you're curious why I asked the two of you to come down here and visit me."

"We did wonder a mite," Clay admitted, reluctant to tell Jefferson how puzzled they had really been. Nor did he mention how close he had come to ignoring the invitation and returning to Ohio. He hoped Shining Moon would understand why he had made the decision to honor Jefferson's request.

As they stepped into the luxuriously appointed parlor, Jefferson gestured toward the ceiling. "Look up there," he said.

On the ceiling was painted a large compass. A metal arrow quivered slightly as it pointed toward the southeast.

"The indicator is attached to a weather-vane on the roof," Jefferson explained. "With this device I know from which direction the wind is blowing even when I'm inside."

"Mighty smart," Clay said, even as he was wondering why in the world anyone would go to so much trouble to invent such a contraption. If Jefferson wanted to know which way the wind was blowing, he could just step over to a window and look at the trees outside.

"I'm rather proud of the floor, too." The former president pointed down at his feet. Instead of planks, the flooring consisted of smaller pieces of wood polished to a high shine and arranged in a distinctive pattern. "It's called a parquct floor," Jefferson said. "They're popular in Europe, but I don't know of another one here in North America."

"Very pretty," Jeff said. He exchanged a glance with Clay, who was starting to grow impatient. Jefferson was understandably proud of his house and clearly enjoyed showing it off, but Clay was chafing to learn why he and Jeff had been summoned.

"Have a seat, gentlemen," Jefferson said. "I'll have some refreshments sent up." He tugged on a velvet bellpull, but Clay didn't hear the bell itself. Given Jefferson's penchant for mechanical devices, a tug on the rope here in the parlor might make a bell ring clear on the other side of the massive house.

Clay and Jeff settled themselves on a divan, and Clay was glad they had put on clean clothes before leaving the inn this morning. He wouldn't have wanted to get trail dust on such fancy furniture.

Jefferson clasped his hands together behind his back and began to pace back and forth in front of the divan. He appeared to be gathering his thoughts. "I've summoned you here on a rather serious matter, Clay," he began. "I'm gratified you came along, too, Jeff. If one Holt brother is good, two are surely better."

"Excuse me, Mr. President," Clay said, aware that he was interrupting but unable to contain his curiosity any longer, "but just how in blazes do you know anything about me and Jeff? I didn't figure anybody outside of our friends and family had ever heard of us."

A smile curved Jefferson's wide mouth. "On the contrary. I heard a great deal about you, Clay, from Meriwether Lewis after he and Captain Clark returned from their journey. Meriwether said you were one of the most reliable members of the Corps of Discovery."

Clay felt a surge of pride. He'd had no idea that Captain Lewis had singled him out for such high praise.

"You probably deserve more credit than you will ever receive," Jefferson went on. He shrugged and shook his head. "But such is the unfairness of fate sometimes. Our greatest heroes are neglected while the trumpets blare for those who are far less deserving."

"I wasn't a hero," Clay said firmly, "just a fella doing the job he signed on to do."

"That makes you a rarer kind of man than you would ever believe, Clay." Jefferson waved a hand. "At any rate, I've also heard about the exploits both of you were involved in when you returned to the Rocky Mountains with Manuel Lisa's fur-trapping expedition. You dealt with what could have been a serious threat to our territory from British forces."

"If you're talking about the London and Northwest trying to move in on the American trappers and stir up the Indians against us, that didn't have anything to do with the government. That was just plain business for some of the folks involved. To the rest of us it was a matter of staying alive."

"Business is government, and government is business," Jefferson said. "A somewhat regrettable relationship at times, but unavoidable." The faint sound of a bell made Jefferson pause and turn toward the wall. "Ah, our refreshments have arrived."

He strode over to what appeared to be a blank section of the parlor wall while Clay and Jeff exchanged puzzled glances. When he reached the wall, Jefferson took hold of a cleverly concealed catch and swung a section of the paneling toward him like a door. Behind the opening was a small chamber, perhaps two feet wide and two feet high. Jefferson reached into it and brought out a silver tray containing a carafe and several glasses. "I don't think it's too early in the day for some brandy, do you, gentlemen?"

Clay pointed at the aperture in the wall and asked, "What is that?"

"I call it a dumbwaiter. Another of my designs. It travels up and down a shaft by means of ropes and pulleys. The shaft connects to the kitchen and pantry and wine cellar underneath the house."

Jeff let out a low whistle of admiration. "You're just about the cleverest fellow I've ever met, Mr. President."

Jefferson smiled again, clearly pleased that his guests were impressed by his inventions. He set the tray on a side table and poured brandy for the three of them. Clay and Jeff stood up to take the drinks from him, and Jefferson said, "To the United States."

Clay and Jeff echoed the toast, and the three clinked their glasses together. Jefferson sipped his brandy, then said, "As I was saying, I've heard about the prowess you both demonstrated on the frontier, and

I think I would be safe in saying that you bear a great deal of affection for that part of the country."

"It's my home now," Clay said simply.

Jeff added, "I live in North Carolina now, but I reckon I love the Rockies, too. I never saw another place like them."

Another faint, rather sad smile appeared briefly on Jefferson's face. "I wish I could see them as the two of you first saw them." He shook his head and drew a deep breath. Then, his manner crisper and more businesslike, he went on, "Someone is trying to steal those mountains from us, gentlemen."

Clay stiffened. "The British?" he asked. Ever since his discovery that the London and Northwest Enterprise, a British fur trading company, had been behind all the trouble that had plagued him and his friends over the past few years, he had harbored an intense animosity toward the former mother country.

Jefferson set down his brandy glass and resumed pacing. "I'm afraid we simply do not know who is behind the effort. An armed invasion would be one thing; we could deal with that by going to war. But this attempted theft is more insidious. Over the past two years, someone unknown has fraudulently gained title to millions of acres in the west, and I fear that he will continue trying to take over more of our land."

Clay frowned. What Jefferson was saying didn't make sense. "How could somebody do that?"

"Through a series of transactions between the government and a number of individuals and companies that apparently do not really exist. These transactions — sometimes purchases and sometimes outright land grants — have transferred title to a huge expanse of government land. The matter was brought to my attention by a friend of mine who believed that the land was ultimately going to wind up in the hands of one man, or a small group of men, who do not have the country's best interests at heart." Jefferson paused to allow Clay and Jeff to mull over this information, then added, "This friend of mine was acquainted with you as well, Clay. I'm speaking of Meriwether Lewis."

Clay's head jerked up. "Captain Lewis is dead," he said harshly. "He killed himself a while back. But I expect you know that, Mr. President."

"Indeed I do. It was a great loss, both to me personally and to the country. Meriwether was a fine man, a man devoted to this nation. That was why he could not tolerate the idea of someone trying to pervert the ideals on which the country was founded. He contacted me and told me in a letter that he believed he had uncovered the beginnings of a land grab in the west. He was going to investigate the scheme and report his findings to me in person." Jefferson shook his head regretfully. "He never reached Washington, of course. Instead, he died in Tennessee, at a place called Grinder's Stand."

"I read about that," Jeff said. "According to the newspapers, Captain Lewis was upset because he'd made such a muddle of his finances. That's why he shot himself."

"Meriwether was not much of a businessman, I'll grant you that." Jefferson smacked his fist into his palm. "But I don't believe for a minute that he committed suicide. I've been told that he was shot twice, in the head and in the side, while he was in the cabin where he was staying for the night. Mrs. Grinder saw him stagger out, and he came over to her cabin seeking help. She refused to open the door, since her husband was away and she was afraid of robbers. Meriwether died the next day. His possessions had been rifled through, and any report that he might have had for me was missing. You can see why I believe he was murdered."

The same thought had leaped into Clay's mind. Now that Jefferson had given him the details of Lewis's death, murder seemed an even more likely scenario. At the same time, Clay could not accept that Meriwether Lewis had come to such a monstrous end.

And yet, he had seen even worse with his own eyes many times — too many times. There was no limit to what men were capable of doing in the name of money and power.

"If Captain Lewis found out who was behind the land grab, that person would have good reason to want him dead," Jeff said. As usual, Clay's reaction had been more visceral and emotional, while Jeff was thinking it through and following the logic behind what Jefferson was telling them.

"That's right," Jefferson said. "Ever since Meriwether's mysterious death, I've been looking into the matter as discreetly as I can. I'm convinced he was right."

"Maybe he was," Clay said, "but what do you want from us?"

The bluntness of the question seemed to take Jefferson by surprise. After a moment he said, "I need someone to take up the investigation and find the truth. A conspiracy such as this, if one actually exists, could have far-reaching effects on our country.

We're still finding our way . . . like a child learning to walk, if you will. If this blatant, illegal land acquisition succeeds, it could damage the nation, even cripple it. This has to be stopped, as soon as possible."

Clay put his brandy glass, still almost full, on a table and turned toward the former president. "I'm just a fur trapper," he said. "There's nothing I can do."

"You can follow a trail. Meriwether Lewis told me that about you."

"Through a forest or across a prairie, maybe," Clay snapped, his irritation and uneasiness making him more abrupt than he meant to be. He understood now what Jefferson wanted him to do, and the prospect was about as appealing as a skunk in the middle of the dinner table. Clay shook his head. "I'm no good in a city."

"Through my own efforts and those of a few trusted associates within the government, we've determined that one of the clerks in the Land Office is involved in the scheme," Jefferson went on, as if he had not heard Clay's protest. "Perhaps this man's involvement is only minor, but at the moment he represents the only starting place we have."

Jeff spoke up. "This Land Office clerk wouldn't be the same fellow who's handling my brother's land grant, is he?"

"No, that gentleman isn't involved, as far as we know," Jefferson replied. "The man we suspect is named Atticus Bromley. He's a minor functionary in the Land Office who works with government maps. But he has access to records that we suspect have been altered, perhaps even destroyed, in order to cover the trail of those higher up who are involved in the plan to steal the frontier from us."

Clay sighed. A large part of him wanted to turn and stalk out of the parlor with its fancy compass and weathervane. Thomas Jefferson clearly had the kind of mind that could follow the twists and turns of a sinister, torturous plot, but Clay had always been more direct in his thinking. He wanted to go home. He didn't want to stay in Washington and try to sort out the strands of some tangled scheme.

But if a land grab really was in the making — if the man, or men, behind the plan succeeded — there might not be an American frontier for him to return to. The Rockies — the whole blasted western frontier — might wind up belonging to some other country.

And if Meriwether Lewis had indeed been murdered, then his death would go unavenged.

Clay looked over at Jeff, the question of what they should do plain to see in his eyes. Jeff responded by saying, "I've been going along with whatever you decided so far on this trip, Clay, but I don't see how we can walk away from this."

"You're right," Clay said, hating the words even as he spoke them but unable to deny the truth. Thomas Jefferson had decided that he and Jeff were the best candidates for the job. Like it or not, they had to try. They would be letting their country down otherwise.

"I'm afraid I cannot promise you any payment for your efforts," Jefferson said, "nor even any public gratitude for your service. If word gets out about what you'll be investigating, the merest rumor that the country is so vulnerable could be damaging in ways we cannot even predict."

Clay and Jeff both nodded in understanding. What they were doing was for the good of the country. That would have to be payment enough.

Jefferson smiled, clearly pleased by their decision to accept the assignment. He picked up his brandy glass. "Good luck, gentlemen. Or perhaps I should say . . . good hunting."

That was more appropriate, Clay thought. He had always been a hunter, from the time Bartholomew Holt had given him his first flintlock. Now he and Jeff would be hunting the most dangerous prey of all: men driven by greed.

Chapter Ten

Bear Tooth, chief of the band of Teton Sioux that lived near the settlement of New Hope, was glad to see his son again, although he did not know what to make of the odd white man who accompanied him. Since Bear Tooth had not known Professor Donald Franklin, as Proud Wolf and Shining Moon had, Abner Hilliard was the first such educated white man he had ever encountered.

Proud Wolf enjoyed the look of bafflement on his father's face as Bear Tooth listened to the seemingly endless stream of words from Professor Hilliard's mouth. Only when Bear Tooth began to look annoyed did Proud Wolf step in.

"Professor Hilliard is my guest here," he told his father in their tongue. "I have promised him that he will be welcomed."

Bear Tooth nodded gravely. "And so he shall be. But he speaks too much. My ears grow tired. Take your friend to your lodge, then return to me, my son. We have much to talk about ourselves."

That was true, Proud Wolf thought. But

Bear Tooth had no idea what they would be discussing. Proud Wolf had not had the chance to mention the offer Professor Hilliard had made him.

They were standing in front of Bear Tooth's lodge. Most of the women and children in the band, along with a good number of the warriors and young men, were gathered around to look at the visitor. Hilliard seemed unperturbed. Some white men would have considered them all savages and feared for their lives, but the professor seemed quite comfortable. Since he and Proud Wolf had entered the village, he had looked around eagerly, taking in all the sights with great interest.

Proud Wolf put his hand on Hilliard's arm. "Come with me. I will take you to my lodge, where you will stay while you are with us."

"Certainly." Hilliard smiled and nodded at Bear Tooth, who merely stared at him impassively. As he and Proud Wolf turned away from the chief's lodge, the professor gestured at the drawings that adorned the tautly stretched buffalo hides of the Sioux dwellings. "You'll have to explain the meaning and significance of all these pictographs for me, my boy. They're rather crudely done, but quite expressive. Surprisingly so, in fact."

Proud Wolf nodded. "Yes, yes, but now you must rest."

"I'm not particularly tired, you know. In fact, I'm rather invigorated by these surroundings. So much to learn, so much to learn. I want to hear everything about the way you and your people live." Hilliard rubbed his hands together expectantly.

"Later," Proud Wolf said firmly. Hilliard might not be weary, but he certainly was. He was convinced that riding on the white man's wagon had made him more tired than walking or running would have.

The crowd of people around Bear Tooth's lodge opened up to let the two men through. Proud Wolf led Hilliard to his lodge and lifted the entrance flap. "Go inside," he said. "Someone will bring you food."

"Thank you. Aren't you coming with me?"

"I must speak with my father."

"Are you going to tell him that you're coming back east with me?"

Proud Wolf grunted. "That decision has not yet been made."

"It's the chance of a lifetime," the professor reminded him. "You can't refuse, Proud Wolf. You simply can't."

"I will speak with you later." Proud Wolf's tone made it clear he would brook no argument. He dropped the entrance flap closed after Hilliard had bent over and entered the lodge.

Since the death of Raven Arrow and his return from Canada, Proud Wolf had had no close friends among the other warriors in the band. But now as he walked back toward Bear Tooth's lodge, two men fell in alongside him. They were Hand in the Face and Runs Far, both of them slightly older than Proud Wolf. He looked at them curiously, and Hand in the Face said, "You should not have brought the white man here."

Proud Wolf stopped, surprised at the harshness of the statement. "There are other white men here," he said.

Both young men shook their heads. "They do not come to our village," Runs Far said, "and we do not go to theirs. They have their own ways, and they are strange."

"Evil," Hand in the Face said.

Their words disturbed Proud Wolf. He and his people had always gotten along peacefully with the white newcomers to the land of big skies and tall mountains and waving grasses. His best friend in the world was Clay Holt, and not only because Clay was married to Shining Moon. Now he saw hostility in the faces of his fellow Sioux and heard it in their voices, and he wondered what had changed.

Perhaps he had been away from the village for too long this time, Proud Wolf thought.

He was not going to allow this insult to his friends to pass unchallenged. He said, "The white men have done us no harm. We have no reason to fear them or be angry with them."

"They catch the beaver, they shoot the buffalo," Runs Far said. "Some even break the ground and plant seeds in it."

Proud Wolf spoke patiently. "There are beaver and buffalo enough to last until the end of this world, no matter how many the white men kill. And though some of their ways are indeed different, that does not make them evil."

"Say what you will," Hand in the Face told him coldly. "You should have left this white man who talks all the time in the village with the other one."

Proud Wolf and Professor Hilliard had stopped in the settlement of New Hope and left Nick Palmer at Malachi Fisher's trading post. Fisher had promised to take care of the wounded guide until Hilliard was ready to begin the journey back east. Proud Wolf had considered bringing Nick to the village of the Sioux, but Nick had wanted to be with his own kind. The professor, on the other hand, had insisted on accompanying Proud Wolf to the village.

"We will speak of this another time," Proud Wolf said curtly. "Now my father waits for me."

"Bear Tooth will tell you the same thing," Runs Far called as Proud Wolf stalked off. Proud Wolf did not turn around or bother to waste his breath on a reply.

But he hated to see ill will toward the white men growing among his people. That could not lead to anything good.

Bear Tooth was waiting in his lodge, sitting cross-legged by the fire. Proud Wolf entered and sat to his father's right. Outside, the shadows were growing deeper with the approach of night, and here in the lodge the flickering flames cast shadows of their own.

Father and son sat in companionable silence for a time. Then Bear Tooth said, "It is good to have you back among us, my son. You have been away from us too often."

"I must go where the spirits lead me," Proud Wolf replied, thinking of the vision of the great white mountain lion.

"This is your home," Bear Tooth said stubbornly. "A child should not leave his home."

Proud Wolf bristled; he did not like being called a child. But he would always show his father the respect he deserved. Calmly he said, "Shining Moon has left us and gone to the world of the white men."

"Shining Moon is with her husband, and that is where she should be." Bear Tooth added gruffly, "You should take a wife for yourself. There are maidens in the village who would look on you with favor."

Butterfly — Raven Arrow — had looked on him with favor, Proud Wolf thought . . . and had lost her life because of it. "I do not wish to take a wife," he said.

Bear Tooth sighed. One attempt at persuasion had failed, but he could always try another. Proud Wolf could hear that sentiment plainly in his father's reaction.

"I grow older," Bear Tooth said. "There will come a day when our people will need another to lead them."

Proud Wolf stiffened in surprise. He had known, of course, that as the only son of Bear Tooth he might someday be called upon to lead the Sioux. But that day was far in the future. At least he had always supposed so. His father was still in a very vigorous middle age; he would be chief for many seasons to come.

"When that day is upon us, I will not turn my back on my people," Proud Wolf pledged. "But until then, I must follow the wishes of the spirits."

"And if they lead you away from us?"

Proud Wolf suddenly thought about the great cat that had appeared when he was pondering whether to investigate the gunfire on the prairie. The message of that vision-become-flesh had been clear: He was to follow that trail wherever it might lead. It had taken him into battle with the Crow and brought him together with Professor Hilliard. Now, abruptly, all doubt regarding the professor's offer vanished.

"Then so be it," he said to his father.

Once again, Bear Tooth sighed. "You are leaving us." It was not a question.

"The white man, Professor Hilliard, wants me to go with him. He will take me to a place where other white men will teach me their ways."

"You will no longer be one of us," Bear Tooth said, unknowingly echoing one of the objections Proud Wolf had raised to the professor.

"I will *always* be a Sioux," Proud Wolf said fiercely, "no matter where I am or what things I learn. And I will always be your son. When I have learned what the white men can teach me, I will come back here and teach to our people."

Bear Tooth gave him a steady, unreadable look, and suddenly Proud Wolf wondered if that would be true. If he left his father — if he left his people — could he ever truly return and be one of them again?

There was no way of knowing. Proud Wolf knew only that he wanted to learn whatever Professor Hilliard and the other white men could teach him. That was the path the spirits had laid before him. He had no choice but to follow it.

"Go, then," Bear Tooth said. He turned his face away, and Proud Wolf knew they would speak of it no longer.

With a heart that was both heavy with regret and soaring with anticipation, Proud Wolf left his father's lodge and went out into the night.

Professor Hilliard was waiting in Proud Wolf's lodge when the young man returned. As Proud Wolf had promised, one of the women had brought food for the visitor. The professor sat cross-legged on a thick buffalo robe and used his fingers to dip stew from a wooden bowl. As Proud Wolf entered the lodge, he looked up and said, "This is delicious! Do you know what's in it?"

"Wild onion and dog," Proud Wolf said.

Hilliard's eyes widened. "Dog?" he repeated. "You . . . you eat dog?"

"It was probably an old dog," Proud Wolf said. "But the stew is cooked for a long time so that the meat will not be too tough."

The professor swallowed hard, then gamely scooped up another handful. "Very well. If such is your custom, then it is my wish to follow it. After all, eating habits are simply a matter of what one becomes accustomed to, and they are not intrinsically good or bad in themselves."

Although some of the words were unfamiliar to him, Proud Wolf caught the gist of what Hilliard was saying. He sat on another robe and said, "I have reached a decision."

Quickly Hilliard set the bowl aside, even though he had not finished the meal. "You're going with me?" he asked excitedly.

"Yes." Proud Wolf's reply was simple and solemn.

"Ah, excellent! You won't regret it, Proud Wolf, I can promise you that. I was so confident you'd accept the society's offer that before I even came out here, I made arrangements with the Stoddard Academy for Young Men for your enrollment there."

"You were so sure that you would find me and that I would say yes?" Proud Wolf asked dryly.

"Certainly. The proposition was simply too intriguing to refuse, wasn't it? And as for finding you . . . well, I've always had confidence in my own abilities. That's one mark of an educated man, you see."

Proud Wolf tried not to smile. As it had turned out, the professor's confidence had not been misplaced, but sheer luck had certainly been a contributing factor. The frontier covered a lot of territory; even with experienced guides, Hilliard might never have been able to find the Sioux village. And it was dangerous, too, as had been amply borne out by the Crow attack on the white party. If the Crow had managed to kill all three white men, Proud Wolf would never have learned of the offer that had brought Hilliard out here.

But instead, Proud Wolf thought as his smile faded, he had heard the distant gunshots, and that stroke of fate had brought him and the professor together. There was no point in denying it. The spirits had guided the paths of all of them. Proud Wolf was more convinced than ever that by going east with Hilliard, he was fulfilling his destiny.

"I will not be attending this college where you teach?" Proud Wolf asked. "It is called Harvard?"

"That's right. The Stoddard Academy is located just outside of Cambridge, so my fellow instructors and I will be able to visit you frequently and monitor your progress."

Hilliard smiled. "I'm afraid the curriculum at Harvard would be a bit too advanced for you at present. Perhaps in time —"

"I will prove myself intelligent enough to go there," Proud Wolf finished, unsure whether or not he should be insulted by the professor's answer.

"You're intelligent enough *now*," Hilliard said, "or at least I believe you are. What you lack is the proper academic grounding, and you'll get that at the Stoddard Academy. If you persevere there, I see no reason why you couldn't attend Harvard in a few years."

"Very well. I will go to this . . . Stoddard Academy," Proud Wolf said, stumbling only a little over the unfamiliar name. "And while I am studying the ways of the white man, you and your friends will study *me*."

Professor Hilliard regarded him uncomfortably for a moment. Then he said, "I must admit, the idea of taking an untutored lad such as you and placing him in a rigorous academic environment . . . well, it promises to be fascinating, simply fascinating."

"I hope you learn much," Proud Wolf said.

"Oh, I'm sure I shall. But in the meantime, I want to stay here for a few days and learn as much as I can about the ways of the Sioux. In fact, I'd like to return here someday and spend some time living with your people. Do you think that would be possible? Perhaps when you've finished your education, we could make the journey together."

That idea had already occurred to Proud Wolf, but as he thought about the hostility Runs Far and Hand in the Face had expressed toward white men, he was not sure it was a good one. If those ill feelings grew, there might well come a day when it would not be safe for any white men to come to this land. But that time, he hoped, was far in the future, and besides, the professor looked so eager that Proud Wolf did not have the heart to disappoint him.

"Perhaps that, too, would be a good thing," he said. "We could learn from each other."

"Exactly!" Hilliard grinned triumphantly, then reached for the bowl. "Now, if you don't mind, I'm going to finish this delicious dog stew."

For the next couple of days, the professor trailed Proud Wolf all over the village, asking questions about everything he saw, from the construction of the lodges to the hunting practices of the warriors to sometimes indelicate subjects such as mating rituals. Nothing seemed too trivial to pique his interest. Proud Wolf rapidly grew tired of explaining everything, but he tried to put himself in the professor's place. When they arrived in Massachusetts, no doubt he would have a great many questions about matters the white men took for granted, and he would want the people he met there to be patient with him.

Unfortunately, the longer Hilliard remained in the village, the more annoyed — and even hostile — people seemed in his presence. It might be a good idea, Proud Wolf decided, for them to leave as soon as possible. Nick Palmer's wound had probably healed sufficiently for him to travel. Proud Wolf resolved that he and Hilliard would leave the Sioux village the next day and pick up Palmer in New Hope. Even if the guide was not ready to leave, it would be safer for Hilliard to remain there until he was.

As night fell, Proud Wolf took Hilliard back to his lodge and said, "Stay inside. Do not wander alone around the village. Some of my people might not understand that you mean no harm."

"I'm not totally blind, you know," Hilliard said with a frown. "I've noticed that the longer I stay here, the less some of your people seem to like it — the less they seem to like *me*. Have I done something wrong?"

Proud Wolf shook his head. The problem

was too complicated to explain. "We will go to New Hope tomorrow," he said. "Tonight, stay in the lodge. I must go speak to my father."

"All right." Hilliard brightened. "This will give me a chance to write up some of my notes."

Proud Wolf recalled that Professor Franklin had spent a great deal of time scribbling in a book. These white men seemed to believe they would not remember anything unless they wrote it down. As for Proud Wolf, an unpleasant task awaited him. He had to say good-bye to his father and the other members of his family.

He left Hilliard in the lodge, closing the entrance flap behind him, and walked toward the lodge of Bear Tooth. No one else was stirring in the village; most of the Sioux had retired to their lodges for the night.

Proud Wolf had taken only a few dozen steps when two figures stepped out from behind another lodge and barred his way. Even in the gloom of night Proud Wolf recognized Hand in the Face and Runs Far.

"We would speak with you, Proud Wolf," Hand in the Face said brusquely.

Proud Wolf shook his head. "I have nothing to say to you. Once I considered you my friends, my brothers, but now we are as nothing to each other." It was a harsh thing to say, but he was losing patience with the grumbling and the resentment of the two warriors. He started to push past them, but Runs Far reached out to grasp his arm.

"You will hear our words!" he hissed.

"The white man must leave our village," Hand in the Face said, crowding Proud Wolf. "And you should go with him."

That was exactly what he planned to do, but Proud Wolf, living up to his name, was too prideful to tell that to the two men. They might not believe he had already decided to depart the next day. They might even believe that they had frightened him.

With a sneer Proud Wolf said, "You act more like white men yourselves than Sioux warriors. I fear you no more than I would a cur snapping at my heels. Now let me pass." He jerked his arm roughly out of Runs Far's grasp.

Suddenly, Hand in the Face's arms shot out, catching Proud Wolf around the shoulders. Before he knew what was happening, Proud Wolf found himself thrown to the ground, the crushing weight of Hand in the Face on top of him. The older warrior's forearm was pressed across his throat, cutting off his breath.

"Little fool," Hand in the Face grated between clenched teeth. "We will teach you not to place the whites above your own people."

Proud Wolf struggled to keep from blacking out. He tried to lift his legs and kick Hand in the Face, but Runs Far caught hold of his ankles, immobilizing him. Hand in the Face kept Proud Wolf pinned down with one arm while he lifted the other above his head. Proud Wolf saw starlight glittering on the blade of a knife.

They did not mean to simply beat and humiliate him. They were going to kill him.

Too late, he remembered that the father of Hand in the Face was one of Bear Tooth's subchiefs. If Proud Wolf was dead, then someday the leadership of the band might pass to Hand in the Face. And Hand in the Face was, had always been, an ambitious young warrior.

Animosity toward Professor Hilliard and whites in general was merely an excuse. Hand in the Face wanted to murder Proud Wolf because of his own ruthless ambition, nothing more.

And as soon as that knife descended in a killing stroke, Hand in the Face would have what he wanted.

As the knife paused, poised at its uppermost point, the scream of a great cat tore through the night. The sound was so close that Hand in the Face jerked his head around and froze, momentarily distracted from his prey. Proud Wolf seized the opportunity and launched a blow, smashing his fist into Hand in the Face's jaw. The older warrior lurched to the side. Proud Wolf arched his back and heaved him off.

Runs Far, also startled by the scream of the great cat, had let go of Proud Wolf's legs. Proud Wolf rolled over and sprang to his feet, gulping air into his lungs through his bruised throat. He looked around, wondering why the people of the village were not coming out of their lodges. Had they not heard the cry of the cat?

Perhaps it had been intended only for his ears and those of his enemies, he thought fleetingly. Who knew what magic the spirit cat was capable of?

In the meantime, he was still faced with two men who were trying to kill him. Seeing no imminent sign of danger from a mountain lion, Runs Far had drawn his knife, too, and was advancing toward Proud Wolf. A few feet away, Hand in the Face climbed to his feet. In the moonlight Proud Wolf could see his features, contorted with frustration and hatred. Both warriors came slowly, menacingly, toward Proud Wolf.

He could have called for help, but the

thought grated on his pride. Had he not killed two renegade Crow by himself? But these were Sioux warriors he faced, not Crow, and even such treacherous dogs as these were more skilled in battle than the Crow.

"I say! What are you doing?"

The voice came from behind Hand in the Face and Runs Far. Proud Wolf knew immediately to whom it belonged. He did not pause to wonder why Professor Hilliard had ignored his command to stay in the lodge; at the moment, Proud Wolf was thankful that the eccentric white man had distracted his enemies. Both men looked behind them.

Proud Wolf launched himself at Runs Far, the closer of the two, and slammed him to the ground. Proud Wolf fell, too, but as he toppled over, he drew his knife from the sheath at his waist. It would have been easy to plunge the blade into Runs Far's body, but instead Proud Wolf flicked the weapon around and struck with the bone handle against Runs Far's temple, stunning him.

At that moment Hand in the Face let out a war cry and ran at Professor Hilliard, knife upraised again, poised this time to strike at the white man. Hilliard stared wide-eyed but did not move.

Proud Wolf scrambled to his feet and

bolted after Hand in the Face. He threw himself into the air, knowing that was his only chance to reach the older warrior in time. He landed on the back of Hand in the Face, who staggered under the unexpected assault but managed to keep his balance. Proud Wolf locked an arm around his throat and jerked back, lifting his chin. The keen edge of his blade kissed the warrior's throat, nicking the skin so that a thin line of blood welled up around the blade.

"Do not move," Proud Wolf said, "or I will kill you. This I swear."

People were finally beginning to emerge from their lodges, drawn by the professor's shout and Hand in the Face's war cry. Among them was Bear Tooth, and as he took in what was going on, he stopped short in surprise. In a deep, booming voice, he barked, "Proud Wolf! That man is a fellow warrior, a brother Sioux. And you dare to threaten him with death!"

"That is what he meant for me," Proud Wolf said, leaving the knife where it was, pressed lightly against Hand in the Face's throat. "He and Runs Far attacked me and tried to kill me."

"That is the truth, Bear Tooth," Professor Hilliard said. Proud Wolf realized with a shock that the white man was speaking in the tongue of the Sioux. "I saw them attack your son."

Bear Tooth frowned at Hilliard. "You speak our tongue?"

"A little. I have been listening while I was here."

More than a dozen warriors were gathered around now. When Bear Tooth said to Proud Wolf, "Release him," Proud Wolf lifted the knife away and stepped back. He knew that now, in front of witnesses, Hand in the Face was no threat to him.

Bear Tooth stood in front of Hand in the Face and demanded, "Is there truth in the words of my son and his friend the white man?"

Hand in the Face spat on the ground. He lifted a hand to the shallow cut on his neck and wiped away some of the blood, scowling. "Your son is a woman," he said. "He finds favor with this white man, with all white men. Only a dog would call a white man friend!"

Bear Tooth stiffened, and for a moment Proud Wolf thought he was going to slay Hand in the Face where he stood. Then Bear Tooth said, "Then you must think I, too, am a dog, because Clay Holt is my friend." He looked over at Runs Far, who was groggily getting to his feet with the help of a couple of warriors. To Hand in the Face he said, "Take Runs Far and leave this village. The two of you are no longer welcome here. You try to kill my son and murder his guest. You are men without honor, and now you are men without a people."

Even in the shadows, Proud Wolf could see that Hand in the Face and Runs Far had gone pale. They would have preferred death to exile from the village and the people.

"My father —" Hand in the Face began.

A tall, mournful-looking warrior interrupted him. "Your father once had a son," he said, "but no longer. The son of Tall Tree would never bring dishonor to his family."

Proud Wolf almost felt sorry for Hand in the Face and Runs Far. Once they had been his friends, but that could never be true again.

Chin up, his face defiant once more, Hand in the Face took Runs Far's arm and assisted him away from the gathering of warriors. Within a short time they would leave the village, never to return, Proud Wolf knew.

Now that the trouble was over, the crowd began to break up as the warriors returned to their lodges. As Proud Wolf sheathed his knife, his father came up to him.

"This white man has caused pain among our people," Bear Tooth said. "He is your guest, so no harm will come to him here.

But I think it would be best if he left as soon as possible."

"He is going tomorrow," Proud Wolf said, "and so am I."

Bear Tooth nodded slowly. "I knew this day would come. I wish you much happiness and good hunting, my son."

Proud Wolf felt a surge of emotion. Unwilling to let his father see it, he curtly returned the nod and then swung around to face Professor Hilliard. "I thought I told you to stay in the lodge," he said in English.

"And I certainly intended to do just that," Hilliard said. "But as I was working on my notes, I found that I couldn't remember several things I wanted to write down, so I thought I might speak with your father quickly while you were with him. I'd say it's a good thing I found you when I did. Those two fellows were trying to do you harm."

"Yes," Proud Wolf agreed, "they were. Now go back to the lodge, and this time, stay there."

"Certainly. We'll discuss those questions I had when you get back."

"I will go with you now." Proud Wolf glanced over his shoulder and saw Bear Tooth striding off into the night toward his lodge, his back straight and unbending. "There is nothing more to be said."

Chapter Eleven

Melissa was seething when she left the emporium. Discovering that the business was having difficulties would have been bad enough by itself. To hear that the company was possibly being sabotaged by a competitor was galling. But would Jeremiah Corbett really stoop to piracy and arson to gain an advantage over Holt-Merrivale? Melissa barely knew the man, so she couldn't answer that question.

She was going to find out, though. She had promised herself that.

"Mama mad?" Michael asked as the four of them climbed back into the buggy. Ned took up the reins and began backing the team around.

"No, darling," Melissa said with a shake of her head. She smiled down at her son and smoothed back his fair hair. "I'm a little worried about something, but I'm not angry."

"Sounds to me like that fella Corbett ought to be horsewhipped," Ned said as he flicked the reins. "I'll take care of it myself if you want, Melissa."

231

"You'll do no such thing," India said to him. "You can't just horsewhip someone because you don't like the way he conducts his business. That would get you thrown in jail."

Ned grinned. "Wouldn't be the first time I've seen jail bars from the inside."

"Hush," India told him, inclining her head toward the avidly listening Michael. She turned to Melissa. "You might be better off talking to the authorities."

"I doubt it would do any good. Corbett's probably too clever to have left any trails leading back to him." Melissa leaned back against the seat and sighed. If Jeff had come back to North Carolina with her instead of going off to Washington City with Clay, he would know what to do about this.

She tried to banish that thought from her mind. For one thing, she wasn't being fair to Jeff; neither of them had been aware of the troubles with the business when he agreed to accompany his brother. For another, Jeff wasn't the only member of the family capable of handling problems. Melissa had taken care of the business while Jeff was in prison, falsely charged with murdering her father. Not only had she kept the store and the freight line running smoothly under very trying circumstances, but she had also helped Ned and

India uncover the identity of the real killer. Surely she could deal with Corbett's underhanded tactics.

The first step, she decided, would be to get a better idea of what the man himself was like. There was only one way to do that.

First thing in the morning, she would pay a visit to Mr. Jeremiah Corbett.

"I don't think you should go alone," Hermione said.

Melissa continued tying on her bonnet. She was wearing a simple gray skirt, white blouse, and gray jacket. She knew the outfit was attractive, though she didn't really care whether it was or not. Her intention was not to dazzle Corbett with her beauty. She simply wanted some answers to her questions, and she thought she knew the way to get them.

"I'll be fine, Mother," she said to Hermione.

"You could take Ned with you," Hermione suggested.

Melissa shook her head. "He might lose his temper and try to strike Mr. Corbett." *That's just what I'd like to do myself,* she thought. She went on, "If I show up at Mr. Corbett's office alone, he won't be suspicious."

The evening before, after returning to the house from the emporium, Melissa had had a long talk with her mother, explaining the troubles with the business and her suspicion that Jeremiah Corbett might be behind them. Corbett certainly stood to benefit the most from the woes that had befallen Holt-Merrivale. Hermione, who knew Corbett only slightly, had been unable to shed any light on the situation. But she had never had much of a head for business, as she was the first to admit. Her concerns now were those of a mother.

"Well, then, why don't you take India with you? She seems such a capable young woman."

"She is, Mother." Melissa turned away from the looking glass above her dressing table and kissed Hermione lightly on the cheek. "But so am I."

She went downstairs, trailed by her fretting mother. "The streets are certainly crowded these days," Hermione said. "Are you sure you can handle the buggy by yourself?"

"Yes, Mother," Melissa said patiently. "I can handle it."

But could she? she asked herself. Could she handle the buggy, or the problem with Corbett, or anything? She might appear calm and confident on the surface, but inside she was a mass of jangled nerves. Her stomach felt as if it was drawn into knots, and her throat was so tight it was a struggle to draw enough breath into her body.

But she smiled serenely, kissed her mother again, and sailed out the front door. The buggy, hitched to the team of horses and brought around by one of the servants, stood waiting for her on the cobblestone street. Melissa stepped up to the seat, unwound the reins from the brake lever, and flapped the lines to get the horses moving.

Hermione was right about one thing: The streets of Wilmington were quite busy these days. The port was crowded with ships, their tall masts visible several blocks away. In a port city, a crowded harbor meant that the entire town was busy. Melissa made her way carefully along streets thronged with other buggies, wagons, men on horseback, and pedestrians. The air was filled with clamor. She could even hear the shouts of dockworkers as they loaded and unloaded the ships anchored at the long wharves.

Jeremiah Corbett's general store was near the docks, and his office was next door in a small building tucked between the store and a cavernous warehouse. Above one of the loading docks of the warehouse was a large sign that read simply RATTIGAN. That was the name of the man who was rumored to be Corbett's new partner, the man who was making it possible for Corbett to drastically undercut all the other merchants in town on the prices he charged for his goods. Given the proximity of the Rattigan warehouse, that rumor appeared to be accurate.

Melissa suddenly wondered if this man Rattigan was the one responsible for the piracy and arson, if piracy and arson had indeed brought about the loss of two cargoes bound for the Holt-Merrivale Emporium. Rattigan was just as likely the mastermind as Corbett, she decided. She knew even less about him than she did about Corbett.

But no matter which of them had decided to employ such ruthless tactics, she felt sure that the two men were working together now. What she had to do was uncover proof of their villainy.

Unless, she reminded herself, it was pure bad luck that the cargoes had been lost. Perhaps the Marsh ship really had gone down in a storm and the fire that had destroyed the warehouse was accidental.

But if that were true, there was nothing Melissa could do to strike back — and right now she needed an enemy. She needed to handle this problem without Jeff's help. It was her fervent hope that by the time he arrived from Washington City, these troubles would be behind them and Holt-Merrivale would be well on its way to recovering its position as the town's leading emporium.

She brought the buggy to a stop in front of Corbett's office. At the same time, a man emerged from the warehouse next door. Without hesitating, he strode quickly over to the buggy and caught hold of the harness on one of the horses. "Let me take care o' these brutes for you, lady," he offered in a heavy Cockney accent. "I'll watch 'em while yer goin' about yer business, wha'ever it may be."

"There's no need for that," Melissa told the man crisply, trying to forestall his next move, which was likely to be a request for payment for the service he had offered. "I can tie them to that hitching post."

"Are ye sure about that?"

"I'm certain," Melissa said firmly as she started to climb down from the buggy's seat.

Instantly, the man let go of the harness and sprang to assist her, taking hold of her arm. Melissa tried to pull away, but his grip was too strong.

"Let go of me," she said between clenched teeth, her voice low and cold.

He released her arm as quickly as he had

grasped it. "No offense meant, mum," he said. He stepped back and tugged on the cap perched on his thick mass of sandy hair.

He was tall and broad-shouldered, with handsome features that probably had all the tavern girls in Wilmington swooning over him, Melissa thought peevishly. She had no doubt he was a sailor. His outfit — white trousers and shirt, dark blue jacket — was evidence of a life at sea, as were the deeply tanned skin of his face and hands and the small lines around his eyes and mouth that bespoke long months spent in the sun and wind and salt spray. His eyes were blue, almost as dark as the jacket.

"I was just tryin' to help out, I was," he went on. "I'm hopin' you'll pardon me if I bothered you. 'Tis not often a seagoin' man such as meself sees a lady like you. Maybe I forgot me manners."

"That's quite all right." Melissa tied the reins to the post, wishing he would stop apologizing and move his formidable bulk aside so that she could go into Jeremiah Corbett's office.

The sailor seemed to be in no hurry to depart, however. He grinned and said, " 'Tis rare a lady such as yerself even comes down this close to the docks. Do ye have business here?"

"My business is none of yours, sir," she told him, but the rebuke only made his grin grow wider. If he wasn't going to move, she would just have to go around him, she decided. She started to do exactly that, saying, "Now, if you'll excuse me . . ."

He moved aside then, tugging his cap off and giving her a mocking half-bow. "Certainly, milady."

Melissa glared at him, forcing down the retort that sprang to her lips, and swept into Corbett's office without looking back.

A clerk behind the counter in the office glanced up at her, then looked again, evidently surprised. Melissa didn't know if he had recognized her or if the presence of any woman in this part of town would have provoked the same reaction. He stood up, laying aside the quill pen with which he had been making entries in a ledger. "Can I help you, ma'am?" he asked.

"I'd like to see Mr. Corbett," Melissa said. "My name is Mrs. Jefferson Holt."

The clerk nodded. He was a lanky man with untidy hair and a well-worn suit. "I'll see if Mr. Corbett is available," he said, turning toward a door behind him. "Please have a . . . well, no, there's no place to sit, is there? Just a moment, please."

Hurriedly, he opened the door, slipped

through, and closed it behind him. Melissa stood on the other side of the counter, looking around the cramped room as she waited.

The skin on the back of her neck began to tingle. Someone was watching her, she realized instinctively. She turned her head and looked through the dirty glass of the single small window. A tall figure lounged on the street outside, gazing through the glass into the office. *That impudent sailor,* Melissa thought. Seeing that she had taken notice of him, he grinned and waved.

She turned around, ignoring him. He could look all he wanted to, she supposed; there was no law against that. But his scrutiny made her uneasy anyway, despite her best efforts to pay no attention to him. Several minutes passed.

Then the door behind the counter opened again, and a paunchy man in a brown tweed suit came bustling out, followed by the skinny clerk. The man was mostly bald, with only a fringe of grayish-brown hair around his ears and the back of his head. He also sported bushy side-whiskers and a mustache of the same drab shade.

"Mrs. Holt!" he said with an enthusiasm that did not ring quite true to Melissa's ears. "How good to see you! Come in, come in. I'm Jeremiah Corbett."

If he was truly guilty of the things Melissa

suspected he might be, her mere presence here would account for his uneasiness. His hearty greeting had been an act. She was sure of it. But she put an equally false smile on her own face and said, "Hello, Mr. Corbett. I've been looking forward to meeting you, since we're in the same business."

Corbett motioned her toward an opening at the end of the counter. Melissa walked through it with as much grace and confidence as she could muster, which she had to admit was considerable. Corbett and his clerk both seemed impressed with her. Corbett also seemed a little intimidated.

She was ushered into the inner office, and Corbett shut the door before the clerk could follow them. Obviously he wanted to keep this meeting private. Melissa would have been willing to wager, though, that the clerk had his ear pressed to the door.

The inner office, as drab and dingy as the outer one, was furnished with a scarred desk and a pair of chairs. Two large cabinets stood on a side wall, and a small window in the other wall looked out into an alley. As Corbett went behind the desk, he gestured at one of the chairs and said, "Please make yourself comfortable, Mrs. Holt."

That was nearly impossible, Melissa thought, considering how hard the chair seat was and how unyielding the back. But she settled herself and looked across the desk at Corbett, who was sitting on the edge of his own chair. She said, "I suppose you're wondering why I've come to see you."

Still smiling weakly, he nodded. "A social call, perhaps? We're fellow merchants, after all. I've had the pleasure of meeting your husband a time or two. By the way, where is Mr. Holt? I understood that the two of you were visiting your family in Ohio for a time."

"Jeff is occupied with other business at the moment," Melissa replied vaguely. She didn't want Corbett to know that Jeff was hundreds of miles away. He might find out soon enough anyway, since it was difficult to keep a secret in Wilmington. For all the bustling activity surrounding the port, in many ways Wilmington was still just a small town, with a small town's proclivity for gossip.

"Why *are* you here to see me, Mrs. Holt?" Corbett asked bluntly, getting to the heart of the matter. That was all right with Melissa. She felt an instinctive dislike for this man and didn't want to be around him any longer than she had to.

So she let her chin tremble a little, allowed a tear or two to well up in her eyes, and said in a shaky voice, "I need your help, Mr. Corbett."

His eyes widened. He might have been expecting to hear many different things from Melissa, but a plea for assistance was obviously not one of them. "My help?" he repeated after a moment. "Mrs. Holt, I . . . I don't know what to say. I hesitate to point this out, but we're competitors. At least, our businesses are in competition —"

"I know that," Melissa broke in, "and I wouldn't ask you to do anything to undermine your own establishment. What I want from you is information. You're a shrewd man, Mr. Corbett, and I know you have a great many connections here in Wilmington and up and down the coast. Have you heard anything about the shipments of goods that my husband and I have lost recently?"

Corbett swallowed. "The . . . the goods? I know about that ship going down in the storm, of course, and the fire at the warehouse. Those unfortunate accidents were the talk of the town for several days, but —"

Melissa interrupted him again. She lowered her voice to a conspiratorial tone and said, "Mr. Corbett, I have reason to believe that they were not accidents at all."

"N-not accidents?" he blustered.

"But who would do such terrible things?" Melissa went on. "You've always been an honest competitor, so you're perhaps the only person I can trust to give me a truthful answer. Have you heard any talk about which of the other merchants in Wilmington might be to blame for these blatant attempts to force my husband and me out of business?"

Corbett blinked rapidly. Melissa could almost see the cogwheels of his brain spinning. Appearing at his office as she had done would have been enough of a surprise by itself, but once she was here, Corbett must have been convinced that she had come to accuse him of sabotage. By taking the opposite tack, by appearing to trust him completely even as she was appealing to him for help, Melissa had totally confused him.

Which was exactly what she had planned to do.

Corbett pulled a handkerchief from his pocket and mopped the sweat from his forehead. He leaned forward and said, "Mrs. Holt, I assure you I have heard absolutely nothing about your terrible problems being anything other than what they appear to be: tragic accidents."

His relief was evident. It glowed on his face like the sun. If she had had any doubts before, his reaction had banished them. At the very least Jeremiah Corbett knew something about the piracy and arson that had claimed the two cargoes, and Melissa considered it quite likely that he had in fact been behind them.

"You're quite sure?" she asked, playing out the game just a bit longer.

"Absolutely positive," Corbett replied, his voice strengthening.

The door behind Melissa opened, and a voice asked, "Positive of what?"

She turned her head and saw another man striding boldly into the room as if he belonged there. He had an air about him that said he would enter any room the same way. He skirted Melissa's chair, went to Corbett's desk, and casually perched on the corner of it. Then he nodded to her and said, "Good morning again, madame."

"The two of you are acquainted?" Corbett asked, surprised.

"We met outside," the sailor said with the cocky grin that was already maddeningly familiar to Melissa, "but we haven't been formally introduced." He held out a hand. "I'm Philip Rattigan."

He still looked the same, and his confident demeanor had not diminished in the least. But his speech was different now, more educated and cultured, though it retained a distinct British accent. The coarse dialect of a common sailor was gone, and Melissa realized with a flash of anger that he had been playing with her outside, pretending to be something he wasn't.

"I'm Mrs. Holt," she said coldly, ignoring his extended hand. "Mrs. Jefferson Holt."

"Ah, yes, one of the owners of the Holt-Merrivale Trading Company," Rattigan said. "I've heard of you and your husband, Mrs. Holt. What brings you here to see Jeremiah, if I may be so bold as to ask?"

"You mean Mr. Corbett, your partner?" Melissa said.

Rattigan shrugged. "We have an informal arrangement, Jeremiah and I. I wouldn't go so far as to call us partners."

Quickly, Corbett jumped into the conversation. He believed he had Melissa fooled, and clearly he did not want Rattigan doing or saying anything that would arouse her suspicions. "Mrs. Holt was asking me about the loss of the Marsh ship and the fire at the warehouse that destroyed some of the goods bound for their emporium."

Rattigan's smile disappeared and was replaced by a look of solicitude. He shook his head and said, "Terrible tragedies, just terrible. Luckily there were no injuries in the fire, but that ship went down at sea with all hands on board, from what I hear. And, of course, all the merchandise was lost in both cases."

It was all Melissa could do not to explode

with the rage that threatened to choke her. How dare he stand there looking so smug with his false sympathy when he was probably at least partially responsible for the deaths of all those seamen?

Instead of lashing out at him, however, she forced herself to murmur, "Yes, it was terrible. I was hoping Mr. Corbett could help me figure out who was to blame for what happened."

Rattigan spread his hands. "Who is ever to blame for such accidents? I haven't the audacity to blame the Almighty, do you?"

No, but he had plenty of audacity to do other things, Melissa thought. She said, "Do you really believe they were accidents?"

"I've no reason to believe otherwise," Rattigan said.

"Someone — one of our competitors — could have caused them."

"Oh, I don't think so. None of the other businessmen in Wilmington would commit such an outrage." Rattigan smirked. "None of them would have the courage or the daring."

"What about you, Mr. Rattigan?" Melissa asked abruptly, tired of the pretense. "Or should I say Captain Rattigan, since you're obviously the master of one of your own ships?"

"Indeed I am. The master, that is." Rattigan's blue eyes dueled with her brown ones. "I'm not a pirate, Mrs. Holt, nor am I an arsonist. *If* that was what you were implying. But if you were simply asking about my courage and daring . . . well, you should probably judge that for yourself."

"I think not." Melissa stood. She had what she had come looking for. She was more convinced than ever that Corbett and Rattigan were to blame for her business woes. She had no proof, but that would come next. "Thank you for your time, Mr. Corbett. Good day, gentlemen."

She turned to walk out the door, but Rattigan was there before her, moving smoothly from his seemingly casual pose. He blocked her way and asked, "Does your husband know that you're here, Mrs. Holt?"

For the first time since entering the office, Melissa felt something other than surprise, anger, or outrage. She was afraid. Philip Rattigan was so tall and capable and, at the moment, so utterly ruthless-looking that she suddenly feared for her life. If she admitted that Jeff wasn't even in Wilmington, would Rattigan think it was safe to deal with whatever threat she might represent by harming her?

Would they murder her right here in Corbett's office and dispose of her body in the harbor?

"My mother knows I came here to speak to Mr. Corbett," she said, avoiding the question about Jeff. She stretched the truth a little by adding, "So do several other people."

"Good," Rattigan said with a nod. "But next time you come to visit us, you should bring someone with you. Sometimes this isn't a very safe neighborhood. There are a lot of sailors about, men who have been at sea for long weeks or months without so much as a glimpse of any woman, let alone one as beautiful as you."

The flattery came easily from his mouth, but Melissa barely noticed it. She was relieved when he stepped aside.

"I'll escort you to your buggy," he offered. "Just to make sure that no one bothers you."

"That won't be necessary," she told him.

"I insist." He took her arm.

Melissa wanted to flinch away from him, but his grip was as firm as it had been before. She had no choice but to go with him as he marched her across the outer office. She glanced over her shoulder and saw Jeremiah Corbett standing behind his desk, his unattractive face made even more so by its pallor and the lines of anxiety etched into his sweaty brow. Rattigan, on the other hand, was still cool and calm.

Outside, still playing the perfect gentleman instead of the murdering cutthroat he likely was, Rattigan helped Melissa up to the buggy seat and untied the reins from the hitching post. He handed them to her and said, "Good day to you, Mrs. Holt. Perhaps we'll meet again. I shall look forward to that day."

Melissa didn't say anything. She turned the horses and flicked the reins to get them started. She was going to drive off without looking back. Philip Rattigan wouldn't be so pleased with the outcome of their next meeting, she vowed. Because when she came back here, she was going to have the authorities with her, and Rattigan and Corbett were going to be arrested for murder, piracy, and arson.

But despite her intentions she turned her head anyway, and she glimpsed him standing there watching her buggy roll away down the street, his sailor's cap shoved to the back of his thick, fair hair, his stance nonchalant but still reminding Melissa somehow of a beast, poised to strike at its helpless prey.

Chapter Twelve

Clay and Jeff spent the rest of the day at Monticello after agreeing to Thomas Jefferson's request that they investigate the possible land grab scheme. Over a leisurely lunch the former president told them everything else he and his associates had uncovered about the plot, which unfortunately was not a great deal.

"We became suspicious of Atticus Bromley when he began to display spending habits well out of proportion to his wages at the Land Office," Jefferson explained. "Government work can be very fulfilling, as you might imagine, gentlemen, but it's no way for a man to enrich himself. So when John Shelby — he's the clerk who handled your land grant, Clay — noticed that Bromley seemed to have more money than he should have, he sent word to me. I trust Shelby — he's one of the few men in the Land Office I *do* trust. Whoever is behind this scheme must have a great deal of money to hand out to his lackeys, to make sure that his actions remain unnoticed."

Clay put down the chicken leg on which

he had been gnawing and asked, "This fellow Shelby — did he have anything to do with our being asked to come out here?"

Jefferson smiled. "Quite perceptive of you, Clay. Yes, indeed, when John mentioned that he was looking into a land grant for a man named Clay Holt, I knew it had to be you. I made inquiries and found that you had come to Washington to claim the land you should have received as partial payment for your service with the Corps of Discovery. Tell me, has that matter been settled?"

"I was supposed to pick up the final papers a few days ago," Clay said. "I reckon they'll be there waiting for me when Jeff and I get back to Washington City."

"Indeed they will. I've asked John to make certain of that." Jefferson sipped from his glass of brandy. "I must say, though, that I'm glad you've decided to stay and assist us rather than heading back to the frontier immediately."

Clay still wasn't convinced he had made the right decision, so he said nothing. Jeff spoke up instead. "So you think this fellow Bromley has been paid off to change the documents and maps in the Land Office and cover the trail of whoever's buying up half of the Louisiana Purchase."

"That's what we're afraid of. And it's not

simply a matter of someone buying government land. As long as it's done legally, that would not be a cause for alarm. What we're concerned about are the false names under which the land is being bought, or in some cases, granted outright. I'm convinced that one person, or one small group of people, will wind up owning half of the western portion of the country. That simply can't be good."

"Maybe not," Clay said, "but I reckon it would depend on what they planned to do with it, now, wouldn't it?"

"An excellent point," Jefferson acknowledged. "That's one of the things we're hoping you and your brother will be able to discover."

Clay frowned as he went back to eating in silence. The whole business was too murky for him. He was going to have to rely on his instincts to guide him in this investigation, and he wasn't sure he had the right instincts for dealing with people adept at moving in the shadowy world of politics and power.

But he would give it a try, and if he could pick up the trail of the land grabbers, maybe he could follow it to its end.

After lunch, Jefferson took great pleasure in giving them a tour of the house and the estate. Monticello had been thirty years in the building. Clay had never seen a house so well constructed, down to the tiniest details. True, some of its features, such as the dumb-waiter and the compass on the ceiling, struck Clay as a trifle odd, but Jefferson clearly derived a great deal of pleasure from tinkering and inventing.

The rest of the estate was almost as impressive as the mansion. The grounds were beautifully designed and cared for, with more specimens of plant and animal life than Clay had seen anywhere outside of a natural forest. He and Jeff hadn't been imagining things earlier. They really *had* seen moose and buffalo wandering the grounds and grazing on the lush grass.

"When you've completed this assignment, you'll have to return for another visit," Jefferson told them when he had finished showing them around. "I own some other property near Lexington, Virginia, which contains one of nature's most sublime wonders, and I should like for you to see it. There is a natural bridge there, spanning the ravine through which Cedar Creek runs. It's over two hundred feet from the bridge down to the creek. A beautiful sight, simply beautiful."

"I'd like to see it," Jeff said.

"Reckon we'd better see if we can settle this other matter for you first," Clay added.

Jefferson nodded. "Yes, that's true. Would you gentlemen care to spend the night here?"

"Thank you for the offer," Clay said quickly, before Jeff could accept, "but I reckon we'll head back to Charlottesville. We've got a room there, and we'll get started back to Washington City first thing in the morning."

"You're certain?" Jefferson asked.

Clay nodded vigorously. He knew that Shining Moon would be wondering why he had not yet returned to Marietta, and he didn't want to prolong this job even an hour longer than he had to.

"Very well," Jefferson said. "Then I'll wish you Godspeed, gentlemen, and the best of luck."

As he thought about the chore awaiting them in Washington, Clay knew they were going to need it.

The trip back to Washington over the next few days was uneventful. Clay set a fast pace, but Jeff didn't complain. He figured that Melissa was beginning to wonder what had happened to him, too. He considered sending her a letter explaining that he and Clay had been detained in Washington, but Thomas Jefferson had asked them to keep their activities on his behalf as quiet as possible. Jeff decided it would be a better idea not to write anything down in a letter that might fall into the wrong hands.

Too, Jefferson, as the former president, had no authority to ask anyone to conduct an investigation. Clay and Jeff were strictly unofficial agents, with no ties to the federal government. If they got into trouble, they would have to get themselves out of it.

Upon reaching Washington, they returned to the Copper Gable Tavern. Harry Ledbetter greeted them with surprise. "I thought you lads had gone back where you came from," he said.

"Is the room we were using still for rent?" Clay asked.

"As a matter of fact, it is," Ledbetter replied. "My trade ain't been as good lately as it was, for some reason. I'm wondering if Rachel quitting had anything to do with it. She was a lusty one, that lass. The men always liked her."

"She quit, did she?"

Ledbetter nodded. "Aye. Said she needed a change of scenery and was leaving town. I think she said she was heading up toward Boston."

Clay and Jeff exchanged a glance. Rachel hadn't wasted any time shaking the dust of

Pennsylvania Avenue off her boots after she and her friends had tried and failed to rob the Holt brothers. Obviously — and wisely — she had taken Clay's threats to heart.

Since it was late in the day, they decided to wait until the next morning to start investigating the irregularities at the Government Land Office. Thomas Jefferson had given them a description of the clerk named Atticus Bromley. Clay and Jeff had discussed the situation at length during the journey back to Washington, and they had agreed that the best way to begin their investigation was to keep an eye on Bromley. He was the only genuine lead they had.

They stationed themselves across from the building that housed the Land Office early the next day and had no trouble spotting Bromley as he walked down Pennsylvania Avenue. He was on the smallish side, with narrow shoulders and a balding head under an expensive beaver hat. Clay and Jeff watched from behind a waiting carriage as Bromley strutted along like a peacock. His demeanor was self-confident, almost to the point of arrogance, yet Clay and Jeff both noted that he quickly deferred to several men he passed on the street.

"Those fellows must be politicians," Clay said. "Senators and the like."

Jeff nodded. "And Bromley wants to curry favor with them, no matter what it takes. Maybe I'm jumping to conclusions, Clay, but I don't think a fellow like that is capable of planning something as big as this scheme President Jefferson is worried about."

"You're right," Clay said. "He's got a boss somewhere. That's the gent we want to find. He'll be the next step up the ladder."

"So we trail Bromley until he leads us to whoever his boss is?"

"That's right. With any luck, it won't take too long."

It didn't happen that day, though. They didn't see Atticus Bromley again until he left the office and headed home that evening. Clay and Jeff trailed him easily to a small cottage south of the Capitol, near the Potomac, where he evidently lived alone. They stood watch outside until the cottage grew dark. Bromley had evidently blown out his candle and gone to bed. A little discouraged, Clay and Jeff returned to the Copper Gable.

Jeff could sense the impatience already growing inside Clay. The next day, Clay went into the building itself while Jeff remained outside to keep an eye on the door. Clay intended to pay a visit to John Shelby, the clerk who was indirectly responsible for their involvement with the land-grab scheme. When Clay returned, he carried a small leather case with him.

"My land grant," he said, holding up the case. "According to Shelby, these documents make me the legal owner of the land on which Bear Tooth's village sits."

Jeff smiled. "I wonder what old Bear Tooth would think if he heard that you were his landlord."

"He won't hear it from me," Clay said. "As far as the Sioux are concerned, that land still belongs to Wakan Tanka, and He's generous enough to let His people live on it."

Jeff smiled again, in appreciation of his brother's own generosity. That was how the Sioux perceived the world, all right, but how many white men would respect their beliefs and surrender the chance to claim so much wilderness for themselves?

Once again the day passed uneventfully, the long hours dragging by as Clay and Jeff watched the steady stream of people going in and out of the building. Any one of them might be involved in the scheme, Jeff knew, but there was no way to connect them with Bromley, not at this point. The possibilities only made the wait more frustrating.

When evening fell, Clay and Jeff followed

Atticus Bromley home. "We're wasting time," Clay groused. "If this keeps up, we might as well go see Bromley, grab him by his skinny little neck, and try to shake the truth out of him."

"It might come to that," Jeff said, "but then the fellows behind the plan would know that somebody was on their trail. The president didn't want that happening if we could avoid it. He's hoping we can sort of sneak up on them and take them by surprise."

Clay sighed in exasperation. "I know. I reckon I'm just ready to go home, and at this rate who knows how long it'll be before we can do that?"

Jeff had no answer for his brother. He returned his attention to Bromley, who was a couple of blocks ahead of them.

Bromley had proven easy to follow. Apparently the idea that someone might be trailing him had never entered his mind. He walked openly along the Washington streets, kowtowing to those he met whom he considered his superiors, brushing rudely past those he thought were beneath him. Jeff had made that assessment about the man just from watching him. He felt a growing dislike for Bromley that had nothing to do with the man's possible involvement with the land grabbers. Bromley was clearly a pompous little popinjay who thought he was better than most folks.

After leading them once more to the cottage where he lived, Bromley went inside, and Clay and Jeff both figured he would soon be turning in for the night. They took up their post half a block away in the deep shadows under one of the trees that lined the street. They could see the light of a candle glowing inside Bromley's house. After an hour or so, when full night had fallen, the light went out.

"He's going to bed again," Jeff said.

Clay's hand gripped his brother's arm. "Nope. Look."

The door of the cottage had opened, and the clerk came out and shut it behind him. He walked toward the tree that hid Clay and Jeff, who drew back a little deeper into the cloaking darkness. Gone now was Bromley's jaunty walk. The man was hurrying along in a gait that reminded Jeff of a slinking animal.

"He's up to something," Jeff whispered in Clay's ear.

"About damn time," Clay responded, his voice equally quiet. Bromley passed the tree without noticing them, and when he was out of earshot, Clay went on, "Let's go. I want to see where he's headed."

Most of Washington's citizens had gone inside for the evening, so the streets were not nearly as busy now. That made it more difficult for Clay and Jeff to follow Bromley unobtrusively. Fortunately, enough pedestrians were still abroad that the Holts managed to blend in as they trailed the clerk from a discreet distance. Bromley's route skirted the Capitol Building. The streets became narrower and darker. The shabby buildings that crowded in from both sides were oppressive. This was not the sort of neighborhood in which a man like Bromley would normally have any business, Jeff thought. He heard the raucous voices of men and the shrill laughter of women coming from many of the buildings he and Clay slipped past.

"He's on his way to a whorehouse," Clay hissed as they struggled to keep sight of Bromley in the shifting shadows.

"Could be," Jeff whispered back.

"Another waste of time," Clay muttered disgustedly under his breath.

Jeff, always the more patient one, counseled, "Let's wait and see." Indeed the neighborhood seemed to be made up almost exclusively of cheap taverns and brothels, but that didn't mean Bromley couldn't have something else in mind besides ale or women.

A few minutes later Bromley stopped in

front of a squat brick building. A sign of some sort hung over the door, but the street was too dark for either Clay or Jeff to make out what it said. They paused at the mouth of an alley about fifty yards away on the opposite side of the street. Garbage choked the alley, and the stench assaulted the senses of both men. Jeff couldn't help but think of the clean, crisp air of the high country. It would be a damned shame, he thought fleetingly — no, more than that, it would be a sin — if certain aspects of so-called civilization were ever allowed to encroach upon the frontier.

They waited until Bromley had gotten up his courage, if that was what he was doing, and gone inside the building. Then they approached the door, and Clay's keen eyes made out the name on the sign even in the bad light.

"Cochran's," Clay read. "Likely a tavern, and that'd be the owner's name."

"And a pretty seedy place, too, from the looks of it. Not the kind of place a fella like Bromley, who's so proud of himself, would spend a lot of time in."

"Unless he was here to meet somebody," Clay said.

"Only one way to find out."

They pulled their hats down low over their eyes. Bromley didn't know them, of course; very few people in Washington did, which was one reason Thomas Jefferson had asked them to take this assignment. Still, they had to be careful about letting Bromley get too good a look at them. If they got no closer to Bromley's superior tonight and had to continue shadowing him, they wanted to make sure he wouldn't recognize them and become suspicious.

The air inside Cochran's was thick with pipe smoke and the smell of stale beer. Candles guttered in tarnished brass sconces along the walls, barely lighting the room. Tables and chairs, none of which seemed to match, were scattered haphazardly. A bar of scarred wood ran along the right side of the room. Kegs lined the wall behind the bar. In the rear of the room were a few booths that, given the dim lighting, looked like the mouths of caves.

Clay and Jeff looked around quickly, trying not to be too obvious about what they were doing. There was no sign of Atticus Bromley, and for a second they exchanged alarmed glances. Then Clay touched Jeff's arm and nodded almost imperceptibly toward one of the booths. As usual, Clay's eyesight had proven sharper than his brother's. Jeff casually turned his gaze in the direction Clay had indicated and saw Bromley. The clerk was leaning forward across the table, his face barely illuminated by the faint light from the candles. He was talking to someone, but whoever was on the other side of the booth was staying well back in the shadows.

"Let's get a drink," Clay said, pitching his voice normally. Anyone overhearing him would think that he and Jeff had just wandered in off the street in search of a mug of ale.

That was what they each ordered after they shouldered their way closer to the crowded bar. A bullet-headed bartender in a filthy apron brought their drinks in pewter mugs. Jeff sipped the sour ale and tried not to grimace at the taste.

He and Clay leaned on the bar, Jeff turned slightly so that he could carry on a conversation with his brother — or so it would appear, at least. In actuality he was keeping an eye on the booth in which Bromley sat, still talking earnestly to someone. Clay watched Jeff's face intently, waiting for a signal that the situation had changed.

It wasn't long in coming. Jeff watched as Bromley slid off the bench, stood up, and leaned back into the booth to make one last comment or ask one final question. Then he straightened and turned toward the door of the tavern.

Clay caught the rapid darting of Jeff's eyes and glanced quickly over his shoulder. He turned his face back toward the bar as Bromley passed behind him.

When the clerk reached the door, Clay said in a low voice, "We'll have to split up. You follow Bromley, and I'll take whoever he was talking to."

Jeff nodded. It was a spur-of-the-moment plan, but he didn't see what else they could do. It was important to keep track of Bromley's movements, in case this meeting tonight turned out to be innocent — or at least unrelated to the land-grabbing business. At the same time they had to find out whom Bromley had been talking to, and why.

Trying not to leave too abruptly, Jeff drained the rest of his ale and set the empty mug on the bar. Then he turned away and headed for the door, leaving Clay at the bar. He saw Bromley step out to the street and turn right. Jeff hung back for a moment, allowing the clerk to gain a small lead.

As he stepped out into the darkened street, he thought about Clay and hoped he would be able to follow whoever had rendezvoused with Bromley. Clay was still not comfortable in the city and probably never would be. He was made for the wilderness. No one was better at dealing with the dangers of life in the wild. But as he had amply proven when Rachel and her fellow cutthroats had tried to rob them, he could handle himself quite well in other situations, too. Jeff knew that if anyone could, Clay would find out what they needed to know.

Then he put that worry aside and concentrated on following Atticus Bromley.

Clay wasn't sure what to expect from the other occupant of the booth. He had guessed from the look on Bromley's face that he hadn't been very pleased with whomever he was talking to. But, Clay reminded himself, this meeting might have nothing at all to do with the land grab. Bromley could have been talking to a woman who was married to another man, or someone to whom he owed a gambling debt; there were any number of possible explanations for the clandestine meeting.

It hadn't been a woman, Clay saw several minutes later as he nursed the last of his ale. A man slid out of the booth and stood up, revealed in the candlelight. Like Bromley he was rather short, but he had a stockier build. He wore a beaver hat, too, and a dark suit that looked expensive. He was as out of place in the run-down tavern as Bromley had been.

That was encouraging, Clay thought. Bromley and the other man must have chosen Cochran's for their meeting to minimize the risk of encountering anyone they knew. That meant the reason for the meeting had to be kept a secret. Bromley's possible involvement with the land grab was motive enough for absolute secrecy.

Clay turned away from the bar as the man passed behind him, keeping his head down so that the brim of his hat would shield his face. Even so, he managed to get a fairly good look at the man who was now his quarry. He was middle-aged, with a round, ruddy face that bespoke a mild demeanor. A pair of spectacles perched on his upturned nose. He looked neither left nor right as he strode out of the tavern.

Clay frowned and headed for the door himself. The man hadn't given the impression of someone who might be involved in a complex and nefarious scheme. He looked more like a genial schoolmaster than someone plotting to steal half the frontier. Maybe Bromley's meeting with him had concerned completely unrelated business after all.

The only way to find out was to follow him and see where he went, Clay reasoned. He stepped out of the tavern and spotted the man strolling along half a block away.

Jeff and Bromley were nowhere in sight.

Clay fell in behind the round-faced man, who was proving to be as easy to trail as Bromley had been. The man reached Capitol Hill and turned north, into an area of larger, grander homes. Clay followed, moving from shadow to shadow, staying in sight of the man but never moving too close.

The houses in this area were smaller and less elaborate than Thomas Jefferson's Monticello, but they were still mansions, at least in Clay's eyes. One of them could hold three of the Holt homestead in Ohio. The houses were set back from the street behind well-kept lawns bordered with hedges and flower gardens. The trees that lined the street provided Clay with plenty of cover, for which he was grateful. Not that the man was looking behind him. Instead, he strode along with all the confidence and self-assurance in the world.

The man turned in at one of the houses and walked up a curving path to the entrance. Lights burned inside the house, giving Clay a clue as to its size. He thought it had three stories, and it appeared to be made of white stone. By any measure it was an impressive structure. Clay stopped across the street in the shadow of a tree and studied the estate. He spotted several outbuildings, probably servants' quarters and a carriage house. A flash of light from the main house marked the opening and closing of the front door. The man Clay had followed had gone inside.

So the trail had come to a temporary end, Clay thought. He couldn't very well march up to the house, knock on the door, and ask whoever answered whether they were trying unscrupulously to get their hands on millions of acres of government land in the west. No, his next step would be to find out who owned the mansion, a task he hoped would not be too difficult.

As he turned away from the house, he wondered if Jeff had had any success following Atticus Bromley, and if so, whether or not the clerk had simply gone back home following the rendezvous at Cochran's. That was the likely scenario, Clay guessed. Bromley himself was unimportant. What mattered was locating his boss, and Clay hoped he had done that very thing tonight.

Inside that house might be the mastermind behind the land grab. If that proved to be the case, Clay and Jeff had to uncover sufficient proof and turn it over to Thomas Jefferson. Once they had done that, they would be free to return to their homes.

That day couldn't come soon enough to

please him, Clay thought, feeling a small sense of satisfaction as he walked off into the darkness.

Chapter Thirteen

Atticus Bromley retraced his steps toward the Capitol and began to circle the hill on which the great, domed building stood. Jeff was about a hundred yards behind him. The night was warm, with only a gentle brccze blowing, bringing with it the faint, muddy smell of the Potomac River. If he hadn't been engaged in following Bromley, he would have enjoyed this evening stroll, Jeff thought.

Suddenly, the breeze brought with it some unexpected noises. Jeff heard a man cry out in what sounded like pain. His attention snapped back to Bromley, and he saw a struggle up ahead. Several men had come out of an alley and attacked the clerk.

"Damn it!" Jeff grated. He knew he was probably witnessing another robbery attempt much like the one he and Clay had thwarted. Bromley's clothes marked him as well-to-do, a temptation for any cutthroat lurking in the shadows. It wouldn't do for him to be killed by thieves before Clay and Jeff were sure they had been led to the next link in the chain of plotters.

Jeff broke into a run, heading straight for the knot of struggling figures.

No one else was on the street. No one was going to come to Bromley's aid. Jeff knew he was going to be outnumbered, but he had no choice. At least he was armed. His North & Cheney flintlock pistol was tucked behind his belt, the butt hidden by his jacket. He swept the jacket aside and pulled the gun free.

The pounding of his boots on the cobblestones apparently alerted the robbers. A couple of them spun toward him, and one of them shouted, "Get out of here, you fool, if you know what's good for you!"

"Stand away from that man!" Jeff called back. In the dim light he saw Bromley struggling frantically to pull away from two men who had hold of his arms.

"Stop that bastard!" one of the men holding Bromley barked at his companions. Jeff skidded to a stop when he saw the two men facing him draw knives from under their coats. He leveled his pistol at them and drew back the hammer as they advanced menacingly toward him.

Brandishing a blade in front of him, one of the men gave an ugly laugh. "You can't shoot both of us," he taunted. "The one who's left will gut you like a fish, mister."

"Yes, but the other one will be dead," Jeff said calmly.

"For God's sake, help m—" Bromley screeched, his plea cut off sharply when one of his captors clapped a hand over his mouth.

"And the gunshot will bring others," Jeff continued. "You'd be better off releasing that man and getting out of here while you have the chance." If these men were common thieves, that was probably what they would do. Jeff's timely arrival would make it more trouble than it was worth to rob Bromley.

And coming to Bromley's rescue like this would put the clerk in his debt, Jeff thought fleetingly; it might give him the opportunity to gain Bromley's confidence.

But then one of the men holding Bromley snapped, "Kill him!" and pulled a knife. Before Jeff could make a move to stop the man, he had pivoted and slammed the knife into Bromley's midsection. Bromley shrieked in pain, the high, thin sound muffled by the other man's hand over his mouth.

One of the men facing Jeff suddenly hurled his knife. Jeff threw himself to the side to avoid the spinning blade. The other man was lunging toward him, knife upraised to strike while Jeff was off balance. Jeff caught himself on his left hand and knee, keeping himself from sprawling helplessly on the pavement. He tipped up the barrel of his pistol and pressed the trigger.

The charge of black powder exploded with a roar. Sparks geysered from the muzzle of the pistol. The heavy lead ball thudded into the chest of the onrushing man and flung him backward.

The man who had thrown his knife followed with a rush. He left the ground in a dive that brought him crashing into Jeff. Jeff went over backward under the impact, and his wrist cracked painfully against a cobblestone. The pistol slipped from his fingers and clattered away into the darkness. It wouldn't have done him much good anyway unless he had the chance to reload it, Jeff told himself, and under the circumstances he doubted he would have had the time. He had his hands full now trying to ward off the punches bombarding him.

He had to worry, too, about Atticus Bromley. The clerk had been brutally stabbed and was probably bleeding to death at this very moment. With a rush of adrenaline Jeff surged up, throwing off the man who had tackled him. He gained his knees and slammed a fist into his opponent's face. The blow rocked the man back and gave Jeff a chance to scramble to his feet. He drove the heel of his boot into the man's chest, knocking him flat.

"Get down!"

Jeff reacted instinctively to the shouted warning. It hadn't come from Bromley; a part of his brain was vaguely aware of that. But he was acting almost solely on his reflexes as he dropped to the street. Two pistol shots blasted, coming so closely together that they were almost one. The glare of burning powder lit the night for an instant, and in that split second Jeff saw one of Bromley's attackers drop a pistol and stagger back a step, clutching at a shattered arm.

If not for the warning, Jeff knew he would probably have been killed. Someone had come out of the night and not only shouted at him but also fired a shot, disabling one of the attackers. The stranger was suddenly at Jeff's side, clutching his arm and hauling him to his feet. A gun was pressed into his hand. "Are you all right?" a voice asked from close beside him. It belonged to the same man who had warned him.

"I'm fine," Jeff said, a little breathlessly. He heard the rattle of footsteps and saw that three of the men who had jumped Bromley were fleeing now, racing away down the street. The fourth man, the one Jeff had shot, was still lying on the ground, a dark, motionless hulk.

Not far away was another sprawled figure. That had to be Bromley.

"I'll go after them," the stranger said. "You tend to that fellow."

Jeff didn't like the idea of letting the stranger pursue the killers on his own, but he had to see to Bromley. There was still a chance the clerk's life might be saved.

As the stranger dashed off, Jeff knelt beside Bromley and knew immediately that he had been wrong. Bromley was lying face down, and judging by the dark, spreading pool beneath his body, it was too late to do anything for him. Jeff gently rolled him over anyway. A low moan issued from Bromley's lips. He was still alive, but Jeff knew he wouldn't last much longer.

"Who did this?" Jeff asked urgently. He had banished the idea that this was a simple robbery that had turned deadly. The four men had intended not to rob Bromley but to kill him. The deliberate way Bromley had been stabbed told Jeff that much.

A grotesque bubbling noise came from Bromley's throat. Jeff leaned closer, hoping the sounds would resolve themselves into words. Instead he heard the distinctive rattling that signaled the last breath. The hapless clerk was dead.

Jeff lowered the man's head to the street

and stood up. He stepped back from the body. No one had come yet to investigate the gunshots and the shouts, but surely the authorities had been summoned by now. A constable would be along soon, and Jeff had no desire to explain what had happened here tonight or his part in it. It would be better, he decided, to return quickly to the Copper Gable and wait for Clay. Jeff hoped his brother had been more successful. All he had managed to do was allow the man who was their best lead to be murdered right in front of his eyes.

There was still the matter of the stranger who had come out of nowhere to help him. That puzzled Jeff, too. Did the man have some connection with Bromley, or was he simply a Good Samaritan who had tried to help because he had seen that Jeff was outnumbered?

Rapid footsteps broke the quiet of the street. Jeff moved quickly to a nearby doorway and lifted the gun the stranger had given him. "Who's there?" he called softly.

"It's me, Mr. Holt," replied the voice he had heard earlier. "I'm sorry, but those killers got away. Is Bromley dead?"

Jeff's surprise was so great that it was a moment before he could answer. This man not only knew who Bromley was, but he knew Jeff's name, too.

"Who in blazes are you?" Jeff demanded harshly, ignoring the stranger's question.

"My name is Markham, sir, Lieutenant John Markham." The stranger stepped closer, and Jeff could make out a young, eager face. "President Jefferson requested that I aid you and your brother, but I'm afraid I've botched the job completely."

That information took a few seconds to digest. Thomas Jefferson hadn't mentioned asking someone else to help them. Nor could Jeff be sure Lieutenant Markham was telling the truth.

But one thing was certain: Jeff had not seen his assailant aiming a pistol at him, and if not for Markham's intervention he might easily be dead now.

"I think we should get out of here," Jeff said. "There's nothing we can do for Bromley. He's dead."

"And we don't want matters complicated by having to explain them to the authorities," Markham finished for him. "I agree completely, Mr. Holt. Should we go back to the Copper Gable? Is that where you planned to rendezvous with your brother?"

Markham was inquisitive. That alone was enough to make Jeff nervous. He also knew more about what Clay and Jeff were doing than anyone should have. Obviously, while they had been shadowing Atticus Bromley, Lieutenant Markham had been spying on *them*.

"Come on," Jeff grunted, deciding not to answer Markham's questions for the time being. Once he and Clay were together again, they could figure out what to do with this eager young man. "By the way, thanks for saving my life."

Markham glanced at the dark shape on the ground that was Bromley's corpse and shook his head mournfully. "That was only part of the job," he said.

As far as he was concerned, Jeff thought, it was an important part.

Clay wasn't sure what to expect when he got back to the Copper Gable. Jeff could have gotten there first, or he might still be out trailing Bromley. When Clay entered the tavern, he headed straight for the stairs, not bothering to stop by the bar and talk to Harry Ledbetter. The proprietor was busy, anyway. His business seemed to be picking up again.

As Clay approached the door of their room, he saw that Jeff — or somebody — was already inside. The tiny sliver of wood Clay had placed between the door and the jamb when they left earlier was now lying on the floor in front of the door, indicating that it had been opened. Maybe the intruder was gone, but Clay's instincts told him that whoever had opened the door was still inside.

He put his right hand on the butt of the flintlock pistol at his waist, looping his thumb over the hammer. With his left he grasped the door latch, then shoved the door in hard. Candlelight lit the room, bright to Clay's eyes after the dim corridor. He stepped into the room and swept his gun up and around, searching for any possible threat.

"It's all right, Clay," Jeff said quickly from where he stood beside the window.

Clay's eyes barely registered his brother. Instead, his gaze was fixed on the young man who stood by the bed. The stranger wore a brown suit and black boots and held a dark brown beaver hat in his hands. He was in his early twenties, Clay judged, with blond hair and an open, friendly face. Clay had never seen him before.

"Who's this?" Clay asked.

"A friend," Jeff said.

The young man stepped forward and extended a hand, ignoring the gun that Clay was still pointing in his direction. "I'm Lieutenant John Markham, sir. I must say, it's an honor to meet you."

Clay stared at him. "Lieutenant," he repeated. "That doesn't look like any military uniform to me."

"That's because I wasn't supposed to reveal my true identity unless I was forced to," Markham explained. "Unfortunately, that circumstance came about even sooner than either the president or I hoped it would."

"The president sent you?" Clay asked sharply. He had made no move to take Markham's hand.

"Mr. Jefferson, actually," Markham said. "President Madison knows nothing of my current assignment. My commanding officer at Fort McHenry is an old friend of Mr. Jefferson's, and of course I was more than willing to volunteer for this mission when the request came from a man of Mr. Jefferson's stature."

Jeff put in, "I think he's telling the truth, Clay. You can put your gun up. I've got a lot to tell you."

That didn't sound too good, Clay thought. He tucked his pistol behind his belt and finally shook hands with Markham. The youngster was persistent, Clay had to give him that. Most men would have dropped their hand by now if it was being ignored.

"As I said, sir, it's an honor," Markham

went on. "I'm told you traveled to the Pacific with Captain Lewis and Captain Clark."

"That's right," Clay said curtly. He didn't want to get bogged down in Markham's evident admiration. There were more important matters at hand. "You know what my brother and I are doing here in Washington?"

"Indeed I do." Markham lowered his voice. "You're investigating some sort of scheme to illicitly gain title to a great deal of government land."

"How did you get involved in it?" Clay asked.

"Well, actually, my role is unofficial, as is your own. According to my commander's records, I'm on leave from the army at the moment. My real orders, however, are to assist the two of you in any way you deem necessary and serve as liaison between you and Mr. Jefferson."

"You mean you're a spy?"

"I prefer to be known as a secret agent," Markham replied conspiratorially.

Clay looked at Jeff, who shrugged. His meaning was clear: For some reason, Jefferson had chosen to saddle them with this youngster, and they would simply have to make the best of it.

"If you're supposed to be skulking around

in secret, what are you doing here tonight?" Clay asked.

Jeff answered for Markham. "It's a good thing the lieutenant was keeping an eye on us, Clay. Otherwise I might be dead now."

"Dead?" Clay exclaimed.

"Like Bromley," Jeff added, his face and voice turning grim.

"Bromley's dead?"

Jeff nodded. "Some men jumped him after he left that alehouse, and one of them stabbed him to death. They might have killed me, too, when I tried to stop them if Lieutenant Markham here hadn't shown up and given me a hand."

These revelations coming almost too quickly for Clay to take in readily. After a moment's thought he asked, "Was it a robbery?"

"I don't think so," Jeff replied, shaking his head. "It looked to me as if all they were interested in was making sure Bromley was dead."

"An assassination," Markham added.

"Why would anybody do that?"

"Maybe Bromley had outlived his usefulness to whoever he was working for," Jeff speculated. "Could be he was demanding more money, or his conscience was starting to act up, and the conspirators decided it would be easier just to get rid of him. It must've been set up before he went to that tavern tonight." Jeff looked intently at Clay. "Did you see who he was meeting there?"

Clay nodded. "It was some fellow I'd never seen before. But I'll know him when I see him again, and I intend to do that. I trailed him to a big fancy house."

"Can you find it again?" Markham asked eagerly.

Clay snorted in answer, and Jeff smiled. "Once Clay's been over a trail, he doesn't forget it, even if it's in the middle of a city," he told the young man.

"Then you can take us there tomorrow," Markham said, his excitement growing. "I shouldn't have much trouble finding out who lives there."

"Sounds like a good idea," Clay agreed. "That fellow I saw tonight must be mixed up in this mess. He could even be the one who gave the order to have Bromley killed. The only way the attack would've been called off would've been if Bromley and that gent had left the tavern together."

"Which didn't happen, so Bromley wound up dead," Jeff finished. "It makes sense, Clay. Even dead, Bromley may be of some help to us."

Clay looked at Markham. "Now that we

know who you are, there's no reason for you to lurk around like an Indian. Come on back here in the morning, and we'll go take a look at that place I found tonight."

"Of course," Markham agreed without hesitation. "I must say, this is going to be a thrilling assignment, working with the two of you."

"Yes," Jeff said dryly. "Thrilling."

The next day, Lieutenant Markham turned up at the Copper Gable earlier than Clay and Jeff had expected him. He was waiting downstairs, sipping a cup of tea at one of the tables, when the Holts came down from their room.

"Good morning, gentlemen," Markham greeted them. "I trust you slept well."

"Well enough," Clay said. He darted a glance at Harry Ledbetter behind the bar. Ledbetter seemed to be paying little attention to them. There were a few other men in the tavern, getting an early start on their day's drinking. If Ledbetter wondered who the young man was who was waiting for Clay and Jeff, he gave no sign of it.

Jeff pulled out a chair at the table and sat down. "I thought you were supposed to keep it a secret that you're working with us," he said quietly.

"That's correct," Markham said. "That's why when I spoke to the tavern keeper about you, I let it slip that I was considering hiring you as guides for a trip I plan to take to the west."

Clay took a seat as well. "You're not really going to the frontier, are you?"

"Not unless my orders take me there. The two of you know who I really am, but to everyone else I intend to present the facade of a wealthy young wastrel." Markham smiled. "I know, that will take quite a bit of acting ability on my part, but I'm confident that I'm up to it. I won't let you — or Mr. Jefferson — down."

"All right, I reckon that story will do," Clay agreed. "As soon as we've had some breakfast, we'll head over to the house I followed that man to last night."

"I've taken the liberty of ordering for you and paying the proprietor for the meal. After all, the two of you are working for me now, as far as anyone else knows, so I can't have you wasting my valuable time."

Clay and Jeff looked at each other, unsure whether to laugh or scowl. They were beginning to understand that working with Lieutenant John Markham was going to take some patience.

After they had breakfasted on the sausages,

eggs, and wheat cakes that Harry Ledbetter brought to the table, the three men left the tavern and walked toward the Capitol.

Clay led Jeff and Markham straight to the mansion north of the Capitol that he had seen the mild-faced man enter the night before. They stopped down the street a ways and tried not to attract notice as they studied the house. "You're sure this is it?" Markham asked.

"I'm sure," Clay said. "The fella who met with Bromley in Cochran's tavern came right here and marched in the front door bold as brass. He belonged here, all right."

A wagon passed by just then, driven by an elderly black man. Jeff stepped forward and raised a hand in greeting. "Good morning," he said. "I wonder if I might ask you something."

The black man hauled back on the reins and halted his team. "Reckon you could," he said, "and I'll tell you if I knows."

The wagon shielded Jeff from the view of anyone in the house. He pointed and asked, "Could you tell me who lives there?"

The man turned his head and looked at the mansion for a few seconds, then looked at Jeff again. "That? That's Marse Maxwell's house."

"You say his name's Maxwell?"

"Yes, suh, Marse Gideon Maxwell. If'n you don' mind me askin', why you wants to know?"

"It's a personal matter," Jeff said. He pressed a coin into the man's hand.

"Well, I reckon that's good enough for me." With a grin, the man got his team of mules moving again, and the wagon rolled away down the street.

"The house belongs to someone named Gideon Maxwell," Jeff reported to Clay and Markham. The young lieutenant let out a low whistle of surprise.

Clay looked sharply at him. "That name mean something to you, Lieutenant?"

"I've been stationed in the Washington area long enough to have heard it before, yes," Markham said. "As you can surely guess from the house, he's quite wealthy, but no one seems to know exactly where his money comes from. He's friends with a great many powerful politicians, and the balls he holds are attended by just about everyone of any importance in Washington City. But I've also heard some rather unsavory rumors about others of his acquaintance —"

"You're saying he's crooked," Clay broke in.

Markham shook his head. "I'm saying I don't know. It's certainly possible. But to my knowledge he's never been charged with a crime or even seriously linked with one."

"That just means he hasn't been caught yet," Jeff said. He looked at his brother. "Sounds to me like this fellow could have something to do with the land grab, Clay. If he's friends with everybody from senators to cutthroats, that's just the type that might try something on such a big scale."

Clay nodded. "That's what I was thinking. We've got to get in there somehow and make sure Maxwell's the one I saw with Bromley, though."

"Let me send word to Mr. Jefferson," Markham suggested. "If Maxwell is having one of his parties in the near future, perhaps Mr. Jefferson could manage to get us invited."

Clay raised his eyebrows in surprise. "Why in the world would a rich man like Maxwell invite a couple of plain folks like Jeff and me to one of his fancy parties?"

"You're not 'plain folks,' either one of you," Markham protested. "You're a famous explorer, a veteran of the Lewis and Clark expedition and a well-known mountain man in your own right."

A smile tugged at Jeff's mouth. "What the lieutenant's saying is that you'd be a curiosity to civilized folks, Clay."

"Not at all," Markham went on quickly. "But people are fascinated with the frontier, and I daresay you know more about it than anyone else in Washington right now. And as for you, Mr. Holt" — Markham looked at Jeff — "you're a successful businessman with a growing commercial empire. Maxwell would no doubt be interested in meeting you because he might want to do business with you someday."

"What about you?" Jeff asked.

"Me?" Markham put a hand on his chest and grinned. "Why, I'm an ambitious young army officer on the rise. That's reason enough to get invited — that and my natural charm, of course."

"Of course," Jeff agreed with a grin.

"All right," Clay said briskly. "How long will it take to set this up?"

"I have no idea, but I'll begin looking into it immediately. I'll ride to Monticello and speak to Mr. Jefferson myself."

"Make it fast," Clay advised him. "I've got folks waiting for me, and I need to get home."

"Of course. But perhaps, in this instance, your country needs you even more."

"Don't lecture me, boy," Clay growled. "Just get us an invitation to one of those parties, and we'll see what Mr. Gideon Maxwell has up his sleeve."

Chapter Fourteen

"And that ol' boar hog took off after that husband o' mine like greased lightnin'!" Cassie Doolittle threw back her head and laughed. "I never seen him move so fast in all his borned days! He shinnied up a tree like he was climbin' up to Heaven to say howdy to ol' Saint Peter hisownself!"

Shining Moon joined in the old woman's laughter. Their friendship was the only thing that brightened Shining Moon's days while she waited for Clay Holt to return from Washington City. Already, several weeks had passed and Clay was not back. Nor had she received any word from him. Clearly something had happened to delay him, and now Shining Moon had no idea when to expect him. The thought that some injury or other misfortune might have befallen him had crossed her mind, but only briefly. She knew better than anyone how capable Clay was when it came to taking care of himself.

She knew, too, that he was still alive, because she could still feel him upon the earth.

The bond between them was so strong that she would be aware of it if he died, no matter where he was, and the same was true for him. She was sure of it.

Cassie stuck a finger in her mouth and worried at something stuck in one of her few teeth. "What d'you call this stuff again?" she asked.

"Pemmican. It is one of the foods my people eat. I brought some with us when Clay Holt and I left the mountains to visit his home."

"It's tasty, I'll give you that, and fillin', too." Cassie stood up. "Well, I'd better be goin'. That place o' mine won't look after itself. Though I'm over here so much these days I reckon it'd be better if it could."

"Your visits are always welcome," Shining Moon assured her. She gestured toward the blueberry pie Cassie had left on the table. "And Castor and Pollux would be very sad if you stopped coming to see us."

Cassie laughed again. "Ain't that the truth!"

She left the cabin as Shining Moon began clearing the table. She was about to take the jug of cider down to the cellar when she heard Cassie screech angrily, "What the hell are you doin', boy? Get away from that mule!"

Shining Moon quickly placed the cider jug

back on the table and hurried out the front door. She found Cassie standing at the base of the porch steps, her hands on her hips, glowering at Matthew Garwood, who stood a few feet away glaring back at the old woman.

"I didn't touch your damned old mule!" he shouted at Cassie. "It stinks, just like you!"

"Matthew!" Shining Moon said sharply. "You will not speak to your elders in this way. You must show respect to them."

"I don't respect this old bitch," Matthew snapped. "I wish she wouldn't even come over here."

Shining Moon put a hand on Cassie's arm. "I am sorry," she said solemnly. "What happened?"

Cassie snorted. "I come out here and caught that little rapscallion about to take a knife to my mule's ears. It woulda served him right if she'd taken a bite right outta his hide or maybe kicked some sense into him."

"That's a lie," Matthew said stubbornly. "I didn't bother her mule. See for yourself."

Cassie stepped forward and inspected both the mule's ears. " 'Tain't cut," she admitted. "But that don't mean he weren't about to go to carvin' on her." She turned and looked at Shining Moon. "You believe me, don't you, Shinin' Moon?"

How could Shining Moon not believe what Cassie was saying? The memory of what the Gilworth brothers had discovered Matthew doing in the woods was all too vivid in her mind.

"I believe you," she said softly to Cassie.

"Damn it!" Matthew burst out. "You always take her side! You never believe me! Nobody ever believes me!"

Shining Moon took a step toward him, extending her hand. She could see the demons in him, yet he was still just a child, and her heart went out to him. "Matthew . . ."

He jerked away before she could touch him. "Leave me alone!" he cried. "You're not my mother! My mother's dead! All you Holts killed her!" He spun around and raced toward the woods.

Shining Moon watched him go. She could have chased him, she supposed. She would have caught him easily. There was no way he could have eluded her; she was still a Sioux, despite her white woman's clothes, and no child — and few adults — could outrun her. But what good would it do, she asked herself, to drag Matthew back to the cabin kicking and screaming? It would be better to let him calm down on his own before he returned.

She prayed that no small animals too slow

to evade him would cross his path today. Surely they would sense the danger and give it a wide berth.

"I'm mighty sorry that happened, Shinin' Moon," Cassie said. "I shouldn't've yelled at the boy. It just got my dander up when I come out and saw him sneakin' around my mule with that knife o' his."

Shining Moon nodded. "Yes. I must take the knife away from him. His heart is too heavy for one so young."

"You watch yourself around him," Cassie advised. Shining Moon was surprised to see something akin to fear in the old woman's eyes. "He's like a wild animal. You can't trust him, and you can't never tell what he's goin' to do."

"Matthew would not hurt me," Shining Moon said quietly. "Clay Holt and I took him in when he had no one."

"An act o' kindness don't mean a damned thing to a wolf. He'll still bite you, first chance he gets."

Shining Moon took a deep breath. "Things will be better when Clay Holt returns and we can go home," she said. She was going to hold fast to that belief.

Otherwise she, too, might start thinking about the things she had seen in Matthew Garwood's eyes . . .

Aaron Garwood was making his way toward Malachi Fisher's trading post when he saw the two men walking into the settlement from the north. A smile flashed across his face. Balancing on his good right leg and the peg he had carved to replace the left one, he lifted his hand and waved. "Proud Wolf!" he called. He had recognized his friend from the Sioux village right away. But who was that funny-looking white man with him?

Proud Wolf and his companion strode up to Aaron. Proud Wolf threw his arms around him and embraced him like a brother. "My good friend Aaron!" he said. "Where are your crutches?" He stepped back and looked down at the pegleg. "What is this?"

"Got tired of being a cripple," Aaron declared with a proud grin, "so I decided I wouldn't be one anymore. I carved a new leg, and I'm learning how to get around on it just fine."

"That's fascinating," said the white man who had come into the village with Proud Wolf. "The power of the human mind is quite compelling. You simply made a decision to improve your lot in life, young man, and by God you're doing it!"

Aaron off took his hat. This stranger with

the bushy white hair and the funny way of talking was quite a bit older than he, and being the youngest in his family, Aaron had learned to respect his elders. In the Garwood family, in fact, lack of what his brothers had deemed proper respect often fetched him a brain-rattling clout on the ear. "I'm Aaron Garwood," he said to the stranger.

The man stuck out his hand. "Professor Abner Hilliard. I'm pleased to meet you, Aaron. I take it you are a friend of our noble red brother here?"

"You mean Proud Wolf? You bet we're friends."

"We have been to see the elephant together," Proud Wolf said solemnly. "Aaron was with Clay Holt and my sister and me when we first met Professor Franklin's expedition."

Hilliard pumped Aaron's hand. "Then I'm doubly pleased to meet you. Donald Franklin was a great friend of mine."

"Yeah, I reckon you remind me of him, at least a mite," Aaron said. "What in the world are you doing out here in the wilderness? If you're a professor, shouldn't you be back east at one of those fancy colleges?"

"A teacher must also be a student," Hilliard said with a smile, "and what better place to learn than the most advanced university of all — the world?"

"It is a long story," Proud Wolf said dryly.

"Well, come on over to Fisher's place," Aaron suggested. "We'll sit down on the porch, and you can tell me all about it."

They walked to the trading post, Proud Wolf and Professor Hilliard carefully accommodating Aaron's slower pace. When Malachi Fisher saw them step up onto his porch, he came out of the building and shook hands first with Proud Wolf and then with Hilliard. With his teeth clamped firmly on his pipe, he said, "Good to see you again, Professor."

"We don't get too many professors out here," Aaron said as he settled himself in one of the chairs on the porch.

"Not that ever'body west of the Mississipp' is uneducated," Fisher added. "I've known mountain men who've read ever' play that Shakespeare fella ever wrote, and they can even recite most of 'em. The same way with the Bible. Some fellas can spout Scripture from the Good Book for hours at a time, right out o' their memory."

Hilliard nodded. "I believe you, Mr. Fisher. The Indians have the same sort of oral tradition, don't they, Proud Wolf?"

"My people are great storytellers," the young man replied. "There are many tales of the olden times and how this world came to be."

"And someday I hope to have the time to listen to all of them and perhaps even write them down. Someone certainly needs to, before the stories are all gone."

Proud Wolf shook his head. "Stories will never be gone. There will always be those who listen."

"Well, I hope you're right." Hilliard brought out his pipe and accepted the offer of some tobacco from Fisher's pouch. "Now, to explain to you gentlemen why I'm here and what Proud Wolf and I plan to do —"

"No need," Fisher said. "Nick Palmer told us all about it."

Hilliard turned to the storekeeper with interest. "How is Nick? I hope his wounds are healing properly."

"He's up and around and ought to be ready to travel whenever you are, Professor. He's staying over at the church so that Father Thomas can look after him. Father Thomas knows more about doctoring than I do."

Aaron spoke up. "Don't reckon I know what's going on here. Who's Nick Palmer?"

"He was my guide out here," Hilliard said. "One of my guides, actually. The other poor fellow was killed in an attack by some Indians."

"Crow," Proud Wolf said disdainfully.

Aaron shook his head. "Don't guess I've met him."

Malachi Fisher gestured at Aaron's peg-leg. "You've been so busy carving on that new leg and practicing with it, you haven't paid any attention to what's going on around you, Aaron."

"I reckon not." Aaron turned back to Hilliard. "You were about to tell me why you're out here, Professor."

"Yes, of course. I've come to meet Proud Wolf and take him back east with me so that he can go to school."

Aaron stared at Proud Wolf, who seemed to be enjoying his friend's surprise. "You're going to *school?* White man's school?"

"Is there any reason I should not?" Proud Wolf asked.

Aaron scratched his head. "No, I reckon not," he said slowly. "But why in blazes would you *want* to?"

"It is always good to learn."

"But those folks back east can't teach you anything you'd really need to know, like how to run a trapline in a creek, or skin a deer, or read sign."

"Perhaps not," the professor said, "but Proud Wolf's instructors at the academy *can* teach him how to read and write and do mathematics, and give him a good grounding in history and philosophy and Latin and all the natural sciences."

"I can read enough to make out my name," Aaron said. "Always figured that was enough."

"A man can never learn enough," Hilliard declared. "There is always more knowledge out there, just waiting to be absorbed by a hungry mind."

Aaron looked at Proud Wolf. "This is really something you want to do?" he asked.

"It is," Proud Wolf said. "I will learn these things not only for my sake but for the sake of my people. I would help them understand the white man."

Aaron stood up and offered his hand to his friend. "Then I wish you all the luck in the world, Proud Wolf."

"Me, too," Malachi Fisher added.

Aaron changed the subject by asking Proud Wolf, "While you were at Bear Tooth's village, did you see Grass Song?"

Proud Wolf smiled slightly. "I saw her. She has grown into a lovely young maiden."

"Well, yes, I . . . I reckon that's so. I haven't seen her lately." He reached down and slapped the wood below his knee. "Been working on this new leg, like Mr. Fisher said. You think Grass Song would mind if I rode up there and paid her a visit?"

Proud Wolf hesitated. He glanced at Hilliard and then said, "There are bad feelings among some of my people now toward white men. But I think it would be all right if you went to the village of Bear Tooth, Aaron. Everyone there knows you are the friend of Clay Holt, and he is our brother, the same as us despite the color of his skin."

"I daresay I simply rubbed some of the Sioux the wrong way," Hilliard put in. "That sort of thing has happened before, even with white men. I tend to be somewhat lugubrious at times."

Aaron had to chuckle. He could imagine that folks would get a mite put out with the professor after listening to him for a while. "I'll go see Grass Song, then," he said, "but maybe I'll wait a few days."

"That would be wise," Proud Wolf agreed.

"Besides, I want to stay down here until you and the professor start back east. It's been too long since we've seen each other."

Proud Wolf nodded. "Yes. Too long." He gazed at the lofty, snowcapped peaks that towered over the valley. "But I fear it will be even longer before I return to this land."

Cassie Doolittle flapped the reins against the back of her mule and rocked gently back and forth to the motion of the two-wheeled cart as it rolled along the trail. She was on her way to see Shining Moon again, and she hoped that Matthew Garwood would be out in the barn or off in the fields with the Gilworth brothers. Cassie had no desire to see the boy again, not after what had happened the last time she was at the Holt place. Nearly a week had passed since she had caught Matthew on the verge of hurting her mule, but she hadn't forgotten. No, sir, not by a long shot.

She liked to think of herself as a good Christian woman, but if it had been up to her, she never would have taken Matthew to raise as Shining Moon had done. Funny, Cassie thought, how a heathen could sometimes behave more like a Christian than a regular churchgoer.

Shining Moon hadn't known the Garwood family as long as Cassie had, though. She had no idea what a sorry, no-account bunch the Garwoods were. Why, that Zach Garwood had been willing to lie with any woman who'd have him — just look how he'd gotten his own sister with child! Gave a whole new meaning to the old saying about being in the family way, Cassie thought with a snort of disgust. And Luther and Pete hadn't been much better.

Of course it was possible that not all the Garwoods were so terrible, she mused. From what Shining Moon had told her, it sounded as if Aaron, the youngest of the four brothers and the only one still alive, had done a heap of growing up since he'd gone west. Aaron was one of Clay Holt's best friends now, so he had to have some good in him. Clay wasn't the sort to take up with a complete reprobate.

Matthew, though . . . Matthew was his daddy's own son, right enough. Cassie could see it in his eyes. Dead they were, as if there was no soul inside the boy, just an emptiness as black as the night . . .

Something flew out of the dense woods that pressed in closely on both sides of the narrow trail. It thudded hard against the rump of the mule, making the animal jump in surprise. Cassie exclaimed, "Hey!"

A laugh floated to her ears, high-pitched, grating.

"Damn it, who's there?" she demanded.

The only answer was another projectile that also caught the mule in the rump. This time Cassie saw it. "Quit chunkin' rocks at my mule!" she shouted as she tried to rein in. Being struck twice had prompted the normally docile mule to pick up its pace. The two-wheeled cart wasn't the most stable vehicle to begin with, and it lurched wildly when the mule went too fast.

"Make me stop!" someone called from the woods. The heavy growth completely hid the speaker. "Make me, you old hag!"

As soon as she had realized what was happening, Cassie had had a pretty good idea who was responsible. The boyish voice confirmed her suspicion. "Matthew Garwood!" she screeched as she sawed at the reins. "You stop throwin' rocks, or I'll tell Shinin' Moon and she'll have one o' the Gilworths tan your bottom!"

Another rock bounced off the mule's flank. The animal broke into a gallop, something it hadn't attempted in ages. Cassie was thrown back in the cart's seat, and she had to let go of the reins with one hand so that she could grab hold of the seat and steady herself. The slacker reins allowed the mule to run even harder.

"The Gilworths won't dare whip me!" Cassie vaguely heard Matthew shriek. "They're afraid of me! They know I'll cut their balls off if they bother me!"

The cart was careening now along the rutted trail. Cassie tried to haul back on the reins with one hand while desperately hanging on to the cart with the other. For a second, as the cart topped a hill, it actually became airborne and then slammed back down with a jolt that rattled the few teeth Cassie had left.

The trail led downhill now, and at the bottom of the slope was a sharp turn to the right. At this speed, Cassie knew, the cart would not maneuver the turn without flipping over. She had to chance letting go of the seat so she could use both hands on the reins again. "Whoa, damn it!" she shouted at the mule. "Slow down, consarn your ornery hide!"

Ironic memories of all the times she had fussed at the mule to quit plodding along and go a little faster flashed through her mind. Now she was praying the brute would stop running so hard.

Matthew was far behind her by now, but he had done his damage. If Cassie didn't bring the mule and the cart under control by the time they reached the bottom of the hill, it would almost certainly overturn, and her brittle old body was too fragile to withstand such a wreck. She was an old, old woman, she told herself as she struggled with the reins, and she should have been ready to go home to the Lord, but she wasn't. Damn it, she just wasn't ready yet —

The mule pounded through the turn, the cart out of control behind it. Cassie felt the vehicle starting to go over, and she tried to throw herself clear. For an instant she seemed to be floating free in the air — like an angel, she thought, just like an angel from heaven above — and then something slammed into her and it felt as if everything inside her was breaking. Blackness engulfed her, shutting out the sunny day, and she knew nothing more.

She didn't see the boy who ran out into the road from the brush at the top of the hill, an expression of shock and surprise on his face. Clearly he had not expected his vicious prank to go this far. He stared down at the scene below: the overturned cart, one wheel still spinning; the mule tangled in the reins, kicking feebly as it tried to get free. Of the old woman he could see nothing but part of a leg poking out from under the cart.

He was silent for a long moment. Then he smiled, and soon delighted laughter began to echo through the forest.

Shining Moon stepped from the sunshine into the barn and looked around, peering keenly into the shadows. Seeing no one, she called, "Castor? Pollux?"

"Yes, ma'am," came the voice of one of the brothers. He looked down at her from the hayloft. "What can I do for you?"

"Have you seen Matthew?"

"Not since right after midday, ma'am. I've been up here all afternoon replacing some planks that've started to rot. He might be over in the east field with Castor, though."

"Thank you, Pollux."

With a sigh, Pollux ran a hand over his bearded face. "I hope the boy ain't gone off in the woods again by himself. After what happened last time . . ."

He did not have to finish the sentence. Shining Moon nodded solemnly and said, "I know. I hope so, too."

As she left the barn, she told herself that it wasn't fair to think the worst of Matthew before she even knew where he was. But that was exactly what she had done. If he was out of her sight these days, she automatically assumed he was up to no good. No wonder the boy resented her, she thought. If he could sense how she felt — and she had no doubt he could — then perhaps his hostility was justified.

Shining Moon took a deep breath. She hoped she was wrong about what he might be doing. Like all her people, she felt no guilt when she killed an animal so that she could make good use of it. That was what the Great Spirit had intended when he placed man and the animals on the earth.

But to torment and kill something for pleasure, a twisted kind of pleasure — that she could not understand. She shuddered.

Shining Moon walked toward the east pasture, knowing she would find Castor there and hoping that Matthew was working with him. Before she could reach the pasture, however, she heard the sound of a horse walking along the path toward her. A moment later the rider came around the bend. A burly, broad-shouldered figure was walking alongside the man on horseback, and Shining Moon recognized Castor Gilworth. She did not know the man on the horse.

"Miz Holt!" Castor exclaimed. "Mr. Sweeney and I were just on our way to the house to find you."

The stranger tugged the brim of his hat as he nodded to her. "Howdy, Miz Holt," he said. He was a stolid-looking, broad-faced man with blond hair and a barrel chest. "I'm Walt Sweeney. Just been elected constable for these parts."

Shining Moon returned his nod. "I am pleased to meet you, Mr. Sweeney." She turned to Castor and saw the stricken look on his face. Something was wrong. "What is it?" she asked. "Why were you looking for me?"

Walt Sweeney had brought his horse to a stop. Now he leaned forward in the saddle and looked uncomfortable. "I'm afraid I've got some bad news for you, ma'am," he said.

Shining Moon remembered Clay Holt describing to her the position held by a constable in the white man's world. He was the keeper of the law, the person who stepped in when there was trouble or when the rules of the band had been broken. Of course the whites did not consider themselves a band, as the Sioux did, but it was the same thing. For Sweeney to have come to the Holt farm, something had to be very wrong.

"Is it Matthew?" Shining Moon barely recognized her own voice as she forced the words out.

"Matthew?" Castor repeated. He frowned in confusion for a second, then shook his head. "No, nothing's happened to Matthew. It's Miz Doolittle. Cassie."

Shining Moon felt her blood turn to ice. "Cassie," she said, speaking the name of her friend as if it were a shaman's incantation, a prayer to the spirits that the old woman was all right.

Constable Sweeney immediately dashed that hope. "I'm afraid she's been killed. There was an accident with that old two-wheel cart she always drove."

Shining Moon bit back the death song that sprang to her lips. She wanted to fall to her knees and tear her clothing and keen the death song for Cassie, to show her mourning and help guide Cassie's spirit to the world that now awaited it.

But these white men would never understand what she was doing. She would have to wait until later, when she was alone, to give voice to her grief in the only way she knew how.

"It looked like a runaway," Constable Sweeney went on after a moment of awkward silence. "I reckon she must've been on her way over here. She was on the road that leads from her place to yours. That old mule of hers must've acted up and started galloping. The cart wasn't made for that. It turned over at the bottom of a hill, and Miz Doolittle went flying. Leastways, that's the way it looked to me. The cart . . . well, the cart landed on top of her." The constable shook his head. "The fall might've been enough to do her in by itself, but with that cart landing on her . . . she just didn't have a chance."

"How . . . how did you find her?"

"One of your neighbors was on his way into Marietta. He found Miz Doolittle and galloped his horse on into town to tell me. I rode out here to take a look for myself, and since I'd heard that you and Cassie had gotten to be friends, I decided I'd come on over and let you know the bad news. If it's all right with you, I'd like to borrow your wagon so I can take the body back to town."

Numbly Shining Moon nodded. There was little enough she could do now for Cassie.

"I saw Walt riding by and hailed him to find out what was up," Castor said. "Soon as he'd told me about Miz Doolittle, we started right on to the house to find you." He shook his head sadly. "She sure could make a fine pie."

For an instant Shining Moon felt a blaze of anger. Her friend — her only true friend here in Ohio — was dead, and Castor was worried about pies! Then she saw the tears shining in the eyes of the big, bearded man and realized that he was dealing with the news of Cassie's death in his own way, just as she would do later when she could chant the death song alone. She reached out to Castor and squeezed his big, rough hand.

Then she asked the question that had sent her in search of him in the first place. "Is Matthew with you?"

Castor frowned again. "The boy? Nope, I ain't seen him since we all ate the noon meal. Isn't he around the cabin or the barn?"

Shining Moon saw the worry lurking behind the tears in Castor's eyes and knew he was thinking the same thing she was. Nothing good ever happened when Matthew disappeared.

"I am sure he is somewhere near," Shining Moon said hollowly. She summoned up a weak smile for Constable Sweeney. "Come. You will take the wagon, as you asked."

"Much obliged, ma'am," Sweeney said.

When they reached the house, Matthew was sitting on the front porch with Pollux. Both of them were whittling, and even in her grief, Shining Moon was glad to see the boy engaged in such an innocent activity. Pollux looked up from his work with a grin and said to Shining Moon, "Here's Matthew, ma'am. He turned up right after you went off looking for him. Ain't that always the way? The little fella was asleep down in one of the stalls . . ."

His voice trailed off as he looked at Shining Moon and his brother, and then his startled gaze fastened on the lawman. "Howdy, Walt," he said. "What brings you out here?"

"Bad news," Sweeney replied. "Cassie Doolittle's been killed in an accident."

"Miz Doolittle? Dead? Lordy!"

Sweeney swung down from his horse. "Miz Holt said I could borrow your wagon."

Pollux stood up, wood shavings falling from his lap. "Surely. Come on, Castor, we'll get the team hitched up."

The Gilworths went off toward the barn with Sweeney, leaving Shining Moon facing Matthew, who was still whittling. He had not looked up, not even when the constable announced the grim news of Cassie's death.

"Matthew," Shining Moon said quietly, "did you hear what Mr. Sweeney said?"

"I heard," Matthew said, still not looking up. "I don't care. I'm glad the old woman's dead."

Shining Moon's breath caught in her throat. "Do not say such things," she said angrily. "The spirits —"

"The spirits don't have anything to do with me," he cut in, finally looking up at her. As his eyes met hers, she knew he was right. None of the spirits, not even Wakan Tanka, the Creator, had breathed life into this boy. He had been given form by something older, more elemental.

Tonight, after she had sung the death song for Cassie Doolittle, she would chant a prayer as well, a prayer to the Great Spirit to protect them all.

Chapter Fifteen

Lieutenant Markham rode to Monticello himself, promising that he would take the fastest horse he could and return to the city as soon as possible. Clay chafed at the prospect of another delay of several days in their investigation, but there was nothing he could do to speed up the process. Now that Atticus Bromley was dead, the murdered clerk's link with the mysterious Gideon Maxwell was the only lead they had. And the best way to uncover more information about Maxwell, Clay knew, was to be patient and hope that Thomas Jefferson's influence would secure them an invitation to Maxwell's next grand ball.

In the meantime Clay and Jeff made use of other sources closer at hand. They decided to ask some discreet questions of the tavern keeper, Harry Ledbetter.

"Gideon Maxwell?" Ledbetter said as he swabbed the bar with a damp rag. "Aye, I've heard of the man. Never seen him, though. The likes o' him don't often come in a place like this, ye understand."

"There's nothing wrong with the Copper

Gable," Jeff said as he nursed a mug of ale.

"It's a right nice place," Clay added. "We wouldn't stay here if it wasn't."

"Well, I appreciate the praise, lads. And I'll tell ye what I do know about Mr. Gideon Maxwell: He's rich. He's got more money than fellas like you and me will ever see in our lifetimes."

"How did he get his money?" Jeff asked casually.

Ledbetter shook his head. "Your guess'd be as good as mine, gents. I've heard it said that he owns a bank, but I couldn't tell you which one, or if that's even true. 'Tis rumored, too, that he dabbles in land speculation."

Clay and Jeff exchanged glances unobtrusively. If that were true, then Maxwell was emerging as a more and more likely suspect in the frontier land grab. Gaining control of half the continent would rank as the largest land speculation deal of all time, Clay mused.

"And he's friends with plenty of folks in the government," Harry Ledbetter went on. "I've heard lots of stories about the parties he throws. There are always a handful of senators there, at the very least. Wouldn't surprise me none to hear that Maxwell's got the ear of the president himself."

Clay and Jeff both hoped that wasn't true.

They didn't want to believe that James Madison, who had essentially been handpicked by Thomas Jefferson as his successor, could be involved in something as sordid and scandalous as illegal land acquisition on such a massive scale.

Ledbetter gave them a puzzled look. "Why are ye so interested in Gideon Maxwell?" he asked.

"His name came up in some business we're doing," Jeff answered vaguely. "We just wanted to find out some more about him."

"I'd say the two o' you are getting to be as mysterious as Mr. Maxwell," Ledbetter commented shrewdly. "At first ye only intended to stay in Washington a few days, and now ye've been here nigh onto three weeks. You're becoming fixtures on the scene, lads."

"Not hardly," Clay muttered. "When the time comes, we'll be gone from here." And that time, he prayed, would come soon.

Two more days passed before Lieutenant Markham returned. Clay and Jeff were sitting at a table in the corner when the young officer entered the tavern. Markham was dusty and trail-worn and had obviously come straight to the Copper Gable. A grin spread across his face when he spotted the Holts.

"Success, gentlemen," he said as he dropped into one of the empty chairs at the table. He leaned forward and kept his voice pitched low. "Mr. Jefferson agrees with us that Gideon Maxwell may be the key to the entire affair. He's promised to wield his not inconsiderable influence to make sure we're invited to Maxwell's next party."

Clay nodded in satisfaction. "Any idea when that'll be?" he asked.

Markham shook his head. "Unfortunately, no. However, it shouldn't be long. Maxwell hosts these soirees quite regularly, and it's been a while since the last one."

"I hope you're right."

Markham scraped back his chair. "I should report to Fort McHenry," he said. "I came here first because I wanted to apprise you gentlemen of the situation. We had best be prepared to move quickly. We may have little notice."

"We'll be ready," Jeff promised.

None of them suspected just how quickly things would move from that point, however. Late that very afternoon, a message was delivered at the Copper Gable. It was addressed to Clay and Jeff, and when Harry Ledbetter brought it up to their room, he said, "You boys are up to something again. 'Twas a different fellow who brought this, but he works for some rich gent. You could tell that by his clothes and the fancy carriage he drove up in."

Clay waited impatiently while Jeff gave the curious Ledbetter a coin and ushered him out of the room. Then he broke the wax seal, unfolded the letter, and read aloud:

"Gentlemen,

"My father and I have just been apprised of your presence in Washington City, and we would consider it a great privilege and pleasure if you would be so kind as to honor us with your company at a small gathering to be held tomorrow evening at our house on New York Street in the city. Two such illustrious guests as yourselves would be most welcome.

> *"Yours most sincerely,*
> *"Diana Maxwell"*

"Maxwell has a daughter?" Jeff said.

"Evidently." Clay handed the paper to Jeff.

Jeff studied the invitation. "From the sound of it, she must serve as her father's hostess for these parties. Maybe Maxwell's a widower."

"Could be. I reckon we'll find out." Clay rubbed his jaw in thought. "Wonder if the lieutenant got one of these, too?"

Jeff grinned. "If he did, I'm sure we'll hear about it." He tapped the letter with his finger. "We're one step closer, Clay."

"Now there's something else we've got to worry about," Clay said solemnly. "What in blazes are we going to wear to this ball? It's not a barn raising, like back home. I don't reckon buckskins would do."

Still grinning, Jeff clapped his brother on the shoulder. "First thing in the morning, you and I are going to have to find a tailor shop and see about getting some fancy suits."

Clay bit back a groan. If anyone but Thomas Jefferson had asked him to get mixed up in this mess, he would have said no. Now, thinking about silk shirts and tight pants and swallowtail coats, he wondered if it was worth it even for Jefferson.

Lieutenant Markham had gotten a similar invitation, also written by Diana Maxwell. He brought it with him when he came to the Copper Gable the next morning and showed it to Clay and Jeff in their room.

"Did you know Maxwell has a daughter?" Jeff asked Markham.

"Once I was reminded of the fact by this note, I remembered hearing her mentioned before," Markham replied. "I'm told she's quite lovely, and looking at the writing on this letter, I can believe it." He held the paper beneath his nose for a moment, inhaling the faint perfume clinging to it. "Lovely," he murmured.

"What about a wife?" Clay asked bluntly. "Does Maxwell have one of those?"

"I believe she passed away some time ago, when Miss Maxwell was young. You understand, I never took any great interest in Gideon Maxwell until I was given this assignment, so there are probably a great many things about him I don't know. I was familiar with him only because I've been posted in the area for the past couple of years, since entering the army. I assure you, though, before we're through we'll learn everything there is to know about Gideon Maxwell."

"What if he's not even involved in the land grab scheme?" Jeff asked.

"I consider that highly unlikely. After all, he — or someone from his household — met with Atticus Bromley just before Bromley was murdered."

"Coincidence, maybe," Clay commented, although he didn't truly believe that. Like Markham, he was convinced that Maxwell was deeply involved in the illegal activities that had kept him and Jeff in Washington. It didn't hurt to play devil's advocate, though, Clay thought — it helped him keep everything objective and logical in his own mind.

"We'll see," Markham said. "In the meantime I think we should deal with the issue of obtaining suitable garb for the party."

"We figured you could lead us to a tailor shop," Jeff said with a smile.

"Indeed I can. Come along, gentlemen. By tonight, we have to look the part as well as act it."

Neither of those tasks was going to be easy for him, Clay thought. He had spent his life being concerned more with survival than with worrying about things like which fork to use or how to tie a cravat. Jeff had more experience than he with such folderol, and Markham evidently had enough social ambition to have mastered all the necessary skills and graces. He would have to rely on the two of them to guide him, Clay decided. He wasn't accustomed to others taking the lead, but in this case he had no choice.

His worries proved to be well founded. He and Jeff and the lieutenant spent the morning in one of Washington's best tailor shops, being measured and fussed over. The news that all three had to have suitable outfits that evening for one of Gideon Maxwell's parties made the tailor shake his head and throw up his hands in disgust. At first he flatly denied that any tailor could work such a miracle, but after Markham quietly laid several coins on his worktable, he grudgingly agreed to try.

"Don't blame me if everything doesn't fit perfectly," he warned them. "I'll have to alter clothing that I already have on hand, and a man can't be expected to do his best work when he's rushed."

"I'm sure it will be fine," Markham said, smoothly adding another couple of coins to the pile.

During the afternoon, the lieutenant attended to renting a carriage so that they could arrive at Maxwell's mansion in proper style. By evening the clothes had been delivered to the Copper Gable, where Markham waited with Clay and Jeff. Clay grew increasingly nervous as he pulled on the new clothes.

He looked down in dismay at the front of his silk shirt, which was decorated with lace. He looped a white stock around his neck and fumbled for several minutes with the gold buckle that fastened it in the back before finally turning the task over to Jeff. His tightly fitted trousers were of white corduroy with straps on the bottom that went under soft black slippers. His tailcoat was dark blue, cut straight across the waist in front and falling in long, divided tails nearly to his knees in the back. A fawn-colored beaver top hat with a narrow, curled brim and a flaring crown completed the outfit.

Clay had never felt like such a damned fool in his whole life.

Jeff and Markham were wearing similar outfits. Jeff's coat was gray, and Markham's was brown. When they were all dressed, Clay looked at them for a moment, then asked, "Do I look as downright silly as you fellas do?"

"The tailor assured me this was the height of fashion," Markham said. "The designs all come straight from London."

"Well, as far as I'm concerned they can go back there." Clay heaved a sigh. "But I reckon we've got to fit in as well as we can tonight so Maxwell won't be too suspicious. If that means looking like a blasted idiot for a few hours, I reckon I can manage it. But right now I'm sure wishing I was back in my buckskins."

"You will be before you know it," Jeff told him soothingly, but Clay didn't believe it for a second. It would be a while, he thought grimly, before he could pull on the sturdy, honest clothes of the backwoodsman he was.

The carriage, complete with hired driver,

called for them just after nightfall. It took a quarter of an hour or so to reach Maxwell's estate. The huge house was ablaze with lights, and colored lanterns had been hung in the trees along the drive that curved up to the front door. The first time Clay had seen the house, he had been following the man who had met with Atticus Bromley just before Bromley's murder. Had that man been Gideon Maxwell, or some subordinate? They would soon know, Clay told himself. He would recognize the man from Cochran's tavern.

A line of carriages was waiting at the porticoed entrance, letting off men and women in fancy dress that put Clay in mind of the British lords and ladies he had seen once in an illustrated book. Looking down at his own finery, he felt like an utter fraud. As the carriage pulled up to the entrance, Clay fingered the stock around his neck and muttered, "I reckon I'd rather go up against a bunch of angry Blackfeet than face this mob."

"Nonsense," Markham said. "This is the cream of Washington society."

"I know it," Clay said bleakly. "That's what I mean."

"It'll be all right," Jeff told him. "Come on, let's see what we can find out."

The carriage door was opened by a servant in extravagant red livery and a powdered wig. The three men stepped down from the vehicle and joined the cluster of guests making their way inside the mansion. More servants were waiting at the door to take their hats. Clay was more than willing to surrender his, and he didn't much care if he ever got it back.

Music filled the air as they walked across a luxurious entrance hall into a large room with a vaulted ceiling. The room was lit by a dozen or more crystal chandeliers. The light was so dazzling that Clay blinked several times as he and Jeff and Markham strolled in. The room was crowded with people, but they hadn't gone more than a few steps when an attentive servant arrived at their side carrying a tray bearing three glasses of pale, sparkling champagne.

Markham took a sip from his glass and murmured, "This reminds me of stories my father told me about the grand parties that used to take place in my family's mansion in Boston, during the time of the War of Independence."

That was the first hint Markham had dropped about his personal history, but at the moment Clay wasn't interested. His nerves were as taut as a bowstring. His eyes darted around the room, searching for some sign of the man he had seen talking to Bromley in the tavern.

A string quartet was playing in a corner of the ballroom, but the music could barely be heard above the laughter and conversation and the clink of glasses. After a moment Markham suggested, "Perhaps we should split up. That way we can mingle better with the crowd."

Clay wasn't sure he wanted to mingle — but he had to admit the lieutenant probably had a point. And anything that would speed things up suited him just fine. He nodded and said, "All right. Be careful, Markham."

The young man smiled broadly. "Of course."

As Markham moved off through the crowd, Jeff leaned closer to Clay and said, "I'll bet he's looking for Maxwell's daughter. The perfume on that note went right to his head."

Clay smiled grimly. "I reckon you're right. But that might come in handy, too, so I hope he finds her."

"Good evening, gentlemen. You would be Mr. Holt and Mr. Holt?" said a male but rather high-pitched voice behind them.

Clay and Jeff turned, and it took every bit of Clay's self-control to keep his surprise from showing on his face. The last time he had seen the short, stockily built man before him was when he trailed him from Cochran's.

They had found the man they were looking for — just like that.

"I'm Clay Holt," he forced himself to say, "and this is my brother Jeff."

The man gave a half-bow, and the light from the chandeliers reflected brightly on his bald, pink head. He was dressed as fancily as Clay and Jeff, but his bearing was that of a servant, Clay thought. He confirmed that a second later when he said, "Mr. Maxwell sends his compliments and asks that you join him for a drink in the library."

"Who are you?" Clay asked bluntly.

"My name is Sumner, sir," the man replied. "I am Mr. Maxwell's butler."

"Oh." Clay didn't know what else to say.

Jeff stepped smoothly into the breach. "It would be our pleasure to join Mr. Maxwell."

"Then if the two of you would follow me . . ." Sumner murmured as he turned toward the far side of the room.

Clay and Jeff glanced at each other, then followed.

Clay's mind was racing. He hadn't known whether or not the man he had followed here several days earlier was Gideon Maxwell, so the revelation of Sumner's identity was not an unexpected surprise. But the fact that

Sumner was the man with whom Bromley had met did not mean Maxwell himself was now above suspicion; he could have ordered the killing.

Sumner led them through the crowd to a mahogany door. He grasped the gilded knob and turned it, opening the door and stepping back so that Clay and Jeff could precede him. They stepped into a room that was small and intimate, only a fraction the size of the ballroom. The walls were lined with bookshelves filled with leather-bound volumes. Clay had never seen so many books in his life, and his first impulse — irrelevant though it might have been — was to ask the man standing on the other side of the room if he had actually read all of them.

"Come in, come in, gentlemen," the man in the library said heartily as the door closed softly behind them. "Welcome. I'm Gideon Maxwell." He put aside the drink he was holding and extended his hand to Clay. "And you'd be Clay Holt, the famous mountain man."

"Don't know about the famous part, but I'm Clay Holt, all right," Clay said as he shook Maxwell's hand.

Maxwell turned to Jeff and shook hands with him as well. "And Jefferson Holt," he said. "I've heard a great deal about your business activities down in North Carolina and Tennessee, Mr. Holt. You're quite an entrepreneur."

"Just a fellow trying to make an honest living," Jeff said with a grin.

Maxwell chuckled. "Aren't we all?"

That's what we're here to find out, Clay thought. He studied Maxwell covertly. The man was a couple of inches shorter than Clay and appeared to be in a very vital and active middle age. His skin had a healthy glow, and his movements were crisp. His dark hair was liberally shot through with iron gray, and he had a neatly trimmed mustache above his wide mouth. Even as Clay studied Maxwell, he sensed that the man's dark eyes were appraising him as well.

Maxwell turned briefly to the desk on which he had set his glass and picked it up again. He said, "I see you already have champagne. I hope you'll join me in drinking a toast."

"Of course," Jeff said. "What are we drinking to?"

Maxwell lifted his glass. "The future, gentlemen. Let's drink to the future."

Clay and Jeff lifted their glasses, then sipped their champagne.

"Now I really must apologize," Maxwell went on. "It was terribly bad manners to send you an invitation to this little party at such a late date. I didn't discover that you were in Washington until recently, though, and I hoped you'd be generous enough to attend anyway."

"It's our pleasure," Jeff said with an easy smile. Once again Clay was glad his brother was here to handle chores like this small talk. Clay had never been good at such niceties.

"What brings you to our nation's capital?" Maxwell asked. "If there's any way I can be of assistance . . ."

"Everything's already settled," Jeff said. "We came here to clear up some questions about a land grant that was due Clay because of his service with the Corps of Discovery."

Maxwell turned toward Clay. "That's right. I was told you accompanied Captain Clark and the late Captain Lewis on their daring journey. That must have been quite exciting."

"It was . . . a very interesting time," Clay said.

"Was there some question about the land grant you were to receive?"

"I didn't get it at all," Clay said bluntly. "Not for a long time, anyway. Then I got a letter from Captain Lewis that he wrote before he died, telling me about the mistake that'd been made, and I figured I'd better come up here and straighten it all out." Earlier, he and Jeff had decided that if Maxwell asked them, they would tell the truth about their trip to Washington — up to the point at which the letter from Thomas Jefferson had arrived.

"And now everything's been taken care of?"

Clay nodded. Jeff said, "Clay's grant was approved and recorded."

"So now you're a country squire," Maxwell said. "I have an estate in Virginia myself where I'm building a new house. Where is your land, Clay?" He had progressed easily and quickly to that familiarity.

"It's in a valley between two mountain ranges," Clay said, the words taking him back to the place he loved best in the world, "where a river runs and the air smells of pine trees and wildflowers and there are antelope and moose and beaver everywhere you look. But it's not really my land, no matter what the government says. It belongs to Wakan Tanka, the Creator, the Great Spirit, and He's good enough to let me live on it."

A faint smile curved Maxwell's lips. "You're a poet, Clay. It sounds like a beautiful place."

"It is," Clay said with an emphatic nod.

"And I mean no offense, Mr. Maxwell, but I wish I was there right now."

"So do I," Maxwell said. "I'd love to see it. Perhaps I will someday." He took another sip of his drink. "By the way, call me Gideon. I'm not a man to stand on formality. I've taken too many hard knocks in my life for such nonsense."

Jeff looked around. "You wound up in a nice place, no matter where you started out."

"True. But I worked hard for every luxury you see around you, gentlemen."

"A fellow has to work for something before he knows what it's really worth," Clay said.

"I couldn't agree more. That's why I don't intend to ever let anyone take anything that's mine away from me."

Clay couldn't tell if this was more small talk or if the conversation had taken a significant turn. He had no time to ponder the question, however, because the library door opened again and Sumner stepped diffidently into the room and said to Maxwell, "Your other special guests have arrived, sir."

"Excellent! Show them in, Sumner."

"Yes, sir." The butler gave another little bow and disappeared.

Maxwell said to Clay and Jeff, "I've taken the liberty of asking three of my friends to join us here in private for a drink, gentlemen."

"That's fine, Gideon," Jeff said. "You're certainly making us feel at home."

It would take more than a glass of champagne and some fancy manners that didn't really mean anything to do that, Clay thought. But he said nothing. A moment later Sumner reappeared, opening the door and then stepping back. Three men came into the room, all of them middle-aged and prosperous-looking.

"Clay and Jeff Holt," Maxwell said as he moved forward to greet the men, "allow me to introduce my friends: Charles Emory, Louis Haines, and Morgan Ralston, all honorable members of that august body, the United States Senate."

Chapter Sixteen

Lieutenant John Markham moved easily through the ballroom, sipping from his drink and nodding pleasantly to the people he passed. As he had told Clay and Jeff earlier, this party brought back memories, though not of occasions he himself had experienced. By the time the American Revolution was over and the United States had won its freedom from Britain, the fortune that had once belonged to the Markham family had been lost. The Beacon Hill mansion in which Markham's Tory grandparents, Benjamin and Polly, had entertained hundreds of guests belonged to someone else now. But Markham's father, Elliot, had told him many stories about those exciting days before and during the struggle for independence, and Markham remembered them well. It was the legacy he had received from his father — a legacy not of wealth but of patriotism and love of adventure — that had led him to enlist in the army and then volunteer for this secret mission. He was carrying on a family tradition.

"Good evening. Have we met?"

The woman's voice, low and husky, broke into Markham's thoughts. She had spoken from behind him, and he wasn't sure if she was addressing him or someone else. He turned around anyway, and as he did, he caught a whiff of perfume. The scent was familiar. It had clung to the note he received inviting him to this party.

"I beg your pardon," he said. "Were you speaking to me?"

"I certainly was," said the young woman who stood there with a champagne glass in her hand and a welcoming smile on her face. "We haven't met, have we?"

Markham shook his head, too stunned by her loveliness to speak.

"Then you must be Lieutenant Markham," she went on. "I believe I know everyone else here."

He swallowed hard and managed to say, "I'm John Markham."

She extended a hand. "Diana Maxwell."

Markham took her hand, marveling at the cool smoothness of the long, slender fingers. He bent and pressed his lips to the back of her hand, then continued holding her fingers as he straightened and met her bold gaze.

She was almost as tall as he, with long, thick hair the color of fresh honey pulled back from a high forehead and framing a face that was striking in its beauty. Her brown eyes were flecked with gold. She wore a long, classically styled gown of cream-colored satin with short, puffed sleeves and a daring neckline that dipped low to reveal the white swells of her breasts. A broad sash of gold silk was cinched just under her breasts. John Markham had never seen a more beautiful woman in his life.

"Diana," he murmured. "The name suits you."

"Goddess of the hunt," she said with a smile. "Is that what I look like to you, Lieutenant Markham?"

"I . . . I would be thrilled to be hunted by a lady of your beauty, Miss Maxwell."

"And when I drove my arrow through your heart?"

"I would die a happy man," Markham declared.

Diana Maxwell laughed as she slipped her fingers from Markham's grasp, and the sound was sweeter to him than the music that filled the air. He had never felt anything like this before. He was enchanted, bewitched, completely overwhelmed by whatever spell she had cast on him . . .

He was also here to do a job, he remembered, and with an effort he forced his thoughts back to the assignment that had brought him to the Maxwell mansion.

He took a sip of champagne and said, "I appreciate your inviting me tonight. I've heard about these parties your father gives, but I never expected to be invited to one of them."

"And why not?" Diana asked. "Father and I enjoy the company of ambitious young men . . . in different ways, of course." Her smile was bold, flirtatious. "Are you an ambitious young man, Lieutenant Markham?"

"Definitely," he answered without hesitation. "I'm also curious. Is this party meant to celebrate any particular occasion?"

She shrugged elegantly. "What's wrong with simply celebrating life?"

"Nothing at all," Markham said. "I just thought perhaps there was a specific reason —"

Diana wrinkled her nose. "Oh, Father is concluding some business deal or other. I pay little attention to such matters, Lieutenant."

"I'd be honored if you would call me John," Markham said, knowing that he was being forward but not really caring.

Diana seemed to take no offense at his boldness. "All right," she said forthrightly, "but only if you call me Diana."

"It would be my *great* pleasure," he breathed. Then he swallowed again and once more forced his thoughts back to the job at hand. "A business deal, you say."

"Yes, something Father's involved in with some friends of his from the Senate." Diana sounded vaguely bored now, as if the idea of her father being associated with some of the most powerful politicians in the land meant nothing to her. "If you're interested in the details, I'll introduce you to Father. I'm sure he'd be glad to discuss the subject with you at great length. However, I can think of more . . . interesting ways to pass the time."

"Such as?"

Diana gave him a sidelong glance. "A walk in the garden?"

Markham couldn't believe his luck. Most men would have killed for an opportunity to walk through a garden in the moonlight with a lovely creature like Diana. He set his glass down on a side table and offered her his arm. "I would be honored, Miss Maxwell."

"Diana," she reminded him as she set her own glass next to his.

"Diana," he said, savoring the way the name rolled off his tongue. That was pleasurable enough, but nowhere near as thrilling as the soft warmth of her body as she linked her arm with his and they walked toward the large French doors at the rear of the ballroom. He felt the tender swell of her breast pressing against his arm, and the heat of her flesh was searing, even through their clothes.

He forgot completely about the senators Diana had mentioned.

"Gentlemen, these are two new valued friends of mine from the frontier of our great land, Clay and Jeff Holt." Gideon Maxwell was completing introductions in the library.

Clay and Jeff stepped forward to shake hands with the three politicians. Charles Emory was the tallest and slenderest of the trio, with gray hair curled tightly on his head. Louis Haines was considerably shorter, with thinning hair and a neat beard. The third man, Morgan Ralston, had a thick shock of pure white hair, a barrel chest, and a ruddy face. There was a trace of a southern accent in his voice as he said, "It's a pleasure to meet you, gentlemen."

"The pleasure is ours, Senator," Jeff said. "I believe you represent the state of Georgia?"

"That is correct, Mr. Holt. You and I are almost neighbors. I know that you're one of the most important businessmen in North Carolina."

"Jeff is a modest man, Morgan," Gideon Maxwell said. "He doesn't like to talk about his accomplishments."

Senator Emory spoke up. "Well, I for one would like to hear about the other Mr. Holt's exploits in the west. You're quite the frontiersman, aren't you, Mr. Holt?"

"I'm just a fellow who enjoys living in the high country, Senator," Clay said. "Nothing special about that."

Emory shook his head and said, "I'm not so sure. There are probably thousands of people who would like to go west and start new lives as you've done, Mr. Holt, but they lack the daring to even attempt such a harsh and dangerous existence. Still, for those who do, the rewards must be great. I'm told the mountain lands beyond the Great American Desert are some of the most beautiful in the world."

Clay could only agree. "That they are, sir."

"It's prime land for expansion, if you ask me," Haines said in his growling voice. "But only if we can get rid of those damned Indians, of course. Until they're gone, the west won't be a fit place for decent folks to live."

Clay's fingers tightened on the stem of his glass. He had to force his muscles to relax before the glass shattered in his hands. He had heard such ridiculous opinions expressed before, of course, but that didn't make them any less annoying. And it was particularly galling that a United States congressman would be so bigoted and narrow-minded.

"A lot of the Indians just want to get along with the whites, Senator," he said, keeping his voice level. "Like my wife's people. They figure Wakan Tanka made the world plenty big enough for everyone to live in peace."

"You're married to a squaw, Holt?" There was an unmistakable sneer in Haines's tone, even if there wasn't one on his face.

"My wife is a woman of the Teton Sioux," Clay replied.

"Who's this Wakan Tanka you mentioned? Some other redskin?"

Gideon Maxwell interceded smoothly. "I believe Wakan Tanka is the Indian name for the Almighty, Louis. They believe in a Great Spirit, just as we do."

"I thought they were all heathens," Haines snorted.

"Gentlemen, let's save our fussing for the floor of the Senate," Morgan Ralston said with a smile. "You can't judge a whole people on the basis of rumors, and none of us except Clay and Jeff here have ever been to the land in question and know the people who live there."

Haines still wore a combative expression on his bulldog face, but he simply nodded and said to Clay, "I mean no offense, Holt."

"None taken," Clay lied.

Maxwell was pouring champagne for the trio of senators. He handed the glasses around and said, "Clay and Jeff and I drank to the future a little while ago. I'd like to repeat that toast and add: To the riches it may bring all of us."

"Hear, hear," Emory said. He lifted his glass, as did the other two politicians, and Clay and Jeff joined in. Clay didn't bother to conceal his reluctance to drink with Louis Haines.

At the same time, he focused on what he and Jeff had discovered so far tonight. They had yet to find anything positively linking Maxwell with the land grab conspiracy, but the fact that Maxwell apparently had three United States senators under his influence said a great deal about the man's power. Clay wasn't convinced that Emory, Haines, and Ralston were simply friends of Maxwell's. One or more of them could be involved in the plot to control the west. Having a senator or two on his side to help him cover his tracks would certainly make it easier for Maxwell to attempt such a bold scheme.

Clay was anxious to discuss the situation

with Jeff in private and see if his brother had reached the same conclusions. That would probably have to wait until they were in the carriage on the way back to the Copper Gable, though.

And then there was Lieutenant Markham, and any pertinent facts *he* might have uncovered tonight . . .

He was going to kiss her. He was definitely going to kiss her. She wanted him to. He was sure of it. She had walked arm in arm with him into the carefully kept garden behind the mansion and commented on how beautiful the moonlight was and leaned close to him as they sat on a stone bench and . . . and by God, he was going to kiss her, right now!

"You know, John, I've been thinking."

Her words, cool and calm, stopped him just as he was about to lean in and press his lips to hers. She didn't appear to notice what she had forestalled. Markham shook his head a little and took a deep breath, then hoped his voice sounded relatively normal as he said, "What were you thinking, Diana?"

"Do you know that my father is having a new house built on some property he owns in Virginia? It will be our country estate."

"That sounds lovely," Markham said,

wondering how that concerned him.

Diana didn't keep him waiting long. She said, "We're leaving tomorrow to spend a few days there, and several of our friends are coming along. I'd be pleased to have you join us, John."

The invitation took him by surprise. He had come to the party expecting nothing more than a chance to find out a little more about Gideon Maxwell. The opportunity he had just been offered to spend several days in the man's company far exceeded anything he'd hoped for. If he accepted, he could try to work his way into Maxwell's inner circle, where he had no doubt he would find the evidence he and the Holt brothers needed to prove that Maxwell was involved in the land grab scheme.

Besides, with Diana looking at him like that, with the silvery moonlight illuminating her face, there was no way he could refuse anything she asked, even if he wanted to — and he didn't.

"Of course I'll come. It would be an honor to join you. But are you certain your father won't mind that you didn't speak to him about it first?"

Diana laughed. "Father knows better than to deny me something I really want. He's taught me well in that regard." She placed a hand on Markham's arm. "Don't worry, John. Father won't mind. I'm sure he'll be happy to have you come along with us."

"Who else is coming?" Markham asked, thinking about Clay and Jeff. If he could manage to get them invited as well, so much the better.

"Several politicians who are involved with Father in business," Diana answered, "and they'll be bringing their families along, too. Some other friends. All the guests will be respected members of Washington society."

Except me, Markham thought. *I'll be the odd man out.* But he would go anyway. "I'll try to fit in," he said to Diana.

She leaned close to him again. "I'm sure you'll have no trouble at all," she murmured. "I'm glad you're going, John. The other guests can be rather tedious sometimes, and I've been dreading the trip, but now I'm actually looking forward to it."

"So am I," he said. She was so close he could feel the warmth of her breath on his cheek. All he had to do was turn his head slightly, and his lips would be only an inch from hers.

"John . . . ?"

He turned his head. "Yes?"

"Please kiss me."

Markham was glad to oblige.

Her lips were as warm and sweet and inviting as he had known they would be. His arms went around her and drew her against him. She clasped her arms around his neck. Markham's pulse thundered in his head, and he was shaken to the core by the intensity of the kiss. At that moment the world could have come crashing down around him and he scarcely would have noticed.

Diana pulled back just enough to break the kiss. "Thank you, John," she whispered.

"Th-thank you?" he managed to repeat hoarsely. He hadn't expected an expression of gratitude. If anyone should be thanking someone, it was he!

"For not disappointing me. As soon as I saw you standing there in the ballroom, I knew you were special." She smiled. "I don't bring every young man who attends Father's parties into the garden and ask him to kiss me, you know."

"You don't? . . . I mean, of course you don't. And I . . . I'm glad."

She slipped out of his embrace and stood up. "Come," she said. "I want to tell Father that you'll be going with us to the country tomorrow."

"All right." Markham would have liked to linger, perhaps to kiss the lady once more and hold her soft form. But he had to meet

Gideon Maxwell sooner or later, and now was probably as good a time as any. He sighed, stood up, and offered Diana his arm.

Pipes were brought out soon after the toast had been drunk. Maxwell kept his guests engaged in small talk. None of the men seemed anxious to return to the party. Morgan Ralston, in fact, was blunt enough to say, "I'd just as soon my wife dance with some of those young bucks from the House of Representatives that Gideon always invites. This old leg of mine hasn't been the same since I got thrown from a balky horse a couple of years ago." He slapped his right thigh.

"And I hear enough talk of politics every day the Senate's in session," Charles Emory said. He was sprawled in a well-padded armchair, long legs thrust out in front of him, pipe in one hand, brandy snifter in the other. He looked completely at ease.

Ralston helped himself to some brandy, then said to Clay, "You haven't told us yet about life on the frontier."

Clay glanced at Senator Haines, who was sitting in an armchair near the fireplace, unlit on this warm night. Haines caught the look and smiled coldly. "Go ahead, Holt," he said. "I promise not to say anything about those savages you seem to care so much about."

"Some of them *are* savages, Senator," Clay said, ignoring the warning look that Jeff gave him. "You're right about that. I've seen a man after the Blackfoot have peeled just about every bit of skin off his body, one strip at a time — while he was still alive."

Haines grimaced. "Good God, man, that's barbaric!"

Clay nodded. "I reckon it is."

"And yet you defend them, after seeing what they do to white men who are unlucky enough to fall into their hands."

"Didn't say it was a white man the Blackfoot did that to. As a matter of fact, it was a Crow. Of course, the Crow do things just as bad to Blackfoot captives they take. Maybe even worse."

Emory sat up and leaned forward. "I thought the Indians were all supposed to be noble savages. They get along with each other and live in harmony with the land. At least that's what some of the natural scientists would have us believe."

Ralston laughed before Clay could say anything. "No race of man is entirely noble, Charles. For God's sake, you've served in the Senate long enough to know that."

"Yes, yes, but I thought the tribes were all friendly to each other," Emory persisted.

"The different bands have been fighting with each other for as long as the rivers have been running, Senator," Clay explained. "They've enslaved each other and wiped each other out since long before we ever crossed the Mississippi. In the eyes of the tribes that are unfriendly to us, we're just one more enemy to be defeated, no different from all the others."

Haines jabbed his pipestem toward Clay. "They'll find out how wrong they are. Once people who know what they're doing get hold of the west, you'll see how these things should be handled. I hate to speak ill of the dead, but I never thought that Meriwether Lewis should have been appointed governor of the Louisiana Territory, and I said so on the floor of the Senate. It's just as well that he blew his brains out. He was always too damned soft on the Indians. Clark's just as bad."

Clay and Jeff exchanged glances, and Clay could tell his brother was thinking the same thing: Haines was all but confessing that he had a motive for wanting Meriwether Lewis dead. As far as Clay had been able to figure, Lewis had never been particularly sympathetic to the Indians; he had wanted them treated fairly, no more and no less. But to a man of Haines's convictions, anyone who believed in even that narrow concept of justice was soft.

Had Meriwether Lewis and his ideas been an obstacle in the way of Haines's plans? Clay wondered.

Before the discussion could go any further, the library door opened. Clay and Jeff turned, expecting to see the butler Sumner. Instead, Lieutenant Markham stood there, next to a lovely young woman with honey-blond hair. She glided into the room, towing Markham along behind her. The lieutenant wore a sheepish smile.

"Father, this is that young officer you were advised to invite by the commander at Fort McHenry. Lieutenant John Markham, this is my father, Gideon Maxwell."

Maxwell stuck out his hand. "Pleased to meet you, Lieutenant. Please, come in and join us. We were just having a drink and discussing the Indian problem in the west."

"No politics, Father," the young woman said firmly. "Tonight was supposed to be strictly for pleasure, remember?"

Senator Ralston came over and gave her an avuncular kiss on the cheek. "For some of us, politics *is* pleasure," he said with a grin.

Maxwell turned to Clay and Jeff. "Gentlemen, I don't believe you've met my daughter, Diana. Diana, this is Clay Holt and Jefferson Holt, two new friends."

She greeted them with a dazzling smile, then asked, "And do you two gentlemen know Lieutenant Markham?"

"We met earlier this evening," Jeff said. He and Clay had decided to keep their relationship with Markham as vague as possible. That way, if Gideon Maxwell were to figure out that the Holts were investigating him, he was less likely to suspect the lieutenant as well.

Diana Maxwell turned back to her father. "I've invited Lieutenant Markham to join us on the outing to Virginia tomorrow, Father."

Maxwell nodded. "An excellent idea. In fact . . ." He turned a speculative gaze toward Clay and Jeff. "Would you gentlemen care to accompany us as well? We're going to be out in the country for several days, camping at the site of my new house. The senators and their families are going, and there'll be plenty of hunting and fishing and picnicking. I can promise you a good time, and the scenery is spectacular. Not quite the wilderness to which you're accustomed, Clay, but the nearest thing you'll find around here."

The idea sounded appealing to Clay for more than one reason. He and Jeff had been cooped up in Washington the past few weeks, spending their time indoors rather than out in the open air. The trip through the Virginia countryside to Monticello had been the highlight of their stay so far. But the most important reason to accept Maxwell's invitation, of course, was to take advantage of the opportunity to find out more about him and his friends from the Senate. Perhaps by the time Clay and Jeff returned from the outing, they would have the proof they needed against Maxwell and, possibly, one or more of the politicians. Clay glanced at Jeff and knew the same thoughts had gone through his brother's head.

"That sounds like a mighty fine idea," he said to Maxwell.

"Very good," Maxwell said. "The carriages will be leaving from here tomorrow morning —"

"We'd just as soon take our own horses, if that's all right with you," Clay said. He wanted to be able to move quickly if the need arose.

Maxwell nodded affably. "Certainly. Whatever you gentlemen wish. You can ride with us out to Forestwood. That's the name of my estate. It's my hope that someday it will rival

President Jefferson's Monticello."

"We've heard a lot about Monticello," Jeff said, hoping to imply that they had never been there.

Maxwell turned to Markham. "And what about you, Lieutenant? Will you travel by horseback, or would you prefer to go with us in the carriages?"

Markham glanced at Diana and said without hesitation, "If there's room, I'll travel with you, sir."

"Of course. The more the merrier, as the saying goes."

Clay wanted to believe that Markham had decided to travel with the Maxwells because of the assignment that had brought the three of them here tonight. He had noticed the look Markham gave Diana Maxwell, though, and he knew better. The young officer was smitten with Diana. As long as Markham's infatuation didn't interfere with the investigation, that was fine.

But Clay hoped grimly that the day would not come when Markham was forced to choose between the job they had been given . . . and Diana Maxwell.

Chapter Seventeen

The first thing she had to do, Melissa Holt thought, was to make sure that no more cargoes bound for the emporium and the trade route with Tennessee "disappeared." She sat Ned and India down in the study one afternoon and asked them point-blank, "Do the March ships sail under arms?"

Ned frowned. "They're not warships, Melissa. Each vessel carries a small cannon for emergencies —"

"Such as being attacked by pirates?"

"The days when pirates roamed the Spanish Main are virtually over and done with, Melissa," India said. "There are no Blackbeards or Henry Morgans around these days."

Melissa stood up, unable to sit still, and restlessly paced back and forth behind the desk. "Perhaps they don't fly the Jolly Roger in this day and age," she said, "but there are still pirates, India. They sail under the flag of so-called reputable companies instead."

As she spoke, the image of Philip Rattigan filled her mind. She could picture him on the

356

deck of a pirate ship, cutlass in hand, shirt open to the waist and revealing a broad, muscular chest, the skull-and-crossbones flapping from the mast above him. The vision resembled an illustration she had seen in a book, and she smiled as she shook her head to clear it. She turned to face Ned and India.

"I'm going to suggest to Lemuel March that he arm his ships more heavily and make sure that the sailors who man them know how to fight," she said. "You may have to give him a hand in that respect, Ned. I have complete faith in you and India, and I know Lemuel does, too."

"I suppose adding a few more cannon won't hurt anything. I've heard rumors that the British privateers are getting more and more daring in their attacks against American ships," India commented.

"I'm only worried about one certain Englishman," Melissa said, then instantly regretted her candor in referring to Rattigan. She hurried on, "Then there's the matter of guarding the warehouses here in town until we can get the goods into the store or loaded on freight wagons."

Ned said, "Most of the warehouses have night watchmen."

"That didn't stop one of them from burning down, did it?" Melissa asked sharply. "I want real guards posted, not just watchmen. I wish we had our own warehouse, instead of being forced to rent space from other people, but until we can afford that, we'll have to do the next best thing, which is to make sure our goods are protected." She took a deep breath. "I'm going to speak to Terence O'Shay about that."

"O'Shay?" Ned exclaimed. "The man's a criminal!"

Melissa smiled slightly. "A smuggler, perhaps, but he was a good friend to Jeff. And he helped catch my father's killer. He has enough connections with the rough element in this town that he can provide some excellent guards for us."

"You'll be lucky if O'Shay and his friends don't clean out any warehouses you set them to guarding," Ned growled. "I'll admit he's a likable sort, but you can't trust him, Melissa."

Dryly India commented, "Of course, I've heard the same thing said of you more than once, Ned."

Ned scowled, then shrugged. "All right," he said to Melissa. "Talk to O'Shay. I suppose it can't hurt — unless he steals you blind. But Jeff *did* save his life, so he may feel he owes you something."

Melissa smiled, trying to appear more confident than she felt. "At least we're taking steps to improve the situation. I'll write immediately to Lemuel and outline our plans to him. I want any suggestions he may have, too, on ways we can expand our arrangement."

"God knows I'm no businessman," Ned said, "but should you be talking about expanding when the business is already having trouble?"

"Sometimes a bit of daring is needed, something that no one expects." Melissa thought again of Philip Rattigan. "There are certain people in the world whom I'd very much like to catch by surprise . . ."

Within a week Melissa had made arrangements with Terence O'Shay. The big Irishman had agreed to provide guards for every warehouse in which Holt-Merrivale goods were stored. O'Shay's men took over the cargoes as soon as they were unloaded from the ships and supervised their transport to the warehouses. The merchandise was guarded continuously until it reached the shelves of the emporium. O'Shay had given Melissa his personal guarantee that the goods would be safe.

"Jeff claims I paid any debt I owed him

when I helped him get out of jail and find your father's murderer," O'Shay told her, "but I know it's going to take more than that to repay the boyo. Anything else you need, ma'am, you just let me know."

What Melissa really needed was time, she thought, time to set all her affairs in order before Jeff returned from Washington. To her surprise, she got it. The days passed with no sign of her husband, and she began to wonder what had happened to delay him. She was sure he was all right, or she would have heard otherwise. He and Clay had probably run into trouble dealing with the Washington bureaucracy. Melissa had suspected that that might happen, which was why she had suggested that Jeff accompany his brother in the first place.

Still, though she was glad to have the opportunity to put her plans in motion before Jeff got back, she missed him. She wanted to hear his voice and feel his touch, wanted to wake in the morning and see his face and know that they would be together forever. The long separation they had endured before had been miserable. Melissa never wanted to go through anything like that again.

The solution to her loneliness, she knew, was to keep busy. She spent part of nearly every day at the emporium, making certain the shelves were once again full of merchandise. Ned and India sometimes went with her, but not always, and she was alone the morning she pulled her buggy to a stop in front of the emporium and saw Philip Rattigan standing on the porch.

He stepped forward quickly and reached up to assist her. Not wanting to make a scene in public, Melissa allowed him to take her arm as she climbed down from the buggy. "Thank you, Captain Rattigan," she said when her feet were planted firmly on the cobblestone street. She looked down pointedly at his fingers where they rested on her arm. "I believe I can manage very well from here."

"In that case, let me see to your horse," he offered, and before she could stop him, he had let go of her and caught hold of the horse's reins. He tied them swiftly and firmly to the hitching post in front of the store. "There you are," he said as he turned back to her. "That animal's not going anywhere until you're ready."

"Thank you again. You're too kind," she murmured. She started toward the steps that led up to the porch, intending to go around him.

Almost lazily, he moved in front of her. She swallowed her irritation, determined not to let him get the better of her. "Excuse me," she said.

He linked his arm with hers. "Allow me."

"That's not necessary."

"I insist." He walked with her up the steps.

Melissa stopped and turned to confront him when they reached the top step. "Is there something I can do for you?" she asked. "Are you here on business, or did you just happen to be passing by?"

A smile split his face as he said, "I wouldn't try to lie to you, Mrs. Holt. I didn't just happen to be in the neighborhood. I came to see you."

"What for?" Melissa asked him bluntly. "Did you want to discuss a business arrangement between your shipping line and my company? Because if you do, I have to tell you I'm perfectly satisfied with Lemuel March and his ships."

She didn't really believe that was the reason for his presence, so she wasn't surprised when he said, "Not at all. I'm as happy with Corbett as you are with March. No, I simply came to see you as a friend, since I'm a bit worried about you."

"Worried about me?" That *did* surprise Melissa. She went on, "And I wasn't aware that you and I are friends, Captain Rattigan."

"My name's Philip. My mates called me

Phil when I was a lad, but I don't much care for it. As for the two of us being friends . . . that's something I *would* like."

The boldness in his eyes prompted her to summon up a modicum of outraged dignity. She drew herself up straight and said, "You forget yourself, Captain. I'm a married woman."

"I didn't forget that for a second . . . unfortunately." He paused and drew a deep breath. "Allow me to start over. We're both business people. In that spirit, I'd like to share a concern I have about one of your current activities."

"What activity would that be?" Melissa asked coolly.

"The hiring of men who are nothing more than common cutthroats."

Melissa fought to keep her face and voice neutral. "You're talking about the men guarding Holt-Merrivale goods in the warehouses?"

"I'm talking about Terence O'Shay's men. They're nothing but bloody criminals!"

"So far, Captain Rattigan, they've been excellent employees," Melissa said crisply, "even if they *were* recommended to me by Mr. O'Shay. I simply don't want any more buildings to burn down, and I'm prepared to take whatever steps are necessary to ensure that doesn't happen."

She could see the frustration on Rattigan's face. He snapped, "You're playing with fire, do you know that?"

"As I just explained, that's exactly what I'm trying to avoid."

"All right." He took a deep breath. "I can see you're going to be stubborn about this. Jeremiah warned me you would be."

"Mr. Corbett doesn't know me very well, Captain Rattigan. Certainly not well enough to make such judgments. And neither do you."

"I can see it with my own eyes," Rattigan shot back. "You think you know more than anyone else, and you're accustomed to getting your own way."

Melissa turned toward the door and tried to move around him, only to have him shift position so that once again he blocked her path. She glared at him and exclaimed, "Will you *stop* doing that?"

"See, you've proven my point. You don't like it when someone crosses you."

"I don't like it when someone is rude to me." Melissa looked around. The street was fairly busy, with several men in earshot. "And if you don't get out of my way," she went on, "I'm going to have to call for assistance. I may even summon the constable and have you arrested!"

He gave her his lazy, maddening smile. "What're the charges, guv'nor?"

"Being the most annoying man I've ever met! Will that suffice for charges?"

Instead of answering her, he moved to one side. "I can see I'm wasting my time here. Good day to you, Mrs. Holt."

"Good day, Captain," she said tightly. She stood where she was, glaring at him and waiting until he had turned away before she started into the store.

There had been nothing sincere about his visit here today, she told herself. He hadn't come because he was concerned about her. He wasn't worried that O'Shay's men might rob her. What bothered him was the fact that it would be much more difficult for him and Corbett to sabotage her business with the guards she now had working for her. She was fighting back, and Captain Philip Rattigan didn't like that one bit.

He had better get used to it, she told herself fiercely, because she wasn't going to let anyone ruin her business without a fight. No matter how handsome he was or how charming he tried to be . . .

When Melissa got home that afternoon, she found a visitor waiting for her. A tall, distinguished-looking man stood up from one of the chairs in the parlor, where he had been talking to Hermione, Ned, and India, and held out his hands. "Melissa!" he greeted her. "It's so good to see you again."

She caught her breath in surprise as she stepped forward to take his hands. "Hello, Lemuel," she said. "It's wonderful to see you, too. But what brings you to Wilmington?"

Lemuel March smiled. "Business, of course. I received your letter and caught the first ship down here. These matters are too important not to discuss face to face."

"You're probably right." Melissa took off her bonnet and shawl and handed them to a waiting servant.

"Sit down, dear," Hermione said, gesturing toward the other half of the divan in which she sat. "I've told the maid to bring lemonade for all of us."

That sounded good to Melissa. The afternoon was warm, and some cool lemonade would be delicious. "Thank you, Mother," she said. She sat down and turned to her visitor. "I'm glad you've come, Lemuel. We need to take action, otherwise we run the risk of being overwhelmed by Corbett and Rattigan and their unscrupulous tactics."

Lemuel settled himself again in an armchair and crossed his legs. "I've heard of this fellow Rattigan, but I don't believe we've ever met. What's he like?"

"Very arrogant, very sure of himself," Melissa said, deciding it would be better not to mention how handsome Rattigan was. That had no bearing on the discussion.

"Do you really think he would sink a ship just to hurt your emporium?"

"I've no doubt of it," Melissa answered. "He's working hand in glove with Corbett, and I'm certain Corbett would like nothing better than to see the emporium forced to close. That would leave him the leading merchant in Wilmington."

Lemuel's normally mild features hardened into a stern mask. "I'll not let any man get away with sinking one of my ships. If Rattigan's a pirate, he'll pay for what he's done."

Ned spoke up then. "In the meantime, we have to stop him from doing it again. That's why Melissa wants your ships to be better armed."

"I agree completely," Lemuel said with a firm nod, "and I've already taken steps to see to that very thing." He looked at Ned and India. "I'm going to rely on the two of you to help me hire extra crewmen who've had experience in such matters."

"We can do that," India said, "but they may be rather hard characters."

"Who better to fight piracy than pirates?" Melissa asked.

Ned smiled appreciatively. "I'm beginning to understand why you went to O'Shay. You're using the same sort of weapons against Corbett and Rattigan that they're using against you."

Melissa flushed. "I suppose that's true. But that doesn't mean we're stooping to their level. We're not going out looking for trouble, and we haven't attacked anyone else. We're simply going to defend ourselves by any means necessary."

"Otherwise we might as well give up," Lemuel said. "And I'm not prepared to do that."

"Neither am I."

Hands fluttering, Hermione said, "All this talk of trouble makes me nervous. If you'll excuse me, I'm going to see what's holding up that lemonade."

Ned and Lemuel stood as she left the room, then resumed their seats. Lemuel looked at Melissa and said, "I hope you'll pardon my curiosity, but where's Jeff? I know you mentioned in your letter that he's away, but I thought he might have returned by the time I got here. Has he gone to Tennessee with a wagon train?"

Melissa shook her head. "He's in Washington with his brother Clay. They're trying to settle some business regarding a land grant that belongs to Clay."

"I see. I know that Jeff trusts you to speak for him, Melissa, but I'd feel somewhat better about what I'm about to propose if he was here."

Melissa wasn't sure whether or not to be offended. Lemuel knew that she was the spokesman for the family business right now, but she supposed she couldn't blame him for wishing that Jeff was here. He was more accustomed to dealing with a man at the helm, as indeed most people were.

"He should be back soon," she told Lemuel. "In the meantime, if you have something else to propose, I'd very much like to hear it."

"All right." Lemuel cleared his throat. "As you know, I don't do business solely with Holt-Merrivale. I have other customers for the cargoes that are carried on my ships. However, due to both the family relationship and the profits of our arrangement, your company has become the most important customer for my line. Now, with the difficulties you've been experiencing and the general unreliability of my other accounts, I find that Holt-Merrivale's problems have had a disproportionate effect on the March Shipping Line."

"In other words, you're in trouble just as we are," Melissa said.

Lemuel smiled. "Exactly. You've summed it up quite well, my dear. In addition, the changes we're going to be making to increase the security of your cargoes will cost money."

"You're suggesting that we foot a larger share of the bill?"

Lemuel leaned forward in his chair and clasped his hands together. "What I'm suggesting is a full partnership in a new endeavor that should prove quite lucrative for everyone involved, just as you proposed in your letter."

"Expansion again," Ned muttered.

"Hush, darling," India told him, patting his hand as she, too, leaned forward. "I want to hear this."

"And I want you to hear it," Lemuel said, "because you and Ned will be a vital part of this plan, India. I think you're going to be quite interested. You've heard, of course, of the Hawaiian Islands?"

India's eyes widened in surprise. "I've been there, several years ago on an English trading ship. The islands are some of the most beautiful places I've ever seen."

"They're also the gateway to the Orient," Lemuel said. He swung his gaze back to Melissa. "The trade routes between east and west in the Pacific are just waiting to be developed. Not only that, but the Russians have established several settlements in the area northwest of Canada known as Alaska. Those settlements offer prime opportunities for trade. There are fortunes to be made in the Pacific, Melissa, fortunes!"

His excitement was contagious. Melissa felt her pulse quickening. But she knew she had to be cautious. "What you're proposing is that, in partnership with the March Shipping Line, Holt-Merrivale should try to open up trade routes in the Pacific?"

"I need your financial backing to do this," Lemuel said. "I'll not lie to you about that. You'd be putting your company, perhaps even your home, at risk. But the rewards may be enormous."

The plan sounded immensely appealing, but Melissa's practical eye perceived the obstacles immediately. "The Pacific is so far away. It took Lewis and Clark — and Holt," she added with a smile, thinking of Clay, "more than a year overland to reach the Pacific from St. Louis."

"It takes far less time than that to sail

around South America to the Pacific," Lemuel said. "Captain Cook and many others have proven it can be done. The English are already doing it, as India pointed out. But we'll have a jump on them, because we're closer. We can make more trips in the same amount of time."

Melissa wanted to make certain everything was clear in her mind. "You'd send ships to the Hawaiian Islands?"

"Aye. We'd load them with trade goods and then, when they got there, trade those goods for a cargo of sandalwood, which I'm told is in great demand in China right now."

Melissa's eyes widened. "You want to sail to China, too?"

"Why not?" Lemuel answered unhesitatingly, with the enthusiasm of the true entrepreneur. "When the ship reaches China, we can trade the sandalwood for silk and jade, which will be brought back here. We can profit at each stage of the trip."

Melissa nodded slowly. What Lemuel was saying made sense. True, the plan was a daring one, but as she had told Ned, sometimes one had to be daring in order to take a rival by surprise — and come out ahead.

"What about the Alaskan settlements?" she asked.

"I know less about them," Lemuel admitted, "but I'm told that the Russians are doing some whaling, so there will be blubber and oil to trade, as well as perhaps timber from the great forests in that territory. I'm confident that the Alaskan trade would prove profitable, too."

"I'll have to discuss this with Hermione," Melissa said, although she knew her mother would go along with whatever decision she made. She looked at Ned and India. "What do the two of you think?"

"I'd like to know what our part would be in this," India said forthrightly. "Lemuel said we would be involved, but I'm not sure how. I've no money to invest in such a plan, and Ned spends his coins as fast as he earns them."

"Now, that's not strictly true," Ned protested. "I've saved a bit."

"Enough to do more than buy a round of drinks for the patrons of the nearest tavern?"

"Well . . . perhaps not."

"I think I can answer your question, India," Melissa said with a smile. "Lemuel has anticipated one of my conditions for accepting his proposal. If everything Jeff and I have built up is going to be at risk, I want a personal representative of the Holt family to be involved. That's you, Ned, and I assume that India will wish to go along, too."

"You want me to go to the Hawaiian Islands?" Ned asked excitedly. "I've never been there. Never even been around the Cape of Good Hope."

"It's not the most pleasant passage in the world," India said dryly. "But I wouldn't mind making it again, especially if that's what you want, Melissa."

"I do," Melissa said firmly. She looked at Lemuel. "I mean no disrespect to you or your men, Lemuel. I trust you, or I wouldn't be doing business with you already. But I want Ned and India along to keep an eye on things and report back to Jeff and me."

Lemuel nodded, clearly unoffended by what she had suggested. "I think it's an excellent idea," he said. "For one thing, I'll be getting two more good sailors out of the deal." He grinned at Ned and India.

"What about China?" Ned asked. "Do we go on to China?"

"Of course. You'll be with the ship all the way back here to Wilmington."

Ned smacked his fist into his palm. "Then I'm the man for the job, Melissa. It sounds like a jolly adventure."

"Do you want to wait and talk this over with Jeff before you commit Holt-Merrivale to the venture?" Lemuel asked.

Melissa shook her head. "If my mother

agrees after I've explained it to her, I think we should move ahead with all due speed. If what you say is true, Lemuel — and I've no doubt it is — and the Pacific trade is just waiting to be developed, then the sooner we get started, the better."

"My thoughts exactly."

"There's just one more thing," Melissa added. The other three people in the room looked at her, waiting. "As far as the trade with Alaska is concerned —"

"Do you think it's too great a risk, trying to open up both routes at the same time?" Lemuel asked. "We could wait on the Alaskan settlements, I suppose, although someone might beat us to it."

Someone like Philip Rattigan, Melissa thought. "No, that's not what I meant at all. But I want the Holt family represented in that part of the enterprise as well."

Lemuel frowned. "If Ned and India are going along on the China route, whom else did you have in mind?"

"Me," Melissa said, enjoying the look of stunned disbelief that appeared on their faces. "When the first ship sails for Alaska, I intend to be on it."

Chapter Eighteen

Lieutenant Markham made no objection when Clay caught a moment alone with him and said, "Jeff and I are going to take the carriage back to the Copper Gable alone. We don't want Maxwell suspecting any ties between us."

"I agree," Markham said. "Besides, that will allow me to spend a little more time with Diana before I leave."

Clay wasn't surprised that Diana Maxwell had something to do with Markham's quick acquiescence. He was going to have to warn the young officer about the dangers of a romantic entanglement. Clay was hardly an experienced investigator, but he had enough common sense to recognize that Markham might risk their entire assignment if he became so enamored of Diana that he grew careless. If Maxwell was indeed the architect of the land grab — and Clay was convinced he was — he could have millions of dollars at stake. All it would take was one careless word on Markham's part to give away their true motives, and then Maxwell would be forced to kill them. Clay wasn't afraid of any attempt on his life, but he didn't want their important investigation ruined.

A little later, after both Holts had danced with several of Washington's society matrons and answered dozens of questions about the frontier, they sought out Gideon Maxwell to tell him they were leaving.

"So soon, gentlemen?" Maxwell asked heartily.

"You said you wanted to get an early start for Virginia in the morning," Jeff reminded him.

"Indeed I did. And so we shall. I'll bid you a good evening, then, and I'll look forward to seeing you in the morning."

The three senators were standing nearby, and they added their own farewells. Ralston was the most effusive; Emory was a bit more restrained. Senator Haines was still cool toward Clay and Jeff, but he nodded civilly and shook hands as one of Maxwell's servants brought their cloaks and beaver hats.

Clay's last sight of Lieutenant Markham was of the young man twirling around the dance floor with Diana Maxwell in his arms. He seemed totally engrossed in her, and once again Clay felt a touch of uneasiness. He hoped Thomas Jefferson hadn't made a serious mistake by arranging for Markham to assist in the investigation.

He would simply have to make sure Markham didn't prove himself a liability, Clay told himself. Once they reached Forestwood, Maxwell's estate in Virginia, he would try his best to keep Markham on a tight rein without being too obvious about it.

The night was still warm, but clouds had blown in, obscuring the stars. A faint mist floated in the air. Clay could smell the salty tang of the tidal basin as he and Jeff walked out to their carriage. The driver was dozing on the seat, and he sat up sharply as Jeff opened the door.

"Ready to go, gentlemen?" he asked.

"Yes, back to the Copper Gable Tavern, please, where you picked us up," Jeff told him.

"What about the other fella?"

Clay said, "He's not ready to leave yet, so he'll be finding his own way home."

"Yes, suh. Whatever you say."

Clay and Jeff stepped up into the carriage, and the driver got the horses moving. As the vehicle swayed and bumped gently over the cobblestone streets, Clay said in a low voice to his brother, "Markham seems to have lost his head over Maxwell's daughter."

Jeff chuckled. "She's certainly pretty enough for a young man to lose his head over. I hope he doesn't lose his wits, too, where she's concerned. Do you think she knows anything about what her father's plotting?"

"We still have no real proof that Maxwell has anything to do with the land grab," Clay pointed out.

"No, but you're as convinced as I am that he does. He sent his butler, Sumner, to meet with Atticus Bromley in that alehouse, and then Bromley wound up dead less than an hour later. That's too much of a coincidence for me to accept."

Clay nodded. "Me, too. Maxwell has to be involved in the scheme up to his neck. He may even be the leader, for all we know. And at least one of those senators is in on it with him."

"Haines," Jeff said without hesitation. "You heard the way he talked about the frontier. All he can see is the money to be made from it. He hated Meriwether Lewis, too, maybe enough to have him killed — especially if Lewis was about to expose his part in the land grab."

"Hell, they could all three be part of it," Clay replied. "That wouldn't surprise me any."

"Maybe we can find out when we join their little outing to the country."

"That's what I'm hoping," Clay said. "I'd like to get this over and done with so we can go home."

Jeff sighed. "I'll wager Melissa is wondering what happened to me. She thought I'd be back in Wilmington before now."

Clay grunted. He knew that Shining Moon was wondering the same thing. He missed her, missed seeing her and hearing the sound of her voice. And once this chore Thomas Jefferson had given them was completed, he would have farther to travel to be reunited with his wife than Jeff would have to be reunited with Melissa. Still, he didn't envy Jeff. Clay had never been to North Carolina, but he knew it couldn't equal the beauty of the high mountain valley he and Shining Moon called home.

Without warning, the carriage suddenly lurched to one side, throwing Clay and Jeff violently against the door. Luckily the latch held. The carriage quickly shuddered to a stop, tilting precariously.

"What the devil!" Clay exclaimed.

Jeff stuck his head out the window and called up to the driver, "What happened?"

The man dropped down from the seat and appeared at the window. "We done lost a wheel," he told Clay and Jeff. "Come right off the axle, it did. Don't know how that could've happened."

Clay reached through the window, grasped the door handle, and opened it. Despite the awkward angle, he and Jeff swung gracefully out of the vehicle and turned to regard it in disgust.

"We'd better get busy and get that wheel back on," Clay said. He took off his hat and tossed it into the carriage, then began shrugging off his cloak. Jeff followed suit.

"You don't have to do that, gentlemen," the driver told them. "You shouldn't be helping me fix a wheel. That's my job."

"You can't do it alone," Jeff pointed out reasonably. "It'll take the two of us to lift the carriage while you get the wheel back on the axle."

The driver looked around, apparently studying their surroundings. "Naw, you don't have to do that, suh. I got some friends in this neighborhood who'll be glad to give me a hand. It's only about six blocks on to the inn where you gentlemen are staying. Why don't you just leave me here to handle this and walk on back to the inn?"

The idea of leaving the driver in this predicament rubbed Clay the wrong way. He'd been raised to give folks a hand whenever and wherever he could. But it was late and he was tired, and the driver seemed almost to take it as an insult that he would need help from the very people he had been hired to deliver to their destination.

Jeff's thinking seemed to parallel Clay's, because he said to the driver, "If you're sure . . ."

"Yes, suh, I'm certain. The two of you just go on along home."

The Copper Gable wasn't his home, Clay thought, not by a long shot. But he nodded and said, "All right. Let's go, Jeff."

They had turned to go when the driver called after them, "Here now, don't forget your hats."

Clay wouldn't have missed the beaver top hat if he had left it behind. The only thing he ever felt truly comfortable wearing on his head was his coonskin cap. But he and Jeff retrieved the hats anyway from the badly tilting carriage and started walking. They carried their cloaks and jackets draped over their arms, since the evening was quite warm, and Clay loosened the stock around his throat.

The great domed bulk of the Capitol loomed upward a few blocks away. It was late enough that the streets of Washington were almost deserted. Clay heard the creaking of wagon wheels somewhere behind them, but he and Jeff were the only pedestrians in sight.

They turned onto Pennsylvania Avenue. The side street on which the Copper Gable was located was three blocks to the west. The Government Land Office, where this whole imbroglio had begun, was across the street.

"I doubt Diana Maxwell knows anything about what her father is doing," Clay said quietly, returning to the subject of their earlier conversation. "I can't imagine that Maxwell would trust her with the details, or even let her know that he's involved in something illegal."

Jeff considered for a moment, then said, "I'm not sure. According to Markham, Gideon Maxwell was suspected of criminal activities even before this business of the land grab came up. Diana's been serving as his hostess for some time, I think. And she seemed to know the senators quite well. Isn't it likely that she'd be familiar with at least some part of her father's dealings?"

Clay shrugged. "Hard to say. Maybe Markham can find out." He laughed humorlessly. "I hope she's not working with her father. If she is, I reckon she can drag just about all our secrets out of Markham without having to work too hard at it."

"He *did* have the look of a man smitten," Jeff said. "Probably the same look I had on my face the first time I saw Melissa."

Jeff's comment sent Clay's mind back to the first time he had seen Shining Moon, in a lodge in the village of Bear Tooth's people, the Teton Sioux. If he remembered correctly, he had stared at her with his mouth damned near hanging open. She was that pretty. But it hadn't taken him long to discover that there was much more to Shining Moon than her beauty. The memories made him miss her even more, and the longing stabbed him like a knife.

He was so caught up in his thoughts that he didn't hear the noises behind him. Suddenly he became aware that the sound of wagon wheels he had noticed earlier had grown much louder, accompanied by the rapid hoofbeats of horses. Beside him Jeff exclaimed, "What in the world —"

Then both Holts were turning quickly to see a wagon racing along Pennsylvania Avenue, drawn by a team of galloping horses. The wagon was carrying several men, and one of them was crouched on the seat, whipping the team into a frenzy.

The horses were coming straight at them.

Instinct took over, as it had so many times in the lives of the Holts. Clay went one way and Jeff the other, throwing themselves to the side so that the careening wagon passed between them. Clay's hat flew off his head as he landed on the street and rolled over. He made no attempt to retrieve the hat or the cloak and waistcoat he had dropped. Instead he surged to his feet and turned to watch the runaway wagon.

Or was it a runaway? he suddenly asked himself. Neither the driver nor any of the other men in the wagon had called out a warning. It was possible they hadn't seen Clay and Jeff. But again Clay's instincts came into play, and they warned him that this was more than a simple accident that had nearly turned tragic.

Jeff was on his feet, too, brushing the dust off his clothing. "Are you all right?" Clay called to him.

"I'm fine," Jeff replied as he came across the street. "Look up there." He pointed along the street to the spot where the driver of the wagon was hauling back on the reins and bringing the heavy vehicle to a stop.

"I see," Clay said flatly.

"You think they're going to come back and apologize for nearly running us down?"

Clay grunted. That wasn't what he expected at all, and a moment later he saw that he was right.

The driver and his companions leaped down and stalked back down the street toward the Holts, leaving one man behind to watch the horses. The driver shook a clenched fist at Clay and Jeff and shouted, "What the hell do you think you're doing? You nearly made me wreck my wagon!"

"Careful, Clay," Jeff hissed. "There's more to this than it looks like."

"I know." Clay stepped forward and called to the men who were approaching, "Stop right there. We don't want any trouble."

One of the other men said, "Well, you should've thought of that before you jumped out in front of our wagon."

"Sorry," Jeff said as he moved up alongside Clay. "It won't happen again."

"Damned right it won't," growled the wagon driver.

Clay knew why Jeff had apologized. Jeff was going to assume that these men were drunk or simply obnoxious. Clearly they had been in the wrong, not Clay and Jeff, but Jeff was willing to apologize anyway in hopes of preventing more trouble. At heart Jeff was a peacemaker, not a brawler. Clay could admire that in his brother — even though he could not truly comprehend it. If these men wanted a fight, he was more than ready to oblige them.

There were four of them, making the odds two to one, but Clay didn't care. He had a fairly good idea what was behind this incident, and a flame of anger burned hot and bright inside him. His right hand moved unobtrusively toward the small of his back.

"I say we teach these swells a lesson," one of the men said. "They swagger about in their fancy clothes and think the world ought to bow to them."

"Yeah," one of the other men chipped in. "We'll show 'em they can't lord it over us just 'cause we're workingmen."

Clay suspected the four men hadn't done an honest day's labor in their lives. His guess was confirmed when they reached under their clothes and brought out short but vicious-looking clubs. "Get 'em!" the driver snapped as he lifted his weapon and charged. "Don't let 'em leave here alive!"

That made it plain enough. These men were hired killers.

So Clay felt no qualms whatsoever when he drew his pistol from his trousers waistband at the small of his back and shot the onrushing driver in the chest.

The heavy lead ball flung the man backward as if he had run into a wall. That cut the odds by one.

Next to Clay, Jeff had drawn his pistol, too. Neither of the Holts had been willing to accept Gideon Maxwell's invitation — venturing into the lion's den, as it were —

without going armed. The long tails of their coats had done an excellent job of concealing the pistols they had tucked away. Now Jeff fired, hard on the heels of Clay's shot, but his target swerved aside at the last instant. Instead of striking him in the chest, the pistol ball only grazed the outside of his left shoulder. But the impact was sufficient to spin the man half around and stagger him, ruining his charge.

Meanwhile, one of the other men slashed at Clay's head with the club in his hand. Clay reversed his grip on the pistol and jerked it up, parrying the blow with the butt of the gun. Then he stepped closer and drove his left fist into the man's belly. Breath sour with ale gusted in Clay's face.

Jeff sprang forward and lashed out with his foot, aiming a kick at the right wrist of the man he had just wounded. His toe connected solidly, and the club went flying out of the man's hand. Jeff flipped his pistol around, caught it by the barrel, and backhanded the butt across the man's face. A satisfying crunch sounded as the blow pulped the man's nose. Jeff had no time to enjoy it, however, because the fourth man leaped forward and landed a blow of his own, bringing his club down hard on Jeff's right shoulder.

As Jeff's arm and hand went numb, the pistol slipped from his fingers. He couldn't feel himself drop the weapon, but he heard it thud to the street. Backing up rapidly, he fended off another blow with his left arm. The man attacking him brought the club back for one more blow.

Before it could fall, Clay kicked the man's legs out from under him, driving the heel of his boot against the side of the man's right knee. There was an ugly snap, and the man howled in pain as he toppled. Clay was still struggling with his own opponent, but he had seen Jeff's predicament out of the corner of his eye and acted instinctively to give his brother a fighting chance. Jeff seized the opportunity, kicking the man in the jaw as he fell. Not very sporting, but Jeff was enough of a realist to know that his life, and Clay's, were at stake in this battle.

Clay threw a short, straight punch that rocked his opponent and set him up for the long, looping overhand that Clay brought around next. The man's head jerked to the side as Clay's fist caught him squarely on the jaw. He folded up, landing in an ungainly heap in the street. All four of the men from the wagon were down now, one of them dead, the others completely out of the fight. Clay stepped back, breathing a little hard but satisfied with the outcome of the brief battle.

Jeff yelled, "Look out!" An instant later, he smashed into Clay with a diving tackle, and both of them sprawled on the ground.

Clay heard the shot as he was falling, and heard as well the ugly sound of a ball whipping past his head. The shot had come from the wagon, where the fifth man had been left to watch the horses. Seeing that his companions had failed in their attempt to bludgeon Clay and Jeff to death, he had pulled a pistol and opened fire, clearly hoping to salvage something from this botched assassination attempt. Instead, the ball had missed, and now Clay and Jeff were scrambling back to their feet.

The man did the sensible thing under the circumstances. He dropped his pistol, bounded onto the wagon seat, grabbed the reins, and shouted at the horses as he whipped them into a gallop. The wagon raced away down the street, its new driver leaving his senseless companions behind.

Clay and Jeff didn't bother giving chase. They quickly gathered up their guns, hats, cloaks, and jackets. "Let's get out of here before the constable shows up," Clay said. "Someone's bound to have reported those shots."

"Probably," Jeff agreed. "I'm in no mood to answer questions."

"Nor am I."

Together they strode off hurriedly into the night.

The Copper Gable was peaceful when they arrived. Several customers were drinking quietly at the bar and at the tables. Harry Ledbetter lifted a hand in greeting as Clay and Jeff entered, but he didn't speak to them as they crossed the room to the stairs. Not until they were upstairs in their own room, with the door firmly shut, did they talk about what had happened.

"No one in Washington City has any reason to want us dead," Jeff said as he tossed his hat and cloak onto his bed.

"No one but the man behind the land grab plot," Clay said grimly.

"Maxwell."

Clay nodded. "I think we can be sure of it now. Somehow he found out that we're looking into the matter, and he wants to get rid of us."

"Do you think Markham let it slip?"

"I think Maxwell knew about it before he ever invited us to that party tonight," Clay said. "He must have spies all through the government, and he found out that we paid a visit to Thomas Jefferson at Monticello.

He was simply toying with us by inviting us to his house before he had us murdered."

Jeff rubbed his chin thoughtfully. "That's quite a leap, Clay. True, all the signs point toward Maxwell, but we have no indisputable proof that he tried to have us killed."

Clay's hands balled into fists. "Proof is one thing, Jeff. Knowing is another. I *know* Maxwell was behind what happened tonight. Those men were supposed to make our deaths look like an accident, but when that didn't work, they tried to kill us anyway."

"Why invite us to go along on the trip to his estate in Virginia?"

"Why not?" Clay asked harshly. "He was already planning to have us killed. He thought we'd be dead before the outing ever began."

"Then Lieutenant Markham must be in danger, too," Jeff said darkly.

"Not necessarily. Diana Maxwell had Markham wrapped around her little finger as soon as he saw her. Maxwell may want to keep him alive, so that he can find out just how much we know about the plan." Clay shook his head tiredly. "I can't puzzle it all out, Jeff. I've said from the first that I'm not the right sort for a job like this."

Jeff smiled. "It seems to me you're doing a pretty good job. We're still alive and still on

Maxwell's trail. Even if he knows what we're really up to, he's not going to withdraw that invitation now."

"You reckon he'd rather have us where he can keep an eye on us than leave us here in Washington to keep poking around?"

"I'm sure of it," Jeff said.

"And once he gets us out there in the country, there's one more thing he can do."

"Try to kill us again." It wasn't a question. Both of them knew they would be risking their lives by accompanying Maxwell to Forestwood. Jeff went on, "I take it we're going anyway?"

Clay thought about the murder attempt tonight and the other killings that could already be laid at the feet of Gideon Maxwell — stretching all the way back, perhaps, to the death of Meriwether Lewis. He looked at Jeff and said softly, "Damn right we're going."

Chapter Nineteen

Shining Moon had never been to a funeral before. She looked around at the people crowded into the small Congregational Church in Marietta and imagined that the hymns they were singing must be like the death songs of the Sioux, but the music rang flat and harsh in her ears. Nor, later, did she genuinely understand why Cassie Doolittle's body, in its wooden box, was buried in the ground of the churchyard. She was aware from past experience with the whites that they usually buried their dead underground, but to her mind Cassie's body should have been wrapped in buffalo hide and lifted atop a scaffold built for that purpose, so that there would be no barriers between her spirit and Wakan Tanka. The body would remain there until it had returned to the elements, leaving behind only the empty bones to be buried in the earth. That seemed much more honorable to Shining Moon than the slow rotting and degradation of the grave.

But the whites had their own customs, and she remained silent during the funeral. She sat upright in the hard, uncomfortable pew with Matthew on her right and Castor and Pollux Gilworth to her left. Both brothers had tears in their eyes as the white man called Reverend Cross spoke of Cassie's life.

Matthew had no tears for Cassie, though, Shining Moon saw when she glanced down at him. His eyes were dry, and his small face was set in lines as hard as stone. His expression never changed — not in the church, not outside in the cemetery as the coffin was lowered into the ground. Castor and Pollux picked up handfuls of earth from the mound by the grave and dropped them into the hole, the clods thudding on the wooden lid of the coffin. Shining Moon knew she was expected to do the same, and even though the idea was repulsive to her, she steeled herself to complete the ritual. Then she moved back to Matthew's side and put a hand on his shoulder.

It was like touching stone. There was no warmth to the boy, no sense of the spirit inside him. And his face might as well have been the carved wood of a totem.

Cassie had no relatives, but she had plenty of friends. Most of them spoke to the Gilworths after the service was over, and a few even murmured condolences to Shining Moon, although she could tell from their averted eyes that many of them thought of her as a heathen, a savage redskin, despite her white woman's clothes and the fact that she had honored all their customs. A bitter taste rose in her mouth. Cassie had been the only one of these settlers to truly befriend her, and now as the prospect of empty, lonely days stretched before her, she wished more than ever that Clay Holt would return and take her away from this place.

Three days after Cassie's funeral, Shining Moon was sitting on the porch of the Holt homestead, rocking slowly back and forth in one of the rocking chairs. There was no more mending to be done; all her clothes and those of Clay and Matthew and the Gilworth brothers had been repaired. Nor did she need to attend to the cooking, because there was a roasted turkey already sitting in a pan suspended above the ashes of the fireplace. In fact, she had nothing to do but sit.

Castor and Pollux were working in the fields, and Matthew was over by the barn, rolling a wooden ball against the wall. Shining Moon could not see Matthew from the porch, but she could hear the ball thudding against the side of the barn.

She would not allow herself to think

about what she suspected might be true. It was incomprehensible that a small boy like Matthew could have caused Cassie's death. Constable Sweeney had said that Cassie's mule had run away with the cart, causing it to overturn. Cassie's death was tragic and senseless, but it had been an accident. It was not murder.

But Shining Moon had seen the satisfaction in Matthew's eyes when he heard how the cart had landed on Cassie and crushed the life out of her frail body. She had not imagined his reaction, she was sure of that. And although she could not bring herself to openly consider the possibility that Matthew had caused Cassie's death, still it lurked in the back of her mind . . .

When the sound of the ball hitting the barn stopped, Shining Moon was not aware of it for a moment. Then the silence penetrated her thoughts, and she looked up from her brooding study of the puncheons at her feet and frowned. It was always best to know where Matthew was and what he was doing. Not knowing could lead to trouble.

She had just gotten to her feet when she heard him call frantically, "Shining Moon! Shining Moon! Help!"

Her heart began to pound heavily in her chest as she hurried down the steps from the porch. For the first time in a long while, she had heard a genuine emotion in Matthew's voice.

Fear. The boy was afraid. But what could have frightened someone like him, someone who was not a normal child? It would have to be something terrible, Shining Moon thought as she broke into a run that carried her toward the barn. He needed her, and she responded to his need, forgetting all her suspicions. "Matthew!" she called out. "Matthew, I'm coming!"

She lifted the cumbersome long petticoats and skirt, and her long brown legs flashed as she rounded the corner of the barn.

"Shining Moon!" Matthew cried again.

She could not see him. He was nowhere in sight. "Where are you?" she called desperately as she slowed.

"Back here! Behind the barn!"

There were woods back there; perhaps a bear or a wolf or a snake had emerged from the dense trees to threaten Matthew. She realized suddenly that she was unarmed. She had no weapons with which to fight off a wild animal.

But with an unexpectedly fierce upswelling of determination, she knew she would fight with her bare hands if she had to. She had taken Matthew to raise, and she would protect and defend him with her own life if necessary.

She reached the rear corner of the barn and rounded it sharply. Still no sign of the boy. "Matthew!" she called. "Where are you?"

His voice floated to her, fainter now but no less fearful. "In the woods! Come quick!"

Shining Moon darted toward the trees, pushing through the underbrush that grew between the trunks, ignoring the branches that clawed at her clothes and skin. Nothing was going to keep her from Matthew's side. She called his name again, and his response was louder this time. He told her she was coming closer to him. With a burst of renewed strength and determination, she broke through a thicket of brush and into a broad clearing.

She saw the black mouth of the hole yawning at her feet but was unable to stop herself in time. She stumbled, her momentum carrying her forward, and suddenly there was nothing beneath her but empty air. She plummeted into darkness.

In the fields half a mile away, Pollux Gilworth paused and leaned on the hoe he had been using to work the ground between the rows of corn. "Did you hear something?" he called to his brother, who was working several rows away.

"Like what?" Castor asked, likewise leaning on his hoe.

"I'm not sure. Sounded like somebody maybe yelling."

Castor stretched his neck, turning his head from side to side as he listened intently. After a moment he shook his head and said, "Nope. I don't hear anything."

Pollux had been listening as carefully. "Neither do I now," he said with a shrug. "Maybe it was just a bird."

"Or maybe you imagined it because you're tired of hoeing and wanted an excuse to stop for a minute." Castor's grin robbed his words of any sting.

"Hah! I'll still be working when you drop in your tracks from exhaustion."

"I doubt that. I doubt that very much."

Pollux chopped at the ground with the hoe. "We'll just see about that," he declared.

"Yes, we will," Castor shot back, resuming his own hoeing.

At first, Shining Moon had no idea how far she had fallen. She knew only that she had come to a painful, jarring halt. Something rough was pressed into her left side, under her arm. It scraped against her skin where her dress was torn. Her left arm and shoulder throbbed, but her right arm was free.

So were her legs, she realized after a few seconds. Her feet dangled in empty air. She kicked them back and forth but could feel nothing. When she flailed out with her right arm, her fingertips brushed against the raw, damp earth of a dirt wall. The precariousness of her situation gradually penetrated her stunned mind, and she tightened the grip of her left arm around whatever it had caught on.

Gradually she became aware that light was filtering down around her from above. She tilted her head back and tried to look up. An unknowable distance above her she saw a ragged circle of brightness, within which several tree limbs were visible. They belonged to the trees that overhung the clearing, Shining Moon realized. She was beginning to understand now.

The creeks and rivers had always provided enough water for her people, but the whites, of course, had different ways. Sometimes they dug holes in the earth, Clay Holt had told her, and when those holes filled with water, they were called wells. The whites would lower buckets tied to ropes and let them fill with water before pulling them back up. It seemed a foolish waste of effort to Shining Moon when one could always go to the nearest stream for water. Now she was convinced that she had fallen into such a well, although she had not been aware of any on the Holt farm.

"Shining Moon?" The voice was faint and hollow, but it belonged unmistakably to Matthew.

"Matthew!" she cried, the boy's name echoing eerily against the earthen walls of the shaft. "Are you all right?" She had been on her way to help him when she had fallen into this hole, and she prayed that whatever had frightened him had gone away.

"You down there, Shining Moon?" Matthew's voice was louder now.

"Yes! I have fallen!"

As she looked upward, she saw his head and shoulders come into the circle of light at the top of the shaft.

"That's a mighty deep hole," he said in a conversational tone.

"Stay back!" Shining Moon warned. "I do not want you to fall, too."

"Oh, I'm not going to. You don't have to worry 'bout that."

His voice was strangely calm and unhurried. A feeling of horror blew through her like a gust of cold wind. Had he known the well was there? Had his cries for help been meant to lure her here?

She did not want to believe that. She could not allow herself to believe it. She drew a deep breath, the rich smell of damp earth filling her lungs, and called firmly to him, "Matthew, go find Castor and Pollux. You have to help me."

He stayed where he was, peering down at her. "You didn't fall all the way to the bottom, did you?" he asked. "I know this well's deeper than where you got stuck. I dropped a rock down and listened for the sound of it hitting bottom."

Evil spirits were gibbering in Shining Moon's ears and gnawing around the edges of her spirit. She forced them away with an effort of will and repeated, "Matthew, go get help. Get Castor and Pollux."

"Sure," he said lazily. "I'll get help." His head disappeared from the circle of light.

Shining Moon breathed deeply again and fought down the panic that threatened to consume her. She was a woman of the Teton Sioux. She would not give in to her own fear.

Matthew would not go for help. She knew that. He would wait for her to fall the rest of the way and die. And she did not think her cries for help, no matter how loud, would carry all the way to the field where Castor and Pollux were working. This hole in the earth would swallow her words.

But she was determined that it would not swallow *her*. And if she was going to get out, she was going to have to do it herself, she realized now. She began to study her surroundings more carefully.

Her eyes had adjusted to the dim light that filtered into the well through the overhanging trees. The object that had stopped her fall was a thick branch that had no doubt fallen from one of those trees sometime in the past. It was a handspan or so in diameter and long enough to have wedged itself at a slight angle between the walls of the shaft. Her left arm had lodged in the narrow gap between the branch and the side of the well. She could see where the weight of her body striking the branch had gouged short furrows in the earthen walls on each end. It was sheer luck that the branch had not dislodged completely and that the wood was not rotten. If it had been, it would certainly have snapped.

She swung around carefully so that she could grasp the branch with her right arm, too, taking some of the strain off her left. Her left arm hurt, but she was fairly confident that it was not broken. She reached out gingerly and pried a clod of dirt loose, then let it slip from her fingers. The faint sound it made when it struck bottom came fairly quickly.

Shining Moon looked up again, studying the shaft above her. She was not good at figuring distances in the manner that the whites did, but she estimated that she was about twenty feet below the mouth of the well. The distance to the bottom was probably shorter than that. If she did drop the rest of the way, she might break a leg, but she doubted the fall would kill her. That knowledge gave her strength — until she realized that if the branch had not broken her fall, if she had plummeted to the bottom of the well, she might have died. At the very least she would have been badly injured.

And that was exactly what Matthew had wanted.

With a deep breath, Shining Moon banished that thought for the moment. She had more important things to think about. She had to find a way out of this trap.

She considered bracing her back against one wall and her feet against the other so that she could climb up the well as if it were a rock chimney. Quickly, though, she realized that the walls were too far apart. That would never work. Perhaps she could dig handholds and footholds in the walls. She reached out with one hand and plunged her fingers into the dirt again. It came away too easily in her hand. Any grips she gouged out would not support her weight.

Her options were slipping away, and she felt her fear growing again. "Matthew!" she called out, unable to stop herself. "Matthew, are you still up there?"

No answer came. Shining Moon closed her eyes for a moment and tried to calm herself. In the language of her people there were no words for the curses the white men used so often, so she drew on her memory and uttered a heartfelt, "Son of a bitch!"

Of course Matthew wasn't up there, she told herself. He had gone off to let her die here. Later, perhaps, after her body was discovered in the old well, he would claim he had gone looking for the Gilworth brothers only to become confused and unable to find them. And except for Castor and Pollux, perhaps, everyone would believe him.

After all, he was only a little boy.

Shining Moon gritted her teeth for a moment, then tipped her head back and shouted, "Castor! Pollux! Help me!" Futile though it might be, she was not going to hang here on a branch and allow herself to die without putting up a fight. Was she not a woman of the Teton Sioux, daughter of Bear Tooth? "Castor! Pollux!"

Nothing. Her shouts had even made the birds fall silent.

And in the end, that was what saved her.

"Something's wrong," Castor said, holding up a big, knobby-knuckled hand.

"What? What did you say?" Pollux paused, his hoe canted over his shoulder, and frowned at his twin brother.

They were near the barn, on the path that led from the fields. "Listen," Castor said.

After a moment Pollux shook his head. "I don't hear a sound. Now you're the one imagining things."

"No, I'm not. And you're right. I can't hear anything, either."

"Something's frightened the birds," Pollux said, catching on quickly to what his brother meant. "A fox, maybe?"

"Or something worse."

Each of the brothers carried a flintlock rifle in addition to their hoes. Civilized though the Ohio Valley might be now, risk and danger were still a fact of life, so as a matter of habit most men went about their business armed. Castor and Pollux were no different.

Castor dropped his hoe and hefted the

long-barreled flintlock. "Come on. Let's find Shining Moon and the boy."

They exchanged glances but left unspoken the worry that nagged at them whenever they left Shining Moon and Matthew alone. Matthew was just a child, of course, but they had seen what he was capable of with small animals. Shining Moon could take care of herself, but she might not suspect Matthew of evil intent until it was too late.

The two burly figures hurried toward the barn. Before they reached it, they heard someone calling from somewhere to their right. "Castor! Pollux!" The voice was hollow and weak, but they recognized it immediately as Shining Moon's.

The woods in that direction were dense with undergrowth, but the Gilworth brothers plunged into the brush without hesitation. Branches bent and cracked before them, and after a moment they broke through into a clearing and saw the black hole that marked the mouth of the unused well.

"Damn it!" Pollux exclaimed. "I thought we covered that up!"

"We did," Castor replied grimly. "Come on."

They dropped to their knees at the edge of the well, and Pollux shouted into it, "Miz Holt! Are you in there?"

"I am here," Shining Moon's voice came back to them. "Thank the Great Spirit you heard my cries."

"Where's the boy?" Castor asked. "Did he fall in there, too?"

"Matthew is not here. Please, you must help me. I cannot . . . cannot hold on much longer."

Castor and Pollux looked at each other. "I'll get a rope," Castor said, standing up. He broke into a run, heading back toward the barn.

Pollux stayed where he was, kneeling beside the well. "You hang on, Miz Holt," he called down to Shining Moon. "Are you hurt bad?"

"No. My arm . . . it hurts. But it is all right. I will hold on . . . as long as I can."

Pollux leaned over as far as he dared. The last thing Shining Moon needed right now was to have him come toppling down on top of her. Squinting into the shadowy shaft, he could just make her out, clutching a broken tree branch that had somehow gotten wedged between the walls of the hole about halfway to the bottom.

"Castor's gone to get a rope," Pollux called down. "We'll lower it to you, and if you can grab on, we'll haul you right out of there. Won't take but a minute."

"I do not know . . . if I can hold on. I have been down here a long time . . . I am tired, and my arm hurts."

"Now, don't you give up!" Pollux said quickly. "We'll find a way. It's just that Castor and me are both too big to start scrambling up and down a rope. Otherwise one of us would sure come down and get you."

"I know. I must . . . help save myself."

Castor pounded up, carrying a thick, braided rope. "Here," he said to his brother. "What do we do now?"

Pollux looked up at him and asked, "Can you tie a loop in the end of that rope?"

"A loop? I reckon. But what for?"

"Make it a good-sized one," Pollux said. "Miz Holt's going to put her feet in it so's she can brace herself while we haul her up."

Castor nodded in understanding and quickly began tying the loop. When it was big enough for Shining Moon to put both of her feet in, he tightened the knot, then tugged hard to make sure it would hold. "I think that'll do," he said as he handed the loop to Pollux.

"Play out the rope and I'll let it down." To Shining Moon, Pollux called, "When this rope gets down there, can you grab hold of it and put your feet in the loop at the end?"

"I will try," Shining Moon whispered.

As Castor played out the rope, his brother lowered it into the well. Pollux stole a glance at the darkening sky. The sun was setting, and the interior of the well was already dark with shadows. He wished he could see Shining Moon and, more importantly, that she could see the rope.

"It ought to be there beside you," he called to her. "Can you reach out and grab it?"

"Yes, I — *oh!*"

Castor and Pollux leaned forward anxiously. "What is it?" Pollux called. "What happened?"

For a long moment Shining Moon made no reply. Then the words came floating up out of the shadows. "I am all right," she said. "I almost slipped, but I have the rope now. I will put my feet in the loop . . ."

"Careful now," Pollux cautioned her. "Be sure and hang on to that branch until you're ready to let go."

They heard faint sounds of movement and a grunt of effort. Both men were holding the rope, and both felt it when her weight pulled it taut.

"I . . . have it!" Shining Moon called.

"Your feet are in the loop?"

"Yes, and I am holding the rope with both hands."

Pollux looked over his shoulder at his

brother, then straightened. "Slow and easy now," he told Castor. "Let's just back up slow and easy."

"That's what I'm doing," Castor replied. He took one step back, then another and another, his strong, blunt fingers wrapped securely around the rope. Pollux joined in the steady, careful pulling.

Slowly they backed away from the hole in the ground until, in the dusky light, they saw Shining Moon's head emerge from the well. "Hang on to the rope!" Pollux called to his brother. He sprang forward and bent over to grab Shining Moon. His big hands went under her arms and lifted her as if she were no heavier than an infant. As soon as she was clear of the well, he swung her to the side, and Castor was there to help steady her. Trembling from the strain and fatigue, she would have collapsed if not for the strong arms of the Gilworths.

"It's all right now, Miz Holt," Castor told her. "You're safe."

She nodded shakily and closed her eyes, drawing deep breaths into her body. Gradually, her trembling subsided. She looked up at the two men towering over her.

"Matthew," she said. "We have to find Matthew."

"You have any idea where he is?" Pollux

asked. "Where was he when you fell in the well?"

"And how'd you come to tumble in there, anyway?" Castor added. "Pollux and me covered it up with planks so that nobody would fall into it by accident. What happened to them?"

Shining Moon shook her head. "I do not know."

"That well never was any good," Pollux said. "That's why we covered it up. Guess we should've filled it in again, or put a better cover on it. Just never got around to it, I reckon."

Shining Moon tested her legs by taking a step. They were shaking, but she could walk. "Matthew was nearby," she said. "We must find him."

Pollux kept a hand on her arm to steady her. "Come on. Let's take you to the cabin, then Castor and me will look for the boy."

They did not have to search for Matthew, though. As they came around the barn and started toward the house, they saw him coming from the other direction. "Castor! Pollux!" he cried. "I looked all over for you!"

"We were working in the fields," Castor said. "You ought to've known that. Your ma fell in an old well and hurt herself."

Matthew didn't say anything. He was

staring at Shining Moon, and Castor and Pollux both would have sworn that he seemed disappointed to see her. But that was crazy, and they marked it up as a trick of the light.

"Are you all right, Matthew?" Shining Moon asked.

"Yeah, I'm fine," the boy said. "What about you?"

Shining Moon was holding her left arm awkwardly and wincing whenever she moved it. But she smiled and said, "I will be all right. My arm is sore, but it is nothing."

Matthew nodded. He seemed to be waiting for something, but whatever it was, he didn't get it. Shining Moon went on, "I will go in the house now."

"You need any help?" Castor asked.

"No, you have done enough." Shining Moon looked at the brothers and forced a tired smile. "You have saved my life. I can never pay the debt I owe you."

"Shoot, you don't owe us nothing," Pollux said. "We're just glad we came around in time to give you a hand. Ain't that right, Castor?"

"It sure is. And if you need anything, Miz Holt, anything at all, you just let us know."

"Thank you." Shining Moon stepped away from them and hobbled painfully toward the house. Matthew started to follow her, but Castor's hand came down hard on his left shoulder, stopping him. An instant later, Pollux grasped his right shoulder.

"You come on with us, son," Pollux said. "Your ma's got enough to do right now just taking care of herself."

"We'll look after you for a while," Castor added.

Matthew turned his head and looked up at them. "She's not my ma," he said coldly.

Castor tightened his grip on Matthew's shoulder. "That don't make any difference," he said. "You'd better be glad she's not hurt any worse than she is."

"That's right," Pollux said. "I'm not sure what happened around here this afternoon, and I don't reckon Miz Holt feels much like talking about it —"

"But we'll be keeping our eyes open," Castor finished.

"Fine," Matthew bit out. "You do that."

The Gilworths looked at each other over the boy's head. Neither of them liked what was going on here.

But neither of them had the slightest idea what to do about it. The only thing they knew for sure was that all of them — the twins and Shining Moon — would have to be mighty careful from here on out.

Chapter Twenty

Proud Wolf had heard Clay and Jeff speak of St. Louis many times, so he thought he had some idea what to expect. But as the wagon came within sight of the city sprawled on the west bank of the Mississippi, not far below the point where the Missouri River joined with the Father of Waters, he found himself staring openmouthed at things he had never imagined, let alone seen with his own eyes.

"So many lodges," he murmured in awe.

Nick Palmer looked over at him and grunted. Palmer was handling the reins of the mule team again while Professor Hilliard rode in the back of the wagon. "I hear tell there's even bigger towns back east," Palmer said.

Proud Wolf shook his head. "That cannot be. There are no villages larger than the one I see now before us."

Hilliard leaned up between them and chuckled. "You'll soon see that you're wrong, Proud Wolf," he said. "Philadelphia, Boston, and New York are all larger than St. Louis. Pittsburgh may well be, and New Orleans, too. The United States is growing by leaps and bounds, my boy, and it's no wonder that more and more people seek to go west. The country needs room to grow."

Proud Wolf thought about that for a moment. "It is like when the Blackfoot or the Crow or the Arikara need a larger hunting ground. Your people will find new land and take it." He shot a glance at Hilliard. "You will kill those who live there now if they oppose you, just like the Blackfoot."

"I'm sure it won't ever come to that," Hilliard said uneasily. "We're a civilized nation. There's room for everyone."

Proud Wolf looked away. He did not agree with what the professor was saying.

Still, he had to admit there was much he did not know. He was learning more every day. The wagon had left New Hope many weeks earlier, and each night during the journey, while the three travelers sat around their campfire, Professor Hilliard had begun Proud Wolf's education in earnest. Inside the wagon was a trunkful of books. Proud Wolf and Shining Moon had learned the rudiments of reading from a Jesuit missionary several years before they first met Clay and Jeff Holt. But with Hilliard's help, Proud Wolf was now much more comfortable with the marks on paper that white men called writing.

Besides reading, Proud Wolf and Hilliard had also had many long discussions concerning history, philosophy, science, nature, and literature. True, these discussions were fairly one-sided, as Proud Wolf listened and Hilliard talked, but some of the professor's ideas lingered in Proud Wolf's mind long afterward. He was learning, and he was so excited that he had no time to miss his village or the people of Bear Tooth's band.

One part of his homeland, his heritage, he had not left behind, however. Though he said nothing about it to the professor or Nick Palmer, several times during the journey he had looked out over the prairie at night and seen a pair of glowing eyes looking back at him. They were the eyes of a great beast, he knew. The spirit cat was following him, and wherever his path led him, the cat would be there as well. That knowledge was reassuring.

As Palmer kept the wagon rolling toward the city, he said, "Reckon we'll be parting company up here in St. Louis, Professor. Got to admit I'll miss listening to you and Proud Wolf talking around the campfire at night. It was mighty interesting, even if I didn't know what you were going on about most of the time."

"And we shall miss you, too, Nick,"

Hilliard said, clapping his hand on the guide's shoulder. "You've been a stalwart companion from start to finish. I hope your arm has healed properly. I'd hate to think that by working for me, you incurred an injury that will haunt you for the rest of your days."

Palmer grinned as he lifted his arm and wiggled his fingers. "Good as new, Professor. That priest fella, Father Thomas, would've made a good sawbones if he hadn't decided to do what he's doing."

"Both are honorable callings, and I've no doubt Thomas Brennan would have succeeded in whatever task he undertook in life." Hilliard and Father Thomas had spent some time together while the professor and Proud Wolf were waiting in New Hope for Palmer's wounded arm to heal. Both were men of learning, and they had naturally gravitated toward each other.

Proud Wolf hoped that someday he would be part of the circle of learned men. He had made a good start on it. Once he had received his education from the Stoddard Academy and then Harvard, he would be ready to take his place among those privileged few.

He smiled to himself as he realized he was beginning to think the way the professor

419

talked. That might not be such a good thing . . .

Nick Palmer drove the wagon to the hotel in which Hilliard had stayed during his previous visit to St. Louis, on his way west. "We'll take rooms here," Hilliard explained to Proud Wolf, "and wait for the next keelboat bound for the east."

"We will follow the Father of Waters?" Proud Wolf pointed toward the Mississippi River, wending its ponderous way south, a couple of blocks from the hotel.

"Only until we reach the Ohio River," Hilliard explained. "We'll travel on the Ohio to Pittsburgh, where we can catch a stagecoach that will take us on to Boston." The professor smiled. "You see, transportation becomes more advanced the farther east one goes, Proud Wolf."

Proud Wolf did not see how anything could be better than a good horse or a well-made canoe, but he said nothing. Hilliard was proud of his civilization, of his people's way of life. Proud Wolf could appreciate many of the things white men had learned to make, but he was still wary of whites themselves.

"Should I engage a room for you as well, Nick?" Hilliard asked Palmer as they climbed down from the wagon.

Palmer shook his head. "No need for that. I ain't much for staying in fancy places like this. I know a place down on the waterfront that's more my style. I'll come 'round tonight, though, and pick up my wages, if that's all right with you, Professor."

"Certainly. And I can tell you now, there'll be a generous bonus waiting for you, Nick."

"Much obliged." Palmer lifted a hand in a farewell wave. "See you boys later."

"Well." Hilliard turned to Proud Wolf with a smile. "Shall we go inside?"

Proud Wolf had already attracted a few curious stares from people passing on the street. He supposed his buckskins and the eagle feather tucked into the beaded band that bound his hair made him a natural object of curiosity. The citizens of St. Louis were no doubt used to the sight of Indians, but an Indian about to enter a hotel was probably rare enough to merit surprise as well as curiosity.

He took a deep breath and said, "I am ready, Professor, if you are."

"Come along, then."

The hotel was three stories tall. Proud Wolf craned his neck and looked up as he and the professor stepped onto the porch. Two men in town suits and beaver hats were sitting on a bench to one side of the doorway, smoking pipes and passing a bottle back and forth. One of them raised his voice and hailed the newcomers. "Hey, what you got there, mister? A tame redskin?"

"Better be careful he doesn't scalp you," the other man chimed in, laughing.

From the corner of his mouth Professor Hilliard said quietly, "Ignore these bumpkins, Proud Wolf."

Proud Wolf nodded and followed the professor to the door. Before they could enter, the two locals stood and swaggered over to them. "Wait just a damned minute," one of the men said. "We were talking to you, weren't we, Coley?"

"That's right, Jud," the second man said. He reached out and grabbed Hilliard's arm. "Don't go acting so high and mighty just because you got a tame Indian, mister."

Hilliard turned to the man and began in a patient tone, "Please, sir, desist —"

Proud Wolf slid between Hilliard and the man who had grasped his arm. Looking into the man's eyes, he asked quietly, "Would you wager your life that I am a 'tame' Indian?"

The man's eyes widened, and his fingers quickly splayed out as he let go of Hilliard's arm.

"Here now, you can't do that!" the first man protested. "Coley, don't let that redskin talk to you like that!"

Coley swallowed and said, "Forget it, Jud."

"But —"

"I said forget it." Coley stepped back and wiped the back of his hand across his mouth. "Come on. We got better things to do."

Jud was still grumbling, but he followed his friend toward a building across the street. Coley glanced back over his shoulder a time or two, then walked even faster.

Professor Hilliard regarded Proud Wolf with amazement. "What did you do?" he asked. "How did you make that ruffian stop acting so belligerently?"

"I looked at him with truth in my eyes," Proud Wolf said. "He saw it and decided his pride was not worth dying over."

"You would have killed him simply because he was crude and insulting?"

"I would have killed him if he had not removed his hand from you." Proud Wolf tapped his chest. "White men keep their truths buried deep inside. It cannot be seen even in their eyes. I let that man see what would happen if he did not leave us alone. That is all."

Hilliard shook his head, both awe and disbelief in his expression. After a moment he said, "I daresay the Stoddard Academy has never had a student like you, Proud Wolf. I have a feeling you will not be the only one receiving an education during your time there."

Proud Wolf and Professor Hilliard spent nearly a week in St. Louis, waiting for a keelboat headed east. The clerk at the hotel had been reluctant to allow an Indian to stay there, but the color of Hilliard's coins had overcome any objections to the color of Proud Wolf's skin. They spent most of the time in the hotel lobby, where Hilliard read every newspaper he could get his hands on, even those that were months old, and pointed out items of interest to Proud Wolf. Listening to the professor for long enough would be an education in itself, Proud Wolf thought.

They also visited the waterfront, where Proud Wolf stood on the docks and looked out over the slow-rolling waters of the Mississippi. Never had he seen such a river. "Truly, I know now why it is called the Father of Waters," he commented. "There is no other river like it."

"Not in this land, anyway. In Africa, there is a river called the Nile which is much like the Mississippi."

Proud Wolf shook his head. "I know nothing of this land called Africa or its

Nile." He waved his hand toward the water. "All I know is that this is a mighty river."

"Indeed," the professor murmured. "Indeed."

They were finally able to book passage on a keelboat called the *Grizzly*. The boat did not look anything like a bear to Proud Wolf. It was some sixty feet long and ten feet wide, and both ends tapered to a point. A long cabin took up most of the deck space. A walkway little more than a foot wide ran along both sides of the cabin, which served as the cargo hold as well as passengers' quarters.

"How do they get it upstream?" Proud Wolf asked the professor as they were about to board. He pointed to four long oars, two on each side, that were set at the rear of the vessel. "The men must have to row very hard."

"They do, but they're not the only ones propelling the boat," Hilliard explained. "Other men use long poles to push against the bottom of the river. They plant their poles and then walk along that narrow area beside the cabin."

"Much work," Proud Wolf said with a shake of his head.

"Yes, but coming downstream is much easier. The boats can cover twice as much distance in the same amount of time as going upstream."

"I would not want to be a boatman."

"Nor would I," Hilliard agreed. "Let's go aboard."

The keelboat's primary cargo on this return trip to Pittsburgh was beaver pelts. This was where the furs trapped by Clay Holt and the thousands of men like him were loaded on boats and taken to the east, where they would be made into hats and robes and coats. Proud Wolf took a special interest in the beaver trade, since he had seen firsthand where the pelts' long journey began, in the cold creeks and rivers of the mountains and prairies.

They traveled downriver from St. Louis, following the Mississippi to the town of Cairo, where the Ohio River flowed in from the east to join the Father of Waters. After the *Grizzly* had made the wide turn into the Ohio, its progress slowed. Proud Wolf spent days sitting on the roof of the cabin with the professor, watching the green banks of the river roll past in a stately procession. When they reached the settlement of Louisville and the Falls of the Ohio, the journey became more exciting as the current quickened.

The captain of the *Grizzly* was a slender, keen-eyed man named Michael Davis. He had become friendly with the professor and Proud Wolf during the voyage, and he took the time to explain to them how the Falls would be negotiated.

" 'Falls' isn't really a good name for them," he said as he pointed the stem of his pipe at the area of rough, rock-studded water that stretched from one side of the river to the other. The boat had put ashore, and the cargo was being unloaded into wagons. "There's a big limestone ledge that goes across the river here, you see, and that causes rapids. The water doesn't actually fall all that much. But it's more than a mite tricky, anyway. Coming downriver, we bring a falls pilot aboard, and he takes us through the Indian Chute." Davis gestured toward the north bank of the river. "That's the channel over yonder. It runs smooth but fast, and you've got to know where you're going or you'll pile up on the rocks, sure as the Devil. Heading upriver like this, we've got to unload whatever goods we're carrying and portage them around the Falls in wagons, specially when the water's a mite low like it is now. As for the old girl herself, we'll tie cables onto her and haul her up and over the Falls from shore. Most captains just use their crew to do the pulling, but I know a fella who's got a team of mules he lets us use. For a price, of course. Once we get past the Falls, though, we'll be in Cincinnati before you know it, then Marietta and Wheeling and Pittsburgh."

Proud Wolf looked at the captain in surprise. "Did you say Marietta?"

"Yup. It's a nice little settlement in Ohio. Heard of it, have you?"

Proud Wolf smiled. "I have . . . family there."

"Yes, I remember," the professor said. "You told me that's where the Holt family lives."

Captain Davis looked sharply at Hilliard. "Is that Clay Holt you're talking about?" he asked.

"Indeed it is."

Proud Wolf said, "Clay Holt is married to my sister, Shining Moon. Do you know him?"

Davis shook his head. "Know of him, that's all. I reckon most river men do. I've carried a heap of pelts Clay Holt has sent back to St. Louis from the mountain country. He still out there?"

"I do not know," Proud Wolf said. "When the professor and I began this journey, Clay Holt was not among my people. He and my sister had gone back to his home in Ohio to visit his family. A reunion, Clay called it. Perhaps they have returned by now, going west as we are going east."

"Perhaps you'd like to stop in Marietta and see if your sister is still there," Hilliard suggested. He looked at Davis. "It won't be out of our way, will it, Captain?"

"Nope, but if you want to go on to Pittsburgh with me, you'll have to get your visiting done in a hurry," Davis replied. "I generally stop one night in Marietta, but that's all."

Proud Wolf nodded. "That will be fine. Thank you, Captain."

"I hope I get to meet this famous brother-in-law of yours," the professor said. "What are the chances he's still in Marietta?"

"I do not know. It is possible." But it was not very likely, Proud Wolf thought. Clay Holt was more at home in the Shining Mountains than any other white man he had ever known. For anything to keep Clay away from the high country for very long, it would have to be very important indeed.

Clay swung up into the saddle and sent the horse down the street in a gentle canter. Jeff rode alongside him. The sun had not been up long, and the air still held a trace of coolness that would disappear later in the humid warmth of the summer day. It felt good to be up and doing something.

Even riding into a trap.

That was exactly what they were doing. Clay was convinced of it, and so was Jeff. They had hashed it all out more than once since the party at Gideon Maxwell's house the night before — the party that had been followed by an attempt on their lives. To think that one thing had nothing to do with the other was to accept too incredible a co-incidence, to Clay's mind. Maxwell had to have sent the men who had tried to run them down and then, failing that, to beat them to death.

They rode straight to Maxwell's mansion and found a veritable parade of carriages and wagons forming in front of the large house. Gideon Maxwell himself was supervising the loading of supplies onto a wagon, and he greeted them heartily. "Good morning, gen-tlemen! Are you ready to enjoy the next few days?"

"Very much," Clay replied. He glanced around. "Where's that young fella Mark-ham?"

"The lieutenant is among us, never fear," Maxwell said dryly. "I imagine that where-ever my daughter is, Lieutenant Markham is not far away."

Jeff leaned forward in the saddle. "Doesn't that bother you, Mr. Maxwell?"

"Diana is a beautiful young woman, gentlemen. I've grown accustomed to having eager young men flitting around like horseflies." Maxwell chuckled. "Don't worry about Diana. She can take care of herself."

It wasn't Diana Maxwell they were worried about, Clay thought.

Maxwell excused himself and went back in the house to attend to some last-minute details. In a voice pitched so that no one could overhear, Jeff said to Clay, "He didn't look much like a man who was expecting us to be dead this morning. I thought he might be surprised when we showed up."

"I reckon that fella who got away came back here and gave him the bad news. He wasn't surprised. He'll just wait until the next chance presents itself and try again."

"While we're out in the Virginia countryside, maybe?" Jeff speculated.

"That wouldn't surprise me a bit."

Clay fell silent when he spotted Senator Morgan Ralston walking toward them. He caught Jeff's eye and inclined his head, and both of them dismounted. Ralston strode up and shook hands, saying, "Good morning, Clay. Good morning, Jeff. I imagine you're looking forward to this little trip even more than I am."

"Why's that, Senator?" Jeff asked.

"Why, you're frontiersmen," Ralston said.

"It must be driving you mad, being cooped up in the city like this. I know that after a while in Washington, I certainly do miss my home in Georgia." He noticed their flint-locks, fastened on the saddles with short lengths of rawhide, and became even more animated. "Those are Kentucky long rifles, aren't they?"

"Not really, but some folks call them that," Clay said. "They were made at the government armory in Harper's Ferry in '03. I carried mine all the way to the Pacific with the Corps of Discovery, and when I got back I got Jeff one just like it."

Ralston rested a hand on the stock of Clay's rifle. "This is a piece of American history, then. Someday you'll have to give it to a museum, so that it can be properly preserved."

Clay smiled. "I'm likely to have worn it out before I'm ever ready to give it up, but I'll keep that in mind, Senator."

Charles Emory and Louis Haines strolled over to join them. Emory greeted Clay and Jeff jovially, and Haines seemed to have forgotten the tension of the night before. He was clearly excited by the trip to Maxwell's country estate.

"I'm a city boy, you know," Haines said. "Come from New York. I've never spent much time out in the wild."

"I was in New York a couple of years ago," Jeff commented. "I've heard that it's grown quite a bit since, and it was a good-sized city even then. You know a fellow named Washington Irving?"

Haines snorted. "Diedrich Knickerbocker himself. What a rascal! I tell you, Irving ruffled a few feathers among the old Dutch settlers when he began publishing those Knickerbocker stories in his magazine. How do you know him?"

"My cousin Ned and I ran into him when we were passing through there. We have relatives in New York, too. Our mother was one of Lemuel March's cousins."

"I know the man well," Haines said. "Runs a shipping line."

"He and I do business together," Jeff said.

"Well, it's certainly a small world." Haines nodded pleasantly to them. "I'll see you later, gentlemen. I should go see if my good wife and our children are ready to depart."

"Yes, I should check on my family as well," Emory said. "We'll visit again along the trail, I'm sure." With a friendly wave, he moved off toward one of the carriages.

When they were alone again, Jeff said to Clay, "All three of them seem like pretty nice gents. Even Haines wasn't a jackass this morning."

"Yep. But that doesn't mean they're not working with Maxwell. A man 'may smile and smile, and be a villain.' I reckon that holds true for politicians more than just about any other kind of folks."

Jeff looked at him in surprise. "Where'd you hear that?"

Clay shrugged. "There's a fella out in the Rockies who can spout just about every word old William Shakespeare ever wrote. He's got them all memorized. I've heard him say that before, and it just popped into my head."

"Well, I'd say you're sure right, no matter who you're quoting."

Diana Maxwell and Lieutenant John Markham emerged from the house and walked over to one of the carriages, where Markham eagerly helped Diana climb inside. The young officer exchanged glances with Clay and Jeff, then stepped up into the carriage behind Diana.

Gideon Maxwell strode out of the house, slapping a pair of riding gloves against his thigh. A groom brought up a saddled horse, and as Maxwell took the reins, he lifted his voice and called out to the other members of the party, "I believe everyone is ready to depart. I hope you all enjoy yourselves, my friends. And now" — he swung up onto the back of his mount — "on to Forestwood." He motioned the line of carriages and wagons forward.

"Almost like a wagon train," Jeff commented with a smile as he and Clay fell in line toward the rear of the procession.

Almost, Clay thought. These people weren't immigrants, though, setting out across the country to settle it and make it a decent place to live. They were rich and powerful, and at least one of them was out to grab as much as he could for himself, and to hell with the rest of the nation.

One way or another, Clay and Jeff were going to see that that didn't happen.

Chapter Twenty-one

Ned and India were discovering something that Jeff Holt had found out long before: Once Melissa Merrivale Holt made up her mind, there was no changing it.

No matter how much they argued, supported by Lemuel March and Melissa's own mother, Melissa hadn't budged from her decision.

"A ship is no place for a woman!" Ned had blustered.

Melissa had simply looked at India and smiled, prompting India to say, "Perhaps that's not such a good argument under the circumstances, Ned."

Hermione had fluttered around as usual, saying, "Oh, my dear, you've done some . . . some *unusual* things in the past . . . but this! To sail halfway around the world on a ship full of ruffians and pirates!"

"The March ships aren't manned by ruffians and pirates," Melissa countered, "at least not yet. I'm sure I shall be perfectly safe."

"Safe from my crew, perhaps," Lemuel had growled, "but what about the elements?

The passage around the Cape of Good Hope is sometimes a stormy one, as India pointed out."

"I have confidence in your ship and your crew, Lemuel."

They had all been unable to dissuade her. Lemuel had given up and gone back to New York, taking Ned and India with him so that they could begin preparing for the voyage to Hawaii. "I'll keep you informed as we go along," Lemuel told Melissa before he left. "It may take some time to secure just the right captain and crew for these new routes and to outfit the ships with more cannon. It could be several months before we're ready to sail."

"I suggest you take along plenty of flint-locks as well," Melissa had said.

Lemuel had stared at her for a moment, clapped his beaver hat on his head, and left.

Melissa knew that Jeff would be back from Washington before this new enterprise was ready to get under way, and she wondered what his reaction would be when he found out she had committed almost all their resources to such a risky venture. Knowing her husband as she did, Melissa hoped he would not be too upset. Of course it was highly likely that Jeff would want to accompany her on the voyage to Alaska, which was what she had had in mind all along. But if she had not acted quickly and declared her own intention of going, Jeff might decide to travel by himself, leaving her and Michael behind. Melissa hoped fervently that would not happen — though she had to admit Jeff might forbid her to go.

In that case, they would simply have to see which of them had the stronger will.

In the meantime, she had to prepare as if she and Michael were going. She had considered leaving Michael with Hermione, then discarded the idea. The voyage would take at least a couple of months, and Melissa didn't like the thought of being separated from her son for that long. But it would entail a certain amount of risk, as Lemuel, Ned, and India had repeatedly pointed out, and Melissa had to ask herself if she was being a poor parent by exposing Michael to the potential of such danger.

But there was danger everywhere, even in the most mundane of settings. Her father's murder in his own store was proof enough of that. And a sea voyage was something an adventurous young boy like Michael would never forget.

In addition to preparing for the trip, there was still a business to run, and Melissa spent a lot of time at the emporium. No more "accidents" had occurred at any of the warehouses in which Holt-Merrivale goods were stored since she had hired Terence O'Shay to provide guards for the buildings, nor had any of Lemuel March's trade ships been mysteriously lost at sea. With the shelves of the emporium fully stocked again, Melissa lowered the prices slightly, just enough to lure back some old customers without cutting too deeply into her profits. It was a risky move, she knew, especially at a time when she would soon need all the funds she could lay her hands on, but she felt that she had to do something to slow Jeremiah Corbett's ascendancy. She was not going to surrender Holt-Merrivale's position as Wilmington's leading merchant without a struggle.

She was in the office at the emporium, going over the books for the preceding couple of weeks, when Mr. Hayward, the chief clerk, knocked on the door and stepped into the room, a piece of paper in his hand. Melissa looked up at him, slightly annoyed at being disturbed. "What is it, Mr. Hayward?"

"I'm sorry to bother you, Mrs. Holt, but . . . aren't you going home?"

Melissa frowned. "What are you talking about? It's not time . . ." A sudden suspicion hit her. "What time *is* it?"

"It's after seven in the evening, ma'am," Hayward told her. "We'll be closing soon."

Melissa sat back in her chair and closed the ledger with a snap. "I had no idea it was so late," she said. "I get so caught up in these figures —"

She broke off with a shake of her head. Hayward wasn't the one she needed to make excuses to. Her mother and Michael would be getting worried about her. She would have to apologize to them when she got home.

As she stood up and reached for her bonnet and shawl, she said to Hayward, "I'm surprised the store is open this late. Don't we normally close earlier?"

"Yes, but I've been working on the restocking list" — he held up the paper in his hand — "so I thought I might as well keep the doors open and catch a little of the late trade."

Melissa nodded in appreciation. Hayward might be something of a toady, but he was a hard worker. "Did you finish the list?" she asked him.

"Yes. I'll send it over to the warehouse first thing in the morning."

Melissa held out her hand and said, "Give it to me, and I'll drop it off there on my way home. Mr. O'Shay's men can start preparing the goods to be brought over here tomorrow."

"Oh, I'm certain that's not necessary. Don't trouble yourself, Mrs. Holt. Besides, Mr. O'Shay's men were hired as guards. They might not want to perform such labor."

"I'm sure they won't mind," Melissa said without withdrawing her hand. "I want our shelves to stay as fully stocked as possible, so if some of the work can be done tonight, so much the better. I'm tired of Jeremiah Corbett stealing a march on us."

Tentatively, Hayward extended the paper. Melissa took it from him, glanced at the items and the quantities he had scrawled on it, and nodded in satisfaction. "I'll deliver this," she said as she picked up her reticule and tucked the paper inside it. Then she pulled the shawl more tightly around her shoulders and nodded to the clerk. "Good night, Mr. Hayward."

"Good night, Mrs. Holt. Would you like someone to escort you home?"

"Hardly. I can manage perfectly well by myself, thank you."

Hayward didn't argue the point. Melissa supposed he was growing accustomed to her independent streak. Most of her family, friends, and associates did, sooner or later.

She left the emporium, climbed into the buggy parked in front of the building, and expertly turned the team around and started the vehicle rolling toward the warehouses that bordered the dock area.

The sun had set, and darkness was settling over Wilmington. At this hour the streets were not nearly as busy as they normally were during the day. Melissa saw a few other buggies and wagons and a handful of pedestrians on the plank boardwalks. As she drew nearer to the harbor, she saw no one about. Large buildings loomed darkly around her. These were warehouses and shipping company offices, now closed for the day. A few blocks away, she knew, the waterfront taverns were full of people, but this particular area appeared to be deserted. Lamps burned here and there, but nearly everywhere Melissa looked there were only deep shadows.

She drew the buggy to a halt in front of the warehouse where most of the goods for the emporium were stored. It was a massive brick building that took up an entire block. Several sets of large double doors ran along the front, giving access to wagons. The doors were closed and locked at the moment, of course. To one side was a smaller door that led into a tiny office area. Melissa stepped down from the buggy and tied the horse's reins to a heavy iron ring she took from the floorboard of the vehicle. An oil lantern hung beside the office door, but its flame had burned low and was guttering now, giving off only a faint, flickering light. Someone needed to refill it.

Melissa expected the office door to be locked, too. She raised her gloved right hand and rapped sharply on the panel. There was no response, so after a moment she knocked again.

That's odd, she thought when no one came to the door. One of Terence O'Shay's men was usually on duty in the office, and several more men should have been patrolling the interior of the warehouse. Melissa knocked again, more loudly this time.

Still nothing. Without thinking about what she was doing, she reached down and tried the latch.

The door opened smoothly under her hand.

She caught her breath. She knew she lacked the instinct for danger that her husband and her brother-in-law possessed, but something inside her brain was warning her that this was wrong. The door should have been barred from the inside. Melissa pushed it open a little farther and saw that the small office inside was dark.

O'Shay and his men will clean you out. Ned had said something like that when Melissa first suggested hiring the smuggler and his men to guard the warehouse. A bitter suspicion was growing inside her now. Had Terence O'Shay simply been biding his time, waiting for the proper moment to strike before looting the very place he was supposed to protect? Had that moment finally come?

Melissa didn't want to believe that the big Irishman could be so treacherous. Yes, O'Shay had been known to skirt the law, but he was fiercely loyal to his friends, and for him the Holts fell into that category. But Melissa knew she could not doubt the evidence of her own eyes. She pushed the door open and stepped inside the office, determined to see for herself if the place had been robbed.

A bit of light from the lantern outside penetrated the room, enough that Melissa could see the desk that took up most of the office. Behind the desk was another door that led into the cavernous, high-ceilinged storage area. That door was closed. Melissa moved around the desk, intending to go through the door into the main room.

Her foot struck something as she rounded the desk, and she caught her breath sharply as a groan sounded. Torn between the desire to bolt back outside and the need to know what was going on, she hesitated, but only for a moment. Then she knelt and reached out to touch whatever it was she had kicked.

She touched human flesh, then something wet and warm and sticky.

Recoiling in horror, she stood up quickly and backed away at the same time, banging her hip against the desk. She barely noticed the pain as she retreated all the way out of the building. Then, shuddering, she stood on the street catching her breath as she tried to decide what to do next.

That was a man lying on the floor in there, a badly injured man. She ought to get in the buggy and drive as fast as she could to summon help. She needed a constable and a doctor. And yet, fetching someone to help would take time, time the man might not have. He was bleeding badly, and he might be dead before she could return with a doctor. If she went back in, she might be able to bind up his wound and slow or even stop the flow of blood.

But she wasn't going back in the dark, she decided, steeling herself for what was to come. She reached up and took down the lantern from the peg beside the door. The flame flared up briefly as oil sloshed in the reservoir. Melissa judged that it would give her a few minutes of light before it burned out. She had to take advantage of that, so she drew a deep breath and plunged back into the office.

The flickering light from the lantern showed her essentially what she had expected to find. A man in rough clothes was sprawled on his face between the desk and the inner door. He had bled freely from an ugly gash on the scalp. He was unconscious but still breathing, Melissa saw as she forced herself to kneel beside him. She reached out with a trembling hand and rested her fingertips for a moment on the side of his neck. His pulse was quick and erratic. The bleeding had stopped, she could tell now, so there was nothing she could do for him.

This man was one of Terence O'Shay's associates. Melissa vaguely recognized him from previous visits to the warehouse. Where were the other men who should have been guarding the building? Surely no one would come in here, batter this man, and then leave. Whoever had committed this act of violence had had even greater mischief in mind.

Melissa stood. Her legs were shaking and her heart thudded heavily in her chest. But her eyes were fixed determinedly on the inner door. She would take a quick look inside the warehouse, she told herself, then quickly drive the buggy into town and find a doctor and a constable.

She moved cautiously around the unconscious guard, holding the lantern high in her left hand while reaching for the latch of the inner door with her right. She lifted the latch, and the door swung back with a loud creaking sound that made her pulse hammer. Anyone who might be waiting in the warehouse now knew she was coming. Of course, the way she had pounded on the door earlier, she had already alerted any intruders to her presence. That thought loomed in her mind as she stepped through the doorway, overwhelming her determination to look around. She stopped short and started to step back, suddenly realizing that she had been foolish to come in here.

Before she could move back into the office, a hand shot out of the darkness and fastened around her wrist. She started to cry out as she was jerked roughly away from the door. Before any sound could escape her lips, another hand was clapped over her mouth. She felt herself drawn inexorably against a man's lean, hard-muscled body. Then she heard a puff of air, the lantern was blown out, and black darkness fell like a shroud around her.

"Be quiet!" a voice whispered urgently in her ear. "Are you trying to get us both killed?"

Melissa stiffened. The voice belonged to Philip Rattigan.

She was almost overwhelmed by a flood of emotions. Foremost among them was fear. The sight of the bloody, unconscious man in the office; the darkness closing in around her, pressing against her; the remorseless strength of the hand on her mouth and the arms that held her — all these things conspired to make Melissa nearly faint with terror.

At the same time, she felt a well of anger and outrage deep within, slowly working its way to the surface. She did not struggle against Rattigan's grasp; she could tell immediately that he was too strong to fight off. But she stood stiff and straight, quelling the impulse to close her eyes and shudder, so that he could at least feel her resistance.

Gradually she became aware that the darkness was not total. From the corner of her eye she could see a faint glimmering of light. With Rattigan's hand still pressed over her mouth, though, she could not turn her head to see where the light was coming from.

That wasn't all. Over the pounding of blood in her head, she heard voices. They were muffled, as if they were far away, and she could not understand what they were saying. She caught only snatches of words that didn't make sense.

Rattigan's breath was warm against her cheek again as he inclined his head closer. "If I take my hand away from your mouth, Mrs. Holt," he whispered, "do you give me your word you won't cry out?"

Melissa nodded, unsure whether she meant it or not.

"Don't lie to me," Rattigan hissed, as if he had read her mind. "You must tell me the truth. You have to be quiet so you won't draw attention to us. If they realize we're here, they'll try to kill us both."

Again Melissa nodded, and this time it was an honest answer. With unknown danger all around her, she wasn't foolish enough to start yelling until she had assessed the situation.

And so far, Rattigan hadn't tried to hurt her. He had simply grabbed her, blown out the lantern, and was now holding her tightly — so tightly, in fact, that she was having a little trouble breathing, especially with his hand over her mouth.

"All right," he whispered. "I'm going to

trust you. I hope I'm not making a terrible mistake."

He lifted his hand away from her lips.

Melissa did not cry out. For a few moments all she did was draw deep breaths of air into her lungs as quietly as possible. "That's it," Rattigan told her, his words so soft she could barely hear them. "As little noise as a mouse."

He would wish she was a mouse before she was through with him, she vowed to herself. How dare he grab her like that? And what was he doing in a warehouse full of Holt-Merrivale goods in the first place?

Getting ready to burn it to the ground? she suddenly asked herself. Perhaps it had been Rattigan who had struck down the guard in the office.

Rattigan's arm was around her waist. He led her away from the office door, his grip unyielding. Melissa tried to move as quietly as she could, twisting her head toward the light. The glow, broken by the moving shadows of several men, barely illuminated the huge stacks of crates that filled the warehouse. The stacks were arranged with a maze of aisles between them, and Melissa's view of the light was suddenly cut off as Rattigan took her around a corner into another aisle. Without the dim light she could not see him, even as a vague shape.

But he was still there. She could feel his hands on her, and even if he had not been touching her, she thought she would have been able to sense his presence, which was almost palpable, it was so powerful. He put his head close to hers and asked, "What the devil are you doing here, Mrs. Holt?"

"These are my goods," she shot back, keeping her voice pitched equally low. "I have a right to be here."

"Do you have a right to get several men killed? Because that's what you've done."

Both Melissa's hands were free. She put one of them to her mouth as she gasped. "The guards?"

"They're all dead except for the lad in the office, and from the looks of that blow he took on the noggin, he may not last much longer."

"You . . . you *bastard!* You killed —"

"I didn't kill anybody," Rattigan interrupted her. "I came in after the dirty work was done. I just heard them talking about it."

"Then you paid the men who did it!"

"You can believe this or not, Mrs. Holt, but I didn't have anything to do with this. The only reason I'm here is to satisfy my curiosity."

"Your curiosity?" she repeated, amazed at his brazenness.

"That's right. I was in one of the dram-shops down on the waterfront having a pint when I overheard some men talking about a warehouse. They sounded like they were up to no good. I heard the name Holt, so when they left, I followed them. I saw them come in here — they got the careless fellow in the office to open up, probably by lying about who they were — and then I heard some noises that told me there was bad business going on. I slipped in behind them . . . and then you show up, pounding on the door like you're the bloody town crier or something!"

She wasn't sure whether to believe any of what he had said. She had a feeling he could be a skillful liar when he wanted to. To give herself a moment to gather her thoughts, she said, "You could have come out and told me what was going on."

"I was hoping you'd just go away," he replied scornfully. "Instead you come waltzing in and waving a lantern around. You're damned lucky those boys are so busy they didn't notice you, that's all I've got to say. Damned lucky. If they hadn't been moving crates around and making banging noises of their own at the same time you decided to knock on the bloody door —"

"Who are they?" Melissa cut in. "Or do you honestly not know?"

"I've never seen them before, but as you can imagine from seeing their handiwork, they're pretty rough lads, the sort whose muscle can be hired for a few coins in any waterfront dive."

Melissa could not stop herself from shuddering. "You said all the other guards are dead?"

"I don't know that for a fact, but I heard one of those men say the guards were all taken care of. I took that to mean dead, or next thing to it."

"They were rough men, too," Melissa whispered. "They work . . . worked for Terence O'Shay."

"That Irish smuggler!" Rattigan hissed, reminding Melissa of their earlier conversation concerning O'Shay. "Set a thief to catch a thief, I suppose you could say."

"You would know all about thievery," Melissa said coldly. "It was you and your partner I was trying to protect my business against."

He chuckled in the darkness, which was a surprising contrast to his grim tone only moments earlier. "I told Jeremiah that you didn't trust us and warned him not to be fooled by that little act you put on when you came to see him a few weeks ago. You're a suspicious little baggage, Mrs. Holt."

She felt a fresh surge of anger. "Watch your tongue, sir."

"I'm just telling the truth, which you seem to value. If I was really trying to ruin your business, would I have come here tonight to try to stop whatever those lads are up to?"

"Is that really why you're here?"

"It is. And I'd be doing just that if you hadn't come blundering along."

"Well, then, if you're telling the truth, let's find out what they plan to do, other than murder my guards."

Rattigan said dubiously, "What we really should be doing is getting you out of here."

"You said yourself I was lucky they didn't hear me coming in. If I try to sneak out, I'm liable to be discovered."

After a moment he said grudgingly, "All right, that makes sense . . . I suppose. Come on, then, but stay behind me — and for God's sake be quiet about it!"

Rattigan removed his arm from her waist, for which Melissa was grateful. Now that she had gotten over her initial fright, she found it disconcerting to be pressed up so closely against a man who was not her husband. Rattigan transferred his grip to her wrist and began leading her back down the aisle. His eyesight must have been keener than hers, because he moved confidently through the warehouse. If not for his guiding hand, Melissa would have groped along helplessly.

Then the light appeared again, and its glow grew steadily until Melissa could make out Rattigan's tall figure in front of her and, beyond him, a narrow gap between two stacks of crates. Rattigan paused when he reached it. He turned his head toward her and touched a finger to his lips in a warning gesture, then drew her alongside him so that both of them could crouch and peer between the crates.

What Melissa saw made her blood run cold. Several of the rough-looking men Rattigan had described were standing there holding lanterns, and soon another man joined the group. Instead of a lantern he was carrying a wooden keg. He tossed it aside, and Melissa could tell from the sound as it hit the floor and rolled away that it was empty.

"Got that powder spread, did ye?" one of the men asked the newcomer.

"Aye. There's a trail of it all around the place, and another one leading from the door to that pile o' kegs we put in the middle of the building. When it blows, what's left o' this place will burn like blazes."

"And nobody'll be able to tell that O'Shay's boys were dead before the fire broke out," added another man. "I'd say we've earned our money tonight, lads."

"I'm ready to collect it," the first man said. "I need a drink and a woman. Let's go touch that powder off and get out of here."

Melissa glanced at Rattigan. She had been unsure whether to believe him when he'd said that he had nothing to do with these men. Now, as she saw the hard planes of his face set in taut, angry lines, she knew he had been telling the truth. He was as outraged as she was by the terrible destruction these men had planned.

They could not allow the killers to set off those kegs of gunpowder. If they did, not only would this warehouse be destroyed, but the entire waterfront district would be in danger. Fires could spread rapidly, too rapidly to be contained. They had to do something, Melissa thought wildly.

Rattigan obviously shared that sentiment. Motioning Melissa back, he stood up and placed his hands against one of the crates in the stack above him. The muscles of his arms and shoulders bunched as he began to shove.

Instantly Melissa understood what he was trying to do. More crates were stacked on top of the one he was pushing. If he could topple the entire lot of them, they would fall on the men who were planning to destroy the warehouse. Unfortunately, the crates weren't budging.

Melissa ignored Rattigan's gestured warning and sprang forward to help him. Her strength was only a fraction of his, of course, but it might be enough to make a difference.

It was. With a grinding rasp, the crates towering above them shifted and began to lean.

"What the hell!" one of the men on the other side of the stack exclaimed.

"There's somebody over there!" another man yelled. "Shoot them!"

Melissa thought she heard the roar of gunshots. She couldn't be sure, because with a mightier roar the crates began to topple and fall. A man screamed, and then someone shouted, "The powder! Look out for that lant— !"

The cry was cut off by the sound of splintering wood as another crate fell. Rattigan grabbed Melissa's arm again and pulled her back. As the echoes of falling crates died away, Melissa heard another sound.

A hissing, almost like a gigantic snake.

"One of those powder trails is burning!" Rattigan snapped. He jerked on Melissa's arm. "Come! We've got to get out of here!"

She pulled away from him, taking him by surprise with a burst of unexpected strength. "No!" she cried. "I won't let them destroy everything!" Without thinking, she darted forward through the rubble of toppled crates.

"Melissa! No!" Rattigan shouted behind her. She heard the pounding of his feet as he ran after her.

All the plotters had been trapped beneath the crates, Melissa saw. A couple of small fires had sprung up from the lanterns they had dropped. It was important that those blazes be put out before they grew larger, she knew, but that danger paled next to another: The hissing sound she had heard and a bright glare that hurt her eyes marked the trail of burning powder that led to a small pile of kegs some thirty feet away. The sparks had already traveled about half that distance.

Melissa was about to throw herself toward the burning powder to snuff it out when a figure flashed past her. Rattigan left his feet in a dive that sent him skidding across the warehouse floor. His hands slapped at the burning powder, scattering it. Several stubborn sparks eluded him, setting off the makeshift fuse once again. Rattigan scrambled after the fire. Smoke and the stench of burned powder filled the air.

Then the hissing, spitting glare died down as he batted out the last of it. The trail of burning powder winked out less than ten feet from the pile of kegs.

Melissa ran up beside Rattigan, her eyes desperately searching for any stray bits of powder that might still be burning. She found none. This fire was out. Now they could concentrate on the others. "Give me your coat!" she said to Rattigan.

He looked up at her from where he was still crouched on hands and knees. He was breathing heavily, and powder smoke grimed his face. His hands were even darker as he pushed himself up off the floor. Realizing what she had in mind, he whipped off his coat and handed it to her, then began tugging his shirt from his trousers.

Melissa ran to the front of the warehouse. A barrel of rainwater was stored there, just inside the closest set of double doors. The barrel was always kept filled in case of fire, and Melissa made good use of it now, dipping Rattigan's coat into it and then running with the sodden garment to the nearest fire. She slapped at the flames with the wet coat.

A few yards away, Rattigan, now bare to the waist, was doing the same thing with his shirt. Both of them worked frantically for several minutes, dashing back and forth to the water barrel and beating out the fires.

When the flames were finally extinguished, Rattigan dropped his ruined shirt and took hold of Melissa's arm. Both of them were coughing heavily from all the smoke they had inhaled. They stumbled toward the office.

The guard Melissa had found there was dead. Rattigan paused long enough to check on him and looked up at Melissa bleakly. She felt guilty for not summoning help immediately for the man, yet she knew that if she had turned around and left the warehouse the first time, the powder kegs probably would have exploded, dooming the wounded guard anyway.

"Let's get out of here," Rattigan said in a voice made raspy by the smoke. Melissa nodded and allowed him to guide her outside.

The smoke in the warehouse billowed out the door behind them. They walked shakily down the street to get away from it, gulping deep breaths of warm, humid, but clean night air into their lungs.

"You . . . you're a foolish woman," Rattigan said as he tried to catch his breath. "You risked your life . . . more than enough times . . . tonight."

"I couldn't let them . . . get away with it," she told him. "And they would have . . . if not for your help, Captain."

"If I'm going to beat someone at business, I want to do it fairly," he said, his voice still hoarse. He inclined his head toward the warehouse. "Who could have done this?"

"Why don't you ask your partner?"

He looked at her intently, his face unreadable in the light that came from moon and stars and distant lamps. After a moment he said, "I intend to."

Without thinking, she reached out and rested her hand on his bare arm. "I believe you," she said.

Then, before she knew what was happening — or at least before she would admit to herself what was about to happen — Rattigan had his arms around her again and was drawing her against his broad, bare chest. His mouth came down on hers in a kiss that rocked Melissa every bit as much as exploding powder kegs would have.

Chapter Twenty-two

Gideon Maxwell's party took a road south-westward from Washington City to the small settlement of Manassas, then westerly along a creek that Maxwell referred to as Bull Run. The stream ran between high, rocky banks lined with trees. A cluster of good-sized hills rose in the distance. Clay heard others in the group calling them mountains, but having seen the Rockies, he knew hills when he saw them. With a grin, he said as much to Jeff.

"This is still pretty country," Jeff said, "and you've got to admit, it's a sight better than being in town."

Clay could only agree. It had grown warmer and more humid with each passing day in Washington. Out here away from the city, the air seemed cooler and fresher.

They had stopped in Manassas for their midday meal, and Clay and Jeff had gotten a chance to meet the families of the three senators. Louis Haines had the most children — seven — and Clay didn't even attempt to keep straight the names of the four boys and three girls. Haines's wife was a woman of fading beauty who looked more tired than anything else. Clay could understand why. Charles Emory and his wife, a graying, still attractive brunette, had three children, two girls in their teens and a boy a little younger. Morgan Ralston was married to a redhead considerably younger than he, and they had only one child, an adolescent daughter of whom Ralston seemed inordinately proud. All three politicians appeared to be devoted family men, and watching them with their wives and children, Clay had to remind himself there was a good chance that one or more of these men was not the upright citizen he seemed.

In addition to the senators and their families, another dozen members of Washington society had been invited along on this outing. Clay scrutinized them as closely as he dared, in case any of them turned out to be connected in any way with the conspiracy. And he couldn't forget Diana Maxwell; Lieutenant Markham certainly hadn't. The lieutenant was quite attentive to her as they shared a picnic basket during the stop at Manassas.

The butler, Sumner, had come along, too, which was a surprise to Clay. He had figured that Maxwell would leave the servant behind in Washington. Evidently, though, Maxwell seldom went anywhere without Sumner.

"My good right hand," he had called the butler during the party in his mansion.

One good thing about being surrounded by such a mess of people, Clay thought as he and Jeff mounted up and fell in line with the procession following the meal: With this many witnesses around, Maxwell wasn't very likely to try again to have them killed.

But an attempt would come sooner or later, Clay was convinced, and he knew from low-voiced conversations with Jeff that his brother agreed with him.

During the afternoon, as they drew closer to the mountains — or hills, as Clay thought of them — Gideon Maxwell dropped back from his place at the head of the party and rode alongside Clay and Jeff for a while. He said, "I'm looking forward to you gentlemen seeing my estate. The house itself is only a shell at the moment, but when it's finished, I promise it will rival President Jefferson's famous Monticello itself."

That was the second time Maxwell had mentioned Monticello. Was he flaunting the fact that he knew about the visit Clay and Jeff had paid to Thomas Jefferson's estate?

They arrived at Forestwood late in the afternoon. The sun was lowering, throwing into bold relief the skeletal framework of a large, unfinished building atop a distant hill.

"That must be it," Jeff said.

"Unless there's more than one half-built mansion out here," Clay said. "I reckon there could be."

The house proved to be their destination. The road now paralleled a smaller creek, a tributary of Bull Run that meandered through a wooded valley dominated by the heights on which Gideon Maxwell's house was being built. The hill itself had been cleared in the center for the house, but a ring of huge, majestic trees had been left intact to surround the mansion on three sides. The road twisted and turned as it climbed the hill, allowing the travelers different views of the valley, all magnificently scenic. This part of the world might lack the rugged grandeur of the Rockies, Clay mused, but it had its own pastoral beauty and serenity.

"Welcome to Forestwood, my friends!" Maxwell boomed as the procession of wagons, carriages, and riders came to a halt in front of the mansion. Most of the walls were completed, and all the rafters were in place. Clay and Jeff could tell from the framework that the mansion, when completed, would be even larger than Maxwell's house in Washington City.

From the top of the hill they noted that the terrain beyond the house was a level plateau. The woods grew densely there, apparently untouched by man.

Maxwell rode over to them and gestured proudly at the forest that had given the estate its name. "I have several thousand acres of woodland here, gentlemen, with all sorts of game roaming in them. I was wondering if the two of you would be kind enough to consent to lead a hunting party tomorrow, since you have the most experience at that sort of thing."

The question took Clay and Jeff by surprise. "A hunting party?" Clay said.

"That's right. We'd stay out several days, and it would be something of a journey into the wilderness for my guests, especially with two such seasoned mountain men as yourselves leading us. You could show us the way men of the frontier really live."

Clay suppressed a snort of disdain. It would be impossible to duplicate frontier life here in Virginia. There were no grizzly bears here, or Blackfoot hankering to take a man's scalp, or howling blizzards out of Canada, or any of the other dangers one routinely encountered in the high country.

But it was entirely possible that Maxwell's request hid something even more dangerous: the treachery of man.

Still, Clay and Jeff had come on this trip

out of a desire to play along with Maxwell, to give him enough rope to hang himself, so they exchanged a glance and then both nodded.

"Sure," Jeff said. "We'd be happy to do that, Mr. Maxwell."

"Gideon," Maxwell reminded them.

"Sure, Gideon," Clay said. "Who's going along?"

"Anyone who wants to. I'll propose the hunting trip tonight around the campfire. I'm sure the senators would be delighted to accompany us, and it wouldn't surprise me if my daughter and Lieutenant Markham want to come along as well."

Markham was definitely coming, Clay vowed. He wasn't going to let the young lieutenant out of his sight, not the way Diana Maxwell had him under her spell.

Maxwell had a campsite prepared for his visitors in front of the house. Several large canvas tents and a handful of smaller ones had already been erected. The carpenters who were working on the house had been told to return after the visit was over so that they would not disturb Maxwell's guests. Half a dozen servants had accompanied the group, including Sumner, who was never far from Maxwell's side. The servants were in charge of preparing and serving meals and attending to any other chores the wealthy visitors might require.

Wagons were unpacked, more tents were pitched, and by nightfall a couple of large fires were blazing. Huge iron pots were suspended over the flames on iron rods, and savory smells soon filled the air.

Clay and Jeff walked to the edge of the plateau where the road began its gradual descent down the slope. The others were gathered around the fire, which gave the brothers an opportunity to speak in private. For a moment Clay gazed up at the stars beginning to appear against the sable backdrop of the darkening heavens, then said quietly, "What the hell is Maxwell up to?"

"You mean why did he bring all these people out here into the country, including us?" Jeff asked.

"That's exactly what I mean. You think he just wanted to get us away from the city so he could get rid of us more easily?"

Jeff sounded dubious as he said, "I'm not sure about that. Seems to me that if he just wanted to kill us, he wouldn't have invited all these witnesses along."

"Could be he already had the trip planned and saw an opportunity to make another try for us."

"That sounds more likely to me," Jeff

said. "And he's willing to risk the witnesses because he's afraid we're getting too close to uncovering his part in the land grab."

"We still haven't tied him to it conclusively," Clay pointed out.

"And he doesn't want us to."

"No, he doesn't." Clay was about to say something else when he heard footsteps behind him and turned around.

Lieutenant Markham strolled to his side. He smiled as he said loudly, "Beautiful evening, isn't it, gentlemen?"

"Yes, it is," Jeff replied, pitching his words so that they could be overheard by anyone around the campfire without seeming unnaturally loud. There was enough open space around them that they could tell no one was closer than the fire.

"Have you found out anything so far?" Markham murmured as he surveyed the broad sky above them.

"Just that Maxwell's a charming host," Jeff said. "What about you?"

"Nothing. Diana's a sweet, lovely girl. I'd stake my life on it that she knows nothing about what her father's planning."

"That's exactly what you're doing," Clay warned the young officer. "You've been careful about what you've said to her, haven't you?"

"Of course." Markham sounded a little offended by the question. "What do you think I am?"

"A young fella who's got his head full of romantic notions," Clay said. "You go to making eyes at Miss Maxwell, you're liable to miss something else you ought to see."

Tautly, Markham hissed, "I assure you, Mr. Holt, I have everything under control. Neither Miss Maxwell nor any other lovely young woman is going to pull the wool over my eyes."

"See that she doesn't," Jeff advised coolly. "Maxwell's going to suggest that some of us go on a hunting trip tomorrow. You'd better volunteer to come along."

Markham nodded. "All right. I'm sure Diana will want to come, anyway. She says that she always goes where her father goes."

"Well, keep your eyes open." Jeff threw back his head and laughed as if Markham had just said something funny. Clay joined in the laughter, a little reluctantly because he doubted his ability to fool anybody.

Markham turned away and rejoined the others around the fire. Clay and Jeff waited a couple of minutes and then followed suit.

The stew the servants had prepared was delicious. Clay and Jeff enjoyed several bowlfuls of the thick, meaty blend as well as a handful of fluffy biscuits. Maxwell had even brought several bottles of red wine for his guests, which Clay and Jeff politely refused because they wanted to stay as sober and alert as possible. They might have walked into Maxwell's trap, Clay thought with grim humor, but at least they were being well fed. He wondered if Maxwell intended this to be their last meal.

When everyone had finished, Maxwell stood up and called for the group's attention. "I've arranged for two of our guests, Clay and Jeff Holt, to lead a hunting expedition tomorrow, and anyone who would like to come along is welcome. We may be gone for several days, however, and the conditions will be more primitive than here at Forestwood. But it should be quite an exciting experience."

"I'm going," Morgan Ralston said without hesitation. "I haven't been on a good hunting trip since I left Georgia."

"I want to go, too," Charles Emory put in.

Louis Haines completed the expected trio by saying, "Yes, so do I."

"Well, I wouldn't miss it for the world," Lieutenant Markham said. He turned to Diana, who was sitting beside him on one of the benches that had been set up by the servants. "What about you, Diana?"

"Of course," the young woman murmured. "As Father said, it sounds quite exciting."

"You enjoy hunting?" Markham asked.

"I have to admit, John, I was a bit of a tomboy when I was growing up," Diana said with a laugh. "Father taught me how to shoot a rifle when I was quite young."

Several more men spoke up, indicating their eagerness to go along. Clay made mental note of each, but he was still convinced that if Maxwell had a partner in the land grab, it was one of the senators — or all three.

None of the senators' wives were interested in joining the hunting party. Emory's son and Haines's three boys were going, of course. That brought the number to fifteen, which was about half of the guests who had set out from Washington. The others would remain at Forestwood with the servants.

Except for Sumner, Clay noted, amending his count to sixteen. Sumner was not going to stray far from Gideon Maxwell's side.

Which probably meant that he knew about the land grab, too. Despite the butler's mild appearance, Clay thought it might be a good idea if he was careful not to allow Sumner to get behind him.

The members of the hunting party rose

early the next morning. Instead of making use of the tent Maxwell had offered them, Clay and Jeff had rolled up in their blankets and slept under the stars. After so many nights indoors, sleeping in the open air felt good to Clay. If he hadn't been on the trail of a killer and a conspiracy that could threaten the entire nation, this excursion into the Virginia countryside would have been quite pleasurable. Not as much as getting back home would have been, of course.

Thoughts of home conjured up Shining Moon's image, and he felt a sharp twinge of regret that he had been away from her for so long. He wondered what she was doing and how she was getting along on the Holt homestead, and he hoped she wasn't too worried about the long delay that had kept them apart. When they were together again he would make it up to her, he vowed.

Bacon was sizzling in a frying pan, filling the clearing in front of the mansion with a mouth-watering aroma. Clay and Jeff retreated into the woods to change clothes, then joined the others at the campfire, which had been allowed to burn down to embers during the night before being built up again this morning. Gideon Maxwell looked up at them and smiled. "My God, gentlemen, you look completely authentic!" he exclaimed.

Clay and Jeff had donned their buckskins. Jeff was a little uncomfortable in his, having grown accustomed to more citified clothes, but Clay felt at home in the outfit, even though the buckskin shirt and trousers were heavier and stiffer than the garments he had been wearing. Both men wore moccasinlike boots that laced up the shins and coonskin caps with tails that dangled down the back of the neck. They carried long-barreled flintlock rifles, had pistols tucked behind their belts, and wore long, heavy-bladed hunting knives in fringed sheaths. Shot pouches and powder horns were slung on rawhide straps over their shoulders. Clay was modest enough not to point out that they didn't merely *look* authentic — they were the genuine article.

The senators were impressed, too. Ralston asked, "Where can I get clothes like those, Clay?"

"My wife made mine," Clay told him.

Ralston laughed. His wife had not yet emerged from the tent in which they had spent the night and likely wouldn't for quite a while, he explained. At least not until the sun was fully up. "And I can't see my darling bride making me an outfit like that," he said, "although she does like to sew."

Clay looked around the fire at the guests

who were going on the hunting trip. "Is everybody ready to travel?" he asked. "Have you got all your gear together?"

He received a round of affirmative answers. Clay intended to check everything himself before they set out, however, and when he announced as much, Gideon Maxwell nodded emphatically. "You and Jeff are in charge here, Clay," he said. "I can't make that too clear. We're putting ourselves in your hands."

Clay didn't believe that for a second, of course, and neither did Jeff.

"As soon as we've eaten and checked over the gear and supplies," Jeff said, "we'll be ready to move out."

That task did not take long. The sun was still below the horizon, though the eastern sky was rosy with approaching dawn, when the sixteen members of the party circled the framework of the mansion and plunged into the woods, following a game trail Clay had spotted with no trouble. To a man of his experience and instincts, the path might as well have been marked with signs.

As soon as they were out of sight of the mansion, Clay felt more at home. Here, as far as the eye could see, there was no evidence of the rapid encroachment of civilization. For the moment, at least, this country was unspoiled, unsullied by the tampering hand of man. Clay shouldered his rifle and tramped along at a fast pace, in the manner of the long hunters of the past who had first penetrated these woodlands over a hundred years earlier, at the beginning of colonial times. And, of course, there had been long hunters even before that, he reminded himself, lean, dusky men in buckskins and feathers, armed with bows and tomahawks, veritable kings of the forest before the European interlopers invaded their territory.

It seemed to Clay that they had barely left the mansion when Jeff said behind him, "Better slow down a mite. You're wearing them out already."

Clay stopped and turned to look back at the other members of the party. Except for Jeff, they were all red-faced and breathing hard, even the younger men. Clay shook his head and said, "Sorry, folks. Reckon I got carried away, being out here in the woods again, and forgot that you're not as used to it as I am."

"That's . . . quite all right . . . Clay," Gideon Maxwell said. "The exercise is . . . good for us. It'll toughen us up, make us more like you."

Not in a hundred years, Clay thought wryly. He and Gideon Maxwell would never be remotely alike.

After a rest the group moved on again, and this time Clay and Jeff set an easier pace for their city-bred companions. The sun rose higher in the sky, its rays slanting down through the heavy growth and casting dappled shadows on the ground. Other than a few more brief stops, Clay kept the party moving until midday. By that time he estimated that they had covered five or six miles from the edge of the plateau.

The terrain was not completely flat; there were areas of rolling hills where the trees thinned out a little and the grass was more lush. Numerous streams ran through the estate, some only a few inches wide. Clay had caught sight of many small animals — raccoons, skunks, badgers, an occasional fox — and the trees were thick with birds. He hadn't seen any larger game, but as he brought the party to a halt next to a creek, he spotted deer tracks on the other side. It wouldn't be difficult now to find the deer.

"We'll set up our main camp here," Clay announced to the group as they sat down wearily, some on rocks, some on fallen logs, the others on the ground. "With any luck, we'll find some deer this afternoon."

"What about a bear?" one of Senator Haines's sons asked. "Do you think we can shoot a bear, Mr. Holt?"

"Well, I wouldn't count on that," Clay told the boy with a smile. "There are probably some bears living in these woods, all right, but they're likely pretty peaceful sorts. They won't bother us unless we bother them, and they'll stay out of sight unless we happen to get too close to their dens. Not like the grizzlies out in the Rockies where I come from. I reckon those old boys hunt human beings just for the sport of it."

"Really?" one of the other children asked, wide-eyed with awe at the thought of encountering a grizzly bear.

Clay nodded. "Old Ephraim — that's what we call grizzly bears sometimes — has put many a good man under for no reason."

"You mean killed them?"

"That's right. The frontier's a dangerous place, son." Clay couldn't stop himself from glancing at Gideon Maxwell. "Beautiful, but dangerous."

If Maxwell read anything into Clay's glance, he didn't show it. He said to the butler, "Sumner, see to preparing a meal."

"Yes, sir," Sumner said. He was still dressed in dark livery and looked quite incongruous in these deep woods. Evidently he was most comfortable in that apparel, just as Clay was in his buckskins.

Lunch consisted of slices of ham from a

haunch that Sumner had packed, together with biscuits left over from breakfast and some wild honey from a hive that Clay and Jeff found. Simple fare but good, and Clay enjoyed it.

Sumner stayed behind at the camp, but the others followed Clay and Jeff as they tracked the deer that had come to the stream to drink that morning. By midafternoon they had located the herd, and after circling on their approach so that the wind wouldn't carry their scent to the animals, the hunting party was in position to make its first kills. The deer were grazing at the edge of a stand of trees. Clay, Jeff, and the others crouched in another line of trees on the other side of a broad meadow.

Clay looked over at Gideon Maxwell. "Want to take the first shot?" he asked in a whisper.

Maxwell shook his head. "I'll leave that honor to my friends," he said, gesturing to the three senators.

Ralston, Emory, and Haines each carried a rifle. Ralston seemed fairly comfortable with his, and Emory had used a rifle before, too. Only Haines handled his weapon somewhat awkwardly. In a nervous whisper he asked, "Are you sure about this, Gideon?"

"Go ahead," Maxwell urged him. "I'm

sure you'll do fine, Louis."

With a dubious sigh, Haines raised his rifle to his shoulder. Ralston and Emory did likewise, and the three men soon picked out their targets.

"The rest of the herd will bolt as soon as they hear the shots," Clay cautioned the others in the group. "Don't waste powder and lead trying to hit any of them. There'll be other chances for all of you to shoot." When he had gotten nods of agreement, he turned back to the senators. "Anytime you're ready," he told them.

Carefully, each man cocked his rifle and drew a bead. They held their breath and squeezed off their shots. The sparks from the flint set off the powder charges packed in each barrel, and the rifles roared as black smoke poured from their muzzles. As Clay had predicted, the herd of deer took off running, vanishing into the woods in the blink of an eye — all except for two bucks, both of whom were down and kicking frenziedly.

"Good shooting," Jeff told the senators.

"Damn it, I missed!" Haines exclaimed. "I had my shot lined up perfectly! What happened?"

"Maybe you didn't allow for the wind," Clay said. "There's not much breeze, but it doesn't take much. Don't worry, Senator.

No one makes every shot."

Haines was clearly upset about missing, though, and he continued to grumble as Ralston and Emory congratulated each other. Maxwell slapped them on the back, and the other members of the party crowded around to offer congratulations. Clay and Jeff walked across the meadow to deal with the two bucks that had gone down under the volley.

Both deer were still alive, though mortally wounded. Clay and Jeff drew their knives and put the animals out of their suffering, then began to skin and dress them as the others gathered around to watch. Judging from the reactions of some of the young men, it was a more gruesome spectacle than they had expected. Folks didn't like to think about that aspect of life, of feeding themselves, Clay mused, but it would probably do them good to witness it and perhaps even learn some respect for the animals they so eagerly hunted and dined upon.

Ralston and Emory each wanted the antlers of the bucks they had killed as trophies. Clay and Jeff obliged. They hung the carcasses from tree limbs and hacked off enough meat to last the party a couple of days. The rest would be left for the scavengers of the forest.

"This is why you frontiersmen can travel

so lightly, isn't it?" Maxwell asked. "There's no shortage of game, so as long as you have plenty of powder and shot, you're in no danger of starving."

"And there are lots of roots and plants that are edible, too," Jeff pointed out. "You're right. Nobody who knows what he's doing is going to starve on the frontier."

"I still say it'll be better when the whole place is civilized," Haines put in. He was still smarting over his failure to down a deer.

The party returned to the camp, where Sumner had been busy all afternoon. He had built a large fire over which the venison would be roasted and set up a small tent for Diana Maxwell. He had also rigged some makeshift shelters with branches and squares of canvas. While most people would hardly have considered any of these things luxurious, this jaunt was nevertheless a far cry from the first fur-trapping expedition up the Missouri River that Clay and Jeff had joined several years earlier, a fact not lost on either brother.

Over dinner that evening, Gideon Maxwell seated himself on the ground next to Clay and Jeff and asked, "Should we keep our camp here tomorrow or move on?"

Clay tore off a strip of venison from the haunch he was gnawing. "I spotted some more tracks on the way back this afternoon. Reckon if you want to leave the camp right here, we can find plenty more game in the area."

Maxwell nodded. "Very well. That will be our plan, then. I can't thank you enough for agreeing to be part of this expedition, gentlemen."

"We've enjoyed it," Jeff said. "Thanks for inviting us."

"It's my pleasure, I assure you."

The trip had been almost *too* enjoyable, Clay thought as he chewed the tough meat. He had to remind himself that he and Jeff and Markham were not out here to hunt animals. They were hunting *men* — the men behind the land grab. Clay had been convinced that Maxwell would make a move against them, but thus far the man had been a perfect host.

Was it possible they had been wrong about Maxwell? Clay knew there had to be some connection between Maxwell and Atticus Bromley, because he had witnessed with his own eyes Sumner's meeting with the doomed clerk. But maybe the connection was an innocent one, and while he and Jeff were traipsing around in the Virginia woods, the conspiracy was going forward full-blast back in Washington. Clay hated to admit to that possibility, but he couldn't deny it.

But his gut instinct still insisted that Maxwell was part of the scheme, and Clay hadn't survived as long as he had by ignoring what his belly told him. He and Jeff would play along a little while longer, he decided, before giving up on Gideon Maxwell as a suspect.

There were no hostile Indians in the area, and the fire would keep any animals from disturbing the group. So there was no need to post a guard. Still, out of habit, Clay remained alert, and he was awake when all the others had rolled into their blankets and gone to sleep. Diana Maxwell had disappeared into her tent. Even Jeff's breathing was deep and regular. The fire had been allowed to die down again, though flames still flickered from it. Clay would feed more branches into it from time to time during the night, making sure it was large enough to keep animals at bay.

He dozed, sleeping so lightly that he was almost as alert as if he had been wide awake. That half-slumber was as restful to him as a deep, dreamless sleep would have been to another man.

So, late into the night, when someone slipped out of camp, Clay was instantly awake. His eyes snapped open when he heard the faint rustle of brush and saw a shadowy figure disappear into the forest. The light from the fire was so dim by now, however, that Clay could not tell who the person was.

He sat up and looked around the clearing beside the stream. To his surprise, he saw that not one but two bedrolls were empty. Someone else had left the camp, but the earlier departure had occurred without Clay's being aware of it. He would not have considered anyone in the group other than Jeff capable of moving that quietly. Obviously he had underestimated someone.

But he would remedy that now. Soundlessly he put his blankets aside and stood up. He was still fully dressed except for his coonskin cap, so all he had to do was pick up his rifle from the ground where it had been lying beside him. Then he stole out of camp on the trail of the two people.

For a moment he stopped and considered waking Jeff. It would be better, though, he quickly decided, to leave Jeff with the others in camp in case of trouble. Nothing was likely to happen to the rest of the group, but Clay couldn't take that chance. As for his other ally, Clay doubted Lieutenant Markham could move stealthily enough to trail the conspirators without being heard.

Clay had no doubt that one of the men he was following was Gideon Maxwell. The other man was probably Maxwell's partner in the land grab scheme. Clay's pulse raced as he thought that he might be on the verge of discovering what he and Jeff were looking for. He moved carefully through the darkness, making less noise than the breeze that rustled the leaves above his head. He didn't stop until he heard the faint murmur of voices somewhere close ahead of him.

Dropping to his hands and knees, Clay moved forward again. Through a screen of brush, he caught a glimpse of two figures. He stopped, lifting himself into a crouch and trying to get a better look at them. Unable to do so, he listened intently to what was being said.

Gideon Maxwell was speaking. "You don't have to worry," he said. "It will all be taken care of."

"When?" Clay couldn't identify the second voice. It was a rasping whisper, and it belonged to a man. That was all he could tell for certain.

"Either during this trip or as soon as we get back to Washington," Maxwell replied. "I won't delay any longer than I have to."

He paused while the other man said something, but this time Clay couldn't make out the words. But Maxwell's reply was chilling confirmation of what Clay and Jeff had suspected.

"Don't worry, Senator," Maxwell said. "I want Clay and Jeff Holt dead just as much as you do. I know you brought me in on this plan, but now I have just as much to lose — or gain — as you do. I'll take care of them just as you had Governor Lewis taken care of."

Clay stiffened, filled with rage. Thomas Jefferson was right: Meriwether Lewis had been murdered so that he could not expose the land grab and the man behind it.

The other man said something, again so muffled that Clay couldn't understand, then laughed. Maxwell responded, "Jefferson's a damned fool. He thought he could stop us by setting a couple of backwoods buffoons on our trail. We'll *own* this country before anyone knows what's happening."

The hell you will! Clay thought as his hands curled tightly around his rifle. He thought quickly about the best way to handle the situation. First he would confront Maxwell and the other conspirator. He would cover them with his rifle while he called for Jeff and Markham. The camp was well within earshot, and the two would be at his side within a couple of minutes. The others in the party would no doubt be shocked, but now that Clay had the proof he needed, he was ready to bring this investigation to an end. He and Jeff and Markham would take Maxwell and the other man into custody and escort them back to Washington, then turn them over to the government. At that point Maxwell and his crony would probably reveal the names of everyone else involved in the conspiracy in order to make things easier on themselves. Clay had no idea how it would all play out, nor did he really care. By that time he intended to be on his way back to Ohio and Shining Moon.

He straightened and was about to push his way through the brush when a ring of cold metal was suddenly shoved against the back of his neck. "Don't move, Mr. Holt," a whispered voice commanded, "or I'll have to kill you. And once you're dead, we'll have no choice but to kill your brother, too."

Clay didn't move — partly because he wanted to protect Jeff, but partly because he was so stunned by the identity of the person who had somehow gotten the drop on him.

"You've been away from the frontier for too long, Mr. Holt," Diana Maxwell told him, continuing to press the barrel of a pistol against his neck. "Otherwise you never would have allowed a mere woman to sneak up on you this way. Now, put your rifle down."

Clay cursed himself mentally for being a damned fool. But he lowered his rifle to the ground. For the time being, he had no choice in the matter.

He was caught good and proper, like a beaver in the steel jaws of a trap.

Chapter Twenty-three

Shining Moon winced as she reached with her left hand for a jar on one of the upper shelves in the cellar. A sharp pain stabbed down her arm and shoulder, subsiding as rapidly as it had come but leaving behind a dull ache in her bones and muscles.

A week had passed since the day she had fallen in the old well. In that time, the injury to her left arm and shoulder had healed well, but she still found it uncomfortable to use the arm too much or move it too quickly, as she just had. She lowered her arm carefully and reached up with her right hand to pluck the jar of green beans from the shelf.

The ache in her arm and shoulder would eventually go away, she knew. The ache inside her was another matter entirely. Clay should have been back by now. She was still confident that he was all right, but something had delayed him, and not knowing what it was only heightened her anxiety. He should not have gone off to Washington City, she caught herself thinking in unguarded moments.

He should not have left her here alone with Matthew.

Not that she was really alone, she reminded herself as she turned and crossed the cellar to the short flight of wooden steps that led to the door. Since the incident at the well, one of the Gilworth brothers stayed close by her at all times. They took turns working in the fields, and Shining Moon was sure the crops were suffering as a result. But she was grateful for their presence, glad to know that if she needed help, all she had to do was call.

She had left the cellar door open, and now, as she reached the bottom of the stairs, a shadow fell across her. She looked up sharply, her breath catching in her throat.

It was not Matthew standing at the top of the stairs; the figure silhouetted there was too tall. But it was also too short and slender to be one of the Gilworths.

"This reminds me of the cave we found as children, at the foot of the mountain of the sleeping warrior."

The voice sent a shock of recognition through Shining Moon. "Proud Wolf, my brother!" she cried as she hurried up the steps. She suppressed the impulse to throw herself into his arms and hug him. She would have done that if she were a child, or a white woman, but a fully grown woman of the Teton Sioux did not display affection so openly. But as she emerged from the cellar, she could not stop herself from reaching out to touch Proud Wolf, to make sure he was real and not a product of her imagination.

She squeezed his buckskin-clad arm. He was real. He caught hold of her left hand. "My sister," he said, his voice husky with emotion. Shining Moon caught her breath again, but this time from pain. Her left arm still hurt.

Proud Wolf's eyes were as keen as ever. He saw her pain, and the joy of their reunion was quickly replaced by concern. "Are you all right?" he asked.

Shining Moon managed to smile. "It is nothing. I am well," she told him. "I am happy to see you, my brother. Why are you here?"

He grinned back at her. "As the white men say, it is a long story." He looked up at the cabin. "This is the lodge of the Holts?"

"Yes," Shining Moon said. "Come inside. We will talk."

She led him around the cabin to the front, where she saw two strange horses tied at the rail in front of the porch. Castor Gilworth stood at the top of the steps with a white man Shining Moon had never seen before.

Judging by the color of the hair under his hat and his lined features, this white man had known many seasons.

He smiled pleasantly at Shining Moon and said, "Ah, Mrs. Holt! I can't tell you how pleased I am to meet you. The lad here has spoken so much of you. I was hoping to meet your husband as well, but I'm told by this estimable gentleman, Mr. Gilworth, that Clay Holt is not here at the moment."

Castor nodded. "That's right. I told the professor about Clay going to Washington. I hope that's all right, Miz Holt."

"Yes, it is fine," Shining Moon said distractedly. "Did you say . . . professor?"

Proud Wolf took her arm — the right one this time — and brought her closer. "My sister, this is my new friend, Professor Abner Hilliard. He knew Professor Franklin."

"Indeed I did, may he rest in peace," Professor Hilliard said. He extended his hand to Shining Moon, who shook with him tentatively. Then he swept off his hat and went on, "The lad and I are on our way to Boston, but we simply couldn't pass through Marietta without stopping to see if you were still here."

Proud Wolf waved a hand at the two horses. "The man at the trading post told us how to find this place and let us use these ponies."

"Rented them to us," Hilliard corrected. "For a rather steep price, I might add."

"Yes. That is Mr. Steakley," Shining Moon said, having no doubt to whom her brother and the professor were referring. She gestured toward the front door. "Please, come inside."

As she turned to follow them, she looked at Castor Gilworth with a question in her eyes: *Where is Matthew?* He simply shrugged his broad shoulders and shook his head.

She decided she would not spoil her brother's visit by worrying about Matthew. She ushered her two visitors inside and placed the jar of green beans on the table. "There is fresh buttermilk," she said, gesturing to a pitcher.

"That sounds wonderful," Hilliard said. "I've always loved buttermilk, ever since I was a boy."

"That must have been many years ago," Proud Wolf said, and although his expression was one of pure innocence, Shining Moon saw the twinkle in his eyes and knew that he was joking with the professor. She could sense a strong bond between her brother and this older man.

Hilliard snorted in mock disgust as he sat down at the table with Castor and Proud Wolf. "I'm not as ancient as you seem to think I am," he declared.

"You were not here when the first buffalo emerged from a hole in the ground?"

"Not even when the second one followed." Hilliard took the cup of buttermilk Shining Moon offered him. "Ah, thank you, Mrs. Holt. You're much too kind."

When they all had something to drink, Shining Moon sat down with the men and again asked her brother, "Why are you here?"

"The professor and I are going to the east," Proud Wolf replied.

"To Boston, actually," Hilliard said as Shining Moon's eyes widened in surprise. "Or, more precisely, to Cambridge, where both Harvard University and the Stoddard Academy for Young Men are located."

"Professor Franklin spoke of this place called . . . Harvard," Shining Moon said, struggling only slightly with the word.

"Yes, we were colleagues there. When the journals he kept during his western expedition were sent back from St. Louis, they wound up in my possession. That was what gave me my great idea."

"Great idea?" Shining Moon repeated. She looked at Proud Wolf.

"I am going to the white man's school," he told her. "I am going to learn to be a white man."

For a long moment Shining Moon was silent. Then she asked in astonishment, "Why would you wish to do this?"

Proud Wolf shrugged. "To prove it can be done."

"Actually," Hilliard put in, "Proud Wolf isn't going to learn to be a white man. We've discussed that very matter, so I suspect he's merely twitting me a bit, as he has a habit of doing. No, he is a Sioux and will always be a Sioux, no matter what he learns at the Stoddard Academy. We are simply — and by 'we' I mean my colleagues in the American Philosophical Society and I — we are simply going to see to it that Proud Wolf receives the same sort of education any young white man might receive who was lucky enough to attend such a prestigious institute of learning. This is in the nature of an experiment, you see, an experiment into the delicate relationship between native intelligence and the influence of one's environment on the development of intellectual capacity."

Proud Wolf leaned toward Shining Moon and said, "The professor has more words than there are pine trees in the Shining Mountains, but he is a good man."

Hilliard drank some buttermilk and then lowered the cup, leaving a small mustache of white foam on his upper lip. "I take that as high praise indeed, coming from your brother, Mrs. Holt."

This was too much for Shining Moon to take in all at once. It had been enough of a surprise to see her brother here, away from the high country where she had thought him to be. To learn that he was on his way east to a white man's school was an even greater shock. She had never pictured Proud Wolf anywhere except in the land that had always been their home.

She looked intently at him. "This is something you want to do?" she asked.

He nodded slowly but without hesitation. "I would do this. I want to learn what the white men know."

"Then you should go." She took her brother's hand. "Can you stay here long?"

He shook his head regretfully. "The boat on which we are traveling will stay in Marietta only one night. We must be back at the river landing by the time the sun rises tomorrow morning."

"But you will stay here tonight?"

Hilliard said, "If you will allow us to impose on your hospitality, madam."

"Yes," Shining Moon said. "You stay."

For tonight, at least, she would not have to be alone with Matthew.

Should she tell Proud Wolf what she suspected about the boy? she asked herself. Almost instantly she knew that she could not. If Proud Wolf thought that Matthew was trying to harm her, either he would insist on staying with her or he would take her back to their homeland. Either course would force him to abandon his goal of attending the white man's school.

There was yet a third option: Proud Wolf might simply kill Matthew and be done with it. He would not willingly kill a child, of course, but he might do so in order to save his sister.

Shining Moon could not allow him to do any of those things. Matthew Garwood was *her* concern. She would not tell Proud Wolf of her suspicions — because they *were* only suspicions, she reminded herself. In her heart she might be convinced of the boy's evil, but the same stirrings of feeling that had prompted her to take him in told her that she must forgive him and keep trying to find the innocent child within him, so that the evil might be banished.

Right now it was important to find out where he was and what he was doing. Shining Moon turned to Castor and asked, "Would you go find Matthew and tell him to come inside?"

Castor did not like being around Matthew

any more than she did. She could see the uneasiness lurking in his eyes, but he nodded and said, "Yes, ma'am." He pushed his chair back from the table and stood up.

It was ridiculous to think that men as large as the Gilworth brothers, men who would make half a dozen of Matthew, would be frightened of the boy. Yet Shining Moon knew that to be the case. Both Castor and Pollux were distinctly wary of Matthew. If he had been a full-grown man, they could have dealt with him directly, even violently, and never known a moment of fear. But he was a boy, and what could they do to him?

When Castor had left the house, Shining Moon turned to Proud Wolf and said, "You must tell me of our people. How is our father, Bear Tooth?"

"When the professor and I left, there was peace in the village of the Teton Sioux," Proud Wolf said. "Bear Tooth is well. The winter was hard, as always, but the spring hunt was good. There are fat, healthy babies in the lodges, and the cries of the children are happy ones as they play."

"And our friends in New Hope?"

"They are well, too. Aaron Garwood has a new leg."

"A new leg?" Shining Moon repeated, her

eyes widening again. "How is such a thing possible?"

Proud Wolf smiled. "He carved it out of wood."

Her brother had been teasing her, Shining Moon realized, and for a moment she wanted to box his ears as she had often done when they were children and he would play mischievous tricks on her. Instead she said, "This is the truth?"

"Yes. Aaron has a peg instead of a foot, but he walks almost as well on it as he did before he was injured. While the professor and I were in New Hope before coming east, Aaron told me that he hopes to go trapping again with Clay Holt when Clay returns."

"That will be a good thing," Shining Moon said.

"Father Thomas says that his flock is growing. There are more cabins now in New Hope than ever before."

"He is well?"

Proud Wolf nodded. "Very well. He is happy in his work."

Shining Moon was glad to hear that. She was quite fond of the priest, who had been her friend during difficult times. The church Father Thomas Brennan had built was the heart of the settlement, as important to New Hope as Malachi Fisher's trading post. That thought prompted Shining Moon to ask about the trader, and she and Proud Wolf spent several minutes talking about Fisher and the other settlers.

The door opened, and Castor brought Matthew into the cabin, one big hand firmly grasping the boy's shoulder. Matthew came grudgingly. He looked with open defiance at Shining Moon, then at Proud Wolf and the professor. He was surprised to see Proud Wolf, but he recognized him and gave him a look of hostile disdain. Professor Hilliard, however, drew a puzzled frown from the boy.

"Who're you?" Matthew demanded bluntly.

"Why, I'm Abner Hilliard," the professor replied. "And who might you be?"

"I'm Matthew Garwood."

"Ah, the little orphan boy. Proud Wolf told me about you."

"Did he tell you I'm an orphan because Clay Holt murdered my mother?" Matthew shot back.

Hilliard's bushy white eyebrows arched in surprise. Clearly he was at a loss for words, which Shining Moon suspected did not happen often. She interjected, "Your mother was killed by the madman, McKendrick. You know that, Matthew."

"But it was Clay Holt's fault," Matthew said stubbornly.

Shining Moon did not feel up to another argument with Matthew right now. She looked at Castor and asked, "Where did you find him?"

"He was in the barn. Playing by himself," Castor hastened to add. "He wasn't fooling with any of the animals."

That was a relief. Shining Moon had taken Matthew's knife away from him, but she felt confident he could devise other methods to inflict torment on any helpless creatures if he chose to.

Matthew turned to Proud Wolf. "What are you doing here, redskin?"

Shining Moon saw the flash of anger in her brother's eyes. "I am on my way to a white man's school in the east," he told Matthew, suppressing his annoyance with a visible effort.

"Won't help you any. You'll still be a filthy redskin, just like her." Matthew nodded toward Shining Moon.

Proud Wolf started to his feet, his face set in taut lines. Shining Moon knew he was going to strike the boy. Sioux children were not allowed to speak in such a disrespectful manner to their elders, and if they did, it earned them a painful cuffing. That was what Proud Wolf intended to do now.

"No," she said, reaching out to her brother.

Proud Wolf glanced at her in surprise. "The boy should not speak so," he said indignantly.

"I will deal with him."

"You are certain?"

"Please, Proud Wolf. This is my problem."

Matthew said, "I'm nobody's problem." He jerked away from Castor's grip. "I don't belong to any of you. I don't belong to no-body!"

Castor grabbed the collar of Matthew's shirt. "Well, you can come with me anyway. It's time to gather the eggs." He glanced at Shining Moon, and when she gave him a weary nod, he hauled Matthew out of the room.

Proud Wolf looked at his sister and said, "The boy is consumed by hate."

She was filled with shame that Proud Wolf and Professor Hilliard had had to witness Matthew's insolence. Without looking at them she said, "Matthew is very troubled. There is . . . an evil spirit inside him."

Hilliard leaned forward, a concerned frown on his face. "Are you certain you don't need any help with him, Mrs. Holt? I mean, the lad's not even really your son —"

"I have taken him to raise as my own," Shining Moon said sharply. "If there is good in him, I will find it." She said nothing about Cassie Doolittle's death or her own fall into the old well. And as soon as she got a chance, she would ask Castor and Pollux not to say anything about either incident. She did not want anything to distract Proud Wolf from his goal of attending the white man's school . . . even though she could not comprehend why a Sioux warrior would choose to set his feet upon such a radically different path.

But Proud Wolf himself had always been different from the other young men of her people. Smaller than most, he had relied on his cunning, his fleetness of foot, and the quick working of his brain to win his battles. If any of her people could understand the ways of the white men and learn the things they taught in their schools, it would be Proud Wolf.

It was late in the day now, so Shining Moon showed her brother and the professor where they would sleep, then began preparing the evening meal. Castor and Matthew came back into the cabin, Matthew carrying the basket in which they had gathered eggs from the chicken house. Matthew was still sullen, but he did not say anything insulting or angry to Shining Moon. A little later, Pollux came in from the fields and was introduced to Proud Wolf and Hilliard.

"Castor and Pollux, eh?" Hilliard commented with a smile. "Fast friends as well as brothers. I wonder if your parents considered naming you Romulus and Remus before settling on Castor and Pollux."

"Our pa's name was Ulysses," Castor said, "and our ma was called Cordelia. It was her idea that they ought to name their young uns after folks in mythology. She'd been educated, you see, and she knew all about such things."

"We've got a sister named Hippolyta," Pollux added with a grin.

"Well, the ancient tales of the Greeks and Romans are certainly rife with noble names," Hilliard said. "Do you intend to continue the tradition?"

"I don't know that there are any gals anywhere who'd want to marry up with a couple of big ugly fools like us," Castor said with a shake of his head. "So I don't know if we'll ever have any children."

"Well, if I ever find a gal willing to get hitched with me, I figure on calling my firstborn son Nestor," Pollux said. "I've always been partial to that name."

"Nestor Gilworth," Hilliard said. "Yes, that will make a fine name for a boy."

Pollux looked a little embarrassed. "Not that it'll ever happen."

"One cannot know these things, Pollux," Shining Moon told him. "We can only follow the path laid out for us by the Great Spirit, Wakan Tanka."

Hilliard turned to her. "I was under the impression, Mrs. Holt, that you had accepted the Christian faith."

Shining Moon nodded. "That is true."

"Yet you still refer to the Deity as the Great Spirit."

"His name does not matter. He is still the Creator of us all." She glanced at Matthew, who had retreated to the corner of the room, where he sat brooding. She found it hard to believe that Wakan Tanka — or Jehovah, or whatever name anyone wished to call Him — could create a child like Matthew, a child of darkness rather than light, hate instead of love, evil and not innocence. Why would He allow such a creature to exist?

It was a question she knew she could not answer, no matter how long she wrestled with it. So she put it out of her mind for now and brought the pot of venison stew she had made to the table. They would eat well tonight, and then in the morning Proud Wolf would once again be on his way. Shining Moon would hate to see him leave, yet she was thankful for even this brief visit. There was no way of knowing when she would see him again . . . if ever.

Where had that gloomy thought come from? She forced it away and smiled as she ladled up bowls of steaming, savory stew.

They talked long into the night, brother and sister, sitting at the table after everyone else had gone to sleep. Proud Wolf spoke of the visions that had come to him, the spirit cat that had told him without words that he must follow the path that led east. Shining Moon was the only one he would ever tell of these things. She told him of the letter from Meriwether Lewis that had sent Clay and Jeff Holt to Washington City and spoke of her hope that Clay would be back soon so that they could return to the mountains. Proud Wolf asked Shining Moon to tell him everything that was troubling her, but just as when they were children, she stubbornly refused. But, even if she would not say it out loud, he knew the source of her pain.

Matthew Garwood.

It had been a mistake for her to take the boy. The bad blood between the Holts and the Garwoods was too powerful to overcome. Matthew would always bear resentment, even hatred, toward the family that he blamed for the deaths of his mother and his uncles. Of course, even though Matthew would probably never know it, the man he had regarded as his Uncle Zach had also been his father. To this day, the unnaturalness of the coupling between Zach and Josie Garwood made Proud Wolf shudder inside. And the whites had the audacity to call his people savages . . .

Somehow Aaron Garwood had been able to overcome the hatred for the Holts that the rest of his family had tried to instill in him. Matthew seemed incapable of making the same hurdle, in spite of the kindness and patience with which the Holts had treated him. Had he been adopted by another family, one unrelated to either the Holts or the Garwoods, the boy might have been able to escape his past and the sins of his elders. But now that seemed unlikely ever to happen.

Nor was it Proud Wolf's place to speak of these things to Shining Moon. She had made her own decision regarding the boy, and he would have to honor it. Still, after he turned in for the night, his sleep was restless, haunted by dark dreams and the fear that he might never see his sister again.

Shining Moon woke her brother and the professor an hour before dawn. She had the morning meal ready, and they ate together in companionable silence. Matthew was still asleep, and the Gilworths were out in the barn, already at work on the day's chores.

When they had finished eating, Proud Wolf asked, "Will you go to Marietta with us and say good-bye at the boat?"

She shook her head. "I will say farewell to you here, my brother. This is my home until Clay Holt returns for me."

"This will never be your home," Proud Wolf said firmly. "Your home is the mountain valley of our people."

"And soon I will be there again." Shining Moon was smiling, but Proud Wolf could tell she had forced that hopeful answer.

"I can stay here with you until Clay Holt comes back from Washington," he said. That thought had been much on his mind during the restless night.

"No!" Shining Moon's answer was immediate and emphatic, allowing for no argument. "You must go to the white man's school." She caught hold of his hand and grasped it tightly. "You know you must follow that path."

She made no mention of his visions, and he was thankful that she respected his privacy.

They stood up, and he embraced her tightly. "May the Great Spirit watch over you, my sister," he whispered, his voice trembling a little.

"And you, my brother," she whispered back.

Professor Hilliard had already slipped outside to let them say their farewells. When they stepped out to the porch, he was shaking hands with the Gilworth brothers. "It was an honor to meet you," Hilliard told them.

"So long, Professor," Castor said. "You come back and see us anytime you want."

Pollux grinned. "Yeah, we like listening to you talk . . . even if we don't always know what you're saying."

The Gilworths had brought the rented horses from the barn and saddled them. Proud Wolf clasped Shining Moon's hand one last time, then stepped down from the porch and took the reins of his mount from Castor. He swung up into the saddle as Hilliard mounted beside him. "Good-bye," Proud Wolf called as he turned his horse around.

He heeled it into a trot, and he and the professor rode away from the Holt homestead. The sky was turning orange with the approach of dawn, and as they neared the Ohio River, Proud Wolf saw mist floating over the smooth surface of the water. It was a lovely sight, and he wished he could have appreciated it more.

Instead he was thinking of his sister and the boy Matthew Garwood. There was an emptiness inside him, a bleak foreboding of worse things to come.

If Matthew Garwood ever brought harm to Shining Moon, Proud Wolf vowed, he would hunt him down . . . and kill him.

Chapter Twenty-four

Jeff Holt knew as soon as he woke up that something was wrong. His instinct for trouble, while not as finely honed as Clay's, perhaps, was sharper than most. He rolled over in his blankets, instantly awake, eyes open as he searched for the source of his unease.

Nothing. The camp on the bank of the small creek was as peaceful as it could be as its occupants began to stir in the reddish-gold light of the rising sun. Nothing was out of the ordinary . . .

Except for one thing, and as he took note of it, Jeff stiffened in alarm.

Clay was gone.

In one lithe motion Jeff threw his blankets aside and came to his feet. Not only was Clay gone, but so was all his gear. The spot on the ground where he had rolled his blankets the night before was bare. There was no sign of his rifle, pistol, powder horn, or shot pouch. If not for the fact that some of the blades of grass were still bent down slightly — a fact that only someone as keen-eyed as a Holt would notice — Clay might as well never have been there.

Several people were up and about in the camp. Jeff swung around, looking for Gideon Maxwell. If something had happened to Clay, Maxwell was behind it. Jeff was sure of that. He spotted their host emerging from the small tent that had been set up for Diana Maxwell. Jeff strode over to him.

"Where's my brother?" he demanded, not bothering with civilities.

Maxwell looked at him, apparently surprised but seeming neither alarmed nor worried. "Didn't he tell you he was leaving?"

"Clay didn't tell me anything," Jeff snapped. "I went to sleep last night and he was here, and now I wake up this morning and he's gone."

"Well, then, you have every right to be concerned."

Maxwell's calm response mystified Jeff. The man certainly wasn't behaving as if he had anything to hide. Maxwell took out his pipe and began filling it as he went on, "Clay started back to Washington early this morning, before dawn."

"What?" Jeff hadn't expected that answer.

"He left. Said that he had remembered something very important that had to be taken care of immediately. I assumed you would know what he was talking about."

"Well, I don't," Jeff said. "Clay wouldn't just go off like that without telling me what he was doing."

Maxwell shrugged. "I wish I could tell you. Clay is *your* brother, Jeff. I thought you would know what he was about if anyone would. And it was none of my business, nor my place to ask him what he was doing."

Maxwell was lying. Jeff was certain of it. He glanced around, looking for Lieutenant Markham. Maybe the young officer had seen what happened — if he wasn't still sound asleep, dreaming of Diana Maxwell.

Even as that thought went through Jeff's head, the young lady herself emerged from the tent, looking fresher and prettier than any female had a right to at this time of the morning. She put a hand on Maxwell's arm, took in the grim set of Jeff's mouth, and asked, "Is anything wrong, Father?"

"Mr. Holt seems to be worried about his brother," Maxwell said.

Diana looked at Jeff with a puzzled frown. "I thought your brother went back to Washington."

"Did you see him leave?" Jeff asked.

"Well, no. But my father told me he did. I was worried that we would have to call off the rest of the hunt, but he said that perhaps you'd agree to continue being our guide and mentor. You have quite a bit of experience as a woodsman yourself, don't you, Mr. Holt?"

Enough to know when a skunk is on the prowl, Jeff thought. And something was sure starting to smell bad around here.

"Until I find out what happened to Clay, I won't be doing any more hunting," he said.

"I'm sure the others will be disappointed to hear that." Maxwell sounded a little angry, as if he thought Jeff was being unreasonable. "I know the senators are looking forward to spending another day or two out here in the wilderness. It's so refreshing after being in Washington."

"Sorry. It can't be helped." Jeff was more than a little angry himself, but he was working hard to control it. He had to keep his wits about him. If he wanted to help Clay, he couldn't afford to lose his temper. He was convinced that Clay was in danger, wherever he was.

A new voice spoke up. "What can't be helped?" someone asked from behind Jeff. "Is something wrong?"

Jeff glanced over his shoulder and saw Lieutenant Markham standing there, his short blond hair tousled from sleep. Markham quickly smoothed it with his palm when he realized that Diana Maxwell was standing with Jeff and her father.

He and Clay were not supposed to know Markham that well, Jeff reminded himself. He said, "My brother is missing."

"I'd hardly call him missing," Maxwell put in. "I told you, Jeff, Clay merely went back to Washington. What else could you possibly be intimating with these suspicions of yours?"

That you killed him, or had him killed, Jeff thought grimly, but again he managed to keep that fear to himself. Instead he said, "It's not like Clay to disappear like this, even if he did just go back to the city. I still say he would have told me what he was doing."

"Perhaps he didn't want to disturb you," Markham suggested. "That certainly seems like a plausible explanation to me. I'm sure that if Mr. Maxwell says Mr. Holt left, that was exactly what happened."

Even as he scowled in response to Markham's comments, Jeff had to admit he was playing his part well. By acting as if he believed without question whatever Gideon Maxwell said, Markham was insinuating himself ever deeper into Maxwell's circle of trusted associates. Either that or Markham was so smitten with Diana Maxwell that he was willing to believe her father's outrageous claims. Jeff wasn't sure which was true.

"I'm going to have a look around anyway," he declared.

Maxwell casually waved a hand toward the forest. "Be my guest."

That was what had gotten him and Clay into this tangle, Jeff thought as he returned to the spot where Clay had slept the night before. That was where the trail, if there was one, would start.

Jeff could see where Clay had stood as he rolled up his blankets and gathered his gear. From there the tracks led back the way the party had come the day before, toward the partially completed mansion. With the experienced eye of a frontiersman, Jeff studied each blade of grass, each leaf, each rock. The story they told was undeniable: Clay had gotten up and left the camp, just as Maxwell said he had.

But why? Jeff's worry deepened as he tried to answer that question. This was completely unlike Clay, and the only thing that could have made him act so oddly would have been some sort of emergency — again, just as Maxwell had said.

"Well?" Maxwell asked when Jeff stalked back to the spot where he had begun his search. "Did you find anything?"

"You know I didn't." The words were out of Jeff's mouth before he could stop them.

Maxwell stiffened. "What do you mean by that, Holt?" He didn't sound particularly friendly now, no longer the good host.

Jeff's brain was working rapidly. As he grasped the beginnings of a plan, he said with deliberate anger, "You've done something with him. I don't know how or why, but you're to blame for his being gone, Maxwell."

Maxwell's face flushed with outrage, but before he could say anything, Lieutenant Markham said, "Here now, Mr. Holt, that's not fair! You can't go around accusing someone of . . . of doing away with your brother!" He reached out to grasp Jeff's arm.

Jeff pulled away roughly from Markham's grip. "Get your hands off me, mister! I don't trust you any more than I trust this oily crook!" He glared at Maxwell, who was now turning purple with indignation.

"How dare you!" Diana yelped. "You can't speak to my father that way."

"There, there, Diana, it's all right," Maxwell said, putting on a magnanimous air. "Mr. Holt's under a lot of strain, so we have to forgive him for these flights of fancy."

Markham said, "You may have to forgive

him, sir, but I don't." He faced Jeff squarely. "Considering the way you feel, Mr. Holt, perhaps it would be best if you went back to Washington, too." With his back to Maxwell and Diana, Markham let one eyelid flicker down and then up in a brief wink.

The young officer was playing his part exactly as Jeff had hoped he would. If Maxwell had any lingering doubts about whose side Markham was on, this confrontation would settle them. Maxwell would believe that his daughter had Markham thoroughly bewitched.

In case Maxwell needed more convincing, Jeff growled, "I'm not going anywhere until I find my brother!" He swung his fist at Markham's head.

The blow was almost full speed and full strength. Jeff pulled the punch just enough to give Markham time to move his head back slightly. His fist grazed Markham's jaw instead of catching it cleanly. Markham staggered anyway, caught his balance, and threw himself forward, tackling Jeff. Both men went down, sprawling on the ground, and Jeff was vaguely aware of shouting as the other occupants of the camp were drawn to the commotion.

"Good job!" Jeff hissed to Markham as they rolled on the ground. That was all he had a chance to say before hands grabbed them and pulled them apart. Jeff was hauled roughly to his feet.

When he was upright, he saw that Senator Ralston was holding him, while Markham's arms were being restrained by Emory and Haines. Ralston said, "I'm accustomed to breaking up fights among my more contentious colleagues on the floor of the Senate, but this is quite undignified, gentlemen!"

"What's this all about?" Emory demanded.

"The two of you were rolling around on the ground like pigs!" Haines added.

Jeff pulled free of Ralston, though he noted the surprising strength of the politician's grip. Instead of answering Emory's question directly, Jeff said, "I'm going back to Washington."

"What?" Emory exclaimed as he and Haines let go of Markham. "You mean our expedition is to be curtailed?"

"Where's your brother?" Haines asked harshly. "Was this his idea?"

Jeff looked at the senator from New York. "Clay is gone," he said. "I don't know where he is. Mr. Maxwell says that he's gone back to Washington, but I intend to find out for myself."

Maxwell cleared his throat. "I must say I'm disappointed in your behavior, Holt.

You're a businessman, not some back-woods barbarian. Yet you've insulted me and jumped to the conclusion that I've done something to your brother." He shook his head. "I'm afraid this outing is over, gentlemen. It just wouldn't be the same now if we tried to continue on our own."

The three senators protested, but Maxwell had made up his mind and would not be dissuaded. He turned to Sumner, who had been hovering in the background, as usual, and said, "Have everyone start gathering their things. We're going to start back to Forestwood as soon as possible."

"Yes, sir," Sumner murmured.

Jeff was already packing up his own gear. He threw an occasional glare at Markham, to preserve the illusion of enmity they had established with their brief struggle. His hope, which he knew Markham shared, was that the young officer would be able to pick up from Maxwell or perhaps Diana some clue as to Clay's whereabouts.

But no matter what Markham discovered, Jeff already knew one thing: He would be returning to Forestwood. At the moment he had no choice but to leave with the others, but he vowed to himself that he would be back. He would not rest until he discovered what had happened to Clay.

But given their suspicions of Maxwell and everything that had happened so far, Jeff feared very much that his brother might already be dead.

Clay awoke gasping and fighting as the cold water splashed in his face. His muscles instinctively strained against the thick ropes binding him, but to no avail. The knots were too tight, and the ropes themselves were too strong to break. He shook his head from side to side, slinging the water away from his face like a wet dog, as he blinked rapidly to clear his eyes.

"I apologize for the rude awakening."

The soft, British-accented voice made Clay look up. The servant called Sumner stood in front of him. To Sumner's right was one of the burly guards Clay remembered from the night before. The guard and another bruiser just like him had slammed punches into Clay's belly and face for what had seemed like hours, demanding answers to the questions they were throwing at him. His stubborn silence had only goaded them on, until finally his head sagged forward and he slid willingly into the arms of the blackness that enfolded him.

But now he was awake, and he had to wonder if they intended to beat him again.

Let the bastards do their worst, he thought. He wasn't going to allow them the satisfaction of seeing how much he was hurting.

And Sumner was the worst offender. While he claimed to be sorry for what was happening to Clay, when Clay looked into his eyes he saw only coldness there, the almost glassy look of a dead man's eyes.

Clay leaned his head back, resting it against the thick wooden beam to which he was tied. He had been brought here to the basement of Forestwood the night before, after being captured so ignominiously by Diana Maxwell. He was trussed up so that he could not move, and a gag tied painfully tight in his mouth had kept him from calling out. Several of Maxwell's men had carried him through the shell of the house, through a trapdoor in one of the rooms, and down a flight of stairs into the basement while the senators' wives and children and the other guests slept peacefully in their tents less than fifty yards away, in front of the mansion. The gag had not been removed until the basement door was closed, and the door was so thick that no sound could penetrate it.

Then the two hulking figures had gone to work on Clay with their fists while Sumner stood off to one side, watching dispassionately, until Clay had blacked out.

Now he was awake again, and he had no idea how much time had passed. Here in the vast, shadowy basement of the great house, the only light came from a lantern sitting on a stool. It might have been the brightest noon or the darkest midnight outside, and Clay would never know the difference.

"I sincerely hope that you've come to your senses, Mr. Holt," Sumner said mildly, his solicitude genuine on the face of it. "There's really no need for you to continue suffering. All you have to do is tell us what you've discovered over the past few weeks."

"Go to hell," Clay rasped, his voice sounding harsh and unnatural even to him. His throat was dry; all he'd had to drink during his captivity had been the few drops that had gone in his mouth when the bruiser threw the bucketful of water in his face to wake him.

Sumner looked sorrowful. "That attitude won't gain you anything, Mr. Holt. We can be every bit as stubborn as you are. More so, I'd wager."

"Go to hell," Clay said again. The sentiment might not be original, but it was heartfelt.

Before Sumner could reply, a squealing noise sounded in the basement. Clay lifted his head and looked in the direction of the noise. The trapdoor was being lifted at the head of the stairs, and silvery light slanted down through the opening. Moonlight, Clay thought. It certainly wasn't sunlight. That told him it was night again. He had been down here all day.

Where was Jeff? he wondered. What had happened to everyone else in the hunting party? Those unanswered questions made him strain once more against his bonds, but this attempt to break free was as unsuccessful as the first, just as he had known it would be.

Clay watched as booted feet appeared on the stairs, followed by long legs in expensive trousers. The rest of the newcomer appeared, clad in a fine waistcoat and ruffled shirt. When he reached the bottom of the stairs, Gideon Maxwell smiled and said, "Ah, I see our guest is awake again."

"But still not talking," Sumner reported. He cast a reproachful glance at Clay.

"I didn't really expect him to. I'd wager Clay Holt has withstood quite a bit of pain in his life. Still, it was worth a try." Maxwell crossed the hard-packed dirt floor and stood in front of Clay. "I'm truly sorry things have worked out as they have," he said. "I've a feeling that under other circumstances, you and I might have been friends, Clay."

"Not hardly," Clay growled.

"Oh, yes. I can see the same determination — some might say ruthlessness — in you that I know I possess. I get what I want, and I suspect you've often done the same."

"Not if it meant being a traitor to my country." Clay restrained the urge to spit at Maxwell's feet. His mouth was probably too dry to manage that, anyway.

"You're speaking of the western enterprise, of course."

"Call it what you want," Clay snapped. "It's still a land grab."

That brought an outright laugh from Maxwell. "Think what you like," he told Clay, "but I assure you, you don't know even half the story."

That comment intrigued Clay. Despite his predicament, he hadn't given up on the idea of escaping, and if he did get away, he wanted to take with him as much information as possible about Maxwell's scheme. Maybe by pretending to know more than he did, he could elicit some useful nuggets from his captors.

"I reckon I know more than you give me credit for," he said. "I know what you've been doing, how you've been doing it, and who you've been working with."

"Is that so?"

"Atticus Bromley," Clay said heavily. "You had him killed."

"Of course I did. He was starting to have doubts. He wanted no more part of the deal. At least that's what he claimed. I think he was just trying to get more money out of me." Maxwell made a dismissive gesture. "He found out how foolish that was. Bromley actually thought he was important to my plans. His only importance was as a link in a chain. I simply replaced that link."

"Another one will break," Clay warned. "The government knows what you're doing."

"Don't be ridiculous. Certain members of the government may suspect, but they have no proof. If they did, that fool Jefferson wouldn't have pressured you to work for him and investigate. My trail is much too well hidden."

"I found it," Clay said.

"You were *allowed* to find it," Maxwell shot back. His mouth quirked with amusement. "I wanted to know how much you had discovered about the plan. That's the only reason you were allowed to get as close as you did before you were captured. I was merely making sure that you and your brother were indeed investigating me before I acted to eliminate that troublesome problem."

Maxwell's mention of Jeff made Clay writhe again. "What have you done with him?" he demanded. "What've you done with my brother?"

"Nothing," Maxwell said. "The last I saw of Jeff, he was on his way back to Washington with the others. I told him that you had left during the night, that you went back to take care of some emergency you had remembered."

"He didn't believe that," Clay said scornfully.

"Of course he didn't. I never expected him to. I simply wanted him out of the way for the time being, until I'd dealt with you. Also, I suppose I was giving him a chance to stop meddling in things that are none of his concern, but realistically, I don't expect that to happen."

Neither did Clay. He knew that Jeff wouldn't give up until he had found out what had happened to his brother.

Maxwell went on, "However, I'll deal with that problem in time. For now, I have plans for you that need to be carried out."

"I'm not telling you any more," Clay declared.

Maxwell laughed. "My good man, I don't care what you tell me. As I said earlier, you have no idea what's really going on in the western territory. When the plan comes to fruition, the face of the entire nation will have been changed."

Clay didn't like the sound of that. Could Maxwell's schemes be more complicated than a simple land grab? It sounded as if he had a larger goal in mind than the acquisition of more wealth and power.

"What are you going to do with me?" Clay asked. Right now, survival was the highest priority. The other matters could be sorted out later — if he was still alive.

Maxwell regarded him for a moment, then smiled expansively. "I'm going to give you a sporting chance."

That answer took Clay by surprise. "A sporting chance?" he repeated.

"Indeed. Do you know of a man named John Colter?"

Clay frowned darkly. "Of course I do."

"Then you've heard the famous story of how the savages captured him and made him run for his life."

Clay knew the story, all right. Anyone who had spent much time in the high country did. John Colter, who had been a member of the Corps of Discovery before becoming one of the first fur trappers in the Rockies, had been captured by the Blackfoot, who decided to taunt him by giving him a chance to outrun them — barefoot, naked, and unarmed. But they had not reckoned on Colter's toughness, ingenuity, and sheer will to live. He had escaped — and killed several Blackfoot in the process.

"I've heard the story," Clay allowed. "What's it got to do with me?"

Maxwell clasped his hands together behind his back and began pacing back and forth. "All the guests are gone," he said. "They're back in Washington where they belong. No one is on the estate at the moment except for me, my daughter, my men . . . and you. So I'm going to have my men take you out of this basement and let you go."

"Just like that?" Clay said, not bothering to mask his disbelief.

"Just like that," Maxwell said. "I'm going to give you an advantage, Holt. I'll let you run for five minutes . . . and then we're going to hunt you down and kill you. My guests didn't get to finish their outing because of you, so now you and I will have a hunting party of our own."

"Like the Blackfoot did with Colter," Clay said grimly.

"Not exactly. You won't be armed, of course, but I *am* going to allow you to keep your clothes and your boots. So you see, I'm giving you better odds than the savages gave John Colter."

For a long moment Clay stared at Maxwell, then said, "If you're waiting for me to say I'm much obliged, you're going to have a long wait, Maxwell."

"Oh, I don't expect gratitude," Maxwell said with an airy wave of the hand. "The only thing I expect, Holt, is for you to die." He turned to his men and jerked a thumb toward the stairs that led out of the basement. "Cut him loose and take him up."

Chapter Twenty-five

Jeff and Lieutenant Markham had maintained their facade of mutual hostility as they prepared to return to Washington. Markham had ridden in the carriage that had brought him to Forestwood with Diana Maxwell, but he rode alone this time, since Diana was staying on the country estate with her father.

"I've a few things to do out here," Maxwell had explained to his guests once they were all back at the half-finished mansion, "so I'll be staying for a day or two. The rest of you will be taken straight back to the city."

"I wish you'd think better of this, Gideon," Morgan Ralston had protested. "I see no reason to end this trip just because you've had a falling out with the Holts." Ralston, like the other guests, cast a resentful glance toward Jeff as he spoke.

Jeff knew the others blamed him for spoiling the expedition. He didn't care. He had more important things on his mind, such as finding out what had happened to Clay — and what Maxwell was planning now.

Ralston's argument hadn't swayed Maxwell, and the party had begun the return trip to Washington at midmorning. Jeff, on horseback, gradually lagged farther and farther behind the others. Finally he decided it was safe to veer off the trail completely and start circling back toward Forestwood. Since the other members of the group were all angry with him, it was entirely possible that none of them would remark on his absence.

John Markham would notice, of course, and Jeff had taken advantage of a moment before the party set out from Forestwood to slip the young officer a hastily scrawled note explaining his plans. In addition, the note had ordered Markham to go back to Washington and wait there until Jeff contacted him again. In the meantime, if Markham could find out anything from Maxwell or Diana without arousing their suspicion, he was to do so.

Jeff didn't think he would have any trouble finding the spot where Clay had disappeared. He wanted to search the area more thoroughly. If Clay had been captured — or killed — by Maxwell's men, there was a good chance that some sign of the struggle would still remain. Jeff intended to scout around the partially completed mansion, too. If Clay was being held captive, that was the most likely place Maxwell would keep him.

By late afternoon Jeff had approached the hill on which Forestwood stood, coming from a somewhat different angle than the party had taken a couple of days earlier. He estimated he was at least two miles north of the main road. This was a rugged, densely wooded area, which served his purposes perfectly. No one was likely to take note of his approach through these woods if he was careful.

The mansion was closer than the hunting camp where Clay had disappeared, so Jeff decided to explore there first. He dismounted and led his horse, picking his way through the trees more slowly and carefully now. If Maxwell was behind whatever had happened to Clay — and Jeff had no doubt he was — then he was likely to be on the alert for more trouble. Maxwell was no fool. He had to assume that Jeff would not meekly give up and abandon his brother.

As dusk was settling, Jeff tied his horse to a sturdy sapling and slipped closer to the mansion on foot. This was not much different from stalking game in the wilderness, he thought — but the stakes were much higher than simply going hungry for a while. Clay's life could be at stake, to say nothing of the very future of the nation. At this point the Holt brothers were the only thing that stood between Gideon Maxwell and the massive land grab in the west.

Most of the tents that had been set up in front of the mansion for Maxwell's guests had been taken down, but the largest of the tents, the one used by Maxwell and Diana, still stood. A light was burning inside it, and as Jeff crouched in the brush, he could see the shadows of two people moving around. One of them was a woman, who he assumed was Diana Maxwell. The other person was probably her father. Jeff continued watching as full night fell and a three-quarter moon rose in the eastern sky. Then his guess was confirmed. Gideon Maxwell stepped out of the tent, strode over to the mansion, and walked toward the center of the building. Jeff lost sight of him in the shadows.

A sudden rattle of brush behind him made Jeff tense and then whirl around. He saw the shape of a man looming there. Jeff's hand moved toward the pistol tucked behind his belt, but before he could reach it, he realized he couldn't afford a shot. That would instantly alert Maxwell that he was nearby. He had to deal with this threat silently. In one smooth motion he launched himself in a dive at the man who was trying to sneak up on him.

The collision brought a grunt from the shadowy stalker, and both men went down, Jeff landing on top. His left hand shot out and closed around the man's throat, cutting off any outcry. With his right hand he slipped his hunting knife from its sheath and brought it to the man's throat, resting the sharp point of the blade against the soft flesh. The man had been struggling, trying to throw Jeff off, but he stopped suddenly as he felt the knife prick his throat.

"Don't make a sound," Jeff hissed. "If you do, I swear I'll slit you from gizzard to gullet."

The man jerked his head in a little nod, indicating that he understood. Jeff lifted the knife, intending to bring the leather-wrapped grip down in a blow that would stun the man long enough for Jeff to tie him up and gag him. It would have been easier simply to kill him, of course, but Jeff Holt was no cold-blooded murderer.

Before the blow could fall, a stray beam of moonlight penetrated the brush, falling on the man's face. Jeff's eyes widened in surprise as he recognized the short blond hair and the eager — but at the moment frightened — features.

It was Lieutenant John Markham whose

throat he had almost slit.

"Markham?" Jeff growled in disbelief. Once again the man nodded. Jeff started to lift his hand away from Markham's mouth, then paused long enough to whisper, "Quiet! Don't say a word until we've backed off a little."

Again the nod. Jeff let go of Markham and slid off. He came to his feet and offered Markham a hand up, then led the way through the brushy undergrowth. When they were far enough away from Forestwood that Jeff felt fairly certain they wouldn't be overheard, he stopped and swung around, saying quietly but angrily, "Just what in blazes are you doing here, Lieutenant? You're supposed to be back in Washington."

Markham shook his head. "I couldn't return to Washington under these circumstances. Your brother is missing, and I was assigned, at the behest of President Jefferson himself, to assist the two of you in your investigation."

"You could have assisted me by doing what I damned well told you!" Jeff drew a deep breath. Losing his temper with Markham wasn't going to help anything. He asked, "How did you get away from the others and get back here?"

"When we stopped at an inn in Manassas

for the noon meal, I noticed that you were no longer with the group, of course. I had a pretty good idea where you had gone, so I told Maxwell's driver to go on to the city without me and rented a horse from the innkeeper. I rode back here and decided it would be best to approach the house stealthily. When I found your horse, I knew you'd had the same idea." Markham grinned in the moonlight. "I suppose great minds work alike, eh, Mr. Holt?"

Jeff bit back the retort that sprang to his lips. The young officer was here, and although Jeff would have preferred that he go back to Washington as planned, there was nothing he could do now but make the best of the situation.

"Follow me," he commanded curtly. "We're going back to the house. Maxwell and his daughter are there, and we're going to keep an eye on the place. Maybe they'll lead us to Clay."

"Not Diana," Markham said. "She couldn't have anything to do with her father's schemes. I'm sure of it."

Yes, but you're blinded by love, you young fool, Jeff thought. He said, "Come on," and started back toward Forestwood without waiting to see if Markham was following him or not.

★ ★ ★

Several more of Maxwell's men had materialized from the shadows of the cavernous basement, and Clay figured that they probably had bunks down here. The ropes binding him were cut. Then, with one of Maxwell's burly henchmen on either side, holding his arms in painfully tight grips, he was taken to the stairs and hauled out of the basement.

"I'm not going to have you gagged this time," Maxwell told him as they went up the steps. "Last night you could have disturbed my guests if you'd called out. Tonight there's no one on the estate to help you, so you can shout as loudly as you'd like."

"No point in yelling," Clay said. "But I'll say howdy to you in Hell when I get there — because you'll be there first."

Maxwell laughed. "Still defiant, I see. Good. That will make things much more interesting. Killing a man who's already given up is no challenge at all."

The men holding Clay released him, shoving him forward at the same time. He stumbled ahead a couple of steps before catching himself and wheeling around to glare at Maxwell. "You're nothing but a damned murderer!" he blazed. "You put on a fancy show, but you're just a low-down criminal like any other cutthroat!"

"I've never really claimed to be anything else," Maxwell said smoothly. "I've never had anything without being forced to lie and cheat and steal — and yes, kill — for it." He shrugged. "Why should I change now? But I'll tell you, Clay, once the deal I'm working on is finished, I'll never have to worry about money — or anything else — again."

"Someone will catch up to you, no matter what you do to me," Clay warned him.

Maxwell chuckled and shook his head. "I think not. The United States government itself won't be able to touch me." He turned to Sumner, who had followed him up out of the cellar. "My gun."

The servant held out a long-barreled hunting rifle, and Maxwell took it with evident pleasure. He turned back to Clay and said, "Five minutes. That's all the time you'll be given. After that, we'll spread out and begin the hunt. We'll shoot on sight, and we'll shoot to kill. I would prefer to tell my men to save you for me, but I have a feeling you're much too dangerous for that, Clay."

"Where's your daughter?" Clay asked tauntingly. "I'm surprised she's not out here. She's as much a killer as you are, isn't she, Maxwell?"

For the first time, Maxwell's facade of control was shaken. "Leave Diana out of this," he snapped. "It's true she knows of my plans and assists me sometimes, but her hands are clean. I intend for them to stay that way."

"The hell you say." Clay gave a harsh laugh. "If you kill me, my blood's going to be on her hands, too, and you know it."

"Shut up." Maxwell controlled himself with a visible effort and then went on, "I'm not going to let you ruin the evening's entertainment, Holt. Now go on. You're wasting what little time you have left on this earth."

Clay glanced around. Four of Maxwell's bully boys stood around, in addition to Sumner, and all of them were now holding pistols. Clay's eyes darted toward the woods behind the mansion. If he had any chance at all, it lay there, in the darkness and the brush. He took a deep breath and broke into a run, heading for the trees. He suspected that as soon as he turned his back to Maxwell and the others they would fire, but no gunshots split the night. A moment later Clay reached the woods and plunged into them, the shadows closing around him.

He plowed through the brush, ignoring the branches that scratched his face and clawed at his buckskins. Now it was up to him to stay alive and somehow turn the tables on Gideon Maxwell. Maxwell thought the deck was stacked against him, but Clay had already decided he was going to have to play a trump card to win this hand.

A trump card bearing the lovely likeness of Diana Maxwell . . .

Jeff crept cautiously toward Forestwood for the second time. Now he had Lieutenant Markham with him, and though Markham was trying to be quiet, he had little experience at moving stealthily through the woods. Jeff had to show him where and how to step, so it took them what seemed an interminable time to get back to the mansion. At one point they heard something moving through the brush about a hundred yards away, so Jeff stopped and stood absolutely still, hoping Markham would do the same, until the noise died away. It might have been a deer, Jeff thought, or even a bear. He and Markham resumed their approach, and five minutes later they reached Forestwood.

They knelt behind the trees just north of the house. Jeff pointed, indicating the cluster of men standing inside the roofless building. Markham nodded. A moment later one of the men spoke, and Jeff recognized Gideon Maxwell's voice.

"It's been more than enough time," Maxwell said. "Let's go." Hefting a rifle, he stepped out of the mansion and strode toward the trees, heading for a spot well to the right of where Jeff and Markham crouched. The other men, all carrying guns, followed Maxwell, but as they reached the trees, they spread out and took different paths.

What in the world were they doing? Jeff wondered. From the look of it, they were acting almost like . . .

A hunting party.

Clay. Clay was out there somewhere in the woods, and Maxwell and his men were going after him. Jeff suddenly wondered if the noises he and Markham had heard a few minutes earlier had been made by his brother.

He leaned toward Markham and whispered, "We've got to get to Diana Maxwell. If we have her, we can force her father to cooperate with us."

"No!" Markham hissed. "You can't mean that you'd actually threaten a woman, Mr. Holt!"

"I think Maxwell and his men have gone after Clay," Jeff said. "They intend to kill him. We have to go out there, too, and stop them, and the best way to do that is to take Diana with us. Maybe we can trade her for Clay."

"You promise she won't be hurt?"

"I give you my word I'll try to see that she's protected," Jeff hedged.

Markham sighed. "I suppose that'll have to be good enough. She's in her tent; I can see her moving around. Let me get her, Mr. Holt. Maybe she won't be as frightened that way."

Jeff considered for a second, then nodded. "All right. But I'll be right behind you."

He slipped his pistol from behind his belt as he and Markham emerged from the trees and started in a crouching run toward Diana's tent. Jeff figured she was alone for the moment, but he didn't want to take any more chances than he had to. He and Markham skirted the shell of the mansion and ran up to the tent.

"Diana!" Markham called in a soft voice. "Diana, are you in there? It's me, John!"

The tent flap was thrust back, and Diana Maxwell stepped out, the look of surprise on her beautiful face clearly visible in the moonlight. "John!" she exclaimed. Then she looked past him and added, "And Mr. Holt! What are you doing here?"

"Please, Diana, don't be frightened —" Markham began.

"But I'm not, John," she broke in. Her right hand came up quickly from where it had been concealed in the folds of her dress and pressed the muzzle of a small, short-barreled pistol against Markham's chest. "I'm not frightened at all, you see. Now, Mr. Holt, I'll thank you to drop that gun you're holding, as well as your other weapons."

Clay had been stalked before. Being the prey was nothing new to him. He had been on the other side, of course, and he knew that hunting men was much more dangerous than hunting animals. An animal nearly always reacted in the same way to anything that threatened it.

But a man . . . a man could do damned near *anything.*

And that was what made him dangerous.

That was why he began circling back toward the mansion almost as soon as he judged he was out of earshot of his pursuers. If he could avoid Gideon Maxwell and the other killers long enough to get back to the house, he might be able to get his hands on Diana, and once he had her, Maxwell would think twice about trying to kill him. Maxwell might be a murderer and a thief on a grand scale, but surely he would not put his own daughter's life in danger.

He wished he'd had the time to familiarize himself a little more with these woods. His years in the wilderness had taught him to re-trace almost any trail once he had been over it, even in the middle of the blackest night. But there was plenty of ground here that he *hadn't* covered during the short time he had been on Maxwell's estate. The moonlight helped a little, but it also cast grotesque shadows that made him stop in his tracks a few times before he realized that what he was seeing didn't represent a threat.

That was what almost got him killed.

He saw a shape looming on his left and thought it was the shadow of a tree or an outcropping of rock, but then the shape moved suddenly and Clay realized it was a man. He lunged toward the shape, knowing it was too late to duck to either side or go back the way he had come. Seeing moonlight glint on the barrel of a pistol, Clay's hand flashed out toward it. He grabbed the weapon around the breech so that when the man yanked the trigger and the flintlock fell, it pinched the web of flesh between Clay's thumb and fingers. Clay grunted at the sharp, sudden pain, but at the same time he lashed out with his other hand, slamming his fist into the man's face.

Silence was of the utmost importance. A shot, a yell, any loud noise would bring Maxwell and the other men charging toward him. Clay struck again as the man was rocked back by the first blow, loosening his grip on the gun. Clay wrenched it away and swung it at his opponent's head. He went down as if all his muscles had suddenly gone limp at the same time.

A moment later, Clay discovered why. His fingers found a depression in the man's skull, and he knew that the pistol barrel had shattered the thin bone at the temple. The man was unconscious and breathing shallowly; he might even be dying.

Clay wasn't going to waste any sympathy on him. He left the man lying where he had fallen but took his pistol, powder horn, and hunting knife with him.

There, Clay thought as he resumed his stealthy trek through the woods, his hand tightening on the grip of the pistol. *This is more like it.* Being armed again made him feel considerably better.

And the odds were one man closer to being even now.

Clay continued on toward the mansion. He had gone perhaps a hundred yards when a branch cracked sharply nearby. He judged the sound came from in front of him, and less than twenty feet away. He froze where he was, next to a tree. More sounds of movement came to his ears, and the next moment another dark shape loomed up out of the night. Clay's hand went to the knife he had taken from the first man and slid it noiselessly from behind his belt. He waited, hoping the shadowy shape would give him some clue to its identity.

A moment later his patience was rewarded when the man muttered in a coarse voice, ". . . tramping around out in the woods . . . Damn Maxwell and his games!"

Clay took a long step forward, bringing the knife up as he did so. He thrust the blade out in front of him, aiming at the sound of the man's voice. The tip of it struck something, then penetrated smoothly and cleanly. The man stopped short and made a muffled, gurgling noise. Clay yanked the knife free, feeling the hot spurt of blood over his fingers, and he knew he had plunged the blade into the man's throat.

The man dropped the pistol he was carrying and staggered to one side, clutching feebly and futilely at his neck. He fell to his knees, made a few more quietly hideous sounds, then pitched forward onto his face and lay still.

Clay knelt over the body and wiped his hand and the knife on the dead man's shirt. A quick check of the corpse uncovered another pistol in addition to the one the man had dropped. Clay took them both.

Straightening, he started forward again. Disposing of the two men had tilted the odds in his favor, but his primary goal was still Diana Maxwell. It would be asking too much to hope that one by one he could kill all six men who had pursued him into the woods.

A shot sounded from somewhere ahead of him, close to where he estimated the mansion to be. Frowning, Clay pushed on, but he moved more quickly now. A gunshot out here in the woods wouldn't have worried him; he would have figured that Maxwell or one of the other men had been too quick on the trigger and had fired at an animal or a shadow, thinking it was Clay. But the idea of a scuffle of some kind at the mansion was much more disturbing. He was counting on Diana Maxwell's being all right when he got there; otherwise she would be of no use to him when it came to bargaining with Maxwell.

He heard voices — loud, angry voices. One of them, shouting commands, sounded like Gideon Maxwell's. Moving both quickly and quietly, Clay threaded his way through the trees and brush and a few moments later reached the edge of the trees that surrounded the clearing where the house stood. He dropped to one knee behind a bush and leaned forward, parting the growth carefully and peering through the opening.

What he saw made him stiffen with surprise, and yet he knew he should not have been shocked. He hadn't expected Jeff to accept whatever cock-and-bull story Maxwell had tried to pass off as the truth.

Jeff and Lieutenant Markham stood between the shell of the mansion and the large tent. Surrounding them and covering them with guns were Maxwell, Sumner, and the other two men who had pursued Clay into the woods. Nearby stood Diana, holding a small pistol. Apparently Maxwell had called off the hunt to deal with this new threat. But two of his men had not returned, and Maxwell was no doubt wondering what had happened to them. The conclusion he would be drawing right about now was equally obvious.

The two men hadn't come back because Clay Holt had killed them.

". . . really should have done the sensible thing, Jeff," Maxwell was saying. "You should have gone back to Washington. And I'm very disappointed in you, Lieutenant Markham. To betray me like this after accepting my hospitality . . . well, I didn't expect it of you."

Even in the moonlight, Clay could see how haggard Markham's face was. He ignored Maxwell's taunts and looked pleadingly at

Diana. "I . . . I still can't believe it," he said. "Diana, I thought that you —"

"You believed what you wanted to believe, John," she snapped. "And I let you believe it. But now you know the truth. I've been part of Father's plan all along."

"Diana's very clever, you know," Maxwell said proudly. "She's made several suggestions that proved to be quite useful. In fact, she's the one who first told me that she thought you were working with the Holt brothers to ruin our plans. Such a pity she was right. Otherwise I might have tried to recruit you to our cause, since you seem to be a bright, ambitious young man."

"I'm not a traitor," Markham said hollowly.

"Traitor, patriot, it's really the same. It all depends on who wins, doesn't it?"

Jeff said calmly, "You won't win. Clay will see to that, no matter what you do to us."

"Clay Holt is already dead or soon will be," Maxwell said, a flash of anger showing through his urbane pose.

"Not hardly. He's already likely killed two of your men. Otherwise they would have come back when you called them in."

Sumner spoke up. "Carr and Johnson *haven't* returned, sir. Perhaps I should start searching for them —"

"Forget about them," Maxwell said. "There's no more time to waste. Kill these two right now, and then we'll hunt down Holt and finish him off."

"Yes, sir." Without hesitation, the ever obedient Sumner took a step forward and brought up the pistol he was holding, aiming it straight at Jeff's head.

Clay couldn't afford to wait any longer. He had already drawn a bead with one of the pistols he had taken from Maxwell's men. Now he pressed the trigger.

The pistol roared, noise and flame splitting the night. The heavy lead ball struck Sumner in the body, spinning him around. The pistol in his hand discharged, but the barrel had already drooped toward the ground, so the shot went harmlessly into the earth. As the echoes of those shots were dying away, even before Sumner had fallen, Clay had dropped the empty pistol and sprung to one side, jerking the other guns from behind his belt. He fired one pistol, kept moving, and then fired the other. The echoing volley made it sound as if more than one man was attacking. Clay saw one of Maxwell's men fall.

At the same time, Jeff was reacting as Clay had expected him to. As Maxwell's men turned instinctively toward the woods, Jeff launched himself at the nearest man, crashing into him and bringing him down. Jeff's left hand closed over the wrist of the man's gun hand and forced it aside. His right balled into a fist and slammed into the middle of the man's face, pulping his nose and bouncing his head off the ground. Jeff jerked the pistol loose from the man's grip. Then, alerted by his own instincts, he threw himself to the side, rolling on the ground as Maxwell fired the rifle at him. The ball whipped through the space where Jeff had been an instant earlier and thudded into the chest of the man with whom he had been struggling. The man was trying to rise, but the rifle ball drove him back to the ground, where he moaned, twitched, and lay still.

Jeff snapped a shot at Maxwell, who was already turning and darting toward the mansion. Maxwell vaulted over a low wall and vanished into the shadows. A figure emerged from the woods and went after him, and Jeff knew that had to be Clay.

Meanwhile, Markham had turned toward Diana as the shooting broke out. His first thought was to protect her from the lead flying around the clearing, but he also realized that she had to be captured. No matter how much he loathed the idea, he knew she was as much a part of the land grab scheme as her father.

"Diana!" he cried as he lunged toward her. "Look out!"

"Get away from me!" she screamed. She jerked up the pistol in her hand and fired.

What felt like a giant fist punched Markham in the shoulder, rocking him back. There was little pain. He was more shocked than hurt. She had shot him. She had actually *shot* him.

Then the world was spinning crazily around him and he knew he was falling . . .

Clay leaped over the wall Maxwell had jumped. He hadn't had time to reload the empty pistols, so he had discarded them. He heard the rapid scuttle of the man's feet over the half-finished floors of the mansion and plunged after him.

Suddenly the sound of Maxwell's footsteps stopped, and Clay hesitated, certain that Maxwell was up to something. Indeed, a second later the wealthy schemer came lunging out of the dark with a furious shout, swinging a long board at Clay's head. Clay dropped beneath the blow, and the board passed harmlessly over his head. Then he reached up, grabbed it, and shoved it forward as he straightened. Maxwell screeched as the board was driven through his hands, leaving splinters embedded in his palms. Then the end of the board thumped heavily into his chest and knocked him backward.

Clay sprang toward Maxwell, intending to seize this momentary advantage. Maxwell was gasping for breath, but he managed to bring his foot up and kick Clay in the stomach. Clay staggered back a couple of steps, startled by Maxwell's ferocity. In that moment Maxwell rolled over, lurched to his feet, and tried to run away, but Clay recovered his balance and threw himself at him in a long, diving tackle.

Both men crashed to the ground. Maxwell twisted around and began fighting like a wildcat, grating a vile curse with each frenzied blow he swung at Clay. Clay blocked some of the punches, absorbed the others, and managed to wrap his hands around Maxwell's throat. Filled with rage, he was prepared to choke the life out of Gideon Maxwell.

But he realized that Maxwell might be the only one of the plotters who knew all the details of the land grab. The authorities would want him alive. He tightened his grip on Maxwell's throat but told himself to hang on only until all the fight had gone out of the man. Then he could drag Maxwell out of the mansion and assist Jeff and Markham with the others.

Too late Clay saw Maxwell's hand come

up, saw the chunk of wood held tightly in the man's fingers. The wood crashed into Clay's head, sending him tumbling to one side. He groaned as the black void tried to claim him. Stubbornly holding on to consciousness, Clay pushed himself up on his hands and knees in time to see Maxwell trying to run away again. Clay lunged forward groggily, reaching out for Maxwell's legs. He caught hold of one of them and yanked.

Maxwell fell, sprawling on the ground in a welter of tools left behind by the workmen. He kicked free of Clay's grip, then tried to get up. As he made it to his feet, he staggered and put both hands to his midsection.

Clay shook his head, trying to clear his vision. Inside the shell of the mansion, among the beams and posts and partially raised walls, it was difficult to see. But as Clay pushed himself upright, he noticed that Maxwell was stumbling around aimlessly. Then Maxwell turned toward him, and Clay saw a dark stain spreading rapidly across the front of his shirt. There was something else there, something that seemed to be attached to his belly . . .

With a gasp, Maxwell pulled it loose, and Clay realized it was an ax. Maxwell had fallen on the blade. Now, with a gush of blood, Maxwell's guts tried to follow the ax blade out of the gaping wound. Maxwell groaned as he clutched at himself, trying to hold his very life in with his bare hands.

He failed, of course. Clay watched grimly as he dropped to his knees, then slowly bent over and curled around himself. He toppled to the side, and Clay heard the death rattle in his throat.

With a harsh sigh, Clay swung around. There was nothing he could do about it now. Gideon Maxwell was dead. Clay hurried back to the clearing to make sure Jeff and Lieutenant Markham hadn't wound up the same way.

Jeff was all right, Clay saw immediately, and a surge of relief washed over him. All Maxwell's men were down, either unconscious or dead. Jeff was kneeling next to Markham, supporting him as he sat up and held a folded piece of cloth to his shoulder.

"She shot me," Markham was saying as Clay came up to them. "She actually shot me."

"You're lucky she didn't kill you," Jeff told the young officer.

"But she *shot* me!"

Clay glanced at Diana Maxwell. She was stretched out on the ground nearby, evidently unconscious. Her chest was rising and falling, and a dark bruise had formed on her cheek.

"I had to hit her pretty hard," Jeff said to Clay. "Don't like hitting a woman, but after she wounded the lieutenant here, I figured it might be a good idea to just take the fight out of her."

"Reckon you did the right thing," Clay said.

"Maxwell?" Jeff asked.

Clay shook his head, then jerked a thumb over his shoulder toward the house. "He's in there. Fell on an ax and cut his belly open. There was nothing I could do for him . . . and even if there had been, I don't know that I would have."

"You would have," Jeff said quietly. He added to Markham, "Keep that cloth on the wound," then stood up and faced Clay. "Maxwell may be dead, but it's not over, is it?"

Clay shook his head again and said, "No. Not by a long shot."

Epilogue

Thomas Jefferson walked into the room, and Lieutenant Markham leaped to his feet, saluted, and said, "Sir!"

The former president smiled and gestured for Markham to sit down again. "I'm no longer the commander in chief, Lieutenant," he said. "There's no need to stand on ceremony."

Clay was also on his feet. "We didn't expect you to come in person, Mr. President," he said. "When we sent that message to you, we assumed you'd reply in kind."

Jefferson shook his head. He took off his hat and cloak and tossed them onto the bed, then sat down in an armchair. "I have information that is too important to entrust to a letter. I assume you haven't been able to discover which of the three senators you mentioned in your message was working with Gideon Maxwell?"

"No, sir," Clay said. "I'm afraid we haven't."

A couple of weeks had passed since the deadly night at Forestwood. During that time,

Lieutenant Markham's shoulder wound, which had been bloody and painful but not life-threatening, had begun to heal. His shoulder, in fact, was in better shape than his pride, which was still suffering from the fact that he had so badly misjudged Diana Maxwell. Clay and Jeff had turned Diana over to Markham's superiors when they reached Washington, and she was now in custody at Fort McHenry. The whole affair had been kept quiet, since not all the plotters had yet been rounded up. At least one of the ringleaders, the senator who had met with Maxwell the night Clay was captured, was still on the loose, his identity unknown. The other conspirators had no doubt concluded by this time that something had gone wrong, however, since Gideon Maxwell had disappeared. Clay and Jeff had sent a full report to Thomas Jefferson via a military courier, and since then Clay had been awaiting word on whether or not he could go home.

Jeff had already departed for North Carolina. He had been reluctant to leave while Clay was still in Washington, but Clay had urged him to do so.

"I got into this whole mess because of Captain Lewis," Clay had told his brother. "Now we know that whichever one of those ʔrs was working with Maxwell probably had Lewis murdered. That's my score to settle, not yours, and you've been away from home long enough."

"So have you," Jeff had pointed out.

Clay couldn't argue with that, but he persuaded Jeff that he could handle whatever new developments might arise concerning the land grab. Besides, Clay had said dryly, he had Lieutenant Markham to help him.

And it was entirely possible that the authorities might decide to dispense with Clay's services altogether and handle the rest of the matter themselves. Clay had been hoping for exactly that. Although it would bother him to leave the job unfinished, he was anxious to return to Ohio and Shining Moon. Ignoring the obsession with secrecy that seemed to infect all of Washington, he had written her a note apologizing for the delay and promising that he would be back in Marietta as soon as possible.

But now, surprisingly, Thomas Jefferson himself had appeared at the Copper Gable, and Clay had the distinct feeling this visit did not bode well for his chances of being reunited with his wife anytime soon.

"Well, I have some news," Jefferson went on, breaking into Clay's gloomy thoughts. "Have you heard of the steam ship *New Orleans*?"

Clay and Markham exchanged puzzled glances, then shook their heads.

"It's the largest, most advanced steam-powered vessel ever to be built," Jefferson went on. "It was designed by a man named Roosevelt, Nicholas Roosevelt, and next month it will be launched in Pittsburgh. It will travel down the Ohio River to the Mississippi, and thence to New Orleans, its namesake."

Clay frowned. "A steamboat's going all the way from Pittsburgh to New Orleans? Doesn't hardly seem possible."

"It's never been done before, that's certain," Jefferson agreed. "But Captain Roosevelt seems confident in his chances for success — so confident, in fact, that he has invited several dignitaries along for the maiden voyage. Senators Ralston, Haines, and Emory will be among them."

Clay and Markham looked at each other again. "Is that a coincidence?" Markham asked. "Or could it have something to do with the land grab?"

Thomas Jefferson smiled. "It will be your job, gentlemen, to find out."

Clay held up his hand. "Now wait just a damned minute." He hadn't forgotten whom was addressing, but at the moment he care. He ignored the warning look

562

Markham gave him and went on, "We found Gideon Maxwell for you and broke up his operation. He won't be getting his hands on any more government land in the west. Now it's time for me to go home. My wife is waiting for me."

"I know, and your country owes you a great debt for what you've done so far, Clay. But Gideon Maxwell's scheme was only the first level of the plan. The man you heard him speaking with can still carry on." Jefferson stood up and began to pace. "You know from the things Maxwell said that something is going to happen in the west, something large and possibly detrimental to the interests of this nation. Until we know exactly what Maxwell's fellow conspirators are planning, you are our best hope for averting that crisis."

"In other words, my country needs me," Clay said heavily.

"Yes, Mr. Holt, that is exactly right." Thomas Jefferson looked steadily at him. "And what is your answer going to be?"

Clay glanced at Markham and saw the eagerness in his face. He probably regarded this as an opportunity to redeem himself.

Clay knew there was only one answer he could give. He looked at Jefferson and said, "I reckon the lieutenant and I will be taking a boat ride."

★ ★ ★

Shining Moon sat in the rocking chair on the front porch of the Holt homestead and looked down at the paper in her hand. She had already read the letter from Clay Holt over a dozen times in the few hours that had passed since Castor Gilworth had given it to her. Castor had picked up the letter at Steakley's Trading Post during a trip into Marietta for supplies.

Clay's writing was cramped and inelegant, but at this moment it was beautiful to Shining Moon. It was the first communication of any kind she had received from her husband since his departure for Washington, and she regarded it as a sign from the spirits that everything would be all right. In the letter he apologized for taking so long to return to Ohio and promised that he would be there soon.

Matthew came around the corner of the cabin. He was carrying a basket containing the eggs he had gathered in the chicken house. For the past few weeks he had performed that chore faithfully, and he had been polite, almost cheerful at times. There had been no more trouble since Proud Wolf's visit.

But Shining Moon kept her hunting knife close to her during the day, and she slept with it next to her side at night. Never again would Matthew take her unaware, and when Clay returned . . .

Shining Moon had no idea what she would tell him. But he would have to know the truth about Matthew, and then, together, they would decide what to do.

Matthew set the basket of eggs down on the porch not far from Shining Moon's chair. "What's that?" he asked, pointing to the paper in her hand.

"A letter," she said.

"Who from?"

"Clay Holt."

"Oh." Matthew paused, then said, "Is he coming back?"

"Soon," Shining Moon said.

Matthew nodded. "Good. I've been wanting to see him again."

Shining Moon had been daydreaming about her reunion with Clay, how he would take her in his arms and kiss her long and hard, and she was looking forward to that very much. She would tell him how very glad she was to see him.

But when that was done, she knew what she would say to him next.

A warning . . .

Proud Wolf had seen many amazing

things during his journey to the east, but none had impressed him more than the cluster of large, redbrick buildings atop the hill that overlooked the village of Cambridge, Massachusetts. The Charles River was visible in the distance, and across the river, the huge city of Boston sprawled over the Shawmut Peninsula.

"This . . . will be my home?" he asked Professor Hilliard, who sat beside him on the seat of the rented buggy.

"This is the Stoddard Academy for Young Men," the professor replied. "And down there — see those buildings? — that's Harvard, where I teach and where you will eventually be a student." Hilliard looked at him. "You still want to go through with this, don't you? You're not frightened?"

Proud Wolf stiffened. He had faced great dangers and challenges in his life. This would be a trifle.

"I am ready," he said firmly.

"Well, then," Hilliard said as he took up the reins, "let's go get you settled in."

A stone wall covered with ivy surrounded the Stoddard Academy. Hilliard drove through the gate and followed a winding path through grounds dotted with trees, neatly trimmed shrubs, and flower gardens. The grounds were pleasant enough, Proud

Wolf had to admit, but there was something unreal about them. They lacked the wild, untamed beauty of his homeland.

That was the way of the white men, he thought. They were never content to let anything remain as they had found it. Always they had to make it over into their own image of beauty, even when it had been perfectly beautiful to begin with.

Hilliard brought the buggy to a stop in front of the main building, which was four stories tall and also covered with ivy. Despite the foliage, the structure had a forbidding look, Proud Wolf thought. The brick walls were not as warm and welcoming as the animal skins his people wove together to make their lodges.

You cannot compare everything to the ways of the Sioux, he warned himself silently. If he did that, he would never fit in here, and he wanted badly to fit in, to receive the education of which Professor Hilliard had spoken so persuasively.

The front door of the building opened as Proud Wolf and Hilliard stepped down from the buggy. A tall man in a dark suit stepped out. Hands clasped together behind his back, which was held ramrod-straight, he marched over to the newcomers and gave them a curt nod. "Professor Hilliard," he said by way of greeting, then looked at Proud Wolf. "I assume this is the young savage?"

"This is Proud Wolf, of the Teton Sioux, Dr. Stoddard," Hilliard said. "I've spent the past several weeks in the young man's company, and I can assure you, he is no savage." The professor turned to Proud Wolf. "This is Dr. Jeremiah Stoddard, founder and headmaster of the Stoddard Academy."

"I am pleased to meet you, Dr. Stoddard," Proud Wolf said, exactly as the professor had instructed him. He bowed slightly, also a suggestion of the professor's, then held out his hand.

Jeremiah Stoddard hesitated only slightly, but enough for Proud Wolf to notice, then took his hand and shook it briefly. "We're glad to have you with us, Mr. . . . ah . . . Wolf," he said.

Proud Wolf was uncertain how sincere the man's words were. He had the feeling Stoddard did not want him here. Perhaps Professor Hilliard had pushed him into an arrangement of which the headmaster did not entirely approve. That could mean trouble sooner or later.

But until any problems developed, Proud Wolf was not going to concern himself with them. Besides, he was going to work very hard, and eventually Dr. Stoddard was sure to realize that he belonged here, that he was every bit as capable as the other students.

Two more people came out of the building. Proud Wolf glanced at them, then looked again, surprised by what he saw. The young man of the pair was a typical white man, tall and fair-haired, but it was the young woman with him who caught Proud Wolf's eye. She was beautiful, slender yet well formed, with green eyes that seemed full of laughter and a mass of thick red curls that tumbled around her shoulders, framing her lovely face. She was as good to look upon as any white woman Proud Wolf had ever seen.

"Is this the new student, Father?" she asked Stoddard, and her voice was like music to Proud Wolf's ears.

"That's right," Stoddard said somewhat grudgingly. "Where are you and Will going?"

"Just for a walk around the pond," the young woman replied carelessly.

Proud Wolf stepped forward impulsively. "I am Proud Wolf," he said as he looked into those green eyes. They were as cool and deep as a forest, but like a forest they also held shadows, shadows Proud Wolf could not quite identify.

"I'm Audrey Stoddard," she said. She extended her own hand, ignoring the looks of disapproval from her father and the young man called Will.

Proud Wolf was about to take her hand when the young man moved between them and grasped his hand instead. "William Brackett," he introduced himself. "Glad to meet you, Proud Wolf. We're pleased to have you with us."

That was a lie, Proud Wolf thought. He could see the truth plainly in the young man's eyes. There was no pleasure there, only uncertainty and perhaps a bit of resentment, even dislike. Proud Wolf tried not to frown as he shook William Brackett's hand. He had done nothing to make Will dislike him . . . except perhaps draw the interest of Audrey Stoddard.

Professor Hilliard put a hand on Proud Wolf's shoulder. "Well, we should take your things in and show you where you'll be living. You'll be starting your classes soon, so you need to learn your way around the academy."

"Don't worry, Professor," Audrey said with a smile. "We'll see that Proud Wolf is made right at home. Won't we, Will?"

"Of course," Will Brackett said, but his expression had grown even colder. "He'll be just fine."

If that was true, Proud Wolf thought, then

why did he feel as if he was about to step into the den of a beast?

Jeremiah Corbett looked up from his desk in surprise as the door of his office opened and a tall, broad-shouldered figure sauntered in. "Philip!" he said. "Where have you been? My God, man, the way you dropped out of sight, I was afraid someone had killed you."

"Almost," Rattigan said. "I nearly died a couple of weeks ago in an explosion."

"An . . . explosion?" Corbett swallowed hard.

"Yes. The warehouse where the Holt-Merrivale Company stores its goods was almost destroyed. But you know all about that, don't you, Jeremiah?"

Corbett blinked rapidly. "I . . . I'm afraid I don't know what you're talking about, Philip —"

Suddenly Rattigan took a long step forward and reached across the desk, snagging Corbett's collar and jerking the smaller man up and out of his chair. "Damn it, don't lie to me," he growled in a low, dangerous voice. "I've spent the past two weeks investigating everything that's happened to Holt-Merrivale, and I know you were behind it, Jeremiah. The warehouse fire, the piracy, the attempt to blow up their ware-house . . . all of it paid for by you." Rattigan shoved Corbett back down in his chair. "Next time you try to sabotage a compet-itor, make sure you pay everyone involved enough to keep them quiet. I've found enough witnesses to have you thrown in jail for murder if I want."

Corbett put his head in his hands and groaned in dismay, not even bothering to dispute Rattigan's accusations. But then, after a moment, he looked up with a feral gleam in his eyes. "If I go to jail, Philip, then so do you, since you knew all about every-thing I was doing."

"That's a damned lie!" Rattigan looked as if he wanted to reach across the desk again and smash his fist into Corbett's face, but he restrained himself. "I knew nothing of what you were doing."

"That's not the way I'll tell the story. And no one I hired — no one! — knows that you were unaware of the plans."

Rattigan's chest rose and fell rapidly as he struggled with his rage. "Damn you, Jere-miah. How could you do these things?"

Corbett frowned, looking genuinely baf-fled. "I don't understand why you're so upset, Philip. After all, Holt-Merrivale is our competitor."

And that was all that mattered to Corbett, Rattigan saw. Winning, destroying a rival, doing whatever was necessary to get a chokehold on the commerce in Wilmington.

Rattigan shook his head. "No more. Our partnership is dissolved, Jeremiah."

"You can't do that!" Corbett came up out of his chair again, on his own accord this time. "We have an arrangement —"

"Which did not include piracy, arson, and murder. I'm walking out of here, and you'd best not try to stop me." Rattigan paused when he reached the door and looked back at Corbett. "You'll be lucky if, for old times' sake, I decide not to tell Terence O'Shay who's responsible for the deaths of his men in that warehouse."

Then Rattigan was gone, slamming the door behind him, and Corbett's face drained of color as he stood behind his desk and began to tremble.

Melissa hesitated as she pondered which of the dresses she was holding she should pack for the voyage to Alaska. There would not be a great deal of room for personal belongings, so she had to weigh each choice carefully.

Then, as it often had these past few weeks, the memory of the kiss she had shared with

Philip Rattigan hit her without warning, filling her mind and producing such vivid, intense sensations that she dropped both dresses on the bed and stood for a long moment, trembling.

There had been no decision made that night, no conscious thought at all, just a simple, instinctive reaching out. She had gloried in the moment and the feel of Rattigan's arms, his lips pressed to hers . . .

She had torn away from him, of course, and her hand had cracked across his face an instant later in a slap of outrage. "How dare you!" she had cried.

And he had smiled that cool, maddening smile and said, "I always dare . . . when there's something I really want at stake."

She had not seen him since that night, had no idea what had happened when he confronted his partner, Jeremiah Corbett, about the murders of Terence O'Shay's men and the attempted destruction of the warehouse. For all Melissa knew, Corbett hadn't had anything to do with any of it. She didn't honestly believe that, but she was willing not to pursue the matter as long as nothing else happened . . . and as long as she didn't have to see Philip Rattigan again. O'Shay was another story; the big Irishman might want to take his own revenge on whoever was responsible for the killings.

So she had turned her attention instead to her partnership with Lemuel March and the upcoming voyages to Hawaii and Alaska. Anything to keep her mind off Rattigan and the fierce longing she had felt while she was in his embrace. She was a married woman, she told herself sternly when these spells came over her, a wife and a mother, and she loved Jeff and little Michael with all her heart and soul, and a woman would have to be insane to even *think* about risking everything she held dear just because a strange man she didn't particularly *like* aroused such heat within her . . .

"Packing already?" a familiar voice asked from behind her.

Melissa caught her breath and spun around, hardly daring to believe what she had heard. But it was true. Jeff was standing in the doorway, a smile on his face. He held his arms out to her, and she was in them in an instant, her own arms going around his waist, her face pressed to his chest for a long moment before she lifted her head for a kiss of homecoming.

Minutes passed while the two of them kissed and murmured soft words and simply held each other. Then Jeff cupped her chin and looked down into her eyes. "What is this?" he asked as he gestured with his other hand toward the bed, where her carpetbag stood open. "You're not leaving me, are you?"

The question was asked in a slightly mocking tone, but there was real concern in his eyes, Melissa saw. She shook her head. "I'm not leaving you," she said. "In fact, we're going somewhere together." It was time for a bold move, something that would ensure Philip Rattigan would be completely forgotten.

Jeff frowned. "We are?" he said. "And where might that be?"

"Have you ever heard of . . . Alaska?"

A grin broke out on Jeff's face, and Melissa's pulse quickened. She knew her husband better than anyone else in the world. First and foremost, Jeff was a Holt.

And the Holts were ready, as they always would be, to answer the siren call of danger and excitement, wherever it might lead them.